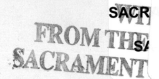

"*Written in the Ashes* is one of those rare novels that sets 'history' afire, to bathe readers in the glow of a greater, hotter truth. Fans of *The Mists of Avalon* will find this romantic/alchemical/feminist/spiritual epic equally captivating."

—**Tom Robbins**, bestselling author of *Tibetan Peach Pie: A True Account of an Imaginative Life* and *Villa Incognito*

"A stunning epic about the burning of the Great Library of Alexandria, Egypt from a brilliant young novelist whose depiction of the ancient world is sure to capture the hearts of readers everywhere."

—**Mark R. Harris**, Academy Award-winning producer (*Crash, Gods & Monsters*)

"Van Zandt's vivid description of the Great Library instantly transported me to a lush fifth century Alexandria. Her lyrical writing style and breakneck storytelling kept me riveted to the very last page."

—**Robin Maxwell**, bestselling author of *Jane: The Woman Who Loved Tarzan* and *Atlantos* (The Early Erthe Chronicles)

"In her captivating debut novel, *Written in the Ashes*, K. Hollan Van Zandt brings to life a fascinating and forgotten woman of history: Hypatia of Alexandria, who may have been one of the greatest female minds of all time. If you've ever wondered what it was like to walk the streets of long ago Egypt, then look no further. You will be enthralled!"

—**Michelle Moran**, bestselling author of *Rebel Queen* and *The Second Empress: A Novel of Napoleon's Court*

Written in the Ashes

K. Hollan Van Zandt

HARPER LEGEND

HARPER LEGEND

WRITTEN IN THE ASHES. Copyright © 2016 by Kaia Van Zandt. All rights reserved. Printed in the United States of America. No part of this book may be used or reproduced in any manner whatsoever without written permission except in the case of brief quotations embodied in critical articles and reviews. For information, address HarperCollins Publishers, 195 Broadway, New York, NY 10007.

HarperCollins books may be purchased for educational, business, or sales promotional use. For information, please email the Special Markets Department at SPsales@harpercollins.com.

ISBN 978-0-06-267368-8

For the librarians of the world,
then and now

Contents

Beneath this well
lay buried the hearts of the fallen gods.
They are rotting into the soil like apples,
sweetening the water.
Come, drink.

—SOFIA GREENBERG

. . . Whosoever would be great among you,
must be your servant: and whosever
would be first among you must be slave of all.

—CHRIST JESUS

MARK 10:43–44

Time Line Prior to This Story

347 C.E.[1]—Birth of Emperor Theodosius I, who in his lifetime will make Nicene Christianity (under the Catholic Church) the official religion of the Roman Empire. He is the last emperor to rule the united eastern and western halves of the Roman Empire.

375 C.E.—Birth of Hypatia of Alexandria.

391 C.E.—Emperor Theodosius I declares by Imperial Edict that all pagan (non-Christian) practice is punishable by death.

391 C.E.—The Serapeum Library (or "daughter library") in Alexandria is destroyed by a Christian mob.

395 C.E.—Emperor Theodosius I dies, leaving his son, Arcadius, on the Eastern throne of Constantinople and his son, Honorius, on the Roman throne in the West. The Empire will never be united again.

408 C.E.—Emperor Arcadius dies, leaving his seven-year-old son, Theodosius II, on the throne of Constantinople. His eldest daughter, Pulcheria, age fifteen, is proclaimed Augusta by the senate and assumes the regency for her younger brother.

---

1 C.E.—Common Era

Map by Shimmering Wolf.

Prologue

All trees hold secrets. From tiny saplings just piercing the earth to the old sentinels that stretch toward the sky until they founder, what the trees have witnessed, we can only dream. They harbor the winds and the changes of time, recording reunions, catastrophes, even unremarkable sunrises in concentric rings that lie concealed in darkness, deep within.

Trees are consummate listeners. A fibrous canopy above the earth, they gather into their taut, hollow bodies all the stories of the world. Like the angels, trees will not interrupt, disagree, or offer advice. Perhaps this is why the ancients thought them wise.

Trees are the first libraries, the oldest houses of wisdom and knowledge.

And they remember everything, even a girl.

PART 1

Alexandria

(410 C.E.)

PART 1

Alexandria

(410 C.E.)

1

Hannah pressed her cheek to the gnarled trunk; silver leaves shimmered around her like netted minnows in the wind. Then stillness. She crouched to make an offering of water that had taken her days to collect, uncapping her water horn and trickling it over the exposed roots. Though it had stood for centuries and bore scars of fire and war, the olive tree had lost its grasp during the dry winter winds. Drought had struck Sinai, lengthening through the dusty afternoons like a deadly shadow, killing everything it touched. The shepherds talked of nothing else. Empty grain sacks withered on the sunbaked clay while scrawny newborn sheep and goats were left to the vultures' talons. Egypt was scoured by dead weeds and hunger; flowing streams atrophied to sand.

Above her, an angel circled and then settled in the eaves of the sky, content to wait. A door would open. The warrior would come. The light had promised it.

Hannah coughed as the warm breeze stirred the dust. There would be no more gypsies dancing to the pounding drums in the spring meadow or stories of the Torah read by the rabbi and his sons. No more familiar shoulders of the mountain at sunrise. Hannah grew impatient with water rations. If only the rains would return.

Hannah discovered from spying on the Bedouin camps that there were sages, wise women who could interpret embers in a fire, read the entrails of animals, or even proclaim that a comet's blue smudge in the night sky would mean the end of a king.

She wanted to find one to interpret the drought and promise its end. She harbored unspoken frustration with her father for his disinterest in the secret language of omens the heavens and stars seemed to speak. He knew only the language of goats. But it was a language he spoke fluently—so fluently he must have a bell for a heart.

When Hannah returned to camp, she reluctantly poured dirt on their fire, packed her rucksack, and joined her father on the deer path.

They walked for days visiting muddy springs already drained by other herdsman. By then, all the youngest and weakest of their herd had fallen; at each mud pit the goats moaned and pawed the ground. At last they found a trickle of water from a crack in a cliff and dropped their possessions to press their lips to the warm wet earth.

Sometime into the night, once her father returned to the fire, Hannah collapsed in exhaustion and had a dream. Birds by the thousands soared above crumbling columns, their wings aflame, spiraling ever higher in blind chaos while far beneath them, men in black robes surrounded a cloaked woman and forced her to the ground; their robes covered her completely until she was lost, screaming in a churning sea of blood. Hannah awoke with a jolt, her breath short. This was no ordinary dream; she felt it portended something evil. She covered her eyes with one hand, and offered the *Shema* as her father had taught her, taught her as if she were not a daughter but a son.

So.

————————

There were centuries of walking. Hannah's heels cracked and bled. Vultures circled their camp day and night. She crouched and felled two small hares with her shepherd's sling and carried them on her shoulders to the fire.

Her father, Kaleb, licked the wine from his beard. "We cannot go toward the roads, Hannah. Thieves may give us trouble, and we have only the one knife between us."

"Then to the sea, Abba?" Hannah prodded the fire with a stick and a shower of sparks lifted into the sky.

"No, to the river in Egypt."

The river in Egypt. Hannah had heard stories about the ancient Egyptians and how they lived on the east bank of the Nile, the direction of life, and buried their dead on the west bank, the direction of death. When the Pharaoh left his corpse, his spirit flew toward the rising sun and the life-giving waters. The pyramid tombs had been designed so he would know his way home. In that way, he was like the geese or the great whales, one of the few among creatures of the earth who knew where he belonged.

Hannah closed her eyes and settled into the comfort of fantasy. She imagined the fragrant baths of the Egyptians inside their glowing temples painted with the blue lotus revered for its beauty and youth-giving properties, the mosaics rimming the pools, the colorful murals of the gods stretched on the walls. There would be strong, bare-chested men standing beside the doors holding papyrus fans and round-hipped women whispering to one another in the water, splashing, laughing. Hannah began to sing softly, feeling hopeful again about their future. Surely the Nile would nourish them.

Kaleb allowed himself to bask in his daughter's reverie until her song trailed off. "Hannah, I have a gift for you. Something I have been saving, and I want you to have it now." Kaleb reached into his leather satchel. Hannah came to sit at his feet. She closed her eyes, held out her hands, and he closed her fingers over the gift. Even without seeing it, she knew what it was. "But Abba, we cannot afford this. Not now."

Kaleb smiled triumphantly. He had saved every coin to buy her the silver Athenian hairpin in the shape of a peacock that she had admired in the market the year before.

Hannah turned the precious gift in her hands, fingering the long sharp prongs, the smooth feathers of the regal bird molded by a talented artisan.

Kaleb kissed and squeezed his daughter's hands. "There is only now," he said, and he nestled the hairpin in one of her burnished curls.

When the fire quieted, Hannah yawned and kissed her father's whiskered cheek. She would sleep with the herd through the night, and he with the fire. She curled up beneath a woolen blanket in the field and shut her eyes, listening to the tinkling of the goat bells, unable to sleep. She wondered if she should go back to the fire and check on her father, lashing and trimming new sinew for the tent poles with his knife, but she knew he would prefer she stay with the herd. Eventually, she fell asleep.

So.

Hannah's eyes sprung open. Rustling grass. The goats bleating, scattering. She sensed a predator and felt for the knife beneath her head, but her father had it by the fire.

Suddenly, there were rough hands at her throat and over her mouth.

She tried to scream, bite the hand at her teeth. Two cloaked men. One with breath that stunk of barley mead grabbed her, the other laughed, clearly pleased. She flailed and was fisted across the face. Once. Twice. She broke away and ran five paces up the hill before they caught her ankles and dragged her backwards. Clawing the earth, her hand found a stone and she turned and struck out, hitting one of the men in the eye, drawing blood but not enough.

She could see two more men on the hill near her father's fire before they covered her head. She struggled desperately, screaming to her father. Abba. Hear me. Stop them. Please. Her heart surged with blood, fierce determination. She kicked at the men in the darkness as they bound her like a lamb, lifted her on their shoulders, and carried her off.

When Hannah awoke, her head pounding, it was in the confines of a wooden cage, sweating, choking, drawing flies. The sack over her face was tied tightly enough at her throat to make her gasp, but she could see through the thin mesh, just enough to make out her captors, the endless barren land, and the silhouettes of the three trembling women beside her, crying softly.

Hannah hugged her knees, knowingly. When the men spoke, she recognized their harsh tongue from the trader's market near the southern sea, and although she did not speak a word of that ugly language, she could guess their conversation. Slave traders. They would be sold, each of them, for the highest price. The drought had brought the men like so many other predators.

All day she cried, wasting water, clinging to whispered prayers and bits of songs as if stringing words together would keep her from drowning in the dark abyss of fear that grew within her by the hour. She hoped her father was alive and tracking them. It brought her some comfort that at any moment he might burst through the cage, sweep her up in his strong arms, and carry her home.

The day was difficult, but the night was unendurable.

At sundown, the men tied their horses to a stake in the ground. They drank fermented mead. Before long, they chose a girl to slake their lust.

Hannah spit in their eyes when they removed the sack around her head. With a desperate burst of strength she managed to bite the hand of one, drawing blood, and kick another in his naked balls. But a knife was drawn to silence her, a cut along her breast, not so deep, but deep enough. A little gift, they called it in their language, the men that gifted her with bruises and semen and hatred so deep that you would think no mother had given them birth.

Hannah wept in hatred, then in shame. There was no word for how much she despised them, these men who gloated in her weakness and took turns upon her naked body from behind. She had never known a man before; she screamed in pain while they laughed, thrusting deeper, splitting her open, pulling clumps of her hair in sport. One, then another, then another. Her knees bloodied the ground, but she continued to strike at them with an intelligent timing to her blows that both angered and frustrated them. Each wanted his turn to punish her, load her with his seed cheered on by the others. But as they fell into drunkenness, they tired of her and set upon the other women, mothers and daughters, who would not be so much trouble. This was before one of them considered that the price brought for fallen fruit would not be as high as for fruit plucked from the branch. And so at dawn they brought out dirty rags and coarse wire brushes meant for horses, and stood over the women with their short swords drawn to let them clean each other's wounds and soak the blood that run from between their legs.

No one spoke. Pain took the place of words. Lips split like firewood, thighs clamped shut, oozing liquid, eyes swollen like ripe plums. The gash along Hannah's sternum blossomed with creamy pus and black silt. A girl, still a child with soft brown eyes and slender fingers, drained it gently. They knew their future, and still they prayed.

That was when the dust storm came. The wagon carrying the cage cracked a wheel, and so Hannah was pulled out to help push it with the other women still inside, her chains cutting her ankle with every step. When she fell on her knees, the men kicked her to keep her walking. Tears washed her burning eyes of sand. Above them, a falcon screamed.

Silt clumped on the horses' eyelashes, and the men paused to tighten the ropes on the wrists of the women until they cut the skin. As if they would run.

A powder fine as flour blew through Hannah's hood with each burst of wind, and her eyes became painfully swollen and red. For strength, she sang, thinking of her father in the hour before the men came: strong, smiling, eyes twinkling with some inner laughter. She could not bear the agony of imagining him helpless, or dead, or left alone and in pain, calling out for her. She told herself she would see him again. He would come for her, or she would escape. She rested her heart in the comforting details of his worn clothes, his wiry beard, his leather rucksack full of fragrant herbs spilling out like entrails beside the fire, and his shepherd's staff beside him, familiar as certain stars overhead. The details of love cannot be lost.

In the early evening, the city of the gods appeared. Hannah was shut back in the cage and left to stare at it from between the bars. She had never seen walls so high, walls that started in the ground and scraped against the sky. The men in their strange language repeated a word like the chorus of a song. Alexandria. Alexandria.

They entered through the Gate of the Sun and were let in by armed guards after payment was made. With their eyes now uncovered, Hannah could see the massive buildings carved from granite and slats of limestone, towering over them. The east-west street they rode through was lined with tall columns so wide seven children holding hands could not wrap their arms all the way round. Under any other circumstances Hannah might have found the city majestic, for she had never seen a city before and never imagined one so great as this. Massive fountains spaced down the center of the boulevard were crowned with gods and spouting dolphins, Nereids and goddesses splashing loudly into limpid pools while Parian marble sphinxes wedged into the architecture watched over the city with bald, lucid eyes.

The shepherd's cunning daughter noted the tremendous city gates, the gates that would lead her back into the desert. By nightfall she would slip between them like a shadow and be gone. Steal a horse. Ride to Sinai. Her head ached with painful thoughts, and the cage jolted as it struck a stone.

Everywhere the street bustled with activity. Horses hitched to chariots trotted swiftly ahead, always managing to avoid the people who passed on foot, many of whom carried chickens and goats in their arms or balanced baskets of sturgeon on their heads, fish tails flopping as they walked. A few shrewd looking gentlemen in flowing robes with papyrus scrolls tucked beneath their arms strode down the street and entered a large meeting hall. Kneeling priests weeded papyrus ponds. Beneath a tattered ecru tent, a woman yelled at a skinny yellow dog as she beat a kilim with a stick. Several soldiers leaned in the shade of an arch in disrepair, weapons at their sides, asleep, while a parade of women with gold hoop earrings walked before them, chattering like brightly colored birds.

As they rounded the final corner toward the market, a sudden commotion came over the street. Before them loomed the most magnificent set of carved wooden doors Hannah had ever seen. The wall they split was itself extraordinary, carved with languages and stories from every known civilization, a living mural of history. But before the wooden doors stood five tall men in black robes, their heads shorn. They shoved a man to his knees who was pleading for his life. There was a stone in the dust before him with a scroll flapping beneath it in the ocean breeze. The man brought his hands together, tears trickling from his eyes. He seemed so pitiful, so small before these enormous men in robes.

Suddenly the tallest priest pulled out a sword and deftly cut the man's arms from his body in two strokes. A guttural scream filled the sky, and everyone turned their eyes as the man fell to the ground. Then the priest pulled a torch from the wall and touched it to the bleeding man's robes, lighting him aflame. The man screamed again and fell to the ground in agony.

The priest threw the torch over the wall and called out, "In the name of the Church of St. Alexander, this man is a pagan, a worshipper of numbers, and he shall die at the door of his master, Hypatia, a heathen witch."

At that, the enormous wooden doors opened, and a furious woman emerged flanked by two guards, her pale hair bound up on top of her head, her eyes condemning. She carried the torch that the priest had thrown.

"This man is my servant," she cried out. "And he has done nothing aside from dutifully attend all of human knowledge with his whole heart. How dare you bring this spiteful war to our gates. You may tell your bishop I refuse to read his letter," she picked up the scroll from beneath the stone and lit it on fire with the torch in her hand, and then tossed it at the feet of the priests. Then she spit, "And I curse him."

Hannah and the others cowered in the cage, afraid of what these priests might do to the beautiful and daring woman who opposed them. But they simply turned and left.

The woman whispered something to one of her guards, who then unsheathed his sword and stabbed the man on the ground who had lost his arms and was still burning, whimpering and close to death. The sword pierced the soft flesh at the top of his shoulder, sunk down into his heart, and he fell still.

That was all Hannah could see before the cart turned the corner and left the mob behind. She thought she could hear the enormous doors swinging shut, bolted from the inside. Hannah was breathing heavily, her whole body trembling. But beside her the young girl broke into heavy wailing, screaming to be set free, throwing herself against the bars of the cage. Hannah pulled the girl into her arms and stroked her head, and then she began to sing to calm her. The song had its effect, and soon the girl was asleep.

 2

So.

It was Tarek who bought the girl in the *agora*.

The slave traders had set her on the block, long dark hair swept in front of her shoulders to hide the ugly gash across her chest, wrists bound so that she could not feel her fingers. The humiliation stung worse than a field of nettles.

Another bidder, an older gentleman with a gilded cane, eyed the girl on the block with her young plump bosom and her long limbs, checking her teeth and running his hand down one of her sinuous arms, then smacking her hip as if she were a horse and clutching her breast in his hand. She spit in his eye. The slave traders kicked her to her knees.

Tarek had been on his way to see a whore, one of the many nameless beauties he preferred. They were to meet beside the city fountain. He had not intended to stop in the market, but he wanted to buy a flute. His was broken. All women love a flute, and he wanted where flutes lead. But instead he saw the trembling girl on the trader's block, and her eyes reached for him and pleaded beauty he had never seen. He forgot the flute and counted his coins.

He knew Alizar would protest. But those eyes. Perhaps he could purchase her and keep her all the same. The mind that wants can reason anything.

Hannah stood in her soiled clothes before a hungry crowd that surged against the block. She was the last to be sold. Her captors had done well. The pretty girl with brown eyes had gone to the wealthy bawd of a brothel on the wharf. The mother and daughter as chattel to a decorated captain on his way to Rome. Hannah was left. Their prize. She was illiterate, but of extraordinary beauty, and the one was worth twice the other. And then there was her talent. Oh, yes. She would bring them a handsome coin.

Sing, beauty.

She sealed her lips.

A knife was pressed to the small of her back.

Sing.

Her lips parted.

Twenty *solidi*.

Fifty.

Seventy-five.

Then a skinny boy with a tangle of dark hair dismounted and led his horse through the crowd, waving a bag of coins. One hundred *solidi*.

Sold.

After surrendering his gold coins to the slave traders, the girl was shuttled from the trader's block and pushed into the hairy arms of a blacksmith who swiftly bound her neck in a bronze collar that read the name and address of where to return her should she escape. His fiery clamp hissed in her ear as metal found metal, and it was done.

The boy took her hands in his, and the cool dampness of them disgusted her; he had fish where hands should be. She looked away.

"You will come with me," he said. "My name is Tarek. I will take you to a bath and a good home. My father's home. Alizar of Alexandria."

Hannah heard the Greek like some new melody. She did not know the meaning of the words but could feel the warmth within them. If this stranger offered some protection, then she would stay with him until he slept, and then escape to find her father. And so she allowed herself to be led, limping barefoot across the cobbles, her toes swollen and bloody from miles of walking the road.

Tarek's regret at spending the money gnawed holes in his gut where certainty should have been. This girl would eat and drink and cost his father's house, and there might be upheaval. The money he had paid for her was to go to supplies for the vineyard: a hundred *amphorae*, a new grape press. Tarek considered other options: he could have been robbed, there were more and more priests demanding bribes, maybe he was swindled by the ceramicist. Better to say nothing. Hide the girl in his room. Give her mending to do and keep her a secret until, until . . . he found some believable excuse.

Tarek guided her through the market district just outside the Jewish Quarter along the narrow alleys that spiraled around a small hill, atop which stood the skeleton of a massive temple library once called the Serapeum. The ruins were flanked with marble statues of Isis kneeling all along the periphery, most of them missing heads or bearing broken wings. At the center of the courtyard stood a tall black column twenty-six meters in height, six meters in diameter, and crowned with the porphyry statue of Diocletian, a ruler now forgotten. It was a latrine for beggars now.

As they wound deeper into the labyrinth of the city, Hannah began to loose her footing. She struggled to hold her head up as a sudden faintness came over her, and the heat surged upward in her blood. Her limbs became heavy and tired. Then her knees buckled.

Tarek cursed her; she could not cost so much only to die.

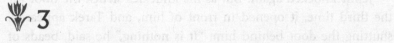

3

Jemir was the first to hear the odd sound from deep within the walls of the house. He looked up from organizing the spices in his kitchen, an activity he greatly preferred to any interruption.

Then it came again.

Had a peacock had gotten into the house and started rearranging the furniture upstairs? He waited several minutes, and, hearing nothing more, took up a handful of fine cinnamon powder and set it on a sheet of parchment, which he then folded lengthwise and carefully tapped into a funnel set precariously on top of a jar. When the powder was half dispensed, a crash came through the wall with such sudden force that Jemir looked up with a start and knocked the funnel from the jar with his elbow, sending aloft an expensive crimson cloud.

With a sneeze and a torrent of obscenities, Jemir threw down the rag resting on his shoulder and went in search of the interruption.

He was not the only one.

Leitah, the young Byzantine maidservant, simultaneously dropped her soggy sponge in the bucket on the stairs and crept through the house with her ear bent to the walls.

Both Jemir and Leitah followed the sound from opposite ends of the house, and came to stand in front of Tarek's door. They shared a conspiratorial nod, and Jemir set his hand on the iron latch. But as he lifted it, he found it was locked.

Jemir knocked. "Tarek? What are you doing in there?"

There was no reply. Then came the muffled, mysterious shrieking.

Jemir knocked again. But as his knuckles struck the door for the third time, it opened in front of him, and Tarek appeared, shutting the door behind him. "It is nothing," he said, beads of sweat at his temples, his sleeves rolled up to the elbow. His bare chest bled where he had been scratched.

Leitah touched the blood on Tarek's skin and recoiled. She showed her burnished red fingertip to Jemir without a word.

"You cannot bring a peacock in the house, Tarek." Jemir pushed the boy aside. "They are stupid birds that will fight their own reflections."

"No." Tarek covered the door with his scrawny limbs and fixed his eyes on the squat Nubian cook with a look that was not to be challenged.

With that, an argument ensued that involved much shoving and yelling of insults between Jemir and Tarek. Even a stranger could have inferred that each held unspoken past grievances against the other. Leitah slipped away unnoticed. When she returned, it was with two enormous red hounds and their master between them.

"Silence!" One ominous word from Alizar ended the squabble between Jemir and Tarek instantly. "Explain yourselves."

Jemir and Tarek bowed their heads.

Alizar set his penetrating gaze on Jemir. "Speak."

"He has a peacock in his room."

"No, there is nothing," insisted Tarek.

"A strange sound disturbed my work," said Jemir. "I came up here to investigate. Leitah heard it as well."

The mute servant girl nodded.

"Tarek, is there something in your room?" Alizar asked. Tarek cringed at the simple question. When punished as a child, Tarek would envision Alizar standing over him like Poseidon at the surf's edge, wild white mane swirling in the storm above him, trident in hand, lightning flashing in the distance as his sonorous voice lashed out. Tarek wanted to lie, but he could not summon any story worthy enough. The truth would have to do.

"Yes."

"Go on. What is it?"

Tarek nudged the door with his foot.

And that was when he revealed to them his secret, the girl he had been hiding in his room for nearly a week. The girl he had purchased for one hundred gold *solidi* in the market who had neither died nor recovered.

"Hermes, Zeus, and Apollo." Alizar swept a hand through his white mane and stopped in the center of the room, for there was Hannah, naked, curled against the wall at the corner of the bed, her knees drawn up to her chest. Her hair was matted and wild about her body as though she had crawled beneath a dead bougainvillea bush. Her skin glistened with sweat, and the sheets beneath her were soaked through. The acrid stench in the room of sweat, urine, and vomit was overwhelming, and drew a curtain of flies.

Alizar did not turn his eyes from the girl. "Jemir, shut the door."

The door clicked shut.

"Tarek, where did she come from?"

"The market."

"I do not mean the market, boy. Tell me where she comes from." Alizar studied the girl before him. This was no Egyptian slave. Her skin might have made her Persian for its smooth sheen the color of sandalwood, but her eyes . . . her eyes were a blue as dark and deep as the Sardinian sea.

"I, I do not know," Tarek stammered. "I bought her."

"You what?"

Tarek bowed his head. "For you."

Alizar's eyes could have impaled the boy. "For me. I hardly think so. And that is a matter I will attend to in fine detail at another time. For now, I must see to this child. What language does she speak, Tarek?"

Tarek shrugged.

A whimper escaped Hannah's lips as a tear slipped down her cheek. Her whole body shook as if in the cold, though the room was an inferno. She was aware that these strange men were discussing her, and the fear she had felt on the road was unequaled by this new wave of terror. What would they do with her now?

Leitah's feminine instincts swelled within her, and she tiptoed to the bed. She reached out tenderly and took the girl's hand. Hannah suddenly jolted to life, and struck out with flailing fists. Leitah stood up and reached forward to take her shoulders, whispering soothing words as Hannah thrashed about until she finally calmed down and began to cry. When Hannah had no resistance left in her, Leitah took the poor thing in her arms and rocked her, wiping the sticky hair back from her shoulders. This revealed the unhealed gash where the raiders had cut her. Hannah trembled soundlessly, her body given over to shock.

Jemir, who stood beside the door, said accusingly, "What have you done to her, Tarek?"

Tarek bowed his head. "Nothing. I swear it. I have tried to feed her and clothe her, and she refuses every piece of meat I give her. She is mad as a dog."

Alizar sat on the bed, touched the sheets, and regarded the deep festering gash that ran along Hannah's sternum. "That needs to be treated by a doctor. Jemir, send for Philomen. Leitah, go and fetch a bucket of warm water and a sponge. Tarek, leave us."

When they had gone, Alizar spoke softly in Greek. "What is your name, child?"

Hannah's expression remained unchanged.

Alizar shifted his tongue to Latin. No response. Then to Egyptian. Then to the few words he could still remember from the northern territories of Gaul, then Persia. Nothing.

Finally, it was Hannah who spoke. "My father is coming for me." She wanted to sound strong, but her voice was hardly a whisper. She lifted her head and spit in Alizar's face for emphasis, which did more to charm than irk him.

Alizar wiped his cheek on his sleeve and smiled to himself, for here was a daughter of Abraham. Although he could see slight traces of that lineage in her, perhaps in the pout of her lips or the way her straight nose rounded and flared at the tip, it was undoubtedly the aristocracy of Rome he saw in her pronounced cheek bones, her well-sculpted jaw, her high brow, and oceanic eyes. Alizar listened closely, turning her words over again in his mind. It was Aramaic, the language of the Jewish shepherds. How did she come to be so far from home? Her bronze collar seemed evidence enough. The metal was still new enough to retain its polish. She must have been captured, taken from her family, and then sold. "Calm yourself," said Alizar in her native tongue. "No one is going to hurt you here. I have sent for a doctor. You are not well. You must rest. What is your name?"

"My father," Hannah pleaded. Her voice was even weaker now, and her eyes had begun the inward collapse of the very ill.

Alizar stood and opened the window to ventilate the stifling room. "I do not know, child. First, we must make you well. Then we will discuss your father, and how you came to be in Alexandria."

"Alexandria." Hannah tasted the beautiful word, the same word the men had spoken when they entered the city, and she knew then where she must be.

She did not remember the days that followed as a torrid fever struck her body, hot rivers of fire flooding her veins. The infection of the wound had taken root, and though Leitah traced a cool rag over her neck and forehead, it did not abate. Philomen, Alizar's preferred doctor from the Great Library, came several times over the week to dress the gash and prescribe herbs and tinctures, but he finally clucked his tongue and told Alizar to secure a small grave. She would not live the night. Pity.

Within the fever's grip, Hannah turned. She dreamed the kinds of dreams that mystics stumble upon at the onset of enlightenment, when the world is luminous and still, staved with a golden light that comes from above and below all at once. Her body housed a shrine to the stars as galaxies unfurled in her belly, and the sun and moon circled like young lovers in her heart. The drum of her pulse became to her inner ear a siege of soldiers marching across a bleak desert, their steps pounding the parched earth. Everywhere she searched for her father, behind doors that blossomed into clouds, and in faces that dissolved into other faces from other times, some familiar and some utterly foreign and disfigured.

Jemir, Alizar, Leitah, and Tarek each came to the girl's bed independently of one another, each performing the same ritual. They stood in the room watching her breathe, unconsciously measuring the length of her inhalations and exhalations, studying the rise and fall of her chest, knowing at any moment she might die, perhaps at the very moment they were standing in the room. They were fascinated by the possibility even as it unnerved them.

In fleeting wakeful moments, Hannah searched for a feeling inside her body that would tell her that her father was alive. Would she not feel something if he was gone? A father abyss in her heart? But she felt only the sickness.

So.

On the fifth morning, her fever broke.

By midday, she was able to nibble on the Roman bread and fig jam brought by Jemir. And then sleep, the deep relief of dreamless sleep.

Her recovery was quick after the infection left her body. The wound closed, leaving a slick scar glossy as a feather, and the doctor seemed pleased with himself and the work of the poultice. When she was well enough to walk, and stand, and dress herself, Alizar appointed Hannah the washing maid and set baskets of laundry in her arms, reluctantly forgiving Tarek's blunder as he had a growing fondness for the intelligent girl. He hoped she would behave.

Hannah humbly accepted her new life as she knew she had to appear complacent in order to plan her escape. There would not be much time. She had already been gone from the waning crescent moon to the full. Perhaps when she found her father, they could repay Alizar with several fine goats from the herd. He had saved her life, and she did not want his generosity to go unrewarded.

In the evening she found an upstairs window and ate her supper alone, conspiring with the moon. True, she could be captured by another slave trader on the road, but it did not matter to her. She knew she could be cunning, for she was raised in the desert. She could certainly escape a city.

Her opportunity came two nights later when Alizar's cistern ran dry. They needed to go to the town well to buy water. It was open all night, guarded by soldiers who collected the fees and tried to prevent theft. Water was rationed and valuable and could be sold by weight on the black market to anyone who could afford it.

Tarek, Leitah, and Hannah left Alizar's house with buckets hanging from sticks over their shoulders, and on a cart pulled by two goats still larger barrels that the buckets could be used to fill. The coins for the water were in Tarek's possession. Hannah eyed them, swinging from a purse at his belt. She would need money. But it seemed wrong to steal from Alizar's purse after he had brought her back from death, and so she decided to steal from someone else if need be. It was something she hated to do, as thieving was something her father always taught her was wrong. Certainly he would make this one exception.

As they neared the well, Hannah began to bounce in place with her hands between her knees. Leitah recognized the gesture immediately and directed her to one of the public latrines in the next alley. Tarek gave Hannah one tiny copper coin to pay the guard at the entrance. As Hannah hoped, Tarek and Leitah turned away to begin the long process of drawing the water. Instead of heading into the latrine, she pocketed the coin, walked down the alley, then turned into the next alley and broke into a run. No one saw her. She made her way through the alleys all night until she could see a promising patch of open desert at the end of Canopic Way and broke into a run.

She was caught trying to leave the Gate of the Sun. The guards there grabbed her wrists as she tried to pass and pushed her hair aside to reveal the bronze slave collar. They simply locked her in a cage until Tarek found her at dawn. The guards opened their palms, expecting payment. Tarek reluctantly complied with a *nummus* each. When they unlocked the cage, he smacked her hard across the face with the back of his hand, and she dropped to her knees. "Do not ever disrespect my father's house again," he said, and she began to cry.

She might have attempted another escape right away had she not discovered the secret door in Alizar's house at the top of the stairs and what lay beyond.

4

Hannah stared at the strange polished brass square in her hands.
She lifted one finger to trace her eyebrows, her rounded nose. She
flared her nostrils, then grimaced, then smiled and curled her
plump lips back to examine her teeth. Hearing footsteps behind
her, she abruptly set the brass mirror back on the table as her
cheeks reddened with shame. Shame, the unbidden emotion that
now followed her everywhere like a hungry dog.

Alizar chuckled, intrigued by the girl whose aura filled the
house like the scent of wild thyme. The ferocity of her sensual
beauty was not lost on him, nor was the pain in her eyes. Somehow, in spite of all that had happened to her, she carried herself
like nobility. No. More than that. He studied her. She stood like
a proud bird of some kind, a heron or a hawk. That kind of grace
could not be learned.

Alizar did not seem upset about the mirror but handed her a
broom and indicated the steps leading from the lower hall to the
roof. "There is a door there at the top of the stairs. You are not to
enter. Sweep the steps and then return to the kitchen to help Jemir
prepare supper. We have important guests tonight."

Hannah nodded. Alizar was still doing her the courtesy of
speaking in Aramaic, but he was gradually mixing in some Greek
so she would learn. When he left, she took the broom to the stairs
and began sweeping the bottom step, gradually working her way
up. The stairway was long and irregular, with three separate land-
ings. It meandered around the perimeter of the house, which was

beset with tiny windows offering views of the market, the fallen Serapeum, and a long and important-seeming wall that shielded five large, ornate buildings. At the first landing, Hannah paused and took a long look out across her new world, the world she would escape at the next available opportunity. She had never been in a city before, only dreamed of them. But in her dreams she frolicked through the passageways and danced beneath the roofs. She cursed the Egyptians that built the city but did not know that it was not the ancient Egyptians who built Alexandria at all. It had been the Greeks seven hundred years before her time, led by Ptolemy, Alexander the Great's revered and trusted general, who upon Alexander's death had taken the legendary leader's corpse with him into Egypt in the hope of founding a new seat for the Egyptian Empire in Alexandria. It was Ptolemy who envisioned and planned the Great Library and Ptolemy whose lineage eventually birthed Queen Cleopatra. Hannah would learn these things and more once Alizar made his decision about her.

Broom in hand, Hannah resumed her task, and then realized that the sweeping would go much better if she started at the top of the stairs rather than the bottom so the detritus would gradually filter down. And that was when she saw the forbidden door, only she was not sure if it was the forbidden door or not, because there was another nearly identical door through a short passage just beyond it. Curiosity overcame her.

The first door she came to was unmarked, and there was a large key stuck in the lock. The second door beyond the passage had no key, and was marked by an unusual symbol burned into the wood: twin serpents ascending a staff toward a winged disk. Hannah decided that this had to be the forbidden door she was not to enter, and so made her way back through the passage.

Hannah had never seen a key before, or a door for that matter, until she came to Alizar's house. In the pastures of Mt. Sinai, no one locked up the moon or threw a roof over the trees. The closest things she knew to architecture were the wooden staves of her father's tent and the branches of the old olive tree on the hill. But by the firelight of many evenings, she had listened to the stories of the gypsies, and the palaces they told of in Persia and the Akropolis in Greece, and all the mighty ships sailed by swarthy men out of the Aegean Sea and the Bosphorus. So she was in no way ignorant of the wonders of civilization; those wonders had simply not included her before.

The key turned, and the door swung open on its own weight. Hannah stepped inside, forgetting her broom, for there on a bed in the center of the room lay an old woman, both hands folded over her ribcage. Was this a corpse? Hannah quickly shut the door behind her. She sensed that she should not be in the room, but she could not bring herself to leave. Who was this woman? And how did she come to be here? Hannah slowly approached the bed, knowing she could at any moment be caught. But she wanted to get closer to the luminous body of this celestial figure laid out before her.

At the foot of the bed, Hannah paused. Though the woman's eyes were closed, a thin thread of breath wove in and out of her nostrils. She was sleeping.

Hannah cautiously edged around the bed, curious. The pale stillness of the woman's face made her look as though she had been carved of marble, and though she was old, her beauty had never faded. The mysterious woman exuded a tranquil peace that seemed to calm all Hannah's fears instantaneously. How could a sleeping body do such a thing? Hannah sat on a velvet-cushioned stool beside the bed facing the woman and watched her for a long time, grateful to be in such soothing company, unaware of the passage of time. It was the first time in weeks Hannah felt safe, a treasured feeling she had nearly forgotten.

A lithe ocean breeze from a north-facing balcony lifted two sheer gossamer veils draped around the bed. The scent of the sea was stronger in that room than in any other Hannah had been in, sweet and salt-laden. She relished it, breathing in and licking her lips. She did not want to leave the woman's bedside in the same way she would not want to draw her cold hands away from a fire. So, she closed her eyes and dozed lightly in the chair.

After a while, a rustling sound woke her, and Hannah glanced down on the floor to see loose pages of parchment fluttering like so many dying fish. Without thinking, she bent to collect them and bound them into a stack with a bit of red string left on a table near the bed. Then she remembered her sweeping, paid the peaceful old woman a long last look, and returned to her chores, turning the key in the lock as she left, relieved she had not been discovered.

Each day, Hannah felt compelled to return to the woman's bedside. She would hurry through her washing to have enough time remaining to sweep the stairs before Jemir needed assistance in the kitchen. Each day it was the same. The pages of parchment had been strewn about the floor by the breeze, and so Hannah would collect them and bind them and set them on the table. Then she would sit for as long as she could on the settee that was turned toward the bed where the woman lay in absolute peace. *In peace.* That she lay in perfect peace was all Hannah knew about her. Of course, she wanted very much to know more but feared that any inquiry would expose her secret visitations to the woman's bedside, and she could not bear the thought of not being able to return to her private refuge. For that was what sitting beside the sleeping woman had become to her.

After several weeks, the secret routine had not changed. There were the loose parchments strewn about the floor, the rectangle of sun where Hannah sat and watched the woman sleep, and then sweeping the stairs. But one day, Hannah did something she had not done previously, and it would not go so easily unnoticed.

She opened her throat in song.

Hannah had simply wanted to give something back to the beautiful woman that had brought her a handful of precious peaceful hours.

So.

Even the angel listened in the eaves, waiting.

Hannah sang a childhood song full of warmth and merriment as tears flowed down her cheeks. Hannah could not remember the last time she had sung. In Sinai, shepherd songs had been the marrow of her days. She did not know who she was without them. Yet in Alexandria, she had forgotten the sound of her own voice and become someone else. A silent, orphaned slave.

Jemir came looking for Hannah when he realized they were running low on water, and more would need to be drawn from the cistern for the soup. He opened his mouth to call her name from the bottom of the stairs, but he heard the singing and froze, for it was the most beautiful sound that had ever reached his ears. He drank it in, closing his eyes. He wanted it to go on as he was transported back to his boyhood, when his mother and his sisters sang together, a time when his family was still alive. A tear sprouted from his eye, which he quickly wiped away.

Alizar passed through the lower hall a few minutes later and saw Jemir standing there with his ear tipped to the wall, and assumed he was listening for a rat. "I do hope you kill it. It has eaten all the basil in the upstairs pots."

"No, come listen." Jemir waved for Alizar to stand in the spot.

"Praise Zeus," Alizar whispered. "Is that girl singing to my wife? I told her that room was forbidden." Alizar nudged him. "Go and get her. Governor Orestes and his wife Phoebe are coming for dinner, and there is much to do." Jemir looked at him. "Go on," said Alizar.

And so Jemir ascended the steps, swinging the empty water bucket, only Hannah met him at the second landing. "Jemir," she said, "I have finished the sweeping."

"Yes," said Jemir. "Good." He did not make any mention of her singing. How could he? He did not want her to stop.

———————

That evening, Jemir and Hannah arranged three place settings at a long wooden Byzantine table in the courtyard beneath a sprawling old fig tree that had seen many gatherings beneath its curling branches. Jemir explained that the governor and his wife were coming for supper, and that it was imperative that all the serving go perfectly. Hannah nodded in understanding.

Alizar was seated within the hour, his twin red Pharaoh Hounds resting at his feet as he enjoyed a cup of Mareotic wine in the mosaic light cast from the candles.

"Orestes, Phoebe, welcome to my table." Alizar stood for his guests and opened his hands, indicating the places set for them. He wore a burgundy robe of fine damask linen, embroidered along the length with edging of golden acanthus, a *corona* of lavender flowers on his head. He looked like an emperor to Hannah, who had never seen such finery. She brought out the baskets of Roman bread and bowed politely.

Orestes and Phoebe took their seats on blue silk cushions that adorned the high backed chairs, and remarked between them that it had been years since they had seen Alizar looking so happy, a reference to his recent gain in weight, a sign of contentment and prosperity. The garrulous old friends chatted happily as the feast was brought out, for they had not seen each other in some time.

There was lamb roasted with honey-pepper sauce set beside leafy cabbage fans cradling a lentil tomato pilaf as well as three large baked hogfish stuffed with cheese and slathered in olive oil and vinegar, served whole on a bed of finely sliced onion. At the center of the table were two amphora filled with the wine from the eastern shores of Lake Mareotis, and on either end, twin ceramic *amphoriskos* carved with scenes of black satyrs, brimming with viscous olive oil. The wine amphora bore a stamp in the clay of two griffins rearing over a chalice resting between them.

Hannah watched from the window in the kitchen, a skein of dark hair plunging between her eyes like a dagger. "Jemir, what does he do?"

Jemir dried his large hands on a rag at his hip and walked to the window. "Alizar? He is a vintner."

"Vintner," repeated Hannah.

"Yes, makes wine."

"Ah, wine!" exclaimed Hannah, understanding this new word that she had learned earlier in the day. She fetched a bottle from the table and brought it to Jemir. "His wine?"

Jemir smiled, his yellow teeth wedged within a face as black as licorice bark, and took the bottle. "*Neh.*" Then he cracked the head of the bottle on the edge of the table and poured two cups, one for each of them.

Outside, Alizar spoke with his hands, gesticulating with the playfulness of the Greeks. There was an ease between him and his guests that comes only with the passing of many years; each finished the sentences of the others, and laughter was as much there for what was said as for what was left unsaid.

Jemir took a sip of the heady dark wine and fingered his mustache contemplatively, then continued his earlier explanation for Hannah's benefit. "His vineyards here in Egypt are twenty-five kilometers outside of Alexandria to the east, on the fertile shores of Lake Mareotis. He owns twelve presses and thirty kilns, and there are almost seventy women who tend them. When he inherited the vineyards from his uncle, he did not have men for the harvest, so he offered to house fallen courtesans and their sons who would have otherwise been left to beg in the street. Everyone in Alexandria called him a madman, but the wine he set on their tables in following years gained him the prestige he now has, of being the finest vintner in the whole of the Mediterranean. When he inherited the business forty years ago, its worth was counted in *tremissis*, but now it is worth a purse of gold *nomisma*. In the last ten years he has acquired more land outside of Athens and planted another vineyard there as well. And I have been with him now for nearly thirty years, as I was with his uncle before him in Epidavros when I was just a boy. The time has passed so quickly." He smiled, the years showing nowhere but in the crinkle of skin beside his eyes. Where silver hair would surely crown his head, his skull was shaved smooth. "The gods have been good to us."

Hannah listened raptly and tried to understand this lyrical language of Alizar's house. So much of it was like a finch's song, meaningless and lovely. She wanted to know more. "What of Tarek?"

Jemir dabbed at the droplets of wine that sprinkled the dome of his belly. "Egyptian. His mother was once a servant in the house, like you and me. She was a frail woman whose cheeks drooped like the jowls of a mean dog." He lowered his voice. "Tarek calls Alizar 'father,' but there is no blood relation. His mother came into the house already with child. Then she tried to insist the boy was Alizar's. No one believed her."

"What happened to her?"

"She left for the fish market when Tarek was a small boy and was never seen again. Alizar's daughter, Sofia, who was perhaps ten years old at the time, despised the woman. She suspected that Tarek's mother fabricated the entire story so that Tarek as the eldest boy in the house would be in line for an inheritance, since Alizar's only son, Theon, was only a season younger than Tarek at the time."

"Alizar has children?"

"Yes. Sofia is the only child now. Her half brother, Theon, was a remarkable gymnast, and had been accepted to compete as an Olympian. He died in a tragic fall from the roof when he and

Tarek were playing a game. Do not speak of him." Jemir's eyes darkened.

Hannah studied Jemir's face. "Do you think Tarek was responsible?"

Jemir sighed, his opinion withheld. "Tarek was devastated by Theon's death. They were practically brothers."

"And Sofia? Is she here?"

"After Theon's death she left Alexandria and has not returned."

"She left? Where did she go?"

"Sofia lives in Epidavros outside of Athens at Alizar's other vineyard. The boy's mother never recovered. Alizar's wife."

"His wife?" asked Hannah.

"Yes." Jemir wiped the red stain from his mustache. "Naomi sleeps at the top of the stairs."

Hannah's eyes came alive.

"What is it?" Jemir asked.

Hannah shook her head and tried to mask her joy at learning the identity of the woman whom she attended to day after day. "Nothing." She did not want anyone to know she had found Alizar's wife. Alizar had been lenient with her about escaping. She did not want to try his patience.

"Jemir?" Alizar called from the courtyard. "Can you bring the coffee?"

"I will get it," said Hannah. She had hoped they would ask for coffee as she loved the potent scent of it. She sometimes carried a coffee bean tucked up under her headscarf all through the day so that she could pull it out and inhale the rich aroma. She dashed out into the courtyard with the tray and a wide smile.

"Alizar," said Orestes, "wherever did you find this charming slave?"

Alizar chewed his food contemplatively, and washed it down with a sip of wine. "She is called Hannah. Apparently, she had family in the desert. A father, I understand. She came here quite by accident."

An Abba.

Hannah set the teacups on the table before Orestes and his wife, her hands shaking so dramatically at the mention of her father that the cups clattered in their saucers. As she poured the dark, aromatic coffee for Alizar, she found it impossible to hold the spout in one place, and it splashed across the table into his lap.

Alizar shoved his chair back from the table with a howl, and then quick laughter.

"Aye!" Hannah set the coffee pot down and quickly untied her waist scarf to mop up the spill. Alizar lifted his napkin and began dabbing at his groin and thigh.

Orestes ignored the incident entirely, so intrigued was he by the beautiful young girl. "She is a Jew?"

Hannah glanced at Alizar, her eyes frantic as she mopped up the coffee, and Alizar set a hand on her wrist. "Stop," he said. "I will take care of it. Go inside."

Hannah bowed her head and ran into the kitchen. She feared this man who stood a full head higher than her father, his taut muscles so well defined he might have modeled for a chart of anatomy, yet he surely had to be a grandfather ten times over. But what struck Hannah most was not Alizar's appearance at all, but his voice. If a mountain could speak, it would sound like Alizar. If all the sonorous waves of the sea broke the shore at once, they could not compete with the resonance in his chest. She wanted to wrap herself in his voice, for it was surely the strongest armor in the world.

"Yes, governor," said Alizar, returning to his chair. "I do not know her story. She attempted to escape not long ago, and so the poor thing must believe her family is still alive."

"She is very dutiful," ventured Phoebe, attempting to be punctilious, hardly masking her seething jealousy at her husband's keen interest in the girl. She repeated a nervous gesture of repeatedly tucking the blue *taenia* in her silver hair behind one of her ears.

"Yes, quite," said Orestes, his eyes merry with desire. "Might I buy her off of you, Alizar?"

Alizar shook his head.

"Just name your price." Orestes shook his purse in his hand.

Alizar looked back to the open doorway of the kitchen where Hannah stood in silhouette, bent over, her face in her hands. Then the door closed. "No," he said resolutely. "The girl is not for sale, old friend."

"But what will you do with her?" asked Orestes. "You told me last month you had too many servants to feed. What if the drought continues? Do us a favor," he glanced at Phoebe. "We could use a girl like her."

"We purchased two like her last season." Phoebe shifted uncomfortably. She certainly did not want a beauty hanging about her husband's quarters. Alizar smiled and ended the discussion. "For now I will keep her." Phoebe looked relieved as Alizar changed the subject and Orestes reluctantly put his purse away. "Speak of Cyril. Tell me, have you made any progress with the Emperor in disbanding the Parabolani?"

"None I am afraid."

"Orestes, I fear for the library."

"Yes," said Orestes gravely, setting down his cup. "So do I. As praetorian prefect I could do far more to protect the treasures of our city, so I have decided to run in the next election. Once I preside over all of Egypt, I believe I will have the leverage I need to gather an army and end Cyril's tirade. Hypatia even seems to think I will win."

"To victory!" Alizar raised his glass, and they all drank deeply.

The candles burned low, and they each took places on divans to recline and recite poetry. Orestes noted the planet Jupiter perched directly above them in the sky and commented on its auspicious placement as they inhaled sweet hashish from Alizar's finest hookah.

Phoebe did not agree with the men that the tide of hatred toward the pagans in the city was changing. She knew in her bones that they were all still in danger. She turned the conversation from joyful banter toward a more serious matter. "Did you hear? Hypatia received another death threat."

Alizar shook his head. "Orestes, pray, when?"

"While you still sailed. Cyril's men cut off Isaiah's arms, lit him on fire, and dropped the lad at the Caesarium gate with a letter tied to a stone before him, demanding that Hypatia turn over the stacks of the library to the church."

"The coward," acknowledged Alizar, his voice softer now that he was stoned, his eyes glowing red as hot coals. "And what was Hypatia's response?"

"You know how foolish Hypatia can be. I believe she cursed him," said Phoebe.

Alizar nodded. "She will never succumb to threats. They merely strengthen her resolve to defend the library." He turned a ripe pomegranate in his hand. "And mine."

"Yes, indeed," said Orestes. "And mine." He smiled triumphantly at his wife and his friend and downed the last of the wine in his *rython*.

That night, Hannah lay curled on her side in her bed of stable straw beside Leitah, who was already asleep. She listened to the market cats in heat as they mewed their prurient cries into the night. Her belly cramped with her monthly blood. At least that concern was over. Now she only felt the silent ache in her heart for her father and the sorrow that she would not have her virginity for a husband, which meant she would likely never marry, even if she were to find her freedom again. Perhaps that was for the best.

She still had dreams of the slave traders' rape, the laughter at her screams. Their hairy naked bodies pressed to her naked thighs. She hated them in disgust, and only in hating them was her shame diminished.

She lifted her hand to her head and withdrew the silver hairpin. Somehow the slave traders had not seen it there, or surely they would have taken that, too. She ran her fingers over the curves of the peacock, the twin pins that emerged from its belly like elongated legs. It was the only thing that remained of her father in her life until they could be reunited. Precious gift. She pressed it to her lips in the darkness and then returned it to her hair.

Her circumstances were maddening. Hannah watched while the drought wore on and reports of the dead came over the walls, and yet she was clothed and fed and slept on a warm bed of straw. Even though she wanted to escape, she was frightened. Everyone knew a slave's collar in the city. She would be punished again, perhaps killed. What good would she be to her father dead? She had always felt so powerful climbing the steep cliffs of Sinai, as capable with the herd as any man. She considered stealing Tarek's clothes and a knife; she could pull a burnoose across her face and walk the roads. It could work if she managed to get out of Alexandria. But what then?

By candlelight Hannah traced twin triangles overlapping, one above, one beneath, just above her pillow. Then she whispered the *Shema*, her hand above her eyes. Sacred prayer.

And though her heart knew little peace, her sanctified whispers carried her to sleep.

So.

Hannah hummed softly, carrying a basket of wet linen sheets on her head as she walked through the white marble halls of the house, past the glistening *impluvium* in the atrium that reflected the enormous stone statue of Hermes, his steely eyes fixed upon the heavens, and down the bougainvillea arbor toward the clothesline. When she had secured the last sheet, Alizar appeared. "Hannah, come see me."

Hannah bit her lower lip and nodded. This was about the coffee incident she was certain. Or worse, what if he had discovered she was secretly sitting with his wife? Hot bile rose in her throat. He would beat her, she was certain, or sell her. Thoughts flew through her mind like raindrops scattered in a flurry. What if he sold her to someone wicked who whipped her or locked her up or made her bear endless children? What if he sent her away on a ship? Each fate seemed more terrible than the last. Hannah gathered the empty reed basket into her trembling hands, set it on her head, and went into the house.

"Come," said Alizar, standing between his loyal red hounds, their tongues lolling against his robes as he rubbed their ears.

He led Hannah across the lower hall toward a south-facing balcony, which overlooked the stable yard and the alleyway that led to Canopic Way. Although the day had only just begun, the sun was already warming the flat stones of the balcony beneath Hannah's bare feet. The hounds sprawled along the wall and closed their eyes. In the street below, traders were setting up their tents. Alizar pointed out the town barber who always took the best spot beside the fountain, his popularity owed to the Alexandrian style of men wearing their faces smooth as geese eggs like its founder—a fashion Alizar had never subscribed to. He showed her the scribe who would take dictations for a *siliqua*, and the cosmetic dealers—plump, cheery women who painted the eyes and lips of the women walking by. Beside the grain merchant's tent, an orange cat was bent over a dead chicken, lapping up the blood as white feathers wafted down the street like dandelion seeds.

Hannah knelt before him, trembling.

Alizar pulled her up. "I am not going to sell you off. Spilling coffee is not a crime, at least not in my house." He lifted an empty cup and poured black coffee from a ceramic pot painted with traditional Greek scenes of Dionysus and his nymphs. He sipped slowly and then lifted one eyebrow and speared Hannah with his ice blue eyes. "I understand you have met my wife."

Hannah threw herself at his mercy. "I am sorry. She was so peaceful there, and so beautiful, and I was curious. Curiosity is a fault with me. My father has always said it."

Alizar settled himself on a divan in the shade and invited Hannah to sit in a chair beside him. "Yes, you are a curious girl, but that is not a crime as I understand it, either. I do not appreciate you going against my wishes to stay out of the room, but I am willing to forgive it this once. Tell me about your father, Hannah, and your family."

Hannah breathed a sigh of relief and sat cautiously in the chair beside Alizar. "My father is a king," said Hannah finally, filled with longing for her Abba at the thought of his name. "A king of shepherds. I never knew my mother. She died giving birth to me just after I was named."

"Your father's name?"

"He is called Kaleb of Sinai."

Alizar narrowed his eyes to slits like a falcon in the wind. "And you are certain your mother was also a Jew?"

"Yes. She was fifteen when she died giving birth to me."

"Hannah, there is not a Mizrahi Jew alive with blue eyes such as yours. Your dark hair, perhaps, but that is all. Was your mother Berber perhaps? Or Greek?"

Hannah's blood rose. "You think because you own me you can insult my family? I was not born into slavery; I was taken from a life of freedom. My father will come for me. He is searching for me even now."

Alizar leaned back on the cushions. He pitied her, so adamant to believe her father was alive. "No, no. I am sorry. But you yourself have looked in the mirror. When you next go into the market to purchase supplies for Jemir, take a look at the Jews there. You do not resemble any of them. Still, you are yourself, regardless of where you came from or how you came to be here. It is not important." Alizar poured another cup of coffee and offered it to Hannah. "I want to talk to you about something else."

Hannah accepted, and blew the steam from the surface of the cup. "I apologize if I insult your kindness, Alizar. I do not forget that you saved my life."

"Acknowledged. Now I have a request. I want you to sing for me."

Hannah nearly dropped her cup. "Sing for you?"

"*Neh*," said Alizar. "I have listened to you from far off when you are hanging sheets out in the courtyard and I want to hear you for myself. You have a beautiful voice. Did you ever play an instrument?"

"A what?" asked Hannah, unsure of the Greek word.

"An instrument. A drum, a lute, a harp."

"Ah, yes, an instrument," said Hannah, understanding. "I had a little lap harp I would play to sing to our herd. It was very worn, and often the strings would break."

"How many songs do you know and in how many languages?"

"I do not know, but it is many." And it was true. She made up new songs every day, and so there were always songs upon songs. "I had a Persian teacher. She knew songs in Arabic, Hebrew, Aramaic, and Egyptian."

"Sing to me."

Just then the hounds sat up and growled at a grey cat that landed on the balcony. The cat realized its mistake at once and leapt for a high branch of the fig tree. As soon as it was out of sight, the dogs settled.

Hannah set down her cup and looked at Alizar.

Alizar smiled. "Pretend I am not here if you like." He turned sideways in his chair and covered his eyes with his sleeve. "Does that help?"

Hannah laughed.

Alizar waved a hand, "Proceed."

Realizing she had no choice, Hannah cleared her throat and began timorously. She sang a Persian song of the evenings when the long grass whispers on the mountain and the goats know they are coming home. As she moved into the second verse, the song overcame her shyness, and she sang more fully.

Down in the market, several people stopped and looked up to the balcony before carrying on their ways. Hannah's voice was from another world, from the same world, perhaps, as the pain in her eyes.

When she finished, Alizar clapped his hands and nodded approvingly. "I have a proposal, if you will accept," he said.

Hannah sat back down on the chair, blushing. She wanted to please him. A song seemed a small gift to give the man who saved her life.

"I propose that through your singing I will help you buy your freedom. It is a great deal of money, I know, but gradually over time it can be achieved."

"You would do this for me?"

"*Neh.*"

It was a generous offer most masters never put forward, yet Hannah knew she needed to find her father at once. Every lost day ached in her bosom. Alizar's offer would take years.

"Well, that is enough to say for now. My wife has been ill a long time," Alizar said. "Tell me, does she wake when you sing to her?"

"She stirs sometimes, but she does not wake. Alizar," Hannah ventured, "What is her illness?"

"I do not know." Alizar closed his eyes. When their son died, Naomi's spirit collapsed into her body like a dying star. No doctor had been able to diagnose her illness, much less cure her. She lost the ability to speak and rarely, if ever, did her eyes open even a thread. Somehow, miraculously, she lived on portions of food and water that would scarcely nourish a field mouse. "Perhaps she subsists only on love." Alizar bowed his head reverently and sighed.

"How long have you been married?"

"Twenty-seven years. We met in Constantinople when I was traveling with my business affairs. Leitah was only six years old then, her cosmetic slave." Alizar spoke with his eyes fixed in some far off direction where the memory lay for him. "If it had not been for a childhood friend insisting Naomi join her on a stroll down to the docks, we might never have met. It was a beautiful day in May, with enormous clouds rolling through the sky. I can still see her standing beside the ship, her smile of light, her laugh that made all the sailors want to humor her so that she would laugh again. I knew she would be my wife. I knew it instantly." Alizar's eyes, heavy with sadness, slowly drew him back to the balcony, blinking back the light as though the memory had not seized him so completely.

Hannah touched his knee with her hand and smiled. "I will clean the teapot," she said, finding her feet.

"Wait," said Alizar. "Sit down. There is one more thing I want to talk to you about."

Hannah sat.

"I want to give you something. A gift." Alizar saw the look of concern in Hannah's eyes. "No, I am not in need of a lover if that is what you are thinking. Nor is this some kind of ridiculous gem you can wear about your neck. No, what I am going to give you is far, far more valuable than that."

Hannah tipped her head. "What is it?"

Alizar smiled. "I will give you the world."

"I do not understand."

"No, not yet, but you will. Tomorrow I will have Tarek take you, and you will begin."

"Begin?"

"Yes, but you must promise me something."

"What?"

"That if I give you this gift, you do not attempt to escape again. It is a foolish thing to try. You would be killed on the road or just sold again to someone with far less patience than I."

Hannah nodded. "I understand."

"And you swear it?"

Hannah shifted uncomfortably. "I swear it," she said.

"Good." Alizar stood up, stretched his arms, and then leaned against the railing of the balcony. "Ah, I only regret I cannot take you myself."

"Where?"

"You will see. I have word that my ship, the *Vesta*, has just been loaded. Her captain, Gideon, and I will sail for Cyprus at dawn. One day I will tell you of my work, Hannah, but not yet." He winked. "You cannot learn all of my secrets today."

At dinner that evening, Hannah found herself seated on the floor in the kitchen at a small table between Jemir and Tarek, both of whom took it upon themselves to entertain the beautiful new girl. Leitah sat with them, peeling a pomegranate. Tarek did his best to translate.

Hannah learned from Jemir that when Alizar was in Alexandria, he rarely came down from the tower unless there were guests, and she learned from Tarek that he preferred it that way so he could be alone with his work. Before she could surmise anything about what a vintner's work might be, the back door to the kitchen was flung open and in sauntered a boisterous man, clearly at home. The stranger hugged Jemir and kissed him like family, and did the same for Leitah. For Tarek, however, the man merely saluted from across the room as he plucked an apple from a bowl in the center of the table, tossed it into the air, and then bit into it. The stranger was tall and toned by the sea; his muscles rippled beneath his *tunica* like a stallion's. Hannah studied him suspiciously—his dark eyes flashed with cunning, his cropped black hair threaded with silver that lent him a distinguished air that proved misleading—this man who whistled through his teeth like a sailor. He bore an angry scar that snaked like a purple vine from the edge of his eye down to his jaw, and his sword hilt was well worn. Hannah shifted in her seat, keen to avoid him.

"Where is Alizar?" asked the man, accustomed to barking commands.

Jemir finished chewing and then said, "Leitah, please go and tell Master Alizar that Gideon has arrived."

Leitah nodded and stood up, but Gideon placed his hand on her shoulder flirtatiously. "No need to disturb him now. Just relay he should meet me later tonight in the harbor to secure the hold." Then he winked at her and took another bite of the apple, his hand drifting to the front of her collar.

"Inform him of Gideon's visit in case there is something Alizar needs of him now," said Jemir to the mute servant girl. The pleasant sound of her gold bangles clinking together followed her down the hall once she had left the kitchen.

Then the stranger's gaze fell on Hannah seated in the corner of the kitchen. "Who is this?" he said, turning to Jemir. "Is everyone so rude that I should not be introduced to a new lady of the house?"

"Our apologies, captain," said Jemir. "This is Hannah, the new washing slave. Hannah, this is Gideon, Alizar's ship captain."

Hannah nodded and smiled at him weakly, which proved to be an instant invitation.

Gideon swept down beside her. "You are lucky to have landed here, lady," he said in a whisper, leaning forward so his lips were at her ear. "You will have the finest sea captain in the world at your service." His pressed the back of her hand to his lips and let his eyes fall on her breasts. Hannah modestly adjusted her *khiton* and drew back her hand. "Thank you, Captain," she said without any feeling.

He smiled and patted her bent knee. "Do not worry, beauty," he whispered. "You and I have all the time in the world."

Hannah dropped her eyes. Beside her, Tarek seethed.

"But for a slave you have no manners," said Gideon. "For one kiss I will be happy to teach you manners, for I am a great teacher of women." He turned his head and tapped his cheek for Hannah to kiss. Realizing she had no choice, Hannah resentfully leaned forward and kissed his terrible scar, inhaling the scent of the sea that lingered on his skin.

Gideon chuckled and smiled and gently patted her cheek. "Forgive me, beauty. Jest is my nature."

"I am a slave to this house and no other," retorted Hannah, spearing Gideon with a glare.

Gideon clucked his tongue at her. "Be careful, girl," he warned, "Or I shall have to teach you a lesson."

"Leave her alone, Gideon. She is mine," said Tarek. He put his arm around Hannah, who glowered at both men.

Gideon laughed at him and stepped to the door, addressing Jemir. "Please tell Alizar to meet me at the docks in an hour. Oh, and tell him to bring *her* with him, while he is at it." Gideon smiled at Hannah. "I find her fury most endearing, and I should like to give her a good jostle on the open sea." As he spoke he made a lewd gesture with his hips and laughed.

Hannah plucked an apple from the bowl and flung it at him, but Gideon had already ducked out the door so the apple glanced off the wall instead. His laughter lingered in the courtyard, and he began to whistle a tune that trailed off into the night.

Jemir turned to Hannah. "Gideon means well," he said. "Do not insult him. You must remember your place here."

Hannah clenched her jaw. "He's dreadful."

Tarek smiled in approval as Leitah returned to the room and sat down on a cushion beside the table.

Jemir clucked his tongue. "Save your fury for someone who deserves it, Hannah. Gideon plays like a giant child. Do not take him seriously, and you might even find him entertaining. Alizar trusts him with his life, and we need no other proof of his honor than that." Jemir retrieved the apple Hannah had thrown onto the floor and set it on the table, then bent to check the flat bread in the oven.

Hannah closed her eyes, her head flushed with thoughts. She turned to Tarek. "Why does Alizar travel? Is it his work?"

"He ships wine all over the Mediterranean," said Tarek.

Jemir reached forward to pour more water into his wine. "That is only partial truth," he said.

Tarek, who hated to be corrected as it was, hated it much worse in front of Hannah. He began to scowl as Jemir began his own interpretation.

"Hannah, Alizar is also an alchemist."

"Sounds like a Bedouin tale." Hannah set her bowl down, leaned back on a thick square cushion, fingering the tassels sewn to the corners.

Jemir chuckled. "Do not say that to Alizar."

"An alchemist knows how to make gold. I saw someone in the market do it once." Tarek smiled his crooked, corn-kernel grin, then rested his hand on Hannah's shoulder.

Hannah's eyes narrowed in suspicion, and she shifted on the cushion away from him.

"You will hear that rumor and many others about alchemists on the streets," said Jemir. "Only the initiated know truth from tale. You see, Hannah, the techniques of alchemy are taught to the monks in the Temple of Poseidon on Pharos, where Alizar spent his boyhood. The seven secrets of alchemy are etched upon a legendary stone called the Emerald Tablet, which was discovered by Alexander the Great when he traveled to the Siwa Oasis."

"Truly?" asked Hannah. "I would love to see such a tablet."

"No one knows where it is. The Nuapar monks on the isle of Pharos guard the knowledge of its location."

"Does Alizar practice these seven secrets of alchemy, then?"

"Indeed. Alizar is attempting to find a remedy for Naomi. He always returns with more herbs from his journeys to boil down into remedies," said Jemir.

"Do you think she will live?" asked Hannah.

Jemir sighed. Leitah nodded. Tarek just stared at his wine.

There was a moment of complete silence in the kitchen until Leitah dished herself a bowl of steaming *fuul*, the bangle bracelets on her wrists clinking as she dipped flatbread in the thick broth.

Hannah looked to Jemir, her eyes full of questions about the mute maidservant.

Jemir understood. "Leitah was studying to be a priestess at the Temple of Serapis under Antoninus, but the temple was burned to the ground by the last bishop. Her mother and only sister were killed. After that she took a vow of silence."

"How did the temple burn?"

Tarek puffed his chest like a pigeon, delighted to tell the story. "Emperor Theodosius the First made an edict forbidding pagan practice, and Bishop Theophilus of Alexandria decided to enforce it without so much as a warning. He attacked the Serapeum temple, killed everyone defending it, and one of his soldiers chopped the statue of Serapis to bits. All the texts were burned, and the Christians erected a church in place of the temple."

"The Christian bishop burned the temple?" Hannah shuddered, thinking of her introduction to the city, how the men in black robes had tortured and burned the man before the great wooden doors.

"Yes, but he is not the bishop any longer." Tarek lowered his eyes. "His nephew holds the title now." *Cyril:* the name was perched on Tarek's tongue, but he refused to speak it in Alizar's house. Instead, he spat on the stone floor.

Just then came a knock at the door, and Leitah rose to answer it. She reappeared a moment later and nodded to Tarek who went to see about it.

Hannah excused herself a moment later to relieve herself, but could not resist her curiosity when she saw the open window near the front door and heard the sound of a young girl crying.

She peaked through and saw Tarek, standing over the girl with his fist raised, and the girl kneeling in the street at his feet.

"I told you never to come here," he said.

"But the child is yours," she cried.

Tarek let his fist fall heavily on her cheek, bruising her other eye as she cried out. "You are nothing but a whore," he said. "You service a hundred men and come to me because we have money. I am not so gullible as that. Go back and tell your bawd that if I see you here again the beating will be worse. Now go." He kicked her to her feet, and she clutched her shawl around her body and fled.

Hannah heard the front door open and shut, and she pressed herself flat against the wall in the shadow, holding her breath as Tarek passed so he would not see her. The light illuminated her feet, and quickly she drew them back beneath her robe.

"Stupid woman," he said, wiggling the fingers he had used to hit the girl. He passed by Hannah without seeing her. When he had gone, Hannah exhaled and looked back out the window to the empty street where the poor girl had been a moment before. She knew then that of all these strangers, it was only Alizar and Leitah she would trust.

5

It was announced to the hall that the meeting of the clergy would be delayed an hour because the bishop was bathing, which was not uncommon, as time spent in the bath was always to alleviate his numerous health complaints: gout, heart murmurs, tumescent bowels. When His Eminence finally arrived, red in the face from an hour of strain, the oblong stone table was surrounded by impatient faces stamped with scowls, which was for most of them the natural angle of repose.

"Heirax, your report." Bishop Cyril took his seat at the head chair of the great table and cleared his throat. The room was deep within the roots of the church of St. Alexander and lacked, above all amenities, light. The stones in the wall absorbed what little the candelabras provided and refused to spit out so much as a spark for the rest of the room. One of the priests (who had traveled all the way from Britannia) loved this damp room that reminded him so much of his home. But the rest took no notice, for their duty involved attending to matters of God and law, not architecture.

Heirax cleared his throat. "The Parabolani have circulated over ten thousand treatises on Hypatia of Alexandria. It has been established further that this heretic remains a threat to our church establishment since an order was sent to her home to disband her private meetings and was ignored."

"I expected as much," said Cyril. "Continue."

"I have held counsel with the Parabolani, Your Eminence, and they inform me that the pamphlets we have circulated mostly end up being used to wrap fish or diaper small children. The populace has simply never seen such an issue before. You realize that most of them do not have access to parchment of their own and are illiterate besides. An expensive waste."

Cyril spread his small, fat hands on the table, grunted, and then stood so that he could pace the length of the room to engage his mind. Forced to sit for extended periods, he always became agitated, tending toward unnecessary fulminations that seldom reflected the weight of the discussion at hand.

"Then perhaps we can supply a small paper merchant in the market who could distribute parchment to the populace so that it is not so rare a commodity when it comes time to spread ideas of importance." The speaker was a young priest called Ammonius, who had a face the others agreed was too handsome for the work of God, though he was an effective preacher.

"No," said Cyril wryly. "I will not have this church gifting the whole civilized world with expensive Pergamon parchment."

Peter the Reader shifted in his seat. His legs were longer than the others, and so his knees pressed uncomfortably against the staves of the table. "I have another idea, one I have considered thoroughly."

"Speak it then," said Cyril, his mouth a thin line where lips should be.

"The populace of Alexandria is well-acquainted with sorcery. Many of them are pagans with secret altars in their homes. Were we in Constantinople, the charge against a sorceress might be taken seriously, but here in Alexandria, it is far too ordinary."

"You propose another charge?" asked Heirax.

"No," said Peter. "I propose we punish the pagan women practicing sorcery. Denounce them publicly. We must educate the citizens of Alexandria that there will be no tolerance for heathens in our midst."

Cyril smiled, and his whole face became lit with the deviousness of a small boy who has cornered a helpless dog with a stick. "Yes, very good. Gather them in a great mass and imprison them."

"With all due pardon, Your Eminence," said Peter, his voice unusually high in pitch for a man of such height and angularity of frame, "Imprisoning the women of Alexandria would be altered in an instant with a pardon from Governor Orestes. They would walk free, and we would look the fools."

Cyril returned to his chair, still standing. The mention of the governor unsettled him. "You have a better idea?"

"We must try them one at a time," said Peter. "Some will renounce their sorcery and take a vow of Christ, and those will be freed. Those who do not take the vow, or who otherwise prove to be involved in witchcraft, must be killed."

Heirax opened the codex before him and read aloud. "Exodus. *Thou shalt not suffer a witch to live.*"

The clergy at the table immediately turned to discuss the matter with one another.

Heirax sat back in his chair and looked at bishop Cyril, who nodded, then raised his voice to speak. "Heirax, the High Counselor of this chamber, has spoken the righteous word of God and reminded us of our true duty as the keepers of His law. I decree that witchcraft is a pagan abomination punishable by death in this city and that any woman thought to be a witch will be brought to trial before the people. If she confesses to her sins and renounces her evil doing and takes up the path of the gospels of our lord Jesus Christ, she shall be forgiven. But if she does not confess or refuses to renounce her sins, she shall be killed in a manner befitting a sorceress of black magic, by stoning or slitting of the throat."

There was silence around the table then, until Ammonius stood and brought his hands before him. Some twenty-odd members of the clergy joined him, facing the bishop. "Praise Christ, our Lord."

"Sit down, Ammonius," barked Cyril. "This campaign will go on until the pagans are vanquished and the witch Hypatia is dead. Alexandria is a Christian city, and we shall make it known to every pagan in that heathen library of theirs. Now go. Leave me to discuss the matter with my Parabolani. Heirax, summon the appointed leaders at once. I have a headache, and I am tired of looking at you." Cyril turned his head.

"As you wish, Your Eminence." Heirax stood. "Peter, gather your men from the square."

"Consider it done," said Peter, who rose to his full height. The gesture always disturbed the bishop further, as his own height was enough of a concern for him that he had special lifts put in his shoes for when he delivered his sermons from the dais.

With Peter out of the room, Cyril's eyes flicked to his High Counselor, Heirax, who was gathering his codices. "See that Peter sits on the other side of the table from me from this point forward. And I demand you leave me at once and return only when you have something interesting to report."

Heirax nodded and stepped out of the room with the other clergy, all the while facing the bishop, never turning his back.

 6

Alizar's ship sailed at dawn as planned. Hannah contemplated his kindness as she went about her morning chores. There was an uncomfortable emptiness in the house without his presence.

Jemir nudged open the window in the kitchen to let in the dirge that lilted down from the balcony. How quiet Alizar's house had been before. He closed his eyes and let himself be swept up in the sweetness of Hannah's voice as if it were an antidote to all that privately ailed him. Later, when she came in and plopped down onto one of the cushions on the floor, he felt his heart warm with affection.

"You sing beautifully."

Hannah's cheeks blossomed. "I did not realize you could hear me all the way in here. I am sorry. I will sing more softly."

"*Kuklamu*, if you sing softly you will offend the gods who gave you that voice."

Hannah turned her eyes down to the floor in modesty, her eyelashes brushing her cheeks.

Jemir threw her a rag. "You know what today is?"

Hannah caught the rag in the air and began wiping the table. She did not know.

"You go to the Great Library and the Mouseion. Alizar has arranged that you will have a tutor." Jemir could see by the expression on Hannah's face that the shepherd's daughter had no idea what a rare privilege this was, especially for a slave—and a female slave at that. Maybe she had not heard the stories of what marvels the library housed. Jemir saw at once his opportunity to build the anticipation for her. She would think he was describing a dream. It did not matter. The library might very well be a dream of the gods.

Hannah took up a long wooden spoon from the table and turned it over in her palms, inspecting it for grime.

Jemir started with something he knew that any girl would love to hear about: the butterfly enclosure. Thousands of blue and yellow and white spotted butterflies with elegant seashell wings collected from all over Africa and Europe. "You put honey on your finger, and they land there." Jemir held out his finger in the air and looked up at an imaginary butterfly that circled and then alighted.

Hannah smiled, almost happy. Jemir stopped short. It was the first time he had ever seen her smile, and it changed her face completely. Her beauty was amplified a thousand fold.

So.

He cleared his throat and continued. "There are enormous lions in cages, one even that lived in the great Coliseum in Rome and ate a hundred men, or maybe it was two hundred. But now the lion is old and has bad hips. The keepers cut the meat into bits for the elderly beast."

Jemir hunkered next to Hannah and waved his hands through the air. He wanted her to feel the greatness of it in his words. He wanted the legendary size of the library to come alive for her right there in Alizar's kitchen.

She laughed at his impression of the lion.

"Then there are the docks in the harbor with the manuscripts piled higher than any building in the city, even Alizar's tower. Imagine. Forty men side by side, all writing translations of the most famous literary and scientific works in the world. Homer. Aristotle. Pythagoras. Plotinus. Euripides. Archimedes. Eratosthenes . . ." Names that would mean something to Hannah once she learned their contributions.

Jemir explained that the fragrant lecture halls had been frequented by the greatest minds of the last three centuries. Mathematicians, philosophers, astronomers, rhetors, physicians, poets. Ptolemy penned his *Almagest* in the garden beneath one of the tall obelisks called Cleopatra's Needles, crumpling the pages he disapproved of and tossing them into the manure pile behind the elephant enclosure.

Hannah's eyes danced with some newly aroused feeling.

"The gardens were even planted by Cleopatra herself in honor of Caesar, or perhaps Mark Antony. No one can remember anymore. She and Antony were both buried beside the pond. It is said that the vine covering her golden tomb that appeared there after her death has lived these hundreds of years as a symbol of Cleopatra's love for Egypt. When the vine blooms, women from all ends of the Mediterranean come to collect its pretty purple flowers and crush them into potions for love."

Hannah hugged her knees to her chest and rocked. "This is Alizar's gift to me?"

Jemir nodded. He had to tell her one more thing, and in the telling, confess his secret love, a love an entire empire shared with him. "Did you know there is a woman who runs the Great Library?"

"A woman? How could that be?"

"It is because she is a star descended to earth. Hypatia, The Great Lady, Virgin of Serapis, daughter of renowned astronomer and mathematician, Theon of Alexandria. She is the most brilliant philosopher alive, a hermeticist said to alone hold the secret teachings of the Chaldean Oracles. She is a friend of Alizar's house. Her mind and her beauty are the envy of everyone in Egypt. And so, as you can imagine, she has hundreds of friends and more than a few enemies."

"Enemies?" As Jemir spoke Hannah remembered the woman holding the torch who had come running from out of the gates when they first arrived in Alexandria. Could it have been Hypatia?

"People cannot abide purity, *kukla*. It offends the poor and the rich at the same time." A lightness entered Jemir's features as he sighed, and for a moment Hannah could see him as a youth, before the deep lines had settled around his eyes and beside his mouth.

Realizing he had become lost in his infatuation with Hypatia, Jemir quickly regained his composure, excused himself, and went outside to check on the bread in the oven.

When Tarek strode into the kitchen and asked Hannah if she was ready, she leapt to her feet. "Jemir was telling me about Hypatia," she said as Jemir came back inside, set the bread down to cool, and busied his hands with a cloth, wiping down the windowsill.

"Oh, I see." Tarek rolled his eyes. Every servant in the house knew about Jemir's affections for Hypatia. Years earlier, when Tarek was a boy spying on the servants, he had seen Jemir writing pages of poetry that he tucked away behind the spice jars whenever anyone came in. Tarek showed the poetry triumphantly to everyone he could think of. After that, Jemir's fondness for Hypatia was no longer a secret. When Jemir had confronted him about the missing pages, Tarek insisted he had no idea they belonged to him. Jemir snatched the pages out of his hand and said, "Who else spices your food?" wielding the words the way he drew a knife down the belly of a small fish.

Tarek took Hannah's elbow and led her down the hall toward the cistern stairs. She stopped to tie her sandal to get out of his grip. "Why are we going this way?"

"I am taking you the secret way. The Parabolani are out."

Hannah cocked her head. "The what?" This city was full of a thousand new things to learn.

"The Parabolani, the bishop's henchmen. He originally recruited them under the auspices of feeding the poor and planting city gardens. Now he uses them to dispose of anyone who threatens his way to power." Tarek slid a large iron key into a lock on a tall wooden door and popped it open. The door swung open easily for its size, as if it were in constant use.

Hannah thought immediately of the men she had seen the first day she entered Alexandria, the ones who cut the man's arms from his body and lit him on fire. "They wear black robes," she said.

"Yes," said Tarek. "They wear their hair shorn to the scalp, dress in black robes, and walk together in threes. If you see them, hide and hide well."

So.

Hannah followed Tarek down the carved limestone steps and through a chthonic passageway lit by flickering torches. Soon she could hear running water and the squeal of rats in the dense walls.

A slow river loomed before her, the brackish water dank and deep.

Tarek strode over to a plank barge tethered to a stone post. Beside him a footbridge arched over the water leading to a stairway on the other side. Taking a torch from the wall, Tarek unleashed the barge, sweeping the long pole up in his free hand. Then he leapt onto the barge, which rocked precariously in the dark water. "Jump," he said.

Hannah stared at the tenebrous tunnel.

"I suppose you expect to float upstream?" asked Tarek.

Hannah eyed the barge. Then she took a deep breath and walked to the water's edge.

"Come on." Tarek leaned the pole on the barge and extended a hand.

Hannah glanced at him. Then she leapt, light as an antelope, without touching the hand floating in her direction, and settled herself on the front of the barge with her legs tucked beneath her.

Once underway, Hannah tugged the hem of her *himation* up over her nose in disgust at the miasma of rotting city refuse dumped in the tunnels: rotten chicken carcasses, excrement, piss, moldy cabbage heads. Tarek steered the barge around corner after corner, until beside a wall lit by sunlight pouring from a grate in the street above, the hairs on the back of Hannah's neck began to tingle, and she sat up, unnerved.

"This is where the poor secretly buried their dead a hundred years ago when the cost of purchasing tombs in the necropolis was raised. Quite illegal." Tarek made the enthusiastic announcement as though he were commenting on a fine frieze decorating a palace wall.

"Ick." Hannah wrinkled her nose, glowering at the honeycomb walls where all sizes of skeletal feet stuck out the ends. Some still had bits of rotted cloth clinging to the twisted toes.

Not soon enough, they floated past the stacks of tombs and turned several more corners before coming to an area in the underground river where seven wide slats of light streamed in from grates overhead.

"We are beneath the theatre district now. Sometimes valuables fall into the catacombs here. I have found coins and jewelry when the water is clear enough to see to the bottom, usually after the annual flood. Once I even saw a whore pissing through the grate." Tarek smirked with pride at this memory, his groin stiffening slightly with the mention of it.

Hannah winced. The noxious assault on her nostrils was making her ill. For a moment she thought she could use the catacombs as an escape—she would just have to steal the barge—but the labyrinth continued, and she became convinced she would get lost and end up dead in the sewer.

Soon there was torchlight on the walls ahead.

Hannah wanted to look presentable, so she undid her dark hair and let it cascade down from her shoulders to the small of her back. Then she began to pick through the tangled curls with the silver hairpin that her father had given her. A few moments later, she looked up from the knots in astonishment.

A pair of enormous twin sphinxes illumined by two torches sat side by side at the base of a wide set of four stone steps. At the top were two tall burnished doors with ebony and brass handles carved to look like vines. Hannah started to stand, but Tarek allowed the barge to float past. She looked back at him in confusion.

"Oh, that is just the zoological entrance." He waved his hand to show insignificance. "One of the lion cages is on the other side of that door . . . Ptolemy's idea, in case his soldiers were followed into the catacombs."

The barge drifted a bit further before the roof of the tunnel dropped to a hand's width above the water, preventing further passage. Beneath it, the river silently drifted into the dark sea beyond. In the torchlight, clusters of barges tethered to posts clunked together, rocking in the gentle current.

As soon as Tarek had the barge secured they leapt off, and he produced a string from under his *tunica* and applied the key at its end to a small lock in one of the doors. It opened with a noisy creak. They ascended a flight of narrow steps and then rounded a corner toward a rectangle of daylight, emerging through a small, unassuming door into a magical garden. Above them stood a tall stone obelisk carved top to bottom in hieroglyphs.

Hannah blinked back the sun. Jemir was right; it was a dream of the gods. She never imagined such beauty existed. Everywhere there were cascades of flowers and fountains, reflecting pools, and immense marble statues. Tarek pointed across the garden to the Shrine of the Nine Muses—a rotunda of columns with beautiful maiden statues in various poses holding writing instruments, masks, lyres, scrolls—and to the thirteen lecture halls beyond it, the medical wing, the zoology and botanical wings, the outdoor theatre, the gymnasium, each more magnificent than the last, painted with intricate murals of Egyptian and Greek myths and set with rows of elaborate Roman tile.

This was the Great Library of Alexandria, more beautiful than heaven itself, conceived by Ptolemy as the repository of all the world's knowledge.

They passed over a little footbridge and then walked toward the palatial structure of the main stacks, rows of rotund, ornate columns propping it up like the sun-bleached ribs of a giant, each decorated with intricate painted scenes at the base, lotus flowers, animals, chariots. Hannah wondered how many camels stacked on top of each other it would take to reach the top. Above the walls, Hannah's eyes reached the large cupola that crowned the high walls where glass of white, ruby, orange, violet, indigo, and emerald scintillated in the sunlight. Tarek proudly explained the Alexandrian technique of variegated ornamental glasswork that was renowned the world over. It was all breathtaking to Hannah. She only wished her father were there beside her to see it. A pang of sorrow shot through her awe and cracked it open like an egg, making it impossible for her to contain her feelings. Tears slipped down her cheeks, and she swiftly wiped them away with her fingertips.

On the ground all around them were marble statues of Zeus, Thoth, Hermes, and Serapis, with rippling muscles and lifelike eyes that watched over the garden as men in long wine-red robes sauntered past, their hands clasped behind their backs, their somber faces preoccupied with scholarly tasks.

Hannah followed Tarek between the widely spaced columns and through a massive and intricately carved teak door that, he explained, Ptolemy and Alexander the Great had brought back from India. It was held open by a chain of stone links as large as ostrich eggs, which were carved from the same granite boulder in a masterpiece of stonework.

Beyond the doors lay the greatest room Hannah had ever seen. It stretched up three stories high, and people were suspended on skeletal ladders that led to narrow catwalks. The walls were speckled with thousands of tiny pigeonholes where thin ivory handles of papyrus and parchment scrolls projected above Greek letters etched in the shelves. Tarek explained that sorting in the library was never-ending.

The librarians who sauntered past, all men, seemed to be accustomed to the magnificence of the place, their thoughts consumed with the business at hand, their arms full of scrolls or odd shaped instruments Hannah had never seen before. There were no beggars within these walls.

Tarek pointed out that the librarians wore wine-red robes and kept their hair shorn to the scalp in a fashion that distinguished them from the philosophers, who wore grey *tribons* and let their hair grow long to proudly display that they never toiled in hard labor but led fortunate lives of intellectual pursuits.

Hannah walked to the nearest wall and let her hand brush the smooth ivory handle of one of the parchments and looked up at the tremendous cupola in awe. A few moments later they were approached by a youthful librarian with a smooth-shaven head, skin the color of river silt, and the penetrating eyes of a hawk.

"Tarek, welcome." The librarian pressed his fingertips together. "And you must be Hannah. Allow me to introduce myself. My name is Synesius. I was appointed by Alizar to be your tutor. You may call me 'Sy' if you wish." He held his hands at his sides and bowed formally in greeting.

Hannah bowed shyly in return.

Synesius nodded his approval. "Tarek, Hypatia needs to see you down on the wharf to discuss the next shipment."

Tarek straightened himself. "Certainly. I will be back in a few hours to gather Hannah."

Synesius spun. "Come, Hannah."

They walked together in silence out into the garden. Hannah followed behind Synesius, who walked so gracefully that not a pebble was disturbed by his sandals. He was rooted in his body the way a tree is rooted in the ground, yet he flowed like wind, the mark of the yogic training Hypatia required of her staff.

The day was exceptionally clear and vibrant birdsong filled the sky. The scent of the sea impregnated the thick breeze, the taste of salt and brine mingling with each breath. As they walked, wide palm fronds shimmered overhead, and busy sparrows darted in and out of the bushes.

The tour began in the zoological park where Hannah was introduced to animals she had never seen before and had no idea even existed. She marveled at the long, spotted neck of the giraffe, the sprightly play of the otters, and the size of the elephants' feet. Although she found all the animals beautiful, the one she favored was not in the zoological park at all but a sole osprey perched on Cleopatra's crypt, tearing open a mackerel, snowy hood strapped to its head with brown bands slung from its intelligent eyes. "I always think of my brother when I see them. Each winter when we were boys the osprey would nest on the cliffs near our home. My mother adored them," said Synesius, a touch of nostalgia in his soft voice that made Hannah wonder where his brother was now.

Then there was the butterfly enclosure which, once inside, Hannah did not want to leave. She could hardly believe the brightness of the colors and the intricate patterns on the wings of the tiny creatures that seemed made of some divine parchment. Nothing Jemir had said could possibly have prepared her for such beauty. "I would love to be as colorful as that," she mused.

"When you learn respect for knowledge and the mind, you will find yourself more colorful even than these." Synesius stretched his palm toward the butterflies. "They would be envious if they knew."

Inside the library, Synesius led Hannah through hall after hall where fist-sized pigeonholes arranged like honeycombs contained scrolls of all sizes.

"Greek, Hebrew, Latin, Aramaic, Nabatean, Avestan, Sanskrit, and Egyptian," declared Synesius.

"How do you know where to put them all?" Hannah asked, overwhelmed by the library's vastness, a human beehive with all its sprawling complexities, each worker knowing what role to fill.

"An excellent question." Synesius clasped his hands behind his back as they walked. His Aramaic was flawless, even his accent. "The documents here are stored in three primary places. The outer library, comprised of three large warehouse rooms beside the docks, holds shipments procured from ships or large caravans. It is in constant chaos, as you will see. Every day we receive hundreds more manuscripts then we are capable of reviewing, and since we always sort the material in the order received, it can be a very long time before the manuscripts get shelved. Right now it takes a manuscript three years to go from the outer library to becoming a scroll and finding a place here." Synesius patted one of the ivory handles and continued walking.

They descended a flight of worn marble steps and entered a wide room with doors open to the harbor docks. Scribes deep in concentration bent over long tables, their sleeves and fingertips—and in some instances, their foreheads—stained with ink. "This is the Reception Hall. These men examine the manuscripts to decide whether or not they will be transcribed for the library's collection. We have some works that are translated into five or six languages, depending on their importance. Translation is often difficult and tedious. There is a law in Alexandria that our library has the right to confiscate all manner of texts, maps, records, and writings that enter the city." Synesius lowered his voice to a whisper. "The owners are given copies, never the originals. Those we keep."

Before them the steps opened to the Great Hall, a multi-story octagonal room with little reading alcoves tucked into corners at the heart of the library. Synesius lowered his voice to a whisper, explaining that above them the magnificent glass cupola magnified sound from one wall to another. For that reason, librarians and visitors were asked to keep silent, as a whisper could be heard as loudly as a shout. The entire hall radiated outward, emanating like a haloed saint, both from the sunlight that poured through the dome and the tall doors lining the inner courtyard, which opened to the Caesarium Gardens.

Hannah glided behind Synesius, her eyes wide with wonder as they passed beneath the dome. She wondered if she would have an opportunity to glimpse Hypatia, why Alizar had chosen this life for her, and if she would be indebted to him in ways she could not yet comprehend for this privilege.

Synesius took them out of the Great Hall and into a narrow passageway that led to another room also filled with pigeonholes where an older gentleman, fingers twiddling his beard, sat at a small desk poring over a pile of scrolls that cascaded onto the floor in disarray.

"This is the first room of the mathematics stacks. We are each in charge of our own sections here in the library." Synesius placed his finger on the Greek letters etched in one of the shelves. "There is so much information that the only way we have found to handle it all is to make each librarian responsible for his own field of expertise. Within that field, certain important works are then selected for the Great Hall and the *Pinakes*. All important works that find their way to the Great Hall are categorized under physicists, dramatists, epic poems, legislators, philosophers, historians, orators, rhetoricians, or miscellaneous. Our system was designed several hundred years ago by Callimachus of Cyrene, and we all find fault with it. I am in the process of expanding the *Pinakes* to include mathematicians and physicians. You see here," he pointed, "This is an initial, and beside it are the numbers that indicate what scroll this is in the order of scrolls that this librarian has worked on. This wall belonged to a librarian called Theon. He was Hypatia's father, a great mathematician and scholar. When he died, his wall was closed, his greatest works removed to be placed in the Great Hall, and a plaque bearing his name was set there on the floor."

Hannah bent down to touch the polished bronze plaque. "Theon." It was the same name as Alizar's son.

Synesius cleared his throat and continued. "In this *armaria*," he opened the door of a cabinet that was set in the corner of the room, "are the codices containing the indexes corresponding to this section. They are alphabetical compendiums. Since Theon was primarily an astronomer and mathematician, these books defer to those subjects." Synesius gave a satisfied smile.

Hannah looked up at him, her brow furrowed.

Synesius pursed his lips and closed the trunk. "I should tell you I have a tendency to get into details too quickly. Come. We shall go upstairs to the study room, and I will give you your first lesson on the Greek alphabet."

Between pronouncing letters and learning to hold a stylus, Hannah learned that Synesius was one of two librarians known as an overseer. This meant he was responsible for going into the sections belonging to other librarians and procuring the most important works from those sections to be brought into the core collection of the Great Hall, where the works of the masters were kept. They had the complete works of Homer and Plato, as well as Aeschylus and Euripides, and all of Caesar's letters to Cleopatra and Mark Antony. Synesius explained his special interest had been creating a compendium of Egyptian culture. He had spent his career organizing the lineages of the pharaohs through the dynasties that led back to the building of the pyramids. Along with bloodlines, he had compiled details of the pyramids' construction and purpose. With that effort now behind him, he had taken a year to travel and recently returned.

"What are you working on now?" asked Hannah.

"In my travels I discovered the teachings of Christ, and I became devoted to new translations of the gospels. It will be my life's work. My soul has found God."

Synesius was a Christian.

So.

7

Hannah felt grateful for the days that put chores and tasks between her and the night in Sinai she was kidnapped from her father's camp. Yet, those same days stretched threadbare her hopes of seeing her father again. The regret, shame, and sadness leached their serums in the loam of her soul, churning inside her like worms. Her only strength was the resolve to find her father and the decision that she would never shed another tear over what happened. Doing nothing intensified the pain, so she must do something, everything in her power.

She knew that the slave traders must have watched their camp for some time before they attacked to learn where she slept, when she would be alone. She shuddered to think how long they must have stood in the shadows of the hills, watching, waiting. If only she had listened to the feeling in her gut that night. Sitting in Alizar's kitchen, Hannah vowed to herself to never disregard that inner feeling again. She did not know how soon she would be tested.

Hannah applied herself with vigor to the tasks at hand. Her Greek improved steadily, and before long she was conversing well. Days became weeks, and weeks drew on. The moon had filled and emptied four times. Hannah knew that in spite of her promise to Alizar, she would attempt another escape. There was no other way.

So.

With Alizar away, there were long-awaited chores: deep cleaning the house, sorting all the supply cabinets, re-arranging and buffing the stable tack. They had run out of barley and honey. Jemir had no patience to wait. For him, maintaining the house would keep the drought at bay, immunize them against dust and decay and every other mortal fright. Leitah was down in the grain cellar, so Hannah volunteered. Tarek pounced to go with her. He would not let her out of his sight, so she was forced to walk the markets around the city together with the wheelbarrow between them. The beggars in the alleys, covered in flies, held out their twisted hands to the beautiful girl. Tarek spat at them as Hannah lowered her eyes.

Barley. Honey. Two sacks of fleshy lentils. One merou fish the size of a child. While Hannah stood at the tent of the barley merchant waiting for Tarek to finish the transaction, she felt her stomach sink, like falling over a cliff in a dream. Perhaps her midday meal was not sitting well with her. She went over in her mind what she had eaten: a handful of figs, a warm bannock, some beans, an apple. The hair stood on her neck as the wind teased the dust into a spiral. This was no indigestion, this was danger. Hannah crouched instinctively to watch from between the stalls.

From nowhere, a commotion came over the marketplace, like the frantic stirring of antelope at a watering hole. Women clutching their children flew past Hannah with panic in their eyes as merchants scrambled to keep their unpaid customers from leaving. A young boy climbed to the top of a tent pole and began shouting. Hannah shifted her position and peered through the slats in a large basket.

Gradually, the street began to clear for a wall of men in black robes: Bishop Cyril's legendary Parabolani. One of them held a girl by the neck who was forced to walk naked before them, her small white hands trying to cover her newly budded breasts, her face streaked with tears.

Tarek appeared at Hannah's side and gave her a start. He tugged her deeper into the tent. "We are too late," he whispered. "Just stay quiet and pray they pass."

The girl pleaded with the robed men who pushed her down on her knees on the cobbles in front of the barley merchant's tent. The Roman barley merchant spluttered prayers and complained to his goddess Concordia. "Why here? Why in front of my shop? I have customers today. I pray, goddess, this malevolence may pass. Favor me."

Hannah clutched the table. "That girl, Tarek. Who is she? What has she done?"

Tarek shook his head. "It does not matter what she has done, if anything. They will make an example of her. A pagan."

"What do you mean 'an example'?" Hannah knew the terror within the girl's eyes all too intimately. She eyed the priests, recognizing one from her first day in the city as the priest called Peter who had cut the arms from Hypatia's servant. He had a menacing face, and he was taller than the rest.

Peter began to speak, calling for the attention of the people in the marketplace. A sullen-faced yet grotesquely interested crowd gathered to witness what the priests had to say.

"This whore has been found guilty in the eyes of God for acts of black magic and sorcery! She will not renounce her heathen worship and take up the path of our Lord, Jesus Christ. God requires witnesses to her sins."

The girl bent her head to hide her tears. "I am not a sorceress," she said. "I am a Jew. I swear it." In response, one of the priests kicked her in the ribs with a sickening crack.

The girl crumpled.

Hannah lunged toward her, and Tarek grabbed her elbow. She wrested herself free from Tarek's grip and crouched near the doorway, fury rising in her blood. She squeezed her fists until her knuckles whitened. The girl spoke in Aramaic. They were sisters in God's eyes.

"Hannah, stop."

Hannah clung to the rim of a clay pot, unable to turn away from the beautiful girl lying in the dust just feet away. The girl met

Hannah's eyes with a look of desperation Hannah had seen before in the other women chained in the cage with her as they traveled into Egypt.

"Hannah," Tarek said sternly. "Step away."

Hannah looked back to Tarek, then to the girl, fear and fury struggling in her eyes. "Why do they do this? She is a child."

"They accuse women of black magic here from time to time."

"Even Jews?"

"It is not our concern."

"Not our concern?"

"Do you want to be next?"

"Tarek, she is not even a woman yet." Hannah remembered the road and the slave traders—their hands on her waist, the way they took turns with their angry thrusts—as if it were the hour before. She shuddered.

"Hannah."

"No." Hannah would not look at him. "No, they cannot do this to any sister of mine."

Hannah stepped from behind the barley merchant's tent and into the crowd.

"And herewith this heretic chooses not to renounce her sins," said Peter, raising his fist. "She will accept Jesus Christ the Lord or be sacrificed in his name."

Sacrificed. Hannah cringed.

A murmur went up through the crowd, and more people joined from the market to watch the unfolding scene, riveted by dark curiosity.

Before she could think, Hannah cried out. "Stop! She is only a child. What kind of sorcery could she possibly know?"

The girl sat up in the dust and looked at Hannah, and her glossy eyes lit with hope.

The four Parabolani turned their gaze to Hannah, and immediately she felt the gravity of her folly.

"Seize her!"

Hannah turned at once and fled.

As Tarek dashed out after Hannah, he heard the barley merchant muttering how this new bishop was going to put him out of business.

Hannah ran swiftly around the corner and down to the end of the next street pushing through hoards of hawkers and camels, fishermen, and donkey caravans. Peter and two other Parabolani were gaining on her, and they had signaled to fellows who were joining in the chase; Hannah could not count how many. It was a sea of black robes.

Peter the Reader shoved a man with his box of chickens out of the way, the flustered birds breaking free of their cages, the man falling to his rump in the street.

Tarek grabbed Hannah's hand and pulled her along at a sprint. At a door in the wall he shoved Hannah through and then stepped in behind her, the narrow dip between his collarbones rising and falling with breath. Hannah made such a panicked sound when she exhaled that Tarek clamped his hand over her lips and watched through the slats in the door as the Parabolani passed. The door they had hidden behind led into a small kitchen. Tarek turned around as an old woman came out of the next room screaming at them in Egyptian, brandishing a broom.

"She thinks we are thieves. We must go," said Tarek, and the door closed behind them with a bang. The old woman was still yelling obscenities at them and shaking her broom as they vanished into a narrow passage strewn with lines of limp laundry hung between blue doors that led to small homes stacked three high in a poorer quarter of the city.

At the alley's end, Tarek peered out from between the houses. Five meters ahead, two Parabolani spotted him and shouted.

Tarek spun back and knocked into Hannah, who tripped on an uneven cobble and stumbled, falling crookedly on the side of her foot. She cried out. Tarek did not give her an instant to waver. He jerked her up and she began to run, limping behind him as he pushed through the lines of wet clothes, the Parabolani now so close Hannah could hear their breath.

Emerging from the lines of laundry, Hannah felt a strong hand grasp her hair. It was Peter. She shrieked repeatedly and with such terror that a line of red hounds tied to a post nearby began braying enthusiastically, and one snapped the line with a twist of his head, dragging the others behind. As the hound bit Peter's thigh, Hannah twisted free, a clump of her hair left in his hands.

The freed dogs barked and snarled mere paces from Hannah's heels. She yanked her *khiton* free from the mouth of one as Tarek found a grate in the street and pried it open with a staff left out for pulling clothes down from the line. "Get in," he commanded.

Hannah swung her feet into the dark pit below the grate, and Tarek took her hands as she lowered herself so that she was hanging onto him and dangling at a great height. "Let go!" he yelled. But Hannah clung to him, shrieking, for she was suspended nine meters over the river of the catacombs, holding to Tarek's arm for her life.

"Tarek!" she cried. "Tarek, pull me up!"

A dog lunged for Tarek's knee and bit straight through his skin to the bone; he kicked at it, but it sprung again, this time for his arm. Two Parabolani nearby were having similar struggles with the dogs that pulled on their robes and growled as they bit the flesh of hands and buttocks. Tarek shook free of Hannah's hands, and she screamed as her fingers slipped and she splashed into the dark, putrid water below. Tarek clocked the dog on the ear, giving the beast a good disorienting blow, and he plunged in after her, shutting the grate as he went.

When he came up for a breath, he looked around and called out into the dark tunnel.

"Here," she sputtered, clinging to a pocket in the slick wall where a brick was missing, her whole body trembling. "I do not swim."

Tarek paddled over to her. "By Poseidon's trident, I do not know whether to save you or let you drown."

Hannah coughed. Tarek brought his arm under her. "The current is swift here. Wrap your arms over my shoulders. I know this place like my mother's pockets. Trust me. I will get us home."

In the vaporous light from the grate, Tarek could see Hannah nodding, her eyes wide in terror. He pried her hands from the wall and put them around his neck.

Hannah stared into the blackness that darkened as they drifted, convinced this was the end of her life. Her breathing turned to short gasps as she dug her nails into Tarek's shoulder.

Overhead, another grate appeared, light streaming in from the street. Above them, Hannah could hear the voices of the Parabolani and the timid weeping of a girl. Shadows shifted across the grate. There was the swish of a blade being drawn and then a gurgling scream.

A body was thrown down and the light was gone.

Then silence.

Water dripped from the roof of the tunnel onto Hannah's head as they floated past. She clung to Tarek's bony frame with numb fingers, terrified.

She heard Peter's voice above them, saying, "... and rid us of the evil pestilence of witches such as these ..." His voice trailed off.

A few minutes later they floated through another patch of light, and Hannah shrieked, splashing in the water.

"Hannah, stop. Stop!" Tarek turned around and saw why she was flailing. She was looking at her arms, fingers streaked with blood.

He tried to hold her still, grabbing her by the wrists so she would not sink.

"The girl! Her blood!" she cried. "What hell have I come to! Curse you. Curse this city that steals children!" She screamed and struggled against Tarek, who fought to hold her head up out of the unctuous water.

"Hannah, you have to try to help me." Tarek pulled up on her lower ribs to help her to the surface. "We are not far from Alizar's landing."

Hannah choked, her face blanched with panic as she went under. Tarek dove after her and pulled her up, but she was heavy as a stone and went under again, swallowing more water as she sank.

Tarek kicked off his sandals and peeled off his clothing in the current, then dove and caught Hannah's hand. He pulled her up and fought to get her *khiton* over her head as she coughed and gasped, but she resisted, fighting him with her fists. "Hannah, the cloth is pulling us under. Do you want to die here?" She shook her head. "Then help me take it off."

Naked in the putrid water, the struggle eased a little, and Tarek began to feel his way along one of the walls for the next turn in the anfractuous tunnels with Hannah's arms around his neck. Her grip weakened with each breath. Tarek thought of nothing other than Alizar's house and focused the full strength of his will that they would reach it—that they would not die in the catacombs. So.

It was an interminably long while before they saw the torches of Alizar's landing and the familiar footbridge. Tarek pushed Hannah out of the water and she collapsed on the stones in exhaustion, her hair strewn around her body like kelp on the beach. Tarek pulled himself onto the stones and struggled up the stairs, his knee trailing blood on each step.

Jemir came at once when he heard Tarek's call. Hannah was barely conscious when they tried to rouse her.

"Hermes, Zeus, and Apollo, what have you done to her?" asked Jemir.

Tarek shot Jemir a nasty look and spit water on the ground. "What have I done? This little cunny challenged the Parabolani in the market. She nearly got us killed."

Jemir's eyes went wide as a lemur's. "They will come here next," he whispered as his hands trembled. "We will all be questioned." But it was not the being questioned he feared; it was the ruthless methods of questioning.

Jemir lifted Hannah up in his arms and she coughed, and then her head fell back. Leitah appeared on the stairs. "Call Philemon," Jemir said to her. "Go at once."

Following the incident in the marketplace Hannah did not leave Alizar's house and slept most of the day and night. Her ankle was black with bruises and throbbed in pain, her spirit even more so. Leitah rubbed a cool mint salve into the joint and bound it with a splint and a strong length of thick linen. The doctor had said the healing would be slow. He was a wise man, though Jemir noticed he counted his coins with a certain glee that seemed inappropriate to his profession.

Hannah could not push the death of the young Jewish girl from her mind. She was full of sickening regret. When the tears stopped, she simply stared at the wall, absently watching the light change as the sun drew down the sky.

For a week, no one in Alizar's house had an enjoyable night's sleep as they waited for the Parabolani to appear. But they did not come. Hannah lay in bed sipping Jemir's willow tea, her leg throbbing with pain. She occasionally limped over to the balcony to look out on the street below. A cot had been placed in Naomi's room for Hannah to rest while she recovered. Sometimes she sat beside Naomi and stroked the tiny hairs on her forearms and lifted a flagon of water to her lips. To be near Naomi was the closest thing she had ever known to having a mother. Hannah found comfort in those hours. Beloved Naomi.

And so Hannah rested and played merles and talked to Naomi. More weeks passed that way until one morning, something unusual occurred. A golden butterfly with dramatic black edging around its wings floated across the balcony and through the doors. It lilted around the room aimlessly for several minutes then settled on Naomi's throat, opening and closing its delicate wings.

And Naomi sighed.

Hannah sat up. Then Naomi sighed again, and her breath wavered on the exhalation, almost as though she were attempting to form words.

"You know it is there," Hannah whispered.

Naomi's lips quivered.

Hannah crept to the bed. "Please wake," she said. "Please, for me." As she watched the butterfly pumping its wings, she slipped her fingers into Naomi's hand and squeezed.

A little breeze crossed the room and Naomi's eyelids fluttered and opened. The butterfly did not stir. Hannah found herself looking at eyes as green as summer grass. Naomi's lips tipped slightly upward, and she squeezed Hannah's hand ever so gently in return. Then her eyes closed as the resting butterfly lifted from her chest and vanished through the open window.

Hannah threw open the door and called to everyone to come quickly. Tarek was out, but Jemir and Leitah came at once. As Hannah told them what had happened, Jemir brought his hands to his heart. "An omen," he said. "She will be well again, Goddess willing. We must pray." And so they each bowed their heads and prayed in a circle around the bed where Naomi lay. Hannah hoped Jemir was right, that the butterfly was an omen. She felt that if

Naomi recovered it meant that everything else would be well also, that her father was alive and that they would be reunited, and the Parabolani would forget the incident in the market.

Later that day a visitor came to the house. When the bell rang, everyone stopped breathing. The servants of Alizar's house flinched at every odd sound in the walls, dreading the coming of the Parabolani. Jemir was the brave one who went to the door to see who it was.

"Hannah, there is a visitor for you." Jemir stood in the doorway of Naomi's bedroom leaning against a pillar, holding a tray of sweet cakes. His heart was heavy for the girl, poor desert child sold into slavery, and now this. She had not spoken a word of what happened that day in the market. Sorrow had tipped the ballast of her heart, and she was sinking. He fussed over her, baking his concern into special cakes to revive her happiness, to no avail. There was no music left in her for Alizar's house.

Hannah gathered the blanket around her body, picked up her cane and found her way downstairs to the atrium. There in the hall, a tall gentleman in a long, wine-red robe stood serenely. Even with his back to the entrance, Hannah knew who it was.

"Synesius." Hannah's lips faltered upward toward a smile. His constant stoic expression that always seemed so cold, in that moment, warmed her like the desert sun. She was glad to see him.

Synesius tilted his head, regarding Hannah's bandaged ankle. "What has happened to you?"

Hannah took a step backward. "We can go into the courtyard to speak. Please."

They stepped into the bright sun of noonday and followed a stone path that led down a slight slope to a lion's head fountain set in a low wall that poured a cool stream of water into a catch basin filled with blue lotus blossoms. Alizar's horses grazed in a pen just beyond it.

Hannah sat on the edge of the wall beside the pond. "I am sorry I missed my lessons."

Synesius glanced at her leg.

Hannah bit her lower lip and looked down at the bandage. "It was in the market. I slipped."

He studied Hannah's face. "Who were you running from?"

Hannah looked up and met his discerning eyes. Perhaps he already knew. "The Parabolani."

"I thought as much."

"We were in the market, and they dragged this young girl out in front of everyone and made horrible accusations. Then they . . . well, they killed her." Hannah teared up. "I was so foolish, taken over by my anger. I actually thought I could stop them."

The flicker in Synesius's eyes showed that her tutor was familiar with the Parabolani and their tactics. "Alexandria contains the greatest extremes, Hannah. This city, like Alexander her patron king, knows only the dramatic circumference of the wheel, rising, falling. Her center stands for an instant, then shifts. Those who study truth must seek to live in the center of the wheel, where there is stillness, unscathed by torment or rapture."

"Do you mean we should ignore what the Parabolani are doing?" Hannah narrowed her eyes.

"We have no choice."

"No choice?"

"The battle is over God, not land or women or gold. It is a fight that can never be won, not in a thousand years or a thousand more."

"But surely something can be done."

Synesius sighed and took a seat on the low wall. "Hannah, do you know who Theodosius the Second is?"

"The emperor."

"Yes, the emperor, a boy of eight years old."

"A child?"

"Yes. Most of the rumors we hear from court say his elder sister, Pulcheria, holds the influence of the Eastern Empire as she is in charge of his education and interests. Emperor Honorius, the western emperor, remains as interested in Alexandria as a baby is in mathematics. It was their father, Emperor Arcadius, and his father before him, Theodosius, who insured the Christian empire would uphold the edict forbidding pagan practice."

"What does it mean?"

"That those who are not Christian, like the followers of Mithras and Osiris, Zoroaster, the Druids, the Romans, and even the ancient hierophant of Eleusis may not worship their gods. There has been some tolerance for the Jews, but even that is waning. They are all deemed pagans." Synesius shook his head. "For all I know, Alexandria may be the last place in the Mediterranean the pagans dare to pray. Elsewhere they have all gone into hiding or embraced Christ to save themselves from persecution."

"Is that why you became a Christian?"

Synesius clasped his hands behind his back and began to pace. "I am a gnostic Christian, not an orthodox Christian. I have particular interest in Christ and his disciples, especially Mary Magdalene. I am translating her writing and the gospel of Thomas now with a team of other Coptic scribes. The practices of the Parabolani are atrocious, true. Our bishop may be a self-righteous man, but Christ himself was and is a worthy teacher, as are his disciples. Christ's emphasis was always on inner knowing, spiritual study, forgiveness, and on love."

"But this girl they killed was practically a child. How can you willingly connect yourself to that?" Hannah squinted up at Synesius where he paused with his head before the sun, an aureole of light illuminating his shoulders as a bee swept past his chin and dove into a purple blossom on the pond.

"As a gnostic Christian, I do not. The teachings of Christ and the church founded in his absence by Paul are not the same. Jesus himself did not create a church; he merely asked his followers to bless others and spread the teachings. Unfortunately, this split among the Christians has sent those of us who believe differently than the orthodox into hiding. Cyril would be killing the gnostics along with the pagans if there were any left to kill. Most students of Valentinus, the teacher of my lineage, were silenced before I was born. I know how to walk in orthodox circles without arousing suspicion, as my life is a work of subtle influence."

Hannah plucked a papyrus leaf and twirled it between her fingers, her lips pressed together in thought.

"I disappoint you?" Synesius asked.

Hannah shrugged. "Perhaps you care more for those scrolls than you do a young girl's life. I do not understand."

Synesius nodded, empathizing with her sentiment. "The Great Library of Alexandria is devoted to uncovering and preserving truth, not resolving human suffering, though the two are certainly intertwined. We study the heavens, the seas, works of all ages, cultures and centuries, and the contributions of great minds that have come and gone and shared their wisdom with us, even those that have made us question our treasured beliefs. The truth is humanity's greatest inheritance, Hannah. And you are right, I would protect it over all else."

Hannah shook her head. It was a philosopher's speech that did nothing to reframe the events in the market for her heart. Feeling neither more nor less consoled, she gazed down into the little pool at the blue lotus flowers swirling like galaxies as water trickled from the lion's stone mouth on the wall.

"Hannah," Synesius stood up. "I have also come today to invite you to sing at a very important lecture this coming Saturn's day. Alizar spoke quite highly of your talent before his departure, and our current musical accompaniment has taken ill. We would like you to take his place. Alizar arranged that it will pay you three *siliquae.*"

"What kind of lecture?" Hannah sat up in surprise. Here then, was Alizar's promise that she could earn her freedom, although three silver *siliquae* were a mere glint on the surface of one hundred gold *solidi*.

"An unveiling of the most important contribution to science to come out of the Great Library in six hundred years." Synesius's calm voice, usually bereft of emotion, welled with excitement.

Hannah tipped her head. "Go on."

Synesius lowered his voice to a whisper. "Centuries ago, Archimedes of Syracuse brought certain drawings to Alexandria of a mechanism he conceived that can discern the position of the entire cosmos, sun, moon, and planets. He was killed before he could construct it. The mathematicians of the Great Library have devoted their lives to its creation. Hypatia's father, Theon, came the closest but failed, and now Hypatia herself has supposedly created a working model of Archimedes's design. She plans to unveil it during her lecture. Magistrates, royalty, rhetors, and prefects have sailed from across the Mediterranean to be there."

Hannah drew a sharp breath. How could she possibly perform before hundreds of people? The thought was paralyzing. "Synesius, it is a very generous offer, but—"

"Hannah, you must. It is expected."

Hannah stood abruptly and hobbled over to the sprawling fig tree with its leaves like giant puzzle pieces twisting in the breeze. "Maybe bravery comes easy to you Synesius, living within the safe confines of the library walls. But that girl's blood covered my face when she lived not moments before. My face!" She threw up her hands, and several silver fish at the surface of the pool darted back into the murky shadows.

"I know it is difficult." Synesius rose and smiled gently. "Hypatia would appreciate meeting another woman of exceptional talent."

Hypatia. Hannah thought of Jemir's description of her, "made of light." In her visits to the Great Library, she had not yet seen the famous female philosopher. If Synesius had come to ask this favor of her, she knew it must be important. "I will be there," she said.

Synesius smiled and bowed to leave. "Good then. Get some rest."

 **8**

When he heard that Hannah would perform at such an important lecture, Jemir secretly shook several coins from the bottom of a leather pouch he wore on his belt and counted them. Then he left the house.

On Saturn's day eve Jemir knocked on the stable door with a fine dress of peacock blue silk in his arms, but Hannah did not respond. He called out to her, and Leitah appeared.

"Where is she?" Jemir asked.

Leitah shrugged. She pointed from the dress to Jemir and mimed walking with her fingers.

Jemir shook his head. "No, she did not come with me. I assumed she was here with you."

Then, in a flash of shared realization, Jemir and Leitah both knew what must have happened. Jemir lay the dress on a saddle rack. "You search the stable and the street. I will call Tarek."

They split up, and Tarek joined them moments later, but he did not have far to look as Hannah entered the stable yard through the lower gate with a fistful of clover. She called to the grey stallion, loose in his pen, and he trotted over. She leaned in to tickle his whiskers with the clover, leaning on the cane Jemir had found for her. His upper lip flapped, and then he gingerly ate every tiny green stem with relish. Hannah smiled in delight; she had come to love the animal.

Tarek stepped out from behind one of the walls. "So you thought you would run away again?" he said, blood rising.

"I went to feed the horses."

"You lie. We know you tried to escape."

"If I wanted to escape I would not be here now, would I?" said Hannah, dusting her hands against her hips. "I would be free of you forever."

Tarek grabbed Hannah's wrist and dragged her into the stable. Her cane clattered to the dust, and she limped after him until he threw her down on the straw. "I tire of your disobedience. You bring shame on my father's house. I curse you to Hades." Tarek spat on her face.

A burst of fear webbed through Hannah's entire body. Curses were serious magic. "I was tending the horses, I swear. Please take it back."

"I paid too much for you," said Tarek. He stood over her, grabbed her by the elbow, and picked her up. She could smell the wine on his breath.

"You are hurting me, Tarek."

"So be it," he said, and he pulled her into him and kissed her firmly on the mouth.

"Stop!" Hannah pushed him back.

He laughed and ripped her *khiton* so he could take hold of her breast. She bit him, and he struck her hard enough across the face that she fell to her knees.

"My father will kill you," she snarled, blood trickling from her lips.

"Your father is dead, and this is your life now." Tarek stood over her. "I own you."

The words stung Hannah's pride.

The angel cringed.

Just then Alizar's stableman appeared at the door with a saddle in his hands. Behind him were Leitah and Jemir.

Hannah wiped her tears and pulled the torn cloth across her bare breast.

Tarek stormed out.

Leitah fetched water and a sponge to help Hannah wash. Jemir brought her a warm cup of red willow tea and then presented her with the *himation* he had purchased for her in the market that afternoon. It was the same color indigo as her eyes.

Hannah thanked Jemir and took it in her arms. She caressed the billowing sleeves that were elegantly slashed open from the shoulder to the wrist where they tied. There was even a gold-braided sash that draped elegantly down along the neckline, swept beneath the breasts, and tied behind the back in the Hellenistic fashion. She had never even seen a fabric so fine. Tarek she would have to face later. For now, she took a breath, and calmed herself. This was an important evening ahead of her, and she wanted it to go well. She pulled it over her head and nodded. She was ready.

A chariot from the Great Library drawn by three sprightly bay desert horses was sent to fetch Hannah. The horses murmured to each other and tossed their heads in the air at her approach. She got in and swiftly kissed Jemir's cheek in thanks as he wrapped a white woolen shawl around her shoulders. She clutched it to her body as the chariot lurched forward.

"Promise me you will remember Hypatia's every word?" Jemir called out from the street to Hannah, who was glowing like the sapphire flame of a glassblower's torch.

Hannah looked back and waved, "I promise it."

So.

When Hannah arrived at the library her palms began to sweat. She had never played for any audience before, much less a large, important one. Her throat tightened and her breath came short. When the chariot lurched to a halt beneath the gates, she noticed the inscription above them in stone: *Knowledge is the Source of the Soul's Freedom.* She sighed. If only knowledge alone would buy her freedom.

Fortunately, the resplendence of the Great Library soothed her agitation. Oil lamps with wicks of Carpasian flax had been set around the perimeter on silver trays, illuminating the magnificent arches and the colorful murals and geometrical patterns the Egyptians fancied. Now and then, a peacock strutted peevishly into the hall from the garden, his bejeweled tail dragging centuries behind him. From the garden came the sounds of insects and frogs humming their spring ragas, mingling with the talk of the people as they found their seats. The Great Hall was already purring with conversation. Overhead, the waxing moon gleamed through the glass cupola like the golden eye of the Cyclops.

"Hannah, welcome." Synesius broke from the crowd and stood before her. "Come with me."

Beside her tutor, Hannah drifted into the swift current of conversation among elegant guests from all over the world. The pulse was unnerving, from the sounds of over a dozen languages in one room to the sheer mass of bodies. Yet, standing in the Great Hall felt peaceful, as if the architecture had sprung from the mind of an intelligent deity—perhaps the same god who authored the orchid's intestines and the moon's distance from the earth.

After an hour of formalities, a gong was sounded. Synesius gestured to the dais, and Hannah froze like a stone in winter. Synesius pulled her aside and whispered in her ear. She softened a little at his words. And so she took a deep breath, and let him lead her to the dais where a lyre waited, lent to her by a bard of the Mouseion. The crowd quieted and found their seats. Synesius guided her to a small stool with a lush crimson cushion, then whirled around to the audience, the sea of faces turned toward them expectantly. "My friends, fellows, and visitors from far away lands . . ." Suddenly there was a thunderous round of applause. He waited for it to die, then spoke again. "Before I introduce Hypatia, it is my pleasure to bring you a new talent from our Great Library, one I know you will enjoy. I give you Hannah of Sinai." Again, applause shook the building.

Hannah's throat went dry. She swallowed and wet her lips. It was time. The slave collar felt so cold around her neck, so constricting. She hoped she would be able to sing.

She had selected an ancient Aramaic song about a woman praying for her husband as he rode into battle. She chose it for its pure and unpredictable melody and the way it made her feel beautiful whenever she sang it.

Early on her voice quavered, but as soon as she relaxed, the melody invited her into its landscape, where her voice found its natural footing. In the refrain, Hannah held the highest of possible notes until the song's ecstasy washed over her. She sang with a voice that flowed from the sunlit mountain streams of Sinai, from the desert's dark sands. It was effortless. The song's emotion reached the secret longings in even the most guarded hearts of the philosophers. As she stroked the lyre, Synesius smiled in pride at his student's courage, and her power. Alizar had been right once again.

When she had let the last note ring out, Hannah opened her eyes. The entire hall was spellbound. She could feel their eyes fixed on her, studying her. Then slowly, one gentleman in the front row began to clap, and then everyone was clapping, standing, and shouting their appreciative applause. The Romans in the crowd pounded the floor with their boots and hooted like shofars.

Synesius, his steps never lighter, returned for Hannah and led her down to a chair where she arranged her dress and then sat. She took a deep breath and touched her trembling fingertips together at her lips.

"Had I known I would have to deliver my lecture after such a voice as that, I might have arranged to speak to you tomorrow." Laughter bubbled up from the crowd as a woman sprung up the dais like a lioness on her prey.

Hypatia.

Hypatia, immaculate star of wisdom, rhetor of heavenly reason, the Virgin of Serapis, so celebrated by the Alexandrian poets. Hannah immediately recognized her from her first day in Alexandria as the brave woman who had cursed the bishop at the gates to the library where the Parabolani had maimed and burned her servant. Of course. This was the Great Lady.

As Hypatia spoke, Hannah regretted her weeks away from the library, since Hypatia delivered her entire lecture on astronomy in Greek. But understanding her seemed inconsequential to hearing her. The audience did not dare to breathe, cough, or shift their feet, so enraptured were they by her presence. Hannah was, like them, entranced, lost in reverie for Hypatia's power, completely suspended in a place time could not touch.

Midway through the lecture, two men ceremoniously carried a tasseled crimson pillow with a circular brass instrument resting atop it to the lectern. Whispers rippled through the crowd.

"Some of you have only heard of it in legend," declared Hypatia, her intelligent gaze more piercing than an owl navigating a darkened wood. "And now, may your doubts be put to rest. Behold, I present to you the Celestial Clock of Archimedes!" Hypatia lifted the heavy brass instrument and held it aloft.

Silence. Shock. Then a wave of sighs and gasps. Then finally applause, but Hypatia raised her hand to quiet them. "I will demonstrate," she said with a victorious smile. Slowly her hand wound the outer wheel to the current date, and then she clicked a small lever into place.

Magically, the dials of the clock began to spin and rotate by themselves, until finally, the position of the planets, stars, sun, and moon for that particular day were revealed on the clock face. The crowd gasped. "Truly automatic!" someone shouted. Hypatia summoned an astronomer who stood at hand to check the accuracy of the clock's calculations. He bent over the instrument to examine it, and then nodded to the audience. "It is perfectly accurate," he said, shaking his head in disbelief.

"Yes, perfectly accurate," declared Hypatia, "in any century, past, present, or future!"

One by one the audience began to clap, and then they stood with awe etched on their faces. Hypatia had achieved the impossible. She had brought legend to life. The world would never be the same.

As the crowd broke and rushed forward to examine the instrument and speak with Hypatia, Synesius turned to Hannah. "I apologize I could not translate during her lecture, Hannah. Thank you for your contribution. History has been made this night."

Hannah smiled. "I am inspired to work harder on my Greek so I will understand her the next time."

"Well said."

Hannah stood and found suddenly she was exhausted. Although she tried to stifle it, a yawn escaped her lips. She reached beside the chair for her cane.

Synesius observed her. "I will call for your chariot." He excused himself with a curt little bow and then disappeared into the crowd.

Hannah settled back down in her chair to wait and watch the people mingle. Here and there among the noblemen, Hannah recognized the librarians in the crowd by their long, wine-red robes, and the philosophers in their heavy grey *tribons*, and noticed again that there was not a woman among them.

Several magistrates saw Hannah and smiled or bowed appreciatively. A few people even came to speak to her on their way to examine the legendary Celestial Clock of Archimedes. The chatter of Greek, Egyptian, Aramaic, Hebrew, and Latin was everywhere. But no Arabic. It would be several centuries before the syllables of that tongue were as abundant in Egypt as grains of sand.

"Hannah?"

It was Hypatia who had broken away from her crowd of enthusiastic followers to thank Hannah in flawless Aramaic for coming.

Hannah smiled feebly, feeling somewhat ashamed of her status as a slave before the renowned Great Lady. "It is I who must thank you, Hypatia," Hannah stammered, fingers adjusting her metal collar.

Hypatia stood before her proud as Athena, clad for the battlefield, her eyes illuminated by the sun. "Then the 'thanks' is mutual. Your music was a divine pleasure this evening, Hannah. Alizar has spoken highly to me of your talent. You hail from Sinai?"

"Yes."

"What an adventure. I have never been beyond the city's walls myself. The knowledge here has been the only source of my travels." Hypatia waved her hand overhead to indicate the stacks.

Then Synesius appeared. "I am most disappointed to have missed the pleasure of introducing the two most brilliant women in Alexandria."

"I was just thanking Hannah for her lovely music. Her considerable talent has been remarked upon all evening by my guests." Then Hypatia turned to Synesius and spoke discretely so that Hannah could not hear.

Synesius's lips curled upward. "I think it is a marvelous idea," he said.

"Lovely then. Hannah, please join me for tea tomorrow in my study," said Hypatia. It was not a question. "Synesius can direct you." Then another guest caught her attention and pulled her aside, leading her into the gardens.

Hannah felt stunned. "Synesius? Why does she want to see me?"

Synesius smiled. "That is for her to say."

9

The next afternoon, Hannah wound through the labyrinth of stacks to the worn marble passage that had been walked by Eratosthenes, Euripides, and Archimedes in centuries before. Her ankle was mending well, though it was still fragile, so she took the steps one at a time. This was her first day without the cane. When she emerged, it was on a wide circular rooftop observatory with views that stretched to the horizon in all directions. There was a long pole erected in the center of the platform with a rope hanging down. The entire turret was surrounded by a waist-high balustrade that bore mysterious vertical markings, probably measurements, all along its inner edge. Hypatia knelt in the west and held a brass instrument to her eye, looking toward the sun, then jotting notes on a scroll in her lap.

"Hannah, how wonderful to see you. When I heard footsteps on the stairs I thought it was my assistant coming to summon me to the docks. It has been madness down there today with so many ships in the harbor arriving all at once." Hypatia completed her observation and stood up, arching to stretch her back.

"I hope I am not disturbing you," Hannah began.

Hypatia waved her hand, "Heavens no, if it were not for welcome interruptions I would be up here all hours of the day and night. My work is never finished. Please come have a look."

Hannah approached. At a closer glance, she noticed that each of the notches in the top of the wall had a Greek name of some kind. "What are these?" she asked.

"The notches? They are named for each of the stars. The ancient Egyptians invented this clever system. You see, far over there is a notch on the east wall, made this morning when the sun rose," Hypatia's fingertip brushed a tiny notch no wider than an apple stem beside her in the wall. "And here is where it will set," she indicated one notch a half meter to the south. "And here is where the sun will set on the summer solstice. All the others are for the moon, the planets, and the stars. This method of precise calculation is how the Egyptians knew when the Nile would flood, by tracking the movement of the stars with each season, especially the star Sirius, as its appearance usually indicates the flood."

Hannah scanned the thousands of notches along the wall made over the years, each monitoring the rise and fall of celestial bodies. What patience it had taken the Alexandrian scholars to observe them so carefully, year after year, century after century.

Hypatia strode over to a chart etched in a basin of plaster that was set on a worktable in the north. "Here is a graph of the movement of the tides with the phases of the moon, made by my student, Pos. He is attempting to calculate how the occurrence of the coming lunar eclipse will affect the sea. Clever dog, Pos. When you come to my lecture this coming day of Mercury, he will present his findings."

Hannah smiled. "I look forward to it." What were these calculations that could embrace the mysterious workings of nature? Was such a thing possible?

Hypatia took a seat on a stone bench, moving as if her bones ached from kneeling for so long. Her eyes were puffy and her golden hair had sprung loose in ringlets all around her face as though she might pose for a portrait of a tired goddess. Her grey philosopher's *tribon* was wrinkled as though it had been slept in. Still, in spite of her overworked appearance, there was a fierce radiance and unsinkable joy about her.

Hannah strode over to the edge of the roof and looked down on the Caesarion gardens, and the many men sauntering past the massive sphinxes set along the path overlooking the long rectangular reflecting pools speckled with lotus blossoms. "May I ask you a question, Hypatia?"

"Certainly. Anything you like."

"Are there any other women philosophers in the Great Library?"

"None. Merely servants and slaves."

"You must be very lonely." For a moment Hannah forgot she was a slave.

"The soul has no gender. But if I could design my life, I might enjoy more women on my staff, which brings me to the reason I invited you here. I was wondering if you might have any desire to become a scholar of music."

"A scholar of music?"

"I think you would benefit from study in the tradition of Pythagoras. Our last music scholar has relocated to Rome, and I was thinking you would make a marvelous fit here in the library. Synesius has spoken of your keen mind. He says you learn quickly, and upon hearing your gift of song, I surmise we have the next Sappho on our hands."

"I am afraid I am not sure what you mean." Hannah's hands began to sweat and she wiped them on her *khiton*. "I am a slave in Alizar's house."

Hypatia smiled, enchanted by the young woman before her who genuinely seemed to be unaffected by, and perhaps even unaware of, both her beauty and her talent. Hypatia cleared her throat. "What I am saying is that I would like you to play regularly at my lectures. Would you like that?"

"It would be an honor, of course, if Alizar consents."

Hannah's innocence about the prestige of the offer gave her all the more merit in Hypatia's eyes. It meant she was not another cloying myopic sycophant maneuvering to be near her in hopes of the attention and purses that could accompany the lives of philosophers and scholars.

"May I speak openly with you?" asked Hannah.

"Certainly."

"Several weeks ago I encountered the Parabolani in the street. I fear them and these public demonstrations."

"Are the Christians so different where you come from?" Hypatia asked, incredulous.

"There are none where I am from, only Jews and gypsies."

"Truly? How unusual. I admit the Alexandrian Christians are extreme, but they are not all this way. Think of Synesius."

"I realize he is a Christian, but then how he can study Plotinus in your school?"

"A philosopher does not accept boundaries with beliefs. He is more gnostic than orthodox, besides."

"You are not afraid, then? Of the consequences?"

"Of course I am. But, Hannah, I learned some years ago it is a waste of one's talent to live in fear. It is true this city is in a state of unrest. The library is in a state of unrest. *Life* is in a state of unrest. I cannot afford to let it interfere with my work, and neither can you. Courage, sister."

"But different philosophies meet with bloodshed."

Hypatia stood and went to the east wall, and Hannah followed her. Far below them a swarthy crew aboard a carrack drew down the ship's red sails in haste. "There is one thing that elevates us here, you know, and it is not our buildings or our walls," said Hypatia.

"What is it?"

"Intellect." Hypatia turned and Hannah could see the swords gleaming in her eyes. "In the mind we are free. It is the body that leads us astray. The mind is the lotus of purity; the body and its demands are merely the mud to be transcended through yoga and contemplation."

"What is that there?" Hannah asked, catching sight of a tremendous island fortress across the eastern harbor.

"It is the Kiosk Palace of Antirrhodus."

"Truly, a palace?" Hannah's eyes danced like a child's.

"Indeed, but the royal family no longer occupies it. The governor, Orestes, keeps his residence there, and the praetorian prefect
of the East Emperor's guard. The palaces Cleopatra once adored
are now mere artifice badly in need of repair. Since the drought,
grain production has dwindled so that there is no money for it."

Another strip of land caught Hannah's eye, in the northern
edge of the harbor, at least seven furlongs from the shore and
crowned with a magnificent building. "And that island there?"

"You have not seen Pharos? There is our lighthouse, designed
by Sostratus the Cnidian, the same architect who constructed the
hanging gardens of Caria. It is of granite and limestone blocks,
but faced with white Calacatta marble, which is why it gleams
so in the sun," said Hypatia proudly. "The base is a tremendous
horizontal rectangle of limestone carved through the center by a
line of three hundred steps, beneath which lived all the laborers
it took to keep the lighthouse functioning when it was in repair."
Hannah could see the first tier was a vertical rectangle of limestone blocks that situated the lighthouse over a hundred meters
above the sea. Above that, an octagonal cylinder of stone ornately
carved and decorated with Egyptian statuary supported a circular
temple at the top crowned by a golden statue of Poseidon leaning on his trident. Hypatia explained that the impressive statues
placed to either side of it facing away from the harbor were of
Ptolemy and his queen, their backs turned to Alexandria so they
could greet arriving ships to the royal harbor. "The hinges of the
lighthouse mirror have become corroded from the salt air, so our
parabolic reflector has not been functional for years. But between
you and me, Orestes says it has now been repaired. There will be
a magnificent party soon to celebrate. It is a miracle the ships do

not founder at the harbor's entrance without it. And you see that smallish blue dome there? It is the Temple of Isis."

"The Temple of Isis," Hannah repeated thoughtfully.

Hypatia's eyes flooded with memories, making her look almost gentle for a moment. "I was initiated there," she said. "When my mother disappeared, my father sent me to the High Priestess to be educated. I still go visit the temple when I need a moment away from this"—she waved her arms—"chaos." Then Hypatia laughed the burdened laugh of those who can never escape their load. "It pains me that the powerful east-west tide of Alexandria is sweeping Pharos away. Beside the Temple of Poseidon, the currents are so swift that anyone who swims there is quickly carried out into the Mediterranean. Some of my staff calculated that in a thousand years, the island will have vanished into the sea."

Hannah looked to the beautiful island that seemed so permanent and found that she could not picture the scene without it.

Hypatia glanced at the sundial at the north end of the observatory and waved Hannah to follow her. "I must prepare for my lecture, come."

They descended the stairs and turned down a narrow passage to a short wooden door, which Hypatia opened with a key strung around her neck. Scrolls and papers were stacked into organized towers on a fine wooden desk that overlooked the harbor, leaving no space to write. "This room used to be a storage closet. It was my father's dream to make it his private office, but he never got around to it. That is his desk, there. It supposedly once belonged to Mark Antony, can you believe? When my father died, I cleared the room and added the window overlooking the harbor. I apologize for the heat. Though late spring in Alexandria is usually quite pleasant, this year the drought has brought dust and swelter. But I have the window, which helps. I see every ship that comes in and goes out of Alexandria. I only hope to be aboard one of them someday."

"Tell me something of your work," Hannah said, sitting on the settee to rest her ankle. Hypatia fell backward into an old Roman chair. Between them a zebra skin was spread on the floor.

"My work. Well, I have had a marvelous commission this week from the bishop of Antioch, thanks to a recommendation from Synesius. The bishop wants a special hydrometer to measure the aging process of his wine. Bit of Dionysus in him, really, though he would never forgive me if he heard me say it." Hypatia smiled, delighted to be able to speak freely.

"It must be exciting to know so many influential people. It was a joy to meet some of your colleagues at your lecture."

"Oh, good, I am glad to hear it. But if you must know, it is a burden at times. Influential people are extremely difficult when they do not get what they want. Look at Cyril."

"The bishop of Alexandria?"

"Yes. He is demanding that we relinquish to him the Celestial Clock of Archimedes—to be destroyed. Of course." Hypatia rolled her eyes to the sky.

"Destroyed?"

"He believes the clock a sorcerer's tool. Excuse me, sorceress." Hypatia waved her arms and batted a tower of scrolls on her desk, a waterfall of papyrus flowing to the floor. She bent to collect them. "I imagine these harsh cosmopolitan ways must seem quite foreign to you. It is not a judgment. To me, the desert you come from, with its scorpions and shifting sands, is the more terrifying place. These walls mean safety to me, even if I must deal with Cyril and his men and their ludicrous requests."

"The desert may shift, but it is always the same."

"Like men. Like time. Like religion and like rulers. Perhaps even like God."

"You risk your life speaking such words." Hannah whispered, now aware that bold speech was a dangerous characteristic in Alexandria.

"Anyone who puts her life in the service of truth must, would you not agree?"

Hannah shifted her position on the settee, and the floorboards creaked. "What does a library need a music scholar for? Musicians have no need for scrolls."

"Hannah, you possess a unique talent. We have hundreds of scribes who can translate and document any language. But how will we preserve the music?"

"Songs are old as the wind and passed down through ancestors. These things cannot be preserved any other way. Fish have songs. Trees have songs. Stones. Waters. How can you capture these? Their beauty is ephemeral."

"What if it were not? Imagine the magic of that! There must be a way to record the music, perhaps with some sort of Pythagorean notation. I feel there is no time to waste. People are relinquishing ancient traditions for the Christian faith. We stand to lose everything I have worked for here. I am sure you can see that."

"But why oppose them? It will only bring their fury, as you have seen." Hannah thought of Hypatia's servant, killed at the gates of the Great Library.

"You misunderstand me. I do not oppose the Christians, and neither does this library. I have many Christians on my staff. We have made more translations of the Gospels than the libraries of Athens, Ephesus, Rome, Tarsus, Antioch, Pergamon, and Constantinople combined"—Hypatia paused—"though many of those libraries have now been destroyed by the same Christians."

"Then why does Alexandria's bishop oppose the library?"

Hypatia selected four scrolls and slid them into a leather satchel. "It is a very complicated matter. The Great Library, like the Serapeum before it, houses far more than just Christian texts. Our scribes have amassed a collection of literature from as far as India, and the content is debatable to some. To others like Bishop Cyril, it is inexcusable. Pornographic, they call it."

There was a light rap at the door.

Hypatia's eyes flicked to the door. "Come."

Soundlessly, the door opened and in strode a magnificently clad gentleman wearing a black silk *tunica* and wide black pants, the ensemble tied together with a wide sash of crimson that bound his slender waist.

The angel brightened. Here at last. The warrior. The door would open and waiting would end. The light had promised it.

The gentleman bowed to Hypatia. She returned his gesture with a nod. "Good day, Julian of Pharos. To what do we owe the honor of this visit?"

"Greetings, Hypatia. The Nuapar have heard of the recent threats on your life. I have come to extend to you from Master Savitur and Master Junkar of Pharos an offer to post our finest Nuapar warriors as sentries at your gates."

Hannah eyed the stranger, curiosity burning in her eyes. Who was this elegant warrior with an animal's grace? She had never seen any man in Alexandria dressed in this costume, his black hair bound into one long braid that hung like a rope down his back. She felt as though she were looking at an Egyptian god brought to life.

"This is most kind of you, Julian. I believe your offer comes at an apropos moment, and I shall discuss it with the other staff. I believe I can speak for us all when I say the library would be most grateful to be under the protection of the Nuapar."

Hannah shifted her legs on the settee and Julian spun.

Hypatia cleared her throat. "Julian of Cyrene, this is Hannah of Sinai. We hope she will be our new music scholar. Hannah, Julian is the younger brother of your tutor, Synesius, a warrior of the Nuapar."

Julian's full lips parted and a tender smile emerged. He bowed to Hannah respectfully. "An honor, lady."

Julian's resemblance to Synesius was evident. They both stood a head taller than most men and shared a warm countenance. But

Julian's face was chiseled through the jaw, and his eyes lacked the squint of hours spent before scrolls in dim light. And of course, Julian's many hours of intense physical training showed in his musculature, whereas Synesius developed the muscle of his mind alone.

When Julian straightened from his bow, his eyes, glowing like ocean agate, locked with Hannah's, and she felt her breath come short. Were the settee any lower she might melt into the floor. "A pleasure, Julian of Cyrene."

Julian glanced at her neck and broke their gaze. "Please give my brother my warmest regards."

"I shall," Hannah said, her fingers unconsciously gliding up to the bronze collar at her throat. She had almost forgotten it, and now she felt choked by an icy claw.

"Hypatia, I must depart. We will speak again soon," Julian purred.

"It is a most generous offer. Please thank your masters for me," said Hypatia. Then she turned to Hannah and added. "You can see what kind of an age we live in when warriors must be employed to protect scholars."

"Do give my regards to Alizar, Orestes, and Gideon. Oh, and please convey to my brother I have passed the final rites."

Hypatia's eyebrows lifted. "Oh? Congratulations. I shall."

Julian nodded to Hannah and smiled curtly at both women, then swept out of the room, quiet as a cat.

Hannah felt the hammering in her chest begin to slow once he was gone.

Hypatia saw the questions in Hannah's eyes. "Only the finest, most committed monks ever reach the rank of Nuapar," she explained. "You know them because they alone wear the black robes with the red sash. The Nuapar have two masters called the *Kolossofia*. They are known as Masters Savitur and Junkar. The Kolossofia always have the same names throughout the ages.

Each chooses his successor, and the successor inherits his master's name."

"Why do the Nuapar need two masters? One would not suffice?"

Hypatia shrugged. "The tradition is ancient. They refuse to write down their teachings no matter how much I prod. With two masters, if anything happens to the first, the teachings are still with the second. But I have never heard of anything happening to a Kolossofia master. There are countless stories of their magical abilities. It is said that they can fly through the air, read minds, make objects levitate, see into the future, and manifest second bodies for themselves. It is all quite superstitious if you ask me. I am a scientist and believe what my eyes can verify."

Hypatia collected one last scroll from the table behind her and added it to the leather satchel. "Time for my class. But there is something I would like to give you before I go."

"Give me?"

"Hearing you sing, I was so deeply soothed. The night you played I was able to forget my burdens for an entire hour and just be swept away. It was such a luxury. You have no idea."

"Singing at your lecture brought me great joy."

"Hannah, you could play for audiences like that one every night. And not just the staff, but visiting magistrates, kings, emperors. You will be everyone's favorite, I am quite certain. We already have requests that you play for my lecture next week."

"You do?"

Hypatia nodded. Then she lifted a large object bound in linen that had lain behind her desk. "For you," she said, setting the bundle on Hannah's lap.

Hannah unwrapped the heavy gift. Beneath the cloth her fingers found the hard surface of polished wood and several taut strings.

A lyre.

Hannah turned the golden instrument in the light admiring the fine wood with a musician's eye. "This is a fine lyre, Hypatia. Olivewood?"

"Yes. It belonged to my mother."

Hannah's breath caught in her throat. "Hypatia, I could not take this from you." She thrust the instrument toward Hypatia.

Hypatia waved her hand. "No, I insist. You need an appropriate instrument to accompany such an exquisite voice. Besides, I am not musical."

Hannah closed her eyes, scarcely able to find the words to express her gratitude. This was not a gift to be taken lightly. "Thank you, Hypatia. What can I do to repay you?"

Hypatia thought a moment. "Write a song that would fit with the theme of one of my lectures and come and play it for us in the library."

Hannah fingered the strings. "What would you like me to write?"

Hypatia paused, turning her eyes up to the sky. "Sing for us of divine Love. Beauty. Truth. That is all I could ever wish for."

"It would be an honor," Hannah said.

Over Hypatia's shoulder another vessel floated into the window frame, past the islands, while a flock of black-headed gulls gyred around the mast, pleading for scraps. There was so much to consider. Hannah had relished playing for the people in the Great Hall. The thought of having an audience like that every night was tantalizing. But then she thought of the Parabolani and how they had killed the young girl in the market. As if to punctuate her thought, a peacock screamed like a woman in peril from the other end of the garden.

Hannah cringed.

10

The Parabolani descended on Alizar's house, Peter the Reader at the front with his cudgel raised, while Hannah was away at the library. Five men in black robes with eyes promising punishment. Jemir saw them at the wall from the upstairs landing and ran to the kitchen. He intended to send Leitah out with two quick missives, but he only had time to write the one to Synesius, to keep Hannah detained. Jemir gathered his strength. He would have to speak to them. Alone.

So.

Hannah poured over scrolls at the library with her tutor, unaware of the brewing storm. Synesius was a devotee of the Socratic method, and so his technique of teaching depended solely upon his student's curiosity. Hannah's swelling stream of questions kept him in a constant state of service to her blossoming intellect, researching the various topics that interested her so that he could prepare her lessons appropriately. He discovered that the empirical girl was never satisfied with philosophical answers alone, and so he found himself recounting stories of Mediterranean lore to help her understand the way civilization, law, war, and politics had evolved. He took her for walks through the Mouseion for their lessons on architecture and to the outdoor gymnasium to practice archery. With her sling she could hit a rabbit at fifteen meters, so the bow fit naturally into her hand.

Synesius never had a student unfamiliar with Greek culture and history. He repeatedly found himself making assumptions about what Hannah must already know, only to discover as he was recounting a historical battle that she had never heard of Julius Caesar, or that she thought Rome was another Greek city. Synesius decided that this afternoon he would unroll a collection of maps so that she could see for herself how the world was laid out.

With her finger, she traced the borders of Greece, Persia, and Asia Minor, Egypt, Nubia, Britannia, Gaul, and Hispania in awe of how large the world had suddenly become to her. They spent hours reviewing cities and conquests and wars until she found with her finger the little triangle beside the Red Sea called Sinai and sighed. "Please. No more maps today, Synesius."

Synesius nodded, rolling up the map. At that moment Hypatia's slave girl appeared with the letter from Jemir on a silver tray. Synesius read the missive and concealed any emotion with the restraint of an actor playing his part. "Thank you. Now take this to Hypatia," was all he said. Then he suggested to Hannah they take a walk out in the garden.

The days were growing unseasonably warm; drought was perched on every tongue as still more grain had to be imported, and households watched their jars of almonds and dried currants run empty. Now everyone feared for the olives and the grapes. The years when the waters of the Nile were low, the upper delta received most of the water of the flood, leaving a mere trickle for the lower delta to irrigate the fields. There was an abundance of fish, but the populace was growing uneasy and restless all the same. But that particular afternoon, worries aside, a rare ocean breeze washed in and gave the merchants an excuse to close their shops early and head to the tavernas on the beaches.

As they walked beneath the wide *peripatos*, Hannah asked Synesius about the Greek gods. He recited those twelve on Olympus that all scholars learn as children: Zeus, Apollo, Hera, Aphrodite, Demeter, Poseidon, Athena, Artemis, Hermes, Dionysus, Ares, Hephaestus. Hannah wanted details about each, but she paused at

Zeus when she heard of his many conquests outside his marriage bed with his wife, Hera. "I do not think he loved her if he could do such a thing to her. What honor could there be in ruining her heart?"

As they walked, their footsteps fell in and out of rhythm. Synesius said, "There are many forms of love. Perhaps Zeus lacked singular devotion, as you have noted."

"You are an expert on the subject then? Of love?" Hannah teased him—she knew he was neither married nor interested in courting.

Synesius laughed heartily, taken by surprise. Something about Hannah's sincerity, however, deserved a genuine answer, not the elusive one he would give any other student. He let his eyes drift up into the sky and then across the sea. When he spoke his voice shed something of the impersonal tone he used while teaching. "When my brother Julian and I first came to the shores of Pharos, it was with one of the Nuapar monks, Kolossofia Master Junkar."

"I met Julian this morning. The resemblance between you is clear."

"Ah, yes. Well, Julian fought in the square in Cyrene for money against any opponent who would challenge him. This is where Junkar found him. It was after our parents died. He challenged Julian, and when he won, for his price, he took us both with him to Alexandria. I will never forget that voyage in the small skiff on the water and the first sight of Pharos, which, in the thick fog of morning, was not a sight at all, but the sound of the priestesses singing on the shore. My brother and I were transfixed by it, like Odysseus. Master Junkar said something to us then that I have never forgotten. He said, 'The fate of love and knowledge are the same: both end with your corpse. Choose what you would fill your days with while you live.' When I came to the library to study under Hypatia, I found she, like the Nuapar, chose knowledge alone."

"She has never loved?"

"One of the other students in her lectures who often sat beside me fell in love with her, and although he tried to keep it a secret, she discovered his affections."

"Yes?"

"On the following day she flung the cloth soiled with her menstrual blood on his writing tablet, saying, 'That is the hideous flesh you love. Flesh that betrays us all.' He never swooned over her again, and she has had no suitor since, which pleases her."

"I do not believe she would ever do something so crude. Not Hypatia."

"Crude indeed. Hypatia would go to any length to illustrate her teaching. She cares nothing for who is offended. The story carried her reputation as far as Londinium, I believe."

They stopped beneath the shade of one of Cleopatra's Needles in the east, a slender granite obelisk perched on a small knoll that overlooked the harbor where moored ships swayed together rhythmically on the shifting sea, their masts almost touching, but never quite reaching.

"Do you suppose that Aphrodite, as the goddess of love, could have enchanted Zeus to remain faithful to Hera?" asked Hannah. She spoke of the gods, but Hannah's heart conjured an image of Julian, his oceanic eyes, the look they had shared. She wondered how often he came to the library and if he would be one of the warriors chosen to protect Hypatia.

Synesius pursed his lips in contemplation. "Love and desire are often mistaken for one another. The first is a praxis of divine origin, one that Christ lived by example; the second, often no less powerful though certainly less pure, an overpowering sentimental sensation. Desire causes one to lose control of the mind, and the mind's peace must be savored and preserved, for once it is lost, it is extremely difficult to regain. Love and peace are the vine and lattice, mutually supporting. Aphrodite was known for her jealousy—and Hera for her stability. I suppose if we take a lesson from the gods, it is to master the mind."

"But not the heart? Would that not be like leaving one of those fine ships in the harbor forever to rot?" As she spoke, Hannah's hair came undone from a knot at the nape of her neck and swirled around her body in the breeze.

"Ships that go to sea are how shipwrecks come to be," Synesius parried.

"Yes, but not all ships that set out of the harbor are doomed to be lost."

Synesius grunted. "Yes. Those that escape a fate on the bottom of the sea are eventually split apart from years of wear."

"I would prefer the bottom of the sea, if it were me." Hannah let her eyes skim over the deeper water beyond the lighthouse, water streaked with wide swaths of deep blues and greys, a sea that could quench the thought of thirst, but never the thirst itself.

One of the library's messengers marched up the walk behind them, thrust a letter into Synesius's hands, and then departed as swiftly as he came. Synesius tore the seal on the letter and read it, then looked at Hannah and folded it up, inserting it in the front pocket in his robes.

Hannah watched his eyes, the animal inside her now aware he was concealing something. "What are you not telling me?"

Synesius shrugged. "It is nothing. We should go to the Lyceum across the garden. I want you to see the gymnasts. Then afterwards, we can begin your arithmetic."

"Today? But the day is mostly spent."

"Yes, today," said Synesius firmly. "And into the evening if need be."

So.

He told her the truth once he had word it was safe to return to Alizar's home. Hannah left at once and ran through the streets until she found the familiar green door in the alley. Inside, Alizar's entire house had been ransacked: pots smashed, tiles stripped from the walls, tapestries shredded like discarded skins left on the floors from room to room. Then the familiar whine and tick-tick-tick of the hounds' toenails on the marble as they came running and buried their noses in Hannah's hands. She knew they had not been fed.

They could wait. Hannah rushed to the upstairs room to check on Naomi. Thankfully she was there in bed, Leitah seated beside her.

"Oh, Leitah! What happened?"

The silent girl shook her head.

"Where is Tarek?" Hannah ventured.

Leitah made a crude thrusting gesture with her hips and pointed out the window.

"He has been at the brothels, then?"

Leitah nodded.

"But Jemir?"

Leitah shook her head, held her wrists together, as though they were tied.

"They have him." Hannah sat on the edge of the bed and placed a hand on Naomi's warm calf. "What should we do? Can we reach Alizar somehow with a letter?"

Leitah shook her head and tears fell down her cheeks.

Hannah reached forward and took the girl in her arms, letting her sob. That was how she came to suspect the private love of Leitah and Jemir.

The project of cleaning the house took most of the evening. Hannah prayed that Jemir had only been briefly detained, but she knew they may never see him again. She felt strangled with guilt. This was all her fault. Had she only held her tongue in the market.

Well after dark Tarek burst in the kitchen door. "What in Hades happened?"

Hannah sat at the table, nibbling some seed bread and hard white cheese. She looked at him, then broke off another chunk, dipped it in a saucer of olive oil. She felt as if she had not eaten in days. "They came."

Tarek sat beside her at the table, his eyes vulnerable, like a boy's. "Where is Jemir?"

Hannah shook her head.

"Leitah?"

"Upstairs in Naomi's bedchamber. She will not come down."

"How long?"

"Earlier today. I was at the library. One of the stablemen is dead."

Tarek hung his head. He reached for her bread and broke off a hunk in his hands and shoved it in his mouth. "This is all your fault, girl."

Hannah got up. "I will make some tea."

Tarek nodded. "If they took him, they wanted him alive. We will wait. He will escape, or we will hear their terms."

The Parabolani did not return, but neither did Jemir. Days passed with no word. Hannah, in addition to her regular duties, helped Leitah scour the house, repair some of the damage, plant herbs in the garden, and attend to chores in the kitchen. There was no need for words, even if Leitah had been in the practice of speaking. They exchanged glances and soft pats on the arm, and when Leitah began to sob while pushing the rag across the steps, Hannah held her and soothed her like a baby. All they could do was wait.

Jemir staggered in at dawn four days later, his face bloody, his wrists bruised and mangled from the chain they hung him by. Alizar's hounds greeted him with loud braying, happy tongues lolling as they pranced circles around his legs.

Leitah was the first to the garden gate. She threw her arms around his neck and kissed him. He savored her embrace. He had thought he may never know her arms again. They hobbled as far as the fig tree when Hannah dashed down the path to assist them to the cushions at the far end of the kitchen where he could lie down.

"How did you escape?" asked Hannah. She poured Jemir a cup of wine and raised it to his lips as Leitah held his head.

Jemir groaned. "I did not escape. I was released."

Just then, Tarek appeared at the door, having been awakened by the commotion of the hounds. "Not by the bishop. Unless you gave him what he asked."

"I did not, and it was by governor Orestes. *Kalimera*, Tarek."

Tarek nodded contemplatively and took another cup of wine from Hannah. "I knew you would make it out. I said so."

"The battle has been taken to higher ground," said Jemir, as he spit out a tooth into his hand. The blood pooled at the edge of his mouth. He tested the rest of his teeth and sucked down more wine with a painful satisfaction. "No one takes interest in a soldier when they can have a king, *Kuklamu*. The governor came and struck a deal."

"What kind of deal?" asked Tarek.

Jemir lay back on Leitah's lap, closing his eyes. "I was not informed, merely released. Cyril's ambitions are great. We should not underestimate his power. He wants Alexandria under Christian rule. He knows the empire is aligned to his interests."

Leitah lifted a wedge of wet cotton to Jemir's face to clean the cuts.

"Did they find the door to Alizar's tower?" Tarek asked seriously.

Jemir shook his head. "No. I sealed the entrance in time."

"And did they learn anything from you about Alizar's work?"

Jemir shook his head. "That I would take to my grave."

Tarek then relaxed back onto the cushions and turned toward Hannah, sipping his wine, daggers in his eyes. "This trouble was all your doing."

"Then perhaps you should not have cursed me while I still live beneath your roof," Hannah said brusquely, helping Leitah by dabbing at the dried blood beside Jemir's eye.

Tarek glared at her. "You forget your place, slave."

Hannah cringed as Tarek left the room. Jemir found her eyes. "Alizar is the master here," he said, reassuring her, "not him."

"Do you think we should all leave the city?" Hannah asked. Inside the question was the veiled hope to search for her father.

Jemir coughed a little and spat again. Then he squeezed Leitah's hand, bringing it to his lips to kiss. "This is our home. Will we fight."

So.

11

Alizar's ship, the *Vesta*, drifted into the harbor on a sea warmed by the sky's sunset palette: gold, scarlet, magenta, lapis blue. Sails were lowered and wrapped so they could be towed into harbor. Governor Orestes thought it might be the perfect occasion for a party, and so he arranged one in the Caesarium gardens behind the Great Library. He hired acting troupes to perform for the feast, with strolling jugglers, acrobats, dancing girls, fire-eaters, and magicians. The finale would be later that evening on the beach, when the new brass reflector—as immense as Hercules himself—was to be hung in the lighthouse crown. The complaints of the sailors who bemoaned that the bonfires on the beach were not bright enough to prevent their ships from foundering would finally be assuaged, for the governor promised that the new beam from the lighthouse would be visible for many lengths out to sea. He would have promised it would bring Alexander the Great back from the dead if he thought it would win him a seat in the Egyptian senate. Orestes was quite fond of the Promethean idea of restoring light to the city, as he was quick to embrace both restoration and progress. But he had not considered Prometheus's fate before he set himself such a high mark. Absent from his memory also was the time that Alizar had confided in him that there was always something to keep him from relaxing upon returning from a long journey. This evening was to be no exception.

As the party began, Alizar strolled into the gardens looking haggard but cheerful, a *corona* of lavender on his head. As the guest of honor, Alizar had many hands to shake and friends to embrace. Every so often someone would push a fresh drink in his hand and distract him from the feast for yet another hour. Soon he could hear his stomach growling over the conversation, and so he excused himself to follow the tantalizing scent of roasted lamb.

As he strode toward the enormous buffet table with its colorful arrangements of cheeses and fresh fruits, breads and olives, Alizar was clapped on the back by Orestes. "Thought I might not even see you this evening!" He laughed, and the men hugged like brothers.

"You have outdone yourself entirely," Alizar chuckled, popping a fat green olive into his mouth, "and I will never forgive you for it."

Orestes knew how Alizar hated to be made a spectacle of, so it was with particular relish he watched Alizar squirm through his sea of admirers. Orestes had told him many times he was too great a man to hide behind such a simple life. He could have been a renowned senator or a general if he had any ambition to leave that tower of his. "Tell me, how is it with the world?"

Alizar stopped chewing. "Word has not made it as far as Alexandria?"

Orestes looked unsure. "Word?"

"Rome has fallen."

"Fallen?"

"Sacked by the Goths. She is lost."

"Alaric."

"Yes, he and his army have succeeded at last."

"Does Emperor Honorius live?"

"The Goths did not bother with Ravenna. They wanted Rome and they got it."

"There will be war."

"No, Honorius is hapless and cowardly. When he was told Rome had been destroyed he thought of his pet chicken Roma and cried out, 'No, how could it be? She just ate from my hand this morning.' The fool."

"What of Alaric and his army?"

"They were sailing for Africa when a storm overtook them. All the ships went down. Alaric is presumed dead, and the Goths have retreated to Gaul, though they have reclaimed Londinium, I hear."

"This will weaken the heart of every true Roman in the city."

"If they do not hang themselves first."

"We best not speak of this tonight. I will prepare something for the morning. A formal statement must be delivered in the *agora*." Orestes downed his wine and dabbed at the sweat now pouring from his brow.

As Alizar stabbed a juicy filet of roasted lamb and hoisted it onto his plate. With or without Rome, a man must eat.

Orestes spied Hannah beside the Caesarium temple speaking with Synesius. "What do you plan to do with the girl now that you have returned, Alizar?"

"I am not certain."

"I hear Hypatia wants her here at the library. But you will certainly give me first consideration."

"At the library?"

"The girl sings like a siren."

"True. I suppose it would be impossible not to be enchanted by her voice. Her talent is extraordinary."

Orestes narrowed his eyes. "Have you heard yet of her scuffle in the market with the Parabolani? Surely you mean to give her up."

Alizar took a measured pause. This meal was getting harder and harder to enjoy. "Tell me."

"She and Tarek interfered with a public demonstration."

Alizar gave a heavy sigh. He was all too familiar with Cyril's barbaric public demonstrations. "They were caught."

"No, but reported."

"My house was put on the watch list?"

"The Parabolani broke in and Jemir was taken prisoner. They tortured him apparently, but he said nothing. That man would die for you. Hypatia called for me, and I met with Cyril to see him freed. Do not worry, he is at home recovering. The herbalist went to see him this morning. But that slave of yours is a troublemaker. Sell her to me. I will make sure she behaves."

Alizar released a heavy breath. "Have I been summoned? Are they speaking of trial?"

Orestes chuckled. "I took care of it, old friend. It is done."

"You and I both know that this is not the end of it. Tell me, is there any word from Empress Pulcheria about recalling the Parabolani?"

"The Parabolani are not at the top of the imperial list of priorities, I am afraid. I am getting nowhere with the court, and of course, Cyril ever resents my working against him." Orestes lowered his voice. Typically there could not be a safer place than the library to discuss things, but Cyril's spies were everywhere.

"He is envious of your popularity." Alizar picked up on Orestes's concern and indicated with a nod that they walk the path to the amphitheatre where they could speak more freely. "But how did you manage to get Jemir freed? Let's not speak of the girl for the moment."

"Cyril has demanded that I return to the Christian church to worship and publicly renounce any affiliation with Hypatia's teaching."

"But you would never agree to such a thing."

"Agreements can be made and broken. I renounced the Christian church publicly in the square instead. I also confiscated Cyril's watch list, which is well within my rights to do, and is the reason why you are no longer on it. I would sooner be put on a cross myself than indulge that spoiled jackass and his railings against the beautiful women of our city. I tire of him." Orestes spat the blasphemous words.

Alizar's eyes filled with warning. "You have done what? Cyril's influence is growing. Whether or not you agree with what he preaches, he must believe you to be an ally. Cyril is not an enemy either of us can afford. I have worked too hard all this time to convince him of my neutrality. You must rescind."

The two gentlemen settled on the top row of the amphitheatre, overlooking the sea. Alizar adjusted his red *klamys* over his shoulder.

"I cannot. I have gained the support of the Jews for my decision, and they are more in number in this city than the Christians. Nearly two hundred thousand by last census. They are how I will attain the prefecture. That, and the Emerald Tablet of Hermes Trismagistus."

Alizar straightened. "The tablet? You know where it is?"

"The Nuapar will disclose its location to me, I am certain."

"Unlikely. They have kept that secret for nearly seven hundred years."

"But never has there been a time such as this."

"The oldest scrolls suggest the tablet will only return to unite the pagan people in the hour of greatest need. It can hardly be used for political gain."

"Ever the alchemist. Can I not persuade you that this is that time?"

"I am doubtful, old friend, but perhaps the prefecture will be enough without it. You really think the position is within your grasp?"

"Our dutiful patience may pay off yet. Anthemius died while you were away. A new praetorian prefect of Egypt is required. I have the nomination already. I need only the Emperor's support by means of Augusta Pulcheria. The ships have sailed with word."

"Anthemius dead? By nature or by poison?"

"What does it matter? His seat must be filled."

"This could be just the edge we need," said Alizar, relaxing on the top bench of the amphitheatre.

Orestes settled beside him and removed five large gold coins from his purse, pressing them into Alizar's hand.

"What is this?"

"The girl."

Alizar thought of Hannah's fate beneath the jealous gaze of the governor's wife. She would be forbidden to read. To go out. To breathe. "I think I will keep her for now." He handed the coins back.

Orestes grunted his displeasure. "Name your price then."

There was silence between them before Alizar spoke. "You know, old friend, we will not overcome the Christians by force. There are too many of them. It seems our only remaining choice is to blend in. Perhaps you should consider honoring your agreement with Cyril and going back to the church to keep up appearances."

Orestes scowled and drained his cup of wine, taking up the flagon beside him to refill it. "I have sent a boy to spy within the church. A trusted boy, called Ignus. He will come to us with anything he hears."

Alizar continued. "A good idea, but not enough. You know as well as I that Cyril is a clever and unpredictable asp."

"Maybe," Orestes sneered, "but I am cleverer still." The ley lines of Orestes's pride had long ago been deeply etched, Alizar knew, and he was the not the kind of man who was wont to shift them, even cosmetically. He changed the subject. "Tell me how your voyage fared."

Alizar's face fell. "I spent twice the amount on bribes as in years past. The trade routes are infested with Christian soldiers while our new emperor is still wetting his bed."

"Ah, if only we could have another Julian the Apostate."

"A lovely fantasy. A pagan emperor would be a welcome change from all of this . . . madness." Alizar waved his hand through the air and then speared another bite of lamb. When he looked up, it was to see Hannah striding toward them with an offering of wine.

"Good evening, Alizar. Welcome home," she said as she paused before them with a little bow and presented the wine. "Governor. Hypatia has requested your presence in the Great Hall."

Both men stood, delighted by her appearance. Orestes clasped the *amphora* of wine. Alizar embraced her and kissed her cheeks. "Hannah, it is wonderful to see you looking so well. Come, I want to introduce you to several friends. Orestes, go easy on the wine, you son of Bacchus."

———————

For the rest of their lives, those who witnessed the restoration of the lighthouse mirror never forgot where they were the moment the blade of light appeared. Little details remained etched in their minds: the feel of a ring on a lover's hand, the cry of a hungry baby, the musky scent of the sea as it mingled with the smoke from the torches, the play of shadows on the archways and painted columns.

The angel watched and waited. Soon.

Alizar knew it was a moment that would stay with him through the rest of his life, a pillar for his memory to lean upon. Once the crowd grew tiresome for him, he returned home. Home. Nowhere he wanted to be more. He was greeted by his two red hounds, licking his hands and whining in glee at their master's return. Alizar swept up the steps, opened the door at the top of the stairs, and carefully lifted Naomi from the bed and brought her to the open window, tipping her chin in the direction of the beach. "We will watch it together," he whispered as he kissed the peach fur of her sunken cheek.

He sat with her in the square of the window long enough to watch the crescent moon drop beneath the horizon, leaving the empty bed of the sky with its scattered clouds like rumpled sheets. The lamps from the street cast a pale yellow glow on Naomi's face. He could feel the slender thread of her breath against his throat.

He watched quietly until a magnificent shaft of light split the darkness and pierced the dark sea. Then it turned toward the beach, making a slow circle. Eventually the light crossed Alizar's bedroom window and fell slantwise across Naomi's eyelids. Her dark lashes fluttered, and then she stirred. The edges of her lips began to quiver and then turn upward as a little sigh rang in her throat. And then her face softened again, the smile slipping away.

Alizar hugged her to his chest again and again, rocking her on his lap, delighted for this little sign of coherence. They passed hours that way until he heard the footsteps of people returning from the beach in the street below. Then he rose and carried Naomi back to the bed. As he pulled the sheet over her chest, he heard voices in the hall. Tarek. Jemir. Hannah. Looking for him.

Alizar left the bedroom and stepped into the bright hall. The instant he saw Leitah's face he stopped short. Something was wrong. Her eyes were worried and hollow. She beckoned him to come.

At the bottom of the stairs Jemir was hollering at Tarek. As Alizar rushed down, both men began incomprehensibly waving their hands and shouting. Alizar quieted them and let Jemir explain. According to his story, Orestes had been announcing the performances of the actors in honor of the restoration of the lighthouse when a group of Jews at the front of the stage began to shout that there were agents of Cyril in the audience planning a riot. "Orestes listened to them, Alizar." The words tumbled off Jemir's tongue in rapid succession.

Tarek picked up the story. "They denounced Heirax, saying his presence was treason against the government. It was merely a drunken provocation, nothing more. But Orestes listened to them. He had Heirax arrested."

"Arrested? Are you absolutely certain?" Alizar studied their faces for the hidden humor. Perhaps they thought to prank him on his first night home. But they remained grave, nodding to him that it was true. Alizar felt a constriction in his chest; after they had just discussed doing nothing to further upset Cyril, Orestes had arrested the bishop's high counselor. "Lock the doors behind me and do not let anyone in under any circumstances." Alizar spun and rushed out into the alley.

Hannah watched the green door click shut behind him and shuddered, feeling nothing good could possibly come of this.

———

Alizar found the governor at ease in his home, the night still thick and unyielding outside. "You must listen to reason, Orestes."

"Alizar, I must appease the Jews. This is my election now." Orestes reclined in his silk evening robe and jute slippers, sipping cinnamon tea. He offered a cup to Alizar, who declined irritably.

"Release Heirax."

"No, he is to be tried tomorrow."

"Under what charge?"

"Sedition."

"Heavens, man."

"Cyril will think twice about dealing with me now. He will see what power government and justice still hold over his little church. It is a move I must make given the fall of Rome. I must establish my authority in Alexandria immediately."

"Have you gone mad? He will retaliate, Orestes. You know Cyril as well as I."

"Let him retaliate. What can he do?" Orestes was besotted. The party had gone well. The lighthouse was restored. Due to his ever-increasing popularity, Orestes was one election from praetorian prefect, and his gleaming reputation had not one mark upon it. All of Egypt was in his hands.

Alizar folded his arms. "He can do plenty."

"You know I respect you old friend, but this time you are wrong. We have won. With Heirax gone, Cyril will withdraw."

"Orestes, you must set Heirax free, or Cyril will unleash the Parabolani on all of us in the name of his Christian God. They are a hundred in number now, and he could conscript two hundred more in a fortnight. What soldiers does Egypt have to offer us in return? We will have no protection. The lamb staked on a hill before the wolves."

"This conversation tires me." Orestes rose from the divan and settled in a deep chair on one side of the hearth, gesturing to Alizar to take the one adjacent, but he refused, preferring to stand beside the fire. He lifted a green malachite sphere from the mantle and turned it in his hands. How many days till these hands were decomposing in the grave? Perhaps few, he thought, but he certainly did not want to be put there by Cyril's men.

Rather than continue to discuss what had transpired, Orestes divagated and brought up Hypatia's latest lecture series on the Enneads and the discussions that had ensued thereafter, all of which Alizar had missed.

But Alizar kept the conversation on Heirax. "You must not kill him. Put him on the wheel for a day if you must, but let it go at that."

"Nothing less than death will serve the intended message."

"That is what concerns me." Alizar excused himself to the kitchen and found, not the cook, but Phoebe pouring from a pot of tea, long silver hair plaited over her shoulder, her hazel eyes bloodshot and fatigued. He spoke quietly. "Phoebe, you must do what only a wife can. Convince Orestes to change his mind about Heirax."

Phoebe laughed. "You know him as well as I, Alizar. He was born under the sign of the Ram. Once he makes up his mind, there is no changing it. Every idea must be his alone."

The following day, it was announced by Orestes in the agora that Rome had fallen to the Goths. He proclaimed the name of

Emperor Honorius as triumphant and elaborated with the death of the Goth leader Alaric and his army at sea. He finished with the words, "Rome shall rise again!"

The effect was unsettling for the crowd. Rome had fallen? Were they next? The people became agitated and restless, eager for a fight to release their tensions.

Several hours passed until Alizar watched from his tower as Heirax was condemned for sedition and tortured. His body was stretched on a large wooden cartwheel, and as the wheel was rotated, one by one, Orestes broke his bones with an iron hammer. First a crushing blow to the knee, then the elbow, then the shoulder, then an ankle, both wrists. The crowd was enormously pleased to hear Heirax screaming over the course of the afternoon. They cheered each time the hammer blow came down. Eventually, once Heirax lost consciousness from the pain, he was eviscerated and, still barely alive, was left strapped to the cartwheel, which was hoisted from a tall column so the crows could eat his entrails.

Cyril wasted no time in calling together the leaders of the Jewish community to threaten them to stop backing Orestes. He even went so far as to insist that the fall of Rome was brought about by the pagans worshipping the Roman gods. But the Jews, who already resented Cyril's maneuvering to take over the city, in turn invested all their confidence in Orestes, tithing their support to the governor for strength and protection just as he predicted.

Alizar and the rest of the house watched uneasily as day after day the tension in the city mounted between the Jews and the Christians. He paid countless visits to Orestes and even considered paying one to Cyril as if he thought it would do any good. Finally, his every move made to no avail, he had no choice but to pace, watch, and lose sleep.

Hannah carried a cup of peppermint tea to Alizar in his tower late one night to find him carving a trail in the available floor, weaving between stacks of dusty leather-bound codices, instruments, unraveled scrolls, and bunches of dried herbs and flowers. "You really think something is going to happen . . ." She shoved aside several enormous codices to clear a tiny spot of table for the teacup.

Alizar grunted. "When you place a kettle on the fire, the water boils." He faced her. "If you press a lid to that kettle, the water boils all the faster."

Hannah nodded. "I feel in my bones there will be trouble," she said.

"Hannah," said Alizar. "You have nothing to fear. This house has stood five hundred years, and it will stand five hundred more. Trust me. These events will pass. Keep your faith."

So.

Their suspicions were confirmed five nights later. It was a warm evening, and most everyone in the city was outside tending their gardens or socializing with family. Alizar was polishing his library shelves with Jemir when he heard the shouting from beyond the walls of the courtyard.

"The church! The church of St. Alexander is aflame!"

Alizar locked eyes with Jemir. St. Alexander was Cyril's church.

Jemir leapt to the door. "Should I call Aziz to ready a horse for you?"

Alizar did not move; he was thinking. "No, not yet. I am not going to ride into the lion's mouth. It might be a trick. We must wait until we know for certain. Call Tarek. We will send him to spy."

"He is out already, I am afraid."

So Tarek was at the brothel again. No matter. They still had time. Another crier would come by the courtyard, and more news would spill over the wall before the night ended.

Time crawled on. Church bells all over the city clanged to announce the fire, so there was nothing to measure the hours.

The sound of pounding on the green door in the atrium brought everyone in Alizar's house running. Leitah peered through the peephole as Alizar strode through the atrium. "Who is there?" His voice reverberated through the marble anteroom.

"Gideon," came the voice from outside.

Alizar threw open the door. "Gideon, tell us the news."

The captain stepped inside, his black *klamys* twirling a circle. Hannah watched him from behind the statue of Hermes, eager to hear what was happening.

"You probably heard that St. Alexander was on fire, but it was a ruse."

"A ruse? You mean it did not burn? Speak."

"Far worse. A group of Jewish fathers hid all around the entrance. When the Christians came to save their church, they were ambushed. The men were angry that the Christians have been killing their daughters. It has to come to this."

"How many killed?"

"Hard to say. Seventy, maybe more. But that is not all. Cyril organized his Parabolani, and they are riding into the Jewish quarter at this very instant, tossing torches into all the synagogues. He is determined to have every Jew in this city dead by morning or else exiled into the desert." Gideon was speaking as rapidly as he could get the words out.

"Tomorrow is Passover," said Hannah, horrified and flooded with concern.

Gideon rested a strong hand on her shoulder, a hand of protection. "Cyril cares not a jot. The Jews are fleeing as the Christian mobs ransack their homes. Some are fighting off the mob. There must be hundreds dead already. Hypatia is hiding as many as she can in the library. I thought you could hide more here."

"I can do far better than that." Alizar said. "Ready my ship to sail at dawn. Find a crew at once, Gideon. I must get to the Gate of the Sun."

Alizar buckled his sword and rushed out the door.

Gideon set both his hands on Hannah's shoulders and met her eyes. "You are a clever girl. Do not be clever tonight."

She nodded.

"Would that I believed you," he said. When he lifted his hands and departed, she could still feel the weight of them there, the soothing warmth. She watched him go until he disappeared and shut the door.

Around the corner the men collided with Tarek, who had been at a full sprint. He careened into Gideon and toppled backward in the dust. Alizar helped him up. "Tarek, come with us. No, better yet, fetch more men and meet us at the Gate of the Sun. And shut the women in the house. Tell them to keep the door locked until I return. If anything should happen, they must hide in the catacombs." Tarek nodded and disappeared.

Alizar and Gideon quickened their steps, rounding the knoll that marked the edge of the Brucheon from the Jewish quarter as smoke flooded their nostrils. The scattered pockets of orange flames rose from several synagogues and spread to nearby homes in a hungry roar. Everywhere, the chaos of bodies churned in all directions as people fled the fires. Braying animals stampeded into the crowds of frightened men and women, crushing whatever they touched; horses, camels, donkeys, goats and chickens were all set loose in pandemonium. At the end of the street, Gideon split off to the harbor, and Alizar tugged his *petasos* over his eyes and continued toward the flames.

At the end of a dark alley, Alizar found the Queen's Theatre still untouched. Several actors quietly ushered Jewish families inside to hide. A little girl in a man's arms screamed and struggled, her hands waving in the air, grasping for some unseen person. The man, his eyes white as a wild horse's, clamped a hand over the little girl's mouth and rushed through the door. Was he an uncle? A father? A stranger?

Alizar promptly forgot the exhaustion from his voyage. There were nearly a quarter of a million Jews in the city. Close friends he had known for over fifty years were somewhere in the chaos, fighting for their lives, their children endangered, their homes being destroyed. Damn Orestes's pride. The death of Heirax had pushed the Christians to eradicate his entire flock of supporters.

Alizar wound his way deeper into the residential district of the Jewish Quarter, which was crumbling into shambles. Two women in the street fought over a wagon, crashing sounds came from behind every door, and a little boy crouched beside a twisted body, crying. There in the midst of the flames, black robes unscathed, were the Parabolani led by Peter, who stood a full head above the others. The priests pounded their fists on the doors of the homes, burst them open and grabbed Jewish families—men, boys, toddlers, grandmothers—and threw them out into the street. Alizar averted his eyes as one of the priests broke an old man's arm, jerking the man away from his door to let a Christian family plunder his home.

"By the will of God, all Jewish property now belongs to the Christians of Alexandria," Peter called out. "Be banished into the desert or face death."

The Jews were realizing they were outnumbered. Some of them had gathered their possessions, herded by the Parabolani like livestock toward the Gate of the Sun and the bleak desert beyond.

"All Jews are now exiled from this city by ordinance of the Bishop," Ammonius shouted, standing beside Peter, black hood concealing his face.

"Ordinance," Alizar hissed. "Cyril cannot make ordinances."

Families scattered in the dark. A veiled woman rushed into the arms of a man who pressed her tightly to his chest. Beside them, a toddler with a dirty face sat in the street, screaming. Everywhere came the sound of crying and fighting, the smashing of walls. The Christians moved in like hungry rats on an abandoned feast. These people, thought Alizar, would claim the kingdom of heaven for themselves even if it meant evicting the current residents. Surely their Christ would never approve, the man who shared all he had and healed the downtrodden that society had cast aside. Alizar pinched the ridge of skin between his eyebrows as the smoke made his eyes water. He had to get to the Gate of the Sun before the Parabolani.

Back at the house, Tarek locked Hannah and Leitah in Naomi's upstairs bedroom. Hannah dashed to the balcony to see what was happening. Then she stepped back into the bedroom and began rummaging through a chest. "I have to help," she explained to Leitah. "Stay here and keep watch over Naomi." She pulled several items from the chest: a broken tray; a set of carved marble horses broken from a wall in Athens; a tiny leather sack of glass eyes of various sizes; a wooden knife, the kind a child might play with. Hannah went on rummaging until she came upon what she was hoping for, some forgotten boyhood clothes belonging to Naomi's son. Leitah helped her bind her breasts with a length of cloth then cinched a *tunica* around her waist and piled her hair up under a cap. A burnoose bound around her head and neck concealed the slave collar. She climbed down the trellis from the balcony and jumped to the street, running as fast as her feet could carry her to the Gate of the Sun.

———

Alizar floated like a phantom through the streets, blending invisibly into the shadows with practiced ease.

Beside an empty, ash-stained fountain, his foot crushed a soft object. He paused and bent down and picked up a dirty cloth doll with black stitches for eyes and frilly yarn hair. He stared at it for a moment, and the little doll stared back. He tucked it into his *klamys* and started toward the east end of Canopic Way.

"Alizar." An old, familiar voice called from the darkness where a door hung from its hinges like a loose tooth.

"Master Savitur." Alizar bowed reverently to the elder Kolossofia master of the Nuapar who was dressed in the traditional black robe, his waist bound by a white sash like a streak of chalk on a slate.

"Your actions will have consequences, Alizar, you know this." Savitur stood serene, though stooped. His eyes glistened magically.

"I do not have time for speeches, however well meaning," Alizar said, his frustration spilling over.

"Come." Savitur walked casually into the empty room behind the door where a single candle illuminated the pale earthen walls.

Alizar did not move. "I mean to follow this through whatever you say."

Savitur chuckled quietly to himself as though he had a secret. "I know. Be cautious."

Alizar stepped forward. "Do you see my death? Is that why you are here?"

"All futures converge in this moment. Possible does not mean inevitable."

Alizar thought of Naomi. He had to live if only for her. "What choice can I make then? What do you see?"

"Use all I have taught you tonight. I can say no more than this."

Alizar almost responded, but Savitur's shimmering form flickered, the molecules of his manifested body dispersing into the room in a thin, vaporous smoke.

Thirty men and Hannah were already gathered at the Gate of the Sun when Alizar arrived just minutes before the Parabolani. He was touched. These men knew the Parabolani would execute them, and still they came.

"Alizar, we cannot stay here," someone cried out. "Cyril's men are chasing the Jews out this gate." Sure as he spoke the ground began to rumble, the footfalls of the throng of people drawing nearer.

Alizar stepped up onto a guard platform so he could see all the men and address them. "You must not let one child pass through this gate, men. Hide outside the walls and take every child not on its mother's breast to my ship in the harbor. My captain is preparing to sail the *Vesta* to Antioch at dawn. I know a woman who tends an orphanage there who will keep the children safe so that their parents may claim them once they make it through the desert." He dared not say *if*. Alizar turned his head toward the darkness that lay beyond the wall toward *Kemet—black*, as the Egyptians called it—the black land of the Nile. Black as a crow's beak. Black as a burned corpse. "Follow the east wall around the outside of the city to the harbor. I do not want Cyril's suspicions aroused. You must not be seen. Now go."

Alizar's men separated but moved with one mind. One by one, they found the children and made swift promises to parents who kissed the cheeks of their little ones again and again and again before they fled, praying they would not be killed.

At the docks in the harbor, Gideon lifted little wriggling bodies up the steps, down the steps, over the gangway, careful now. The children clung to each other in fright like startled bats in a sudden light. Librarians who heard of the exile of the Jews from the city dashed to the harbor with bundles of clothes, sheets, bread, wine, and cheese. Antioch was ages away. There were thirty children when Gideon counted in the beginning of the night. By dawn his count had reached nine hundred and three.

Smoke billowed out of the city, swirling in dark edged spirals that filled the air with the unmistakable scent of loss. No one spoke. The only task was to do what must be done.

Near dawn on her third trip to the harbor, in a dark alley behind the fish market, Hannah was spotted with three small Jewish children, running to Alizar's ship. Peter secretly followed her, urging two other Parabolani to join him. When the priests saw the ship, and the men working urgently on the docks, they exchanged words and departed in haste.

The angel, weighted by the pull of the earth, could not prevent them.

What struck Alizar as he confronted the scene in the streets was that Cyril's power was far greater than he had suspected. In the years that had passed since the destruction of the Temple of Serapis, Alizar had seen the Christians grow in number, but it had not occurred to him how completely outnumbered they would be in the event of a crisis such as the one that occurred the night Cyril exiled the Jews from Alexandria. This meant the end of free worship in Alexandria, a thought that seemed unfathomable to Alizar in a city that stood for freedom of worship. If this was their, "Do unto others as you would have them do unto you," then the religion had hollow bones indeed.

Soon, thoroughly exhausted, Alizar stood on the docks tossing the last of the supplies up to be secured in the bilge of his ship. His heart pounded furiously every second she was still docked.

Gideon called down that they had reached the maximum capacity in the bilge just as Hannah rushed to the ship with the three children. "You must take these, captain," she called out.

"Not possible," a sailor on board called back. "There is no more room."

Gideon leaned over the edge and hurled a wine-filled *pythos* into the sea. "Let them up, hurry."

Hannah lifted the children to Gideon's waiting hands. "You must think of it as a great adventure," she whispered to the last, a tiny boy clinging to her hands. "Have you ever been on a ship before?" He shook his head, no. "Well, the captain has a real sword. There he is now. I bet he will show it to you if you ask." She lifted him to Gideon, who locked eyes with hers. "Lady, you should not be here," he said, recognizing her. "Get back to Alizar's at once."

"You have done what you felt was just," said Hannah. "And so have I."

Gideon scowled at her.

Then Hannah heard the heavy footsteps on the dock behind Alizar, The Parabolani. "Look out!" she yelled.

Alizar shoved the gangplank into the water and cut the ropes with his sword. "Go!"

Gideon threw a knife down to Hannah. "Take it, woman!"

It clattered on the dock, her only weapon, and fell through to the sea.

Gideon rushed to the helm as the sailors clamored down to row the longboat and tow the *Vesta* slowly toward the open sea where they could raise her sails.

On the docks, a dozen of Cyril's Parabolani swept toward Alizar, led by Peter, their black robes snapping behind them. "His Eminence, Cyril of Alexandria, commands you to halt your ship," declared Peter.

Then he thrust a letter marked with the wax seal of the bishop into Alizar's hand. Behind Peter, the Parabolani lifted their swords and loaded their bows. Each was on the ready for Alizar's response.

Alizar took the letter and pried it open with a finger, then pretended to read. He nodded to the men before him in defeat. As they approached him to bind his wrists, he spun and knocked one man with his elbow, the other with his head, and plunged into the sea. The Parabolani were caught off guard for a moment, but then they retaliated. Alizar swam holding his breath, unseen in the dark water. They searched the docks, the beaches. A hundred priests, maybe more, swarmed the harbor.

Hannah pulled the burnoose over her head and fled to the Great Library's harbor entrance. They did not bother with her in their search. Not this time.

The Parabolani held torches to their arrows and the wicks caught fire. Then they released their rainbows of death on the ship. The crew worked frantically to put out the flames as they slowly slid out of the harbor. The arrows fell. The children screamed for their lives. Several sailors were struck dead and fell into the water like limp dolls.

The archers loaded their bows again and let them fly. Some fell in the sea as the ship slipped further away, but others landed in the lines where the sailors doused them with water. Praise Zeus the sails had not yet been raised.

Alizar came up for air at the ship's stern. But as he raised his hand to catch the rope thrown to him by Gideon, Peter spotted him and grabbed a bow from the Parabolan beside him. Then he lifted it, aimed, and let the arrow fly.

One silent streak of accuracy. Alizar was speared through the right shoulder, and he released the rope as the *Vesta* glided away on the silver sea beyond the breakers. The Parabolani ceased fire as the ship unfurled her sails in the wind; she was now untouchable.

12

"Alizar, how good of you to come." Cyril stood from behind the desk to his full height of far less than most men, his dark eyes shining with the confidence of a gambler who has won a bet. His thin black hair was clipped shorter than usual, and he had shaved his beard since Alizar had last seen him. Alizar wondered how anyone capable of such malice could put on such pleasant airs. But then he reminded himself that Cyril had probably not left that very room all night. He had the Parabolani to do all his unpleasantries for him. Cyril himself had probably spent the evening sipping wine and watching the fires in the Jewish Quarter as if it were all a trivial theatre show.

"Not my choice."

Cyril dismissed the Parabolani with a polite nod, and Alizar fell to his knees, the arrow still lodged.

"Alizar, you are an intelligent man. I think we both know you are in a great deal of trouble. I gave you orders to halt your ship, and you disobeyed."

Alizar attempted to stand. "There was nothing I could do to stop my ship. It had already sailed."

Cyril came around his desk and leaned one hip against it, thoughtfully turning a small jar of ink in one hand. "Punish him," said Cyril to one of the guards, who then grabbed the arrow's shaft, and broke it.

Alizar crumpled to the floor like wet paper, his teeth clenched against the pain that tore through the right side of his body. He forced himself to keep his eyes open, for fear he may lose consciousness. Breathe. More slowly. Do not waste breath.

Cyril set down the jar and whirled around to face a long row of tall windows that overlooked the city's square, his hands clasped behind his back. "I can charge you with paganism and kill you now or perhaps treason against the church and have you imprisoned for the rest of your life. But I must say I am disinclined." Cyril leaned down so his spittle sprinkled Alizar's face. "You see, I believe you and I can make a deal that will let you walk free. If you even survive, which I rather doubt."

"What do you want, Cyril?" Alizar growled.

"You will address me as 'Your Eminence,'" Cyril barked. "And what I want is for you to tell me the truth, namely, that you were persuaded in your actions to sail your ship with the Jewish children on board by Governor Orestes."

So that was it. Cyril wanted Orestes put on trial, not him. Alizar's testimony could sentence him. With Orestes eliminated, Cyril would take control of the Alexandrian council, align church and state, and gain complete reign over the city, the treasury, the grain stores, everything.

Alizar fought the pain to try and think. He had to find another bone for this hungry dog to chase. "I tried to save Heirax."

"Why should I believe you?"

"Bloodshed is bad for business." Alizar struggled to his knees.

"Ah, your winery. For which I care not a ewe's tit. Heirax was a fine Christian and a close friend. His death does not sit well with me, or with God. I am a reasonable man, Alizar. Tell me what else Orestes has planned, and I will free you, or you will meet the fate of Heirax yourself."

"I cannot tell you . . . what I know nothing of."

"You try my patience, old man. Hypatia and Orestes conspire against me, and I want to know the full extent of their plans. If you speak, I will spare this little whore of yours. She is yours, is she not?" Cyril smiled at Alizar, generously.

A guard stepped forward and thrust Hannah to her knees next to Alizar with a knee to her back. Alizar looked at Hannah, her boy's clothes, her hair come undone. Why would this slave leave the safety of his house dressed as such? But then he knew.

"Orestes and Hypatia are guilty only of philosophy." Alizar winked at Hannah.

Cyril stood before them. "As I recall, I captured another servant of yours, Alizar, by the name of Jemir. And to ensure his release, Orestes bargained to publicly denounce the pagan witch of the Great Library. Instead he denounced my church and gained the popular vote in the city with the help of the Jews in order to assure his election to praetorian prefect. You think I do not know this? Do you think me a fool? Do you?"

Alizar shook his head. "No."

"You will tell me all you know. And you will admit that Orestes ordered that you sail your ship with the Jews on board. May God save your soul, or I will kill this girl before you."

Hannah closed her eyes. May death come swift.

"Kill her, then," Alizar snarled. He hated to be threatened with God. He personally preferred the sanity of the Goddess, with her beautiful breasts on which to cry all tears of human suffering, though this was neither the time nor place to raise her name.

Finally Cyril spoke. "Call Peter!"

One of the guards left, and a beautiful youth emerged from an adjacent room carrying a small dagger. Then Peter followed, his sandals hissing against the stone floor, conviction burning in his eyes.

Two gruff Parabolani hoisted Hannah up by the elbows. Ammonius presented the blade to Peter, who took it gladly.

"Kill us both," said Alizar. "I will never assist you."

"Is that so?" Cyril's eyes flickered to Hannah, then back to Alizar. "I hear your wife is ill. Beautiful Naomi. I know how disappointed you would be if anything happened to her. Perhaps I should even put her on the breaking wheel and let her suffer as Heirax suffered. This is your final opportunity to comply."

Alizar bristled, and a feverish sweat broke out across his brow. Peter set the cold blade against Hannah's throat.

Cyril took a seat at his desk and leaned back in the chair with his hands folded over his chest. "Kill them both, then," he said.

Alizar calculated, and struck. In one swift sideways motion he brought his fist down as hard as he could on Peter's naked toes. There was a sickening crack and Peter dropped the knife instantly. Behind him, the beautiful youth, Ammonius, snatched the knife and swept it through the air where it collided with Alizar's hand as he attempted to defend his face, his thumb tumbling to the floor.

Hannah leapt in and stole the bloodied knife from the young boy, who was unskilled at fighting. She slid it to Alizar across the slick marble floor, who pressed the tip to young Ammonius's throat with his good hand.

The other Parabolani surrounded Cyril to protect him. This left the door unguarded and Alizar saw his chance. With Hannah on one side of him, the boy as their captive, they stepped out the door, slamming it behind him and kicking a large wooden bench before it to block it.

"Guards!" Cyril yelled from inside the door. There had to be other entrances. Other exits.

The threesome limped down the passageways of the church, dripping blood, unholy stigmata. Ammonius, the point of the knife still on his flesh, led them through the halls to the back door that let out into the garden.

"The key," said Hannah, holding out her hand.

Ammonius complied, dropping the iron key into her open hand. She kicked Ammonius down to his knees, and she pulled Alizar out into the garden, locking the door behind them.

The garden was empty. All the priests and the Parabolani had taken part in the looting of the Jewish Quarter.

Hannah wrapped her burnoose around Alizar's thumb and helped him to the far gate beyond the palms. She lifted the latch and found it open. Once in the street, she looked back twice as they sidled past the church's sidewall with its rows of peaceful papyrus all in bloom. They moved slowly but did not stop until they arrived out of breath at the little green door that led to the atrium.

"Tarek? Jemir? Leitah? Call the doctor!" Hannah pulled Alizar inside as he lost consciousness.

 13

No one answered. Hannah left Alizar in the atrium and ran to the stable, grabbed one of the bridles from the wall, and caught the sprightly stallion. Then she hoisted herself up, grabbed a clutch of mane, and pressed her heels into his sides. The stallion lurched forward, and she galloped towards the library, praying it was not too late.

So.

The poets of the Mouseion suggested it was the tears of all the Roman women in the city that brought the flood that year. The waters of the Nile, as though lifting up to cradle the heavy hearts of the people, spilled from her banks and overflowed the flood-plain. All the entrances to the catacombs were sealed with stone doors to prevent leakage as nature ran her course.

Then came the most welcome miracle of all, clouds. Prayers that rose into the air on the smoke of temple joss sticks were met by storms that snuffed out the remaining fires in the Jewish Quarter, adding to the feeling that the city was, in effect, crying. Besides, sunlight would have been an insult. Dark skies were more suited to grief.

Everyone waited to see if Alizar would live or die.

As the days wore on, Hannah walked silently beside Leitah through the empty marketplaces assisting those families in need. Even Tarek joined them on occasion. The city seemed deserted by all but flies and rats as the remaining people gathered indoors, in temples or in their flats, to mourn the dead.

In the end, over a hundred and fifty thousand Jews had been exiled into the wilderness of the desert, while another thirty thousand had been slain, their bodies buried in the massive necropolis to the west of Lake Mareotis by those friends and family who had survived and remained behind to pick through the unclaimed bodies in search of a familiar ring on a hand or some other identifying mark.

Hannah found her only solace in helping people. Her anxiety and sadness abated a little more at every house where a woman needed a hand with the wood for her kettle fire, or a baby required changing, or an extra arm to lift stones from the rubble of a fallen room was appreciated. Hannah was able to lose her own concerns in the concerns of others; for the first time in months, she stopped thinking of her father and whether or not he was alive, forgetting even her life of slavery. None of that mattered now.

Beautiful memorial shrines appeared overnight beside the charred and ruined synagogues and in the *agora*, so that those who lost their lives in death or exile could be remembered and cherished. But the shrines were increasingly vandalized, and so the few remaining Jewish men kept watch beside the memorials to defend the dead. Hannah dropped a kiss with her palm on each shrine when she passed.

Like many cities once occupied by Rome, Alexandria had a short memory for the many tragedies that had befallen her. Synesius had once explained to her that even the fury of Caracalla, who had once killed every boy in the city, had been forgotten. So it was that merchants became anxious for business to resume, and children could not be kept indoors forever. After weeks of mourning, the people realized that they would have to put their grief behind them and carry on with work whether they felt like it or not. Such was the power of necessity.

And so it was that when the rains arrived and the populace began the arduous task of forgetting what can never be forgotten, something unusual occurred.

Strangely, it seemed the stray cats of Alexandria had multiplied their numbers by the thousands and were suddenly a formidable presence in every pocket of the city. Lily-white, ginger, brindle-striped, calico, and black as the space between the stars, they roamed freely, marking their territories with pungent urine and shitting in the lush church gardens where they were chased by outraged priests. At night their stentorious cries were so inexhaustible that the populace of Alexandria became completely sleep-deprived and short-tempered. Politicians with bloodshot eyes arrived late for government meetings, soldiers grew too weary to lift their weapons, and frustrated mothers burned their stews as babes cried into the night.

People began to grumble to one another, claiming the cats were a curse laid upon the city. There was no one who had not fallen victim to the cats' mischief. They crept into kitchens and stole whole chickens off the spit. They knocked over clay pots, spilling the winter supply of grain into the dust. They gave birth to wide-eyed kittens in the stables, spooking the horses. It was even said they extinguished candles set on family altars just by gazing at them.

For Hannah, the cats were welcome companions. A ginger cat slept beside Hannah in the stable night after night and finally gave birth to a litter of five tiny kittens that Hannah coddled and kissed. The elderly Jewish woman across the alley whose husband had died in the exile toddled outside every morning to set a bowl of fresh goat milk out for the cats in order to woo them inside to sleep on her lap, which they did. Children cradled little kittens in their arms in hopes that they would fill the air with purring, which they did. Fishmongers adopted the cats, convinced that they could keep the rats away. Which they did.

So.

On the first clear morning after the rains, Alizar awoke. He lay in bed beside Naomi watching a black cat with glassy emerald eyes wash her ears with her paws. His mind was empty without even so much as a dream fragment to ripple the gloss. Alizar meditated on the movements of the cat as she passed her paws over her face, behind her ears, licked down her front and shoulders, then back again to face and ears. Face and ears.

Alizar gently adjusted his wounded shoulder, which was gradually mending. The arm corresponded to his bandaged hand, now missing much of the thumb. At least it was not his sword hand.

Alizar looked at Naomi, taking in the comforting familiar curves of her profile, her neck, her rising chest.

"Naomi?" Alizar sat up.

Her eyes were open.

She smiled at him.

Alizar turned and kissed her again and again. "A miracle!" he shouted, tears of jubilation in his eyes. And he held her. "Can I get you anything?" he whispered.

Naomi cleared her throat, her pale green eyes illuminated as if in the moonlight. "Water."

Over the weeks that followed, no one remembered Alizar so happy. Naomi's recovery was his recovery. Soon she was sitting up and then slowly walking across the room. His shoulder mended well, the doctor said. Miracle they got the arrow out.

Hannah bonded to Naomi even more deeply through her songs. Naomi often asked her to stay and sing in the evening, and there was nowhere else Hannah would rather be. Afterwards, she would lay her head in Naomi's lap as Naomi played with her hair and told her stories of her own childhood in Constantinople. With her health, Naomi's youth returned.

Late one afternoon Hannah came in from running errands and found Leitah at Naomi's bedside washing and dressing her. "The apothecary acted strangely today," she said, setting the bag of medicines on a brass tray on a low table near the bed. One by one she pulled out and arranged the colorful glass vials.

Leitah drew a sponge of warm water along Naomi's arm, down again.

"How is Marcus?" asked Naomi, lifting her head to inquire after the apothecary. "I have not seen his family in ages. Are the children well?"

Hannah counted and arranged the vials. "He was not himself. His children looked hungry and thin. His wife also. She asked me repeatedly if there was anything else I needed. And he nervously rubbed his hands, as if I were a ghost in the room. Could I have offended them in some way?"

"Perhaps it was a quarrel with the wife's sister. She always wanted Marcus for herself. She is a tall, thin woman. Was she there?"

"Actually, there was a woman there by that description," Hannah said. "She stood by herself near the window, away from the rest of the family."

Naomi smiled. "You see? There. Not so strange."

Hannah sighed, realizing she had become suspicious of everyone. It was an exhausting way to live.

Leitah began to trim the nails of Naomi's hand, filing them with a course wedged tile. Naomi set her other hand on Hannah's cheek. "You are such a dutiful girl. I do hope you earn your freedom and find your father, if that is what you wish."

The sudden, surprising words were spoken with such love that Hannah felt tears fill her eyes. No woman had ever spoken to her so intimately. She fell on Naomi's neck, hugging her. Naomi kissed her forehead and rocked her like a child.

The weeks that passed in delight brought unfounded hope. Naomi grew weaker again. She collapsed back into her bed, needing more and more time to sleep and rest. Hannah came every hour, and Leitah never left her side.

The medicine failed.

Alizar, suspicious of Naomi's decline, investigated the vials. He smelled them. He studied them. He tasted them. Then he knew: water. Salt water. All of them. There had never been medicine. Either the apothecary knew and lied for the money, or he was put to it by Cyril.

"I never lived by medicine," Naomi reassured him. "I love you."

Alizar smashed the tray to the ground and threw the vials against the wall. "This cannot happen to you. Not now. I forbid it."

"I am ready," she said, "to see my mother's face again."

Alizar looked up and wiped his tears on his bandage. "I will miss you."

They embraced.

Within the week, Naomi died.

Her spirit passed very near the angel, who guided her to the light.

Alizar held his wife as her eyes turned to stone. It was a graceful, peaceful death, which was what he wanted for her, as much as he hated to see her go. She had assured him of her love again and again. And that she would be happy.

Her death fell hard on Hannah, who had adopted her as a mother. Each night she lay awake in the stable straw and mourned, for should it not be divine law that anyone who is loved, live?

Alizar's house became black once again. He wanted no more visitors, no more light. He shut and locked his tower door. He knew the only tonic that would work on his grief. It was solitude.

So.

Tarek found a moment when Hannah was alone, washing the stairs, and stood before her, shifting his weight from one foot to the other, looking like a vulnerable little boy.

Hannah glanced up and when Tarek did not walk past, she set her rag down. She had thrown herself into cleaning as if scraping the crud from every corner would do the same for her heart. She sat on her heels and wiped her forehead. "What is it, Tarek?" she asked, and her voice sounded harsher than she intended.

"I am sorry I cursed you," he said. His eyes were laden with grief.

Hannah smiled, knowing how hard those words must have been for him to say. "I forgive you," she said.

He took three halting steps forward, then began to cry. She caught him as he fell into her arms, ugly sobs wracking his body.

If only he could always grieve so, she thought. His grief was the open window to the goodness in his soul.

So.

At all hours after Naomi's death, friends came to call, and Jemir tried to console them with little cakes and sighs of understanding. Hannah helped him kneading bread and preparing hot *fuul* and tea. Tea. Endless tea. Hannah became the tea-bearer, bringing it even when it was not needed, setting hot cups beside everyone all through the day and into the night. There was no consolation better in all of Egypt.

Alizar did not come down from the upper floor. Hannah visited in the evenings, her footsteps so light in the hall, as if she were concerned she might disturb the floor by walking on it. She squeezed her master's hands, ardently kissed his knuckles, served him wine and warm Roman bread with olive spread. "Can I help you with that?" or "How about with this?" and so much fussing he thought she meant to help him breathe and beat his heart and blink his eyes for him all at once. He finally shut her out.

After another month had passed, Hannah decided that Alizar needed to at least have a walk, after all it was unhealthy to remain indoors for so long, just watching the light change across the floor. She knew that kind of pain. It did not abate on its own; effort must be made, a pushing from within, enough to break the skin.

She put on a fine indigo tunic that matched her eyes and bound her hair back into a long braid with a scarf of the same color.

When she glided into Alizar's sitting room he looked up from his tea and smiled his approval. "So the rumors are true," he said.

Hannah looked at him, perplexed.

"We have a goddess in our midst." Alizar stood, the two red Pharaoh hounds standing with him, eager for the outdoors.

Hannah bent her head down and fibbed a little. "Jemir thought that you should have a walk." She had not seen Alizar for a month, and in truth, his gaunt appearance startled her. He was so thin that his clothes hung on him as if his shoulders were tree branches. But the bandage was off his hand, if not his heart.

Alizar winked at her. "Jemir is right. I should walk." He did not move. The hounds, however, turned their ears toward him, tongues lolling. They knew the word immediately.

Hannah waited.

Alizar said nothing.

Hannah picked up his sandals from beside the door and set them beside his chair. A walking gesture.

The hounds whined in high-pitched expectation and wagged their tails.

"Bother," said Alizar. "Wait a moment and I will put on a robe in case I should see someone who wants to pester me with unwanted sympathy."

Hannah smiled, and the red hounds shot out the door ahead of them.

––––––––

The market was busier than usual. The merchants seemed irritated, each trying desperately to draw potential customers into their stalls. There were no Parabolani about. But no one thought of the priests for the moment as the need to make up for lost business in the stalled economy had everyone scurrying, trying to please, please, please, which only meant the customers felt pestered.

Rather than push their way through the bustling market-place, Alizar purchased two ripe plums from a fruit merchant, and they walked toward the Gate of the Moon at the other end of Canopic Way, sucking the sweet red juice as it ran down onto their fingers.

Hannah could not think of what to say that had not been said already, and so she decided to go back, back before the riots, and the deaths, and the fires, and so many nights without sleep, and Naomi's death. "Tell me about Athens," Hannah said as they stepped onto the beach where the tall, thin waves fell over on the shore like so many fainting women. Before them, a jagged berm appeared along the shoreline, so they walked along the surf instead, their garments trailing circles in the sea foam.

"Athens?" Alizar repeated. "Athens is the home of many sages and still many more boasters and charlatans. Piraeus is full of filth and charm, and the Akropolis is another word for beauty. The people are mad when they are not riveted by some new phi-losophy that offers them a fresh kind of madness. The only thing Athenians love more than fish is women, and the only thing Athenians love more than women is wine. We Greeks argue over things that do not matter to anyone. But they do to us. Once I had an argument with my head gardener that took the better part of a month over what color bougainvillea to plant in the courtyard. He planted red. I wanted a fuchsia-colored one. He refused to plant the fuchsia. I planted it myself and came back to find it missing. We went on like that for weeks."

"And what happened?"

"He planted the red, of course." Alizar chuckled. "It was the right color."

Hannah bent down and picked up a cracked mussel shell that looked like a blue goat hoof broken in half, the inside gleaming pink where it was not covered in sand. She rubbed it dry in her palms, and turned it to the sun to admire.

"How are you faring with the upheaval in the city, Hannah? I hear you had more than just a little excitement while I was away. And after I returned, of course."

They laughed.

Hannah did not reply after that, lost in what to say, what not to say.

"It is a question that requires response," Alizar insisted. He had come to adore this girl, but knew also that her impetuosity may get them all killed.

Hannah had thought every day of the girl the Parabolani killed, her beautiful, pleading eyes. "I acted without thinking. I am sorry. It was my fault Jemir was captured. My anger. The girl. What they did was so unjust."

"I want you to know that I am grateful you and Tarek survived the incident. And I am also grateful Orestes was able to free Jemir. And from our meeting with Cyril, I owe you my life."

"You do not owe me that."

"Well, leave that for me to say. But now the danger is increasing. Cyril has a memory for us both now. He will not forget. He will hunt for you."

Hannah nodded in understanding.

"I am considering arrangements. I want you to be ready."

"I do not understand this city, Alizar. I was not born for this kind of life. I keep thinking of my father and our herd, and I regret not keeping his knife with me the night we were attacked, because maybe then we would still be together." Hannah rubbed her hands together, massaged the back of her neck unconsciously, the guilt with a life of its own in her flesh.

"You do not know that for certain. You punish yourself. It is the past. It cannot be undone."

Hannah cleared her throat. "I know, but it torments me still."

"I have a gift for you that may help." He drew a bundle of red cloth out from his robe.

Hannah unfolded it, and withdrew a small dagger, bone handle, a good size for a woman, blade as long as her fingers and palm put together.

"You cannot be out in this city without protection."

Hannah smiled and lifted the hem of her *himation* so she could affix the dagger with its leather strap to her calf. "Thank you, Alizar. I may have been cursed to come to Alexandria the way I did, but I was blessed to come to you. I am terribly sorry for the trouble I have caused you. I have appreciated my lessons in the Great Library. Synesius is a fine tutor. Thank you."

The sky changed then, the wind chasing the clouds that scattered like nervous fish into a shoal. Then the horizon turned black. More rain. Soon.

"I am impressed with your Greek, Hannah. You have learned our difficult tongue quickly." Then Alizar stopped and faced the waves. Hannah paused beside him, sensing that his next words would be important. "So you have given up thoughts of escaping back to the desert?"

"I never stop thinking of my father, Alizar. Never. But I know I cannot return. He would not want me to die in search of him. I am certain of that."

"Good. I feel your education should continue. I can think of nothing more important, especially for a woman. Women possess powerful minds. I feel they should be given more opportunities in government and as scholars. Look at Hypatia. Anything is possible."

Hannah picked up the hem of her dress in both hands as she walked through the swirling saltwater to where the sand was dry. A white gull soared from the waves toward the beach and landed gently, folding her wings across her back. The hounds rushed it at once, and it lifted into the breeze out of reach, screeching in irritation.

Hannah tried to read the lines in Alizar's face, so deeply etched with fatigue: unsettled thoughts, questions, many journeys upon the sea, a childhood full of laughter. "How are you faring, Alizar?"

He stopped again, having climbed the berm above the ocean's edge, looking west toward the horizon and the northern tip of Lake Mareotis. "Still among the living, it seems. After I lost my first wife, Mona, I found the soil, and the grapes, and a private, unspeakable relationship with sunlight. And I came to know that I do not define myself by my losses but by my victories." Alizar went to tug his beard in his once characteristic gesture, forgetting he had shaved it. A nuisance. He would have to grow it back.

So.

They had come to the jetty then, at the south end of the harbor. Alizar stepped up first and gave Hannah his hand to help her. She was so light he thought she must have the hollow bones of a bird. How in the world did she help carry him all the way from the Church of Saint Alexander?

"Have you heard news from Antioch? Of the Jewish children?" Hannah asked, and her thoughts went to Gideon, his strong hands lifting them onto the ship. His same hands on her shoulders. She touched her fingers to her collarbone, remembering.

"No word. Not yet. My ship will return within the month, and then it will sail again. I am short on time in this life, and my work is never ending."

"Shipping wine?" Hannah asked. "I would like to see your vines one day, if you would allow it."

Alizar thought a moment and then said, "Hannah, the time has come to make you aware of my real work." Then he winked.

Once at the house, Alizar gestured for Hannah to follow him to a small door at the other end of the kitchen she had always assumed led to a storage closet. She had never actually seen anyone in the house open it before. She felt a childish delight watching him unlock it.

They passed through the door and climbed a set of stone steps up a narrow, dimly lit passageway that would have been much less dreary had there been a few windows along the walls. At the top of the steps a corridor led off to the east and into a small loft with an elegant transom at one end, the sunlight illuminating a massive altar beneath it. Several urns stood ceremoniously beside slender white candles. There were pots, and reliquaries, and little ancient figurines. Alizar paused and lit a stick of frankincense and fixed it upright in a little bowl of ashes. Then they continued down the passage.

At the end, Hannah recognized the hall at the top of the stairs and the large wooden door she was forbidden to enter that stood across from Naomi's bedroom.

Hannah touched her fingertips to the winged staff emblem entwined by two serpents carved into the door.

Alizar explained. "It is the seal of Hermes, the caduceus, an ancient alchemical symbol with many layers of meaning. You must never show anyone to my tower, Hannah. You must forget it is even here." Alizar's tone was stern. Hannah understood. She could keep a secret, especially if Alizar asked it of her.

With that said, Alizar unlocked the door.

From nowhere, Hannah was gripped with a sudden memory of a canyon in Sinai that had been her secret haven. She imagined Alizar would open the door and she could walk into the deep familiar ravine with rocky crevices that led into a stone canyon where boulders loomed like ancient people walking side by side, joined like shadows at the shoulder. In the winter the water rushed down with a deafening roar. But in the summer the stream dried up and formed a path to a high cliff that overlooked the valley. Hannah could almost breathe the spring pine in her nostrils, reach down to collect a smooth stone to rub between her thumb and forefinger that she could pocket on her way back down the trail to the goats, the ting-tong-ting of their bells the happiest sound in the world, the most peaceful. All behind her now. Her favorites, the black, the silver, the tawny, all surely dead. Her eyes focused back into the present, the weight of the dagger against her calf a comfort.

Alizar shoved open the door to reveal six stalwart Doric columns evenly spaced around the room in a circle. Between them a mandala of the planets stretched across the floor, painted in vibrant detail. Tall windows offered views of the city. In the rear stood an alcove of ever expanding bookshelves, Alizar's private collection, a lifetime of his painstaking codex-binding successes and failures. In front of them was a sea of scrolls spread out on every available surface. Hannah recognized the scent of musty papyrus, joss sticks, and ocean spray that seeped out of the stones as the same that always lingered on Alizar's robes. A large brass armillary was set on the table, an improvement on previous models from Alizar's candlelight vigils of undisturbed concentration.

Under the windows were enormous clay pots large enough for a small child to hide in, each brimming with scrolls. On the tables nearby, scrolls were stacked in piles, bundled with string, spilling out of wooden boxes, and strewn across the floor. Alizar reached into a pot and lifted one out and unfolded it, inviting Hannah to have a look.

Hannah tipped her head and tried to discern the odd symbols, but found she could not.

"The teachings of the great Egyptian alchemist, Hermes Trismagistus." Alizar returned the scroll to the pot. "So are all the rest." He went to the next clay pot. Alizar fished out another scroll and opened it, then another. "And this is the Gospel of Mary Magdalene. This the Gospel of Thomas."

Hannah looked confused. "So you are a collector?"

Alizar shook his head. "These scrolls are copies of scrolls in the Great Library, should the Christians ever decide to burn our library like they did those in Pergamon, Tarsus, Antioch, and Ephesus, which I believe they will. It is only a matter of time."

Hannah nodded. She thought of Cyril and shuddered.

"I decide what is significant enough to be kept, I sponsor the copying, and then I send these pots aboard my ship to be concealed in hidden locations around the Mediterranean. Gideon buries them and maps them. Then he returns here with the maps, and I load another shipment of wine."

"So this is your work." Hannah was beginning to think Alizar was probably the Emperor of Africa and just had not gotten around to telling her yet.

"Yes, this is my work, and it is a secret I entrust to you. You must tell no one, and defend it with your life if you must, for all of this is far more important than you or I."

Hannah nodded. "I promise."

Alizar picked up his pipe from the table and lit the bowl with a nearby candle. "Well, would you like to see the view of the city from the roof?"

"Very much."

Alizar palmed a nautical brass weight that hung by a manila rope from a pulley, slowly lowering a set of small stairs from the ceiling. On top of the roof, looking east to the Jewish quarter, the city sprawled before them like an open wound. In the north, the isle of Pharos and all the sea beyond it lay concealed behind a curtain of mist hovering at the shoreline, whether it would bring more rain, still unseen.

"*The breath of Nereus,* the sailors call it." Alizar said, gesturing toward the hidden sea. "By legend it is said to conceal the interference of gods in the lives of men. I suppose we must entertain the gods. If life were not a spectacle for someone, why live?"

Hannah walked to the edge. Beyond the city's walls the desert stretched south, yellow as a lion's back. Somewhere, perhaps her father still lived, or died. "What will we do?" The question was as much to herself and to God as to Alizar.

"Orestes has a greater plan in place, but I do not trust it entirely. He believes we can be unified by the Emerald Tablet."

"What is that?"

"Legend, possibly. Possibly a real stone tablet created by Hermes Trismagistus and encoded with the secrets of alchemy. It is guarded by the Nuapar. Or its secret is. No one knows where the tablet may be hidden. Some believe its magic is strong enough to unite the pagan people against the Christians. To prevent the fall of our world."

"Do you believe it?"

"I do. Yes."

"But is it really magic?"

"Possibly. The Emerald Tablet is said to hold the teachings of alchemy, the secrets to immortality for those who can interpret it. It is legend. It is a symbol, but I believe it is real. Still, even symbols have the ability to unite people, to divide them. That is the real magic, Hannah. When enough people believe, there is change. You will find a symbol at the heart of every great revolution, at the center of every evil masquerading as justice. I share the hope that the Emerald Tablet might be ours."

Hannah turned toward the sea. Alizar was wise as a rabbi. Her father would have liked him, she felt. She hoped they could find this Emerald Tablet of the Nuapar, that it had the necessary magic to defeat the Christian soldiers. But deep inside, the discomfort at the thought of even something as beautiful as hope ate a hole in her stomach, like acid, like swallowing piss. She locked eyes with Alizar, then broke his gaze and let her hands move along the stone parapet like a blind woman, feeling for the ledge. "You are eye level with the birds up here," she said, changing the subject as several seagulls dipped and soared down beneath her line of sight to the docks.

Alizar smiled at the white bird shit that streaked the stone ledges. "Yes, I suppose I am."

 14

The merciless summer light blurred the edges of the short nights, and annual customs jolted everyone in the city into buying and selling and sharing alcohol as though it could cure every ill, satiate every desire, make one immortal, raise the dead. Hannah, Leitah, and Jemir wound through the city as two trumpets blew at either end of Canopic Way to signal that the opening ceremony of the Mid-Summer Chariot Race was about to begin. Everywhere people scrambled into viewing positions on top of the city's walls, pushing and wriggling against each other for a patch of stone to squeeze onto. Each successive year always brought one or two fatalities as people crowded in the front were pushed off the top of the high walls by those in the back, like penguins huddled on an ice shelf. No one could remember who first conceived the unusual idea of running this particular race around the periphery of the city instead of in the hippodrome like all the other chariot races. But the popular tradition had held up for centuries.

This year, however, the festivities only thrust the exile of the Jews to the forefront of everyone's minds when they saw the bald patches of seats along the wall where families and friends had gathered every year for generations. The population of Alexandria had been reduced by one quarter. No more synagogues. No more Aramaic chatter in the market. No more craftsmen to repair the streets and build the monuments. No more lenders to support the needy. Alexandria had lost a limb. And limped on.

The three moved along the wall to sit above the Gate of the Moon on the west side of the city, where Tarek was already waiting. He held out his hand to Hannah so that she would sit beside him, his eyes sweet with the request. Hannah swallowed and sat down, unable to refuse him when he was kind. Below her the empty street was lined with barrels from Alizar's vineyard, mostly to keep the chariot wheels from striking the walls. Alizar's was the most envied box of the west end, as the finish line would be drawn across Canopic Way directly beneath them.

Tarek was already inebriated and in the mood for telling stories. He recounted how in the previous year he had urinated on a wheel of one of the losing chariots. The chariot driver, screaming profanities, had flogged him with his whip while chasing him down the street, but the man fell in a puddle of horse piss as Tarek escaped. "Piss for piss," Tarek said with an inebriated giggle. This story got a few laughs, even from strangers listening in.

Behind Hannah, Leitah soaked up the heat with her eyes closed, wearing a wide brimmed hat woven from palm fronds to prevent the sun from burning her northern complexion. The hat was a wonderful idea, and soon Hannah was wishing she had one as well since the sea had not offered up even the stingiest breeze. In the west, the ever diminishing outline of Lake Mareotis captured the sun with a mirror's intensity, making the day uncomfortably bright. To block out the glare, some took to wearing eye masks of black horsehair that tied behind the head.

"Where is Alizar?" Hannah looked over her shoulder.

"He will be here. He never misses this race." Tarek smiled as he lifted another flagon of wine.

However it was not Alizar who appeared weaving through the crowd, but Gideon carrying several shoulder bags. Hannah had not recognized the ship's captain, but once she did, she felt grateful to see him. She had thought often of his valor in saving the children, and realized she must have misjudged him the first time they met. She had seen him as rather coarse and arrogant, yet he had made certain every child had been able to fit on Alizar's ship. She stood up to make more room for him so he would sit beside her and share how the Jewish children fared in the journey to Antioch.

"For you, goddess," Gideon said as he pulled a palm frond hat out of one of the bags and bent down to kiss Hannah's cheek, fitting the hat to her head. Then he proceeded to greet everyone in his teasing manner that always made the people around him feel special. After placing the fruits and wine and bread he had brought with him down before his friends, Gideon settled beside Hannah on one of the kilims they had brought from the house. She folded her legs beneath her like a fawn to make room for him.

Hannah brushed her hair back and set her hand over her eyes to scan the crowd.

"Alizar is at the opening ceremony," Gideon said to her.

"Oh? Will he join us?"

"I do not know."

Around them, the impatient crowd took to smoking a great deal more hashish than they would have if the races had begun on time. But the races never began on time, so this was only an excuse to smoke more hashish and drink more wine. Soon everyone was crimson-eyed and calm, joking among friends as they waited.

Hannah thought of her father, somewhere in the desert, alive surely, searching for her. A familiar ache shuffled between her ribs like a pigeon in the eaves. Nothing would excite him more than a chariot race.

The afternoon wore on with no sign of the race beginning. Hannah learned that Gideon's voyage to Antioch had been smooth and that the children had been received with tremendous compassion by the orphanage there. As she took the wine Gideon offered her, she watched him. The scar down his cheek seemed compelling now, whereas before she had found it menacing. How had he gotten it? She wanted to trace it with her finger from his eye to his jaw. She touched his shoulder, smiled at him without even meaning to. Her gesture did not go unnoticed, but his expression did nothing to betray his sudden arousal of interest.

More wine. More waiting. Alcohol, warm and welcome, stroked her fingers along Hannah's spine, puddled in her knees, burned in her sex. Alcohol, powerful as a spiritual revelation, numbing as snow, and deceptive as a serpent. So much smiling Hannah's cheeks hurt. For the first time in her life, she longed for a man to kiss her. This man.

Then breaking her reverie, Gideon spilled the wine and it was all over them, his lap, her *tunica*, his arms, her hands. She squealed and he groaned. The wine dripped from his fingers, and she laughed, but she yearned to put them in her mouth and suck them clean. Such thoughts. Wine brings them so easily to the surface, suggestions from Dionysus, whispering his wanton lust. Hannah, sickened by this new unbidden desire, offered him a cloth so he could dry himself and turned her gaze back to the street, determined to triumph over the surge of warmth in her blood.

Gideon tickled Hannah's shoulder with a ripe fig. "You will never believe who the mystery entrant is in the races this year."

"Who?"

"Hypatia."

"Hypatia!" Tarek, who had been eavesdropping, blurted.

Gideon narrowed his eyes at him in irritation.

"It is really true?" Jemir asked, rousing himself from a midday snooze.

Gideon nodded. "*Neh*. Her father once kept chariot horses, and she is riding to honor his memory." He chewed on a piece of dried, salted meat as he unlatched the buckles on his other bags to offer the rest of the wine and water to everyone.

Hannah tried to picture Hypatia letting her hair down in the havoc of a chariot race and found it difficult. "Hypatia is racing, for certain? Has a woman ever raced before?"

"Oh yes, but not for ages. The last time was thirteen years ago," said Jemir with a smile. "It was Alizar's wife, Naomi."

Hours crept by and the sun seemed to hold its position directly overhead. Gideon traveled down the wall three times to refill their flagons of water and wine. Leitah purchased a lovely peacock fan for six *nummi* from a merchant along the wall, and they all took turns with it.

Then, suddenly, the drowsy crowd came alive.

"All hail Bishop Cyril!" came the cry from the lookout box on the top of the wall.

Hannah looked around in confusion as everyone stood, but then Gideon grabbed her hand and pulled her up. "Our city's bishop has found yet another occasion to remind us to bow before him," he said sarcastically, and then added, "He also has the Parabolani take notes on any houses who do not stand to honor him so they know who to put on the watch list and pay visits to, Christ be damned." He was clapping as he spoke, his face so full of admiration that in any other century he might have been a great stage actor.

Below them Cyril, in his finest violet and white ecclesiastical robes and headpiece—which resembled a beehive in size and shape—rode by in a golden chariot pulled along by a team of five well-groomed chestnut horses flanked by ten priests carrying tall staffs, their faces more somber than serene.

The crowd on the walls of the city exploded with cheers, a sea of hands waving the blue city flag or articles of clothing that had been removed in the heat. Anticipation blazed in their bloodshot eyes.

A few minutes later, the horns sounded at the other end of Canopic Way. No one in Alizar's box on the wall above the Gate of the Moon could see the start, as they were over the finish line. But the race had begun.

Moments later the first chariot rounded the bend. The crowd pressed forward. "It is our Aziz!" Jemir pointed to the blue chariot, a sleigh design with gold edging pulled by two black Arabian horses. "It is Alizar's chariot!" someone else shouted. The crowd marveled at his lead.

Then two chariots—one black, one glaucous green—rounded the corner neck to neck, and a shrill squeal erupted as their wheels caught and sparked. The black chariot fell back as the green chariot toppled sideways into the row of barrels, the horses tumbling to their backs, legs kicking as they tried to regain their footing. The charioteer lay crushed by his own chariot, his body splayed crookedly across the cobbles, the side of his face mashed beyond recognition as his blood spurted onto the street. Three men ran to move the body out of the way and pull the horses to their feet. The crowd seemed simultaneously horrified and entertained by the accident, murmuring and spreading the news of the incident along the wall as the unfortunate charioteer's blood drew flies.

Then a red chariot pulled by two large bays in a full gallop with ears flattened in the wind bolted past, driven by a man called Nicaeus, who had been the favorite in the race. He was followed closely by three others. Gideon rapidly explained that Nicaeus would play it easy the first few laps before letting his horses open up. His were long-legged geldings from Rome, horses made for running. Hannah gasped as their thunderous hooves shook the wall beneath her.

And then another chariot rounded the corner: a chariot of pure white, gliding like a swan above the street.

Hypatia.

The Great Lady had donned a pure white *khiton*, her mane of golden curls streaming behind her. Her two white mares were perfectly synchronized, mirrors like a lake of clouds reflecting the sky.

Gasps flew up from the crowd, and a flock of pigeons all departed their roost at once, circling in the air. A few Christians at the back of the wall shouted obscenities, throwing anything they could think of. Hats, shoes, bottles, and fans rained down onto the street below. Hannah was clocked in the head with a boot.

"Whore!" they cried. "Heretic! Witch!"

But the crowd was also comprised of Hypatia's secret admirers, her students and colleagues, saluting the bravery it took her to appear publicly after Cyril's threats. She was their hero, their goddess come to earth. Jemir's hands went to his heart, and then he drew Leitah into his arms, pointing.

With each lap, the chariots grew closer together in a dangerous cluster. Hypatia dropped back, which proved to be a moment Cyril's Parabolani had lain in wait for.

"What are those two doing?" Hannah said to Gideon, pointing down to the street where two men pounded spikes into a barrel. Gideon looked over the edge of the wall and then vaulted down to the street below. Hannah shrieked, and everyone leaned down to see what happened.

But Gideon had landed squarely on his feet on a rug merchant's balcony, and then leapt to the street with astounding agility. Still, he was too late. The barrel was rolled into the street to capsize the next charioteer, Hypatia. She carved the corner with ease, and then saw the barrel, yanking back on her reins. Gideon made a dive for the barrel, and managed to shove it to one side, but was left facing down Hypatia's horses himself.

The crowd on the wall gasped and groaned, prepared to see him trampled. The horses hardly slowed as Hypatia maneuvered them to swerve beneath the rug merchant's balcony, and back out into the street, a hundred rugs scattered and rolling behind her.

Gideon leapt up and rushed after the two men who had set the barrel. He caught one by the ear in the next alley and gave him a punch that sent him reeling. The other vanished completely.

When the chariots rounded the corner in that final lap, there was not a man, woman, or child still sitting down. Nicaeus had stolen the lead, and Aziz was running second, a half-length behind. The other chariots were still four lengths behind, crowded together, with Hypatia bringing up the rear. Men rapidly cleared the street of the carpets. The crowd rose to see the finish and screamed, overcome by the realization of their fevered anticipation.

Alizar's stableman, Aziz, leaned so far forward his nose was perched above the rumps of the horses as he pressed them to their fullest stride. *Come on. Run you.*

Still, Nicaeus was untouchable. His red Roman horses seemed to fly like Pegasus. For the seconds before he crossed the finish line the people held their breath in awe, some feeling as though they had seen the sun chariot of Apollo, some the chariot of Ra, depending on the story that lived in their hearts.

"Nicaeus has taken the chest! Victory to Nicaeus!" the crowd cheered. Hypatia was completely forgotten in the winner's triumph by everyone except Jemir, who, Hannah noticed, was reluctant to turn his eyes away from the last chariot in the race, his eyes flooded with unspoken admiration.

"Victory to Nicaeus!" shouted Gideon. Then he leaned down to Hannah and whispered, "With what I just won from my bet, I will buy you the necklace of a queen."

Hannah blushed. "Why, though, would you bet against Alizar's horses?"

Gideon bristled, then shirked it. "Where I wager follows who I expect to win. To be fair, I did also bet on Alizar's horses, but the Roman-bred horses are unstoppable."

"If we go now we can make it to the winner's circle to see the closing ceremony," Gideon said to Hannah.

"No one wants to go anywhere with you, Gideon," said Tarek. "And besides, she is my slave, so she comes with me," and he grabbed Hannah's wrist and jerked her to him.

"Tarek, you are hurting me," Hannah said.

Gideon, twice the size of Tarek, released Hannah's wrist with one quick tug, placing his fingertips in the center of Tarek's chest to distance him. "She is in my charge today."

Tarek glared at Gideon, then at Hannah, spit, and disappeared into the sea of bodies all jammed together above the only ladder, waiting for a turn to descend.

When they reached the street, Tarek had disappeared. Gideon led Hannah away to the winner's circle to see she was properly entertained. Alizar greeted them with a warm hug when he saw them approach, happy to see Gideon had returned. Then he went off to greet other friends and check on his horses, leaving Gideon and Hannah free to wander. Hannah told him of the concerts she had given in the Great Library for Hypatia since he had been away and of her studies with Synesius. He listened with interest, asking her intelligent questions, leaning in to hear more, absorb more of her, the light leaping from her body into his hungry eyes.

As they walked through the street, weaving in and out of the onlookers, they rubbed the sweaty foreheads of the horses, but they did not find Hypatia.

"She must have gone back to the library." Gideon shrugged. "She probably wanted to leave before the festival of Osiris begins. She despises the debauchery, poor girl."

"The festival of Osiris?" No one had mentioned anything about a festival to Hannah.

Gideon corrected himself. "The Festival of Light—that is what the Christians have us calling it now. It used to be the day we celebrated Osiris coming back to life to make love to Isis so she could conceive Horus. For the first two days we celebrated Osiris's death with wine and masks and loads of sex, and then on the third day when the god was reborn, the hierophant would erect a long pole in the ground to represent his enormous cock." Gideon smiled, and Hannah saw again the cavalier and raunchy captain she had met that first night. Did she adore or despise him? She did not know. He caught her hand to kiss her open palm. His eyes flicked to her bronze slave collar as he released her hand; it had lost its polish and looked like part of her now. Wilderness girl, shepherdess. Even he could see it was not in her spirit to be kept.

"How did you come to Alexandria, Hannah?"

"I am from Sinai. My father and I are shepherds."

"Does he live? Do you know?" Gideon knew the ways of slave traders. The story of these girls usually led to the brothels. She was fortunate.

"I do not."

"What about your mother? Where is she?"

"I never knew her," said Hannah, lowering her eyes. "She died giving birth to me. What of your family?"

Gideon waved away an Egyptian boy selling three white doves in a small brass cage. "I come from Epidavros, which is how I met Alizar." Gideon sensed Hannah's sorrow and stroked her arm. "I think you and your father will find each other again. Life is long, Hannah. Do not give up hope."

Hannah nodded, tears welling in her eyes. Gideon suddenly wanted to kiss her, but not here, not yet.

The angel bent like a reed, a hollow body full of music, to be near her.

15

As dusk fell on Alexandria, the city experienced a celestial transformation. All the walls, low and high, were adorned with glowing lanterns that burned all through the night, spilling amber light through the streets so that faces, *tunicas*, fountains, the eyes of cats and rats reflected the golden glow.

Vendors stayed open all through the night to hawk their wares while the pubs down on the wharf swelled with sailors, politicians, and merchants in lavish costumes carrying amphorae of wine and singing sailor tunes. Some people wore masks in honor of Osiris, but more and more every year people were going without them, not wanting to be associated with any pagan traditions, no matter how personally revered, for fear of being persecuted by the Christians.

Street acrobats gathered attentive audiences as they flipped from each other's shoulders and folded themselves into clay pots in feats of flexibility while their children held out plates. Magicians circulated through the crowd, amusing some with coin tricks and stealing coins from others. Fire-eaters lit torches with flaming tongues. Some houses lay shuttered and black, others bubbled with music and wine, while in the darkness above the street, thieves crept across the rooftops hoping to discover an unlocked transom in a house where the residents were out.

Every year Alizar hosted a party on the first night of the Festival of Light. Usually the party was a large and open to the street with friends visiting from all sides of the Mediterranean, but this year he decided to keep the gathering small, only inviting a few close friends and family. He simply was not in the mood for a celebration. Naomi was gone, and there were too many friends who had left the city, either in exile or to avoid what was looking politically like a dim future for Alexandria.

Hannah and Jemir kept bumping into each other in the kitchen as they readied plates of sardines, olive paste, crackers, and figs. "You should go out, Hannah, and see the lights. I have everything ready here." Jemir steadied a tray of stuffed *dolmas* on his palm.

"No, it is Shabbat tonight," Hannah protested. "I must finish my work before sundown and then say prayers."

"You would not have to work if you came out with me." Tarek stuck his head into the kitchen.

Hannah eyed him suspiciously. "Jemir has too much to handle by himself for now, and I still need to make the *challah*. The sun has nearly set." Hannah began kneading a lump of dough on the table. As she spoke she reached into a small bowl and took out a pinch of flour to sprinkle over the top.

Tarek collapsed on the pile of pillows in the corner. "There is a very famous musician from Memphis playing at the taverna tonight," he said. He was attempting to grow a beard, and although it was sprouting in thin patches, he stroked it with pride. Hannah presumed he was growing it to look older, but unfortunately it had the opposite effect. Still, he had put on a fine olive grey *tunica* with a wide leather belt that fit him quite well, even if he was sprawled across the cushions like a dog.

Hannah set three lengths of rounded dough on a large wooden paddle, braided it, and dusted her hands together over the table.

"Have you heard of Garzya of Cyprus?" Tarek propped his head up on his elbow, waiting for her reaction, hoping to entice her. "He plays the kanun."

The Egyptian harp. Hannah had never heard one, although she had been longing to ever since she learned of it: the most difficult instrument in all the Mediterranean to master, played with finger picks on all ten fingers and the harp set horizontally on a table. The Egyptians likened the kanun to the body of a lover, as it was not played, but tickled, caressed, and stroked languidly into song.

When Tarek saw the light in Hannah's eyes he knew he was defeating her resistance. "Come with me."

Hannah weighed her choices. Tarek had been kind recently, much like he had been to her when he first bought her and tried to make her well. But he was two people sharing the same bones: one, punishing and cruel, and the other, vulnerable and sweet, still just a boy. And she longed to hear the kanun. Going out would not be working. She could say her prayers before she left. Her father would never approve, but then, she was the only Jew in Alizar's house. No one else noticed her observances. And truly, she would rather have spent the evening with Gideon, but he had work aboard the ship and would not be about. She nodded to Tarek. "I will go."

Tarek smiled triumphantly. Truthfully, he could have commanded her as he did with his whores, but he longed for her willing company. Even he had a heart. "Meet me in front of the taverna on the wharf in an hour. The owner is a friend of mine. He will give me a fine table."

As Hannah set out from Alizar's house, Jemir tapped her on the shoulder and dropped several copper coins in to her palm. "Enjoy yourself," he said.

She tried to give them back, but he smiled and went out to secure the chickens in their roost.

Hannah pinned her hair up and put on a flowing pale pink *khiton* and wandered down to the hawker's bazaar where women, young and old, were gathered in tents by candlelight, their jewelry flashing as they laughed. Others stood beside tables attracting customers by holding up their goods and thrusting them toward the passersby.

"Nothing more beautiful than this shawl! Finest linen in Egypt!"

"For you, madam, it matches your eyes."

"Pure silver. Here, try it on. Ah, see how it suits you."

"Necklaces and bangles worn by Cleopatra herself!"

"Best prices in all of Alexandria!"

Displayed neatly on carpets and tables were reed baskets, alabaster vials of kohl, glass perfume flasks, small hinged seashell boxes filled with powdered azurite and selenite for painting the eyes, elegant garnet, amber, and turquoise beads. Colorful *tunicas, pallas,* and *himations* lay folded on tables beside elegant *fibulas* and *penannulars* of different metals and shapes in Roman and even Celtic styles. The women bantered cheerfully as they made their purchases, weaving in between the *gabbehs*, examining linen with eyes that could find every flaw in perfect thread.

Hannah swooned at the sight of so many beautiful things. Each time she entered a tent, the merchant would rush to put a teacup in her hand so that she would stay and buy something. In one tent she met a kind Jewish woman and her three daughters selling exquisite hand-beaded necklaces, apparently taking the night of festival to heart even if it was *Shabbat*. Hearing her own language spoken, Hannah felt her heart melt. It was like hearing a favorite song after an interminably long time without music.

"*Yaffe*, such a beautiful girl." The plump woman smiled as she cupped Hannah's cheek in her palm and then insisted she take a beaded bracelet as a gift.

Around the rim of the hawker's bazaar, fortunetellers solicited their customers with promises of life's mysteries revealed. Hannah slipped past, wanting to make her way down to the taverna. But one of the Bedouin children, a crippled boy with withered legs that hung like seaweed between his wooden crutches, clung to her skirt and looked up at her with hungry eyes. "You want to know your fortune?"

"No, no. Thank you." Hannah turned and walked away, but the child came after her, tugging her sleeve and looking up at her. "Special deal tonight for the beautiful lady. Your future revealed."

Hannah smiled and shook her head, but pressed a coin into the boy's dirty hand. "No one but God can reveal the future."

"Yes," said the boy. "But even God sends messengers. When the doe is hunted, she must lose the dogs in the water."

Hannah looked at the earnest boy for a moment, and then nodded. The Bedouin children were full of enchanting riddles.

She decided to walk along the west beach on the way to the taverna, tracing the route she and Alizar had taken the week before from the north end of Canopic Way. At the end of the street she unlaced her sandals and strolled down to the waves where the wet sand made it easier to walk. Ahead of her, two lovers, drunk and tripping on the sand, laughed and leaned on each other. Hannah could not help but watch them, though the sight of their amorous gestures gave her pause. She thought of her life in the Great Library and all the music she could make there. Though music might be a loyal companion, even Hannah knew a lyre could not warm the bed at night or replace the laughter of children. But without her freedom, how could she find a husband?

Hannah turned her eyes away from the man and woman and looked to the luminous crests of the waves and the wide amber beam that stretched across the water from the lighthouse, penetrating the darkness, beckoning the ships. She tried not to let the laughter of the lovers pierce her, tried not to think of another year bringing her swiftly to the age of twenty, an age that made a man seek out a younger wife. As she passed beside the lovers, she saw that they were two men, not a man and woman at all. She laughed at her own folly. The Greek men often kept a boy, she knew, even those with wives, but still it shocked her to see their revelry. They ignored her and retreated to the sea wall to make love, standing one behind the other. Hannah looked away.

At the end of the beach Hannah neared the lively banter of the crowd, a woman shrieking with laughter, a cluster of men drunk and talking over one another. Hannah's breath hitched, realizing her calf was bare. Her knife! She had left it tucked beneath the stable straw where she slept. Ever since Alizar had given it to her she had not been without it for a moment. She wondered if she should turn back. But Tarek was waiting, and she did not wish to anger him. Besides, the evening washed over her, warm and gentle. All around her, Alexandria glowed like a promise. The Parabolani were not out. She would enjoy the first half of the performance and then return to Alizar's before it even ended.

She climbed over the seawall, realizing as she looked around that this was the street to the *agora* where she had seen Tarek that first day, the day the men had set her on the block to be sold. Somehow that moment seemed like ages ago. It could have been much worse, she knew. Much worse.

The wharf was only mildly cooler than the rest of Alexandria, which made it stifling. The pungent scents of rotting seaweed, sweat, and cinnamon wafted through the air and made it difficult to breathe. The taverna stood at the other end of the docks, and Hannah made slow progress through the thick sea of bodies. More than once a sailor leaned over to steal a kiss or request a dance.

Just one, just one, come on. Come.

You are so beautiful.

For me.

Come.

Hannah smiled politely and sidled past. Tarek was waiting for her at the door of the taverna when she arrived.

"Where were you?" he demanded.

"The crowd." Hannah said, and then narrowed her eyes at him. Tarek was drunk already, swaying side to side. Hard to believe sometimes that Alizar could look on him as a son.

"Come, Hannah." Tarek snatched her hand, pushing past a bearded Greek sailor with arms the size of two cannons. He grunted as Hannah and Tarek entered the taverna but let them by.

Hannah withdrew her hand from his to adjust the sleeve of her dress, glowering.

Three sailor friends of Tarek's joined them and presented a goat-horn pipe and a lump of hashish the color of dried snake blood. Tarek filled the bowl and passed it to Hannah, who stared at his hand for a moment before deciding to try. One toke and she began to cough uncontrollably, pressing her palms to her chest. Tarek just laughed and polished off the rest.

Either from the effects of the hashish or the events that followed, Hannah took away only a single, distinct memory of the kanun player, whose name was Garzya.

The young musician curled his body over his instrument like a snail, strands of long black hair plastered to his sweaty forehead and cheeks, his eyes pinched tightly shut, his hands dancing across the strings of the kanun in a blur. The music he created was so immense that no walls could contain it. It bound the audience together in a sea of music and light. No one could take their eyes away from the handsome musician as they felt themselves moved by the intricacies of his caress, each wanting to be his instrument, even for an hour. It was so intimate that Hannah found herself unable to look at him for very long without blushing, so she looked at the table and the tufts of pipe ash spread like windblown seeds between the wine cups.

Walking home after the performance, Hannah could still hear the music echoing in her mind. His melodies had raised her vision of what was possible. The night was young yet, and she had inspiration to pick up Hypatia's lyre and compose a new song. Tarek staggered along beside her, besotted.

As they approached the familiar green door, Tarek caught her arm and pulled her body into his to kiss her. She pushed him away, but he caught her by the hair. "I have waited long enough for you," he snarled.

She looked him squarely in the eye. "Tarek, let me go."

He laughed and grabbed her by the collar, the metal cutting into her neck. She shrieked as he kissed her greedily, forcing his tongue into her mouth, his groin stiffening as he held her, his breath a vile mixture of alcohol and smoke.

Hannah struggled to break free, but he did not relinquish his grip. "Stop it, you little cunny," he demanded. "Tonight I get what is mine."

Hannah cried out, pushing at his arms, his chest, wielding her hands like claws. "You get nothing from me," she said, wishing for her knife tucked in the stable straw. She had been wrong to trust Tarek.

Tarek pulled her toward the darkest nook in the alley, turned her around and hoisted up her *khiton* from behind. "You will give me what I want," he said. "And you will beg."

She pleaded. "Tarek, stop! You are drunk, now let me go." She struggled to break his grasp, but his fingers held her collar firm.

"Beg, slave," he said, and he spit in his hand and slid it to his cock.

Hannah cried out.

Tarek smacked the back of her head. "Beg!"

"No."

He hit her again, and her hair came undone, the silver hairpin her father had given her clattering to her feet. "I said beg, slave."

Hannah began to cry. "Never."

Tarek's face reddened, and his pride smarted. "I will teach you to beg," he said, and he pressed himself against her bare buttocks but lost his seed with a groan before he could deliver his full intention.

And in that instant his grip fell slack giving Hannah reach, her fingers searching desperately for the silver peacock hairpin at her feet. There. Her eyes closed to slits, full of fury. Never. Never again. She turned and plunged the prongs deep into Tarek's knee, splitting muscle from bone.

Tarek screamed and released her as he fell to the ground, pulling the hairpin and angrily hurling it into the street. "Look what you have done!" he said, indicating the wound pouring blood.

But Hannah did not look. "Do not ever touch me again," she said, and then she left him curled up in a ball in the street like the dog he was.

"I own you!" Tarek yelled at her. "And you owe me your life."

Hannah turned back to him, her eyes dark and hollow. "My debt to you is paid."

But as she reached Alizar's door, a new menace presented itself.

Peter and the Parabolani came around the corner, sweeping up the alley toward Alizar's house.

"There she is!" called Peter, and the five Parabolani broke into a run.

Tarek whimpered, unseen by the priests, his hands clutching his knee as his blood poured into the street.

Hannah pivoted and fled, running around the back of the house to the stable entrance, but the door was locked. "Aziz! Jemir! Leitah!" Hannah screamed to be let in, but no one heard as they were all in the house for the party. Peter was mere steps away.

She had to run elsewhere. She sped down one alley after the next, turning carts over behind her as she passed, angering the merchants. She could feel that Peter and his men meant to draw blood. Tonight would be their revenge.

Hannah dashed through the *agora*, trying to lose the Parabolani in the crowd. They easily closed on her, and more priests joined in the chase. Hannah was not as fast as they were, and she realized she was losing ground. The Christians meant to make an example of the pagans on this night of debauchery, of course.

Cyril had already decided Alizar's slave would be their victim—
punish the master and the girl together.

As she ran, she could feel the same fear as the antelope running from the lion, knowing that this was the last chase, the last
distance that her legs would carry her. She prayed as she fled,
praying to God for her life, to her father to help her.

When she reached the Great Library, the gates were locked.
She pulled at the enormous iron handle and screamed for help,
but there was no response. Behind her, the Parabolani grabbed
torches from the walls and closed in.

When the doe is hunted, she must lose the dogs in the water.

The Bedouin boy's riddle echoed in her ears. Yes, the water.
Hannah ran out onto the wharf that led to the harbor. The *Vesta*
was moored somewhere in the royal harbor, a ship in a sea of
ships. She had to find it somehow. But there were so many ships in
the darkness.

The Parabolani saw they had her cornered on the wharf. Peter,
the tallest among them, caught her in her moment of hesitation.
He grabbed her clothing and pulled her backwards on the wooden
boards, skinning her knees. But she found her footing, and spit
in his face, which momentarily blinded him, though he did not
relinquish his hold on her.

And then, suddenly, she was gone.

Peter was left holding her dress, and the girl was nowhere.

The Parabolani turned circles on the wharf, calling out and
scanning the sea. They would have heard her plunge in, but there
had been no sound.

They did not consider the angel, who smiled in triumph.

Beneath them, Hannah hung from one of the beams in the
structural support of the wharf, holding her breath. And she
waited until her fingers began to slip, and it was just long enough.
Peter called out, "There is nowhere to run, slave! We will spill your

pagan blood tonight or another night. It is no matter." And he gathered his men, and they walked back down the docks as Hannah slipped into the sea, a large wave crashing on the beach muffling her splash.

The cold ocean enveloped her. She sank lower and fought for the surface. A wave washed over her, and she sputtered for breath, the bronze collar heavy and cold about her neck. Where, oh where, was the ship?

Hannah swam toward Pharos, toward the royal harbor, but she could not make out which ship was Alizar's from all the many moored that night.

She swam across the harbor, circling each ship, growing fatigued as the heavy collar at her throat threatened to pull her under. Finally she paused to rest, treading water. But her limbs lost strength and she began to cry out.

Then a black shape surfaced beside her in the water letting out a puff of steam and she shrieked in terror. Something brushed her foot. She struggled to remain at the surface with renewed vigor. But the creature circled her. Hannah began to cry, pleading for her life. She struggled mightily for breath, and the panic of drowning overcame her. And she sank below the water, the sleek animal dove beneath her and lifted her to the surface. It had to be a seal, or a dolphin, she did not know, but she relaxed against the creature's smooth skin.

"Who goes there?" Shouted an oarsman, his little skiff clipping across the harbor.

"Hannah. Of Alizar's house," Hannah stammered, reaching out a hand. "Please help me."

Hannah was pulled aboard by the oarsman, but she forgot she had been speaking Aramaic. He looked at her in confusion, then in desire. She pulled her wet clothing to her body, and pleaded. "Alizar. His ship. The Vesta. Please."

Gideon was on the deck of the Vesta, checking the lines when he leaned his head over the aft rail, torch in hand, and heard the oarsman shout in approach.

"Praise Zeus, Hannah!" Gideon unrolled the ladder so that it dangled from the stern to the sea. Then he descended and reached his hand out to clutch the wet girl to his body. "Thank you," he said to the oarsman, who pushed away with a grunt, disappointed not to be thrown at least a coin.

Gideon knelt on the deck, Hannah cradled in his arms. "The Parabolani," she coughed and sputtered. "They chased me onto the wharf."

Gideon smiled his astonishment at her arrival, more beautiful than any siren. "Let me fetch you a blanket."

He took her to the captain's berth and made her a strong cinnamon tisane to warm her up. Though the night was warm enough, still she trembled like a fallen bird. As he wrapped another blanket across her shoulders, the story come rushing out of her about the Parabolani, and she sputtered her tears and gradually began to calm down, and then even to laugh a little at how absurd it all must seem. She did not mention Tarek. She knew she could be severely punished for what she had done to him.

"Woman, you are safe now," he said. "Though how you find so much trouble is uncanny. You are drawn to it like surf to shore."

"I thought the leviathan would eat me. What creature was it?"

"There is a playful dolphin called Apollo that tends this harbor, if that is what you mean. He is our omen of good fortune." Gideon looped his fingers through one of the handles on the ceiling as the ship rocked in the gentle wake of another vessel. "I will take you back to Alizar's in the morning. For now, I will ready a sailor's bunk for you and see to it you get some clothes."

As Gideon turned to go, Hannah stood up, shivering, and touched his face with her hand, tracing the purple scar that snaked down from his eye like a vine.

He needed no more encouragement than that. Curse modesty.

He hoisted her in his arms and carried her to his bed as the blankets fell from her naked shoulders.

Hannah had never known a man by her own choice, and what majesty there could be in that. He gave her the depth of his presence; his calloused hands squeezed her buttocks, her breasts, making her cry out in ecstasy again and again as he ravished her. Their bodies entwined as though each was familiar to the other, an unspoken language arising effortlessly between them. He lost himself in her before the sun crested the sea.

Alizar could wait for them another hour.

Gideon rose to fetch tea and coffee, eggs and spinach leaves. Her mind blissfully free of thoughts, of fears, Hannah felt she might know contentment in Alexandria at last, but even she knew this would be only a respite. Cyril still hunted her.

A single sunbeam played in the folds of Gideon's *tunica*, illuminating a gold medallion pressed with the image of a rearing lion. She lifted it in her fingertips to admire.

"I found it in a shipwreck. Dove for the gold myself off the island of Icarius."

"What do the letters say?" asked Hannah, her eyes lit with curiosity.

"Ah, a girl with an inquisitive mind, eh? You know what we do to women such as thee," Gideon teased. "We feed you to the lions!" And he grabbed her, pretending to eat her arm until she kicked and squealed and howled with laughter.

"Please tell me," she insisted.

Gideon pinned her. "You must promise not to laugh."

"I promise."

"It says that the bull shall piss wherever he pleases."

"It does not."

"All right, then." He tucked the medallion in his *tunica*. "I presented it as a gift to my father, originally, as the lion is the symbol of our family crest. But when he was called to the grave, it was left again to me. If I have a son one day, I will give it to him."

Hannah smiled, and kissed him. "Tell me what it really says."

Gideon laughed, unyielding. He wondered how any one woman could be so beautiful, so nearly perfect. As they made love again, swept away, Gideon pulled the girl on top of him and imagined never wanting another but Hannah. This woman. This moment. He shut his eyes and let himself go until their bodies were still again. But the thought lingered, at first tiny and beautiful, then compelling and terrifying, eventually humming in his mind like a hornet. Wanting this woman more than any other pricked him to his senses, and he knew it would be better their passion did not make two slaves of one. He swung his legs off the side of his bunk. Love was not a complication he favored.

"Come, dress yourself," he said, standing abruptly and throwing her some sailor's clothes. Hannah smiled, aware that she had unsteadied him. So, the fierce captain could not resist her. Beauty must be his weakness. She leaned forward and took his fingers in her mouth, her tongue sliding across his knuckles, but he pulled his hand free. "We must see Alizar, woman."

"You are taking me back? Just like that?" Hannah sat up. She had hoped they might have more time.

He nodded, gruff. "The Parabolani. Alizar must know at once."

Hannah tugged on the man's tunic he offered her. "Did I offend you somehow, Gideon?"

"Offend? No. We must go, come."

Hannah had to live with his answer as the unspoken thoughts he held threw up a wall between them. Did he not feel this abrupt turn of affection or care? She swallowed hard and tried to run her fingers through her knotted hair, the seawater dried and salty in the strands. Perhaps he was just eager to speak with Alizar. She chided herself for taking his sudden coldness to heart. What would he be like as a husband, she wondered? Surely after the night they had shared, that would be the outcome. She felt sure if there were a baby from it, he would have to marry her. Hannah smiled inwardly, knowing at last her future would bear fruit. Her heart lifted, soared, carved happy circles inside her ribcage like a hawk in the open sky.

They took a small oar boat to the docks, then slunk through the polished alleyways of the Brucheon. Gideon tethered her to him, pulling her near whenever a Parabolan passed them. But the priests were not looking for a girl clad in a sailor's costume, and so the pair found their way to Alizar's door without incident.

"What do you plan to say to Alizar?" Hannah whispered.

"Leave that to me."

Gideon pushed open the little green door. But when Hannah passed the threshold she caught her breath. A voice in the atrium. Could it be? She paused and waited, clutching Gideon's arm, but there was nothing.

Then she heard it again. The voice she knew the way she knew the fields and the sky. The voice that had been calling inside her heart these many moons apart. She flew through the atrium and out into the courtyard.

And there he was.

16

"Abba?" Hannah asked, blinking her eyes at the impossible apparition of her father sitting cross-legged beside the fountain, talking to Alizar.

Kaleb stood weakly with the help of a cane and held out his arms. "Hannah."

For a moment Hannah could not move, so deep and sudden was this new shock, but then she ran to him, just a few short steps to close the distance that had separated them—the time, the miles, the terrain like it was all a dream now, and father and daughter fell into a long embrace that was followed by a greeting that had no words. Kaleb placed his hands on either side of Hannah's cheeks, kissed them several times, and professed how she was more beautiful than he remembered, while Hannah touched her father's heart, kissed his knuckles, and wept.

They each noted what had changed with the other, eyes moving up and down. Hannah touched the cane her father carried in concern, and then swept her hand up to his beard, his pale gaunt cheeks. She met his sunken eyes, and her breath stopped short.

He was not well.

Alizar, seated on the divan with his legs crossed at the knee, nodded in satisfaction at their reunion. Although he had not thrown his usual banquet party, still guests had come, many unexpected, such as the humble shepherd who knocked at the little green door, pleading in Aramaic to find his daughter, "Hannah.

Hannah. Have you seen my daughter?" Alizar had shown him in, and they had waited all night for her return.

"Abba, how did you find me here? I feared you were dead, but then I knew, something in me knew you were alive." Hannah hugged him, kissed him again and again, this new joy melting through her, erasing all the grief, the loss, the unspeakable sorrow she had lived with since the night she was captured.

Kaleb laughed, though he was tired, though he had been awake all night. Alizar's house still hosted guests when he arrived in the dark, some standing, some reclining on divans with glasses of wine, all bantering about the city's politics and the emperor's bedwetting and a thousand other things that matter only to the people who have the luxury of concerning themselves with more than meals or the lack thereof. Kaleb explained he had known where to find her, but only because of this: he handed her the hairpin that Tarek had thrown into the street. He had found it wedged in the cobbles, gleaming like answered prayer, and asked at the nearest door.

So.

Hannah took the hairpin from his hands, washed it of Tarek's blood in the fountain, and proudly nestled the peacock back into her hair. Alizar and Gideon nodded to one another and left father and daughter alone to speak. Hannah, supporting her father's weight, helped him to a comfortable chair. "Abba, when did you arrive? Are you well?"

"In the night. The party only ended just before you came. Arguing is a favorite sport of the Greeks. I am surprised they have not put it in their Olympics." He coughed.

Hannah fetched him a cup of water from the nearby table. Something was wrong; he drank it as though he could drink the Nile in one sip.

"The slave traders were clumsy," Kaleb explained. "They were clumsy with their knives and clumsy with their trail. I knew I would find you. I sold our herd, not knowing how long I would need to travel the road. I had the money sewn into the sole of my boot, but my boots were stolen like everything else. I am so sorry. I know now it would have meant your freedom." Kaleb sighed, eyeing her bronze collar, his eyes sunken with loss. "One of the merchants in the market remembered you. 'Hard to forget a pretty girl like that,' he said. The barley merchant, I believe he was." Kaleb turned to face her with a wince and a grunt, his hand moving to his ribs.

Hannah hugged him. "Abba, you are hurt. Where? We can get a doctor. What is it?"

He shooed her away with his outstretched hand and took some breaths in and out of his mouth, the pain spreading, and then receding. "I am all right. I have come this far. I have found you. I am all right." He looked up and cupped her cheek. "My baby."

Hannah held her father close, smelling him, hearing him, stroking the familiar fur on his arms. He patted her hand, and then turned to face her, his expression deeply serious. "Hannah, there are things I must tell you now. Things that, since I have found you, you must know."

"No, Abba. Whatever it is can wait until tomorrow or the next day. You are tired, and Alizar can send for the doctor. We must make you well. And you need sleep."

"No," said Kaleb, his happy eyes creased with pain. "I must tell you now. I have walked a century, and I only made it this far with my heart set on finding you. You must be quiet and listen to me."

Hannah promptly knelt on the smooth flagstones of the court-yard before her father, resting her head on his knees the way she had since she was a girl.

Kaleb tugged at a worn canvas bag over his shoulder, set it on his lap, and uncinched the leather straps. Then he reached in and pulled out a smooth white alabaster jar and thrust it toward her. "For you," he said.

Hannah reached out and caressed the cool glossy surface of the jar. Then she turned the lid. Inside was crumbled sand, bits of bone. Suddenly Hannah recoiled her fingers. "These are ashes."

"Yes. Your mother's ashes. Your father's. And your grandmother's. Maybe sisters and brothers, I do not know. I have kept it all this time. I must tell you the truth now."

"Abba, I do not understand."

Kaleb rested his forehead in his hands. "I was traveling with the herd when I found a camp that was still smoldering from a fire. Robbers. Clearly the people were wealthy, as they were traveling with Roman soldiers among them. I found helmets and several swords. Hannah, everyone was killed. The robbers had tied the family to their carts and lit them on fire. I was picking through the rubble, looking for anything useful that was left, and then I heard your cry."

A tear swept down Kaleb's cheek. He brushed it away. Hannah said nothing, her eyes like two huge holes, disbelieving, her hands feeling the weight of the smooth alabaster jar on her lap, cold as death itself.

"There was a baby hidden in the deep roots of the olive tree. Your mother must have hidden you there and covered you completely in a brown woolen blanket. The raiders took what they wanted and did not find you."

Hannah could hardly believe his words. "You are not my Abba?"

"I am your Abba, Hannah, just not by blood. I thought I would carry the child to a couple I knew in the meadows on the eastern flank of Sinai who were childless. And so I carried you, and you never slept but only cried, and it was difficult. When I reached the woman's house, I stood for a long time in the field. I told myself that she would be a good mother to you. I told myself that she could do what I could not. But when I looked into your eyes, I could not do it. I found a wet nurse for you. I raised you, selfishly."

"Not selfishly, Abba. Never."

"I kept the herd nearby, thinking perhaps someone would come looking for you, but I hoped they never would. I wanted you for myself. A daughter from God."

Hannah rested her head on her father's knees. She looked up, the realization in her eyes that Alizar had recognized her as a Roman, and it was true. "I am not a Jew."

Kaleb sighed. "I raised you as one of my people, and I feel that you are as much a Jew as any born by blood, but the rabbi would disagree."

"Abba, all these months I wanted only to be with you." Hannah wiped her eyes, flowing with tears. "I have always wanted only to be with you. I do not care what story you tell me or who I am. You are my Abba. We must never be separated again."

Kaleb stroked his daughter's head. "I am sorry I lied to you. Somehow I thought it would be better if you had a different story, a story that made me your Abba. But I thought all this time on the road praying to find you, that if I found you, you must know the truth. You cannot be in this world and not know where you came from."

Hannah shook her head. "I do not care. I belong with you."

Kaleb smiled and patted her arm, then winced against a wave of pain.

Hannah sat up. "I will call Alizar. We must get the doctor at once. Philemon is a good doctor. He saved my life when I first came to this house."

And though Kaleb tried to protest, Hannah ran into the house. But she found that Alizar had already called for Philemon.

Jemir and Leitah followed Hannah outside to the courtyard, and they helped her father into the house to lie down on the pillows in the kitchen, which was the nearest room. Hannah never left his side except to complete her chores.

———

Kaleb died with his eyes open, smiling, perhaps at peace that he had found his daughter. Before that hour, Hannah told him everything that had happened since they were separated, and he listened. She lifted water to his lips, cradled him. She wept and cursed.

Kaleb consoled her. "I want to go now. It is time for me. I can feel it. I regret I lost the money that would have freed you. This is the only pain I take with me. You must know I am proud of you for learning to read. You have made your Abba so happy."

But Hannah just cried and held his head in her arms and pleaded with him to stay.

"I will watch over you, I promise." It was as if he thought he was just walking into the next room.

When she returned with the rabbi, Kaleb was gone. Hannah fell upon her father's body. "Abba," she wailed, trying to rouse him, but he would not move. Her gentle nudging turned to frantic tears. She threaded her fingers into her father's hand and pleaded softly, her cheek pressed to his heart. He was still warm. How could this be? His body was still warm, but his heart was not beating. "Abba, do not leave me. Please."

The rabbi stepped forward, closed her father's eyes, and began to pray.

Hannah knelt at her father's bedside, weeping in sorrow and confusion, trapped in the story of her life: orphaned by her parents not once, but twice. Her Abba was gone, and there was no one else in the world she knew as family.

Outside, the sparrows rustled and twittered in the branches of the fig tree, the clouds passed soundlessly by, the lion spat his stream of water into the fountain. No going back, the world seemed to say. No going back. There is only this day.

Jemir clucked his tongue, shook his head. "Her father comes all this way to die. So sad."

Alizar took a seat on the large wooden table beneath the fig tree, resting his boots on the bench, his elbows on his knees. Gideon and Jemir stood before him. "Naomi and now Hannah's father. Two deaths," Alizar said. Then he looked up into the webbed branches of the tree. "Make no mistake. There will be another. There is always a third. Send for a seer to bless the house and ward away the evil eye. We need spiritual protection, someone who will portend the future. For the house and for my ship. Jemir, go."

Jemir set his gaze intently on Alizar and then left to do his bidding.

Gideon turned to Alizar. "As long as Cyril and his Parabolani hunt for Hannah, she will be in danger. We must send her away." This had been hard for him to say, but he set his jaw; this is how it must be.

Alizar groaned, shifted his legs. Stood. "You want me to send her away?"

"For her protection. To protect your work. With Cyril's dogs sniffing our door, we will not succeed with even one more shipment."

"It is loyalty, then, why you suggest this," said Alizar, testing him. "Not love?"

Gideon did not answer. In the time since Hannah had been with her father, Gideon had gone to visit the brothel night after night, throwing his coins to the prettiest girls, girls he took to bed two and three at a time. He teased them and played their games, made love to one as she kissed the full lips of another. He learned their fabricated names—names after pretty flowers like Jasmine and Rose, Lilac and Lily, taking each of them in turn. He had no need of a slave girl, though the persistent thought of Hannah still haunted his quiet hours. He had the cure for thinking of her in his grasp, and he would grasp it indeed. "Loyalty."

Alizar nodded, taking Gideon at his word. He would make the arrangement that would carry Hannah off to another world, away from them. A twinge of regret passed between the men silently, like a gust of wind.

This was not preference they were discussing, but necessity.

So.

PART 2

The Emerald Tablet

17

On a colorless morning when the birds were quiet, Gideon accompanied Hannah to the harbor, his hand on the hilt of his sword. However, where there should have been the island of Pharos with its lighthouse and temples, a thick wall of marine mist whorled as it brushed the surface of the water, obscuring the island from view: *the Breath of Nereus*. What had Alizar said about it? That it concealed the workings of the gods? Hannah sighed. So be it. The Greeks and their mad, many gods.

She touched the bottom of her haversack to find the white alabaster jar that held the remnants of her relatives, all except for her Abba, who had been buried in the Jewish necropolis beneath a mulberry tree in the far eastern corner nearest to Sinai. Alizar made certain he was tucked under the first patch of earth to be illuminated at sunrise. Hannah traced the bronze slave collar at her neck with one finger. She was a not a Jew. She was a Roman, a shepherdess, a pagan, a slave. A slave with every decision made for her, whether it was to learn to read, to play on her lyre, or to gather her things at once. Go.

Hannah wrapped her arms around Gideon's neck, and he kissed her for the last time, quickly, his mind elsewhere. Then he stepped back and called the skiff. Her beauty and her spirit, however enchanting, was not a sea he wished to drown in.

Hannah shivered. The captain's passion for her had waned to perfunctory gestures such as this kiss. She wiped her lips and tried to remember their night together, a once perfect night now swallowed by disappointment by his cool avoidance. She wanted to look at him, feel his warmth, wrap her hands inside his own, but could not bring herself to meet his eyes again knowing he would spurn her. She felt grateful there had been no sign of a baby, as clearly he wanted nothing of a husband's duties.

The boatman pocketed Gideon's coins and lit a torch at the front of the skiff to prevent any approaching ship from plowing blindly into them. The erratic orange flame licked at the mist and danced across the surface of the mirrored sea, the only color in the endless expanse of grey, just as the dip and lift of the oars in the water was the only sound in the silence.

Gideon disappeared without a backward glance.

Once in the skiff, Hannah gathered her woolen shawl tightly around herself and hugged her knees up to her chest, tears breaking free of her restraint as she gulped for air. She was still unused to the way the ocean's dampness burrowed into her bones. The cold of the desert was never so penetrating. She looked back to the dock, but it had already been swallowed in the mist.

No going back.

Hannah felt a pang of loneliness. The cold fog did nothing to reassure her, yet somehow it was apt. Winter was the season for loss. Beside her skiff the silver dolphin called Apollo surfaced for breath. His presence was an omen of good fortune, she knew now, and so she whispered words of thanks to him in Aramaic for helping her to Alizar's ship. Still, the sea unsettled her. Only when the bottom of the skiff scraped against the strand did she fully exhale.

So.

Standing on the beach with her things at her feet, she scanned for the little path that Alizar had said would take her to the Temple of Isis. He had made it sound like he was sending her away for further instruction, but she knew the truth. She was now a burden, a dangerous expense. She knew she should be grateful he did not sell her at the market to the highest bidder. This was not a gratitude she could feel, though, just a weak thought to blunt the sharp edge of the pain of being sent away, and being thoroughly unwanted.

Hannah walked the length of the beach. Beneath the lighthouse, a sheer cliff rose up from the sand and sea caves. Beyond it, the beach was choked with bramble bushes. She startled a flock of cormorants, and they swept out across the harbor like displaced letters on a scroll, flowing off the page.

Hannah re-pinned her *fibula*, gathered up the ends of her *himation*, and began to pick her way through the bushes toward the escarpment. Thorns slashed her calves and drew streaks of blood. Twigs that snapped back at her tangled in her hair and snagged the fringe of her shawl.

Hannah had to use her hands to pull herself up the white jagged stones that jutted out from the slope like milk teeth from gums. When she finally clamored to the top, the lapis blue dome of the Temple of Isis appeared from behind the mist, nested like a robin's egg against the back of a rounded hill of dry grass.

Hannah set her things down and went to work on rescuing her appearance. She combed the twigs out of her long thick hair and plaited it down her back. Then she picked the thorns from her shawl and moistened a corner with spit, dabbing at the stinging scratches on her legs.

When she looked up she saw the thin dusty path just beyond the thicket, snaking between the palms. It seemed to come from the west and wind its way uphill. Hannah collected her haversack and lyre and took a breath to steady herself. She did not want a new life, yet another new life, but a new life she would have.

As she wound her way up the first knoll, the landscape grew barren and rocky, speckled with low-lying ground cover that clung to patches of dirt, the succulent leaves growing luminous purple flowers that seemed even more vivid in the mist. When Hannah paused to rest, a black lizard with golden eyes darted beneath a rock at her feet.

To the east, a barren hill stood between the lighthouse and the temple, blocking the lighthouse beam from the rest of the island, forming a quaint rural backdrop for the little cloister with its white lime-washed walls and tall trellises overgrown with scarlet bougainvillea. There was a palpable peace about the place that Hannah could feel easing her mind. Then she realized this was the first time she had felt safe since she could remember.

As she approached the temple, Hannah could hear water splashing into a fountain. She walked around the high walls until she reached a set of tall wooden doors that were locked from the inside. Hannah set her satchel and lyre down at her feet and rapped loudly.

From behind the wall came the braying of a goat, the tinkling of a bell, and light footsteps on a stone path. Behind the doors, a child spoke. "Who is there?"

"I am Hannah."

There was no response.

"I just arrived from Alexandria."

A little finger poked through a knothole in the gate. "Look through here."

Hannah knelt and peered through the hole. An eye with long lashes and a brown iris looked back at her. The child giggled.

Hannah stood up. "What is your name?" she asked sweetly.

"Suhaila," said the child. By the sound of her voice she was no older than four or five.

"Suhaila, can you open the gate for me?"

"I am not allowed."

"Oh, I see. Could you get someone to open it for me?"

Suhaila ran from the gate, calling the name "Mira" again and again.

Hannah heard two sets of footsteps and then the clanging sound of a key being turned. The gate opened a fraction, and a beautiful girl peered through, everything about her golden, flawless. Her long hair swirled around her gleaming skin like bronze water, her amber eyes so luminous they might belong to a hawk more than a woman, although her nose was red and swollen, as if she were sick. Mira eyed Hannah's slave collar and her full breasts with a slight look of, was it disapproval? Hannah shifted nervously.

"You are Hannah?"

Hannah collected her things into her arms and nodded. "I am."

The woman opened the gate wide enough for Hannah to pass and then closed it behind her and locked it again from a key that hung from a cord around her neck. She withdrew a handkerchief and blew her nose modestly, then tucked it away. "I am Mira," she said, bowing slightly, her palms pressed together in front of her heart. "And this is Suhaila." Mira placed one delicate hand on the head of the small, dark-haired child standing beside a white goat with a bell around its neck.

Suhaila fingered the ends of one of her curls and introduced the goat. "This is Cleopatra."

Hannah smiled and returned the bow. "A pleasure."

"Come, I will show you the grounds and the gardens, and then you will meet Mother Hathora, our High Priestess," said Mira. As she led Hannah around the temple, the diminutive priestess carried her head high and walked with the same sprightly gate as the Arabian horses Alizar adored. Hannah felt awkward by comparison. Still, this was a fresh start, a new beginning, untainted by any mistake, pure as the smile of a babe. If only Hannah knew how tainted it was destined to become.

They crossed the wide stone steps of the temple, weaving between the tapered columns. Several ancient olive trees stood watch over the garden where, between the vegetable rows, women in long colorful robes were gathering bunches of herbs and flowers into their arms or digging with small spades.

On the far side of the vegetable and herb gardens, opposite the lapis dome of the temple, stood a quaint split-level stone house that adjoined several other structures. "Those are mostly rooms devoted to study." Mira indicated the smaller buildings covered in creeping vines. "Before us is the Garden House, where we sleep. Up on the knoll, behind the fire circle, there are much older gardens and a beautiful outdoor chapel that overlooks the sea in the north."

Hannah forced a smile, trying to think of this new place as her home.

The angel above her tried to soothe her with an intention of warmth. The door had been promised. The warrior would come.

Mira kissed Suhaila's head and pushed her off toward another priestess who took her by the hand. "Come, Hannah."

The entry of the Garden House opened to a sparsely decorated room, called the common area, with some large cushions set on the floor and a glowing brazier at one end.

"We mostly use this room for meetings, meals, and occasionally crafts. We have no need to work the way the monks of Poseidon do with their stone carving. The Great Library completely sustains us. We perform some of their translations."

"Is there water here on the island?" Hannah asked.

"There was a flowing spring once when the Heptastadion bridge was still in place some fifty years ago, but then we had to dig a well. We send our requests for items like candles and incense by skiff when we pick up the morning wood. You will see." Mira sneezed, and blew her nose in the kerchief she kept tucked up her sleeve.

Beyond the common area was a small kitchen. Beyond an open door, two red hens scratched at the damp ground beneath a sprawling belladonna tree, pink blossoms swaying. Mira paused to explain the various kitchen duties the priestesses performed, and then they crossed the common room and ascended a flight of winding stone stairs to the sleeping quarters where ten or more doors opened at angles into the wide stone hall. "That door at the end leads to the room where the children sleep. The other rooms are for the priestesses. You will share my room." Hannah could not tell by the look in her eye if Mira was happy about the arrangement.

Down several steps in the center of Mira's cozy room hung a worn white tapestry with a peacock feather design that acted as a divider. All around were a number of candles set on stone pedestals and tucked into recesses in the wall that cast a warm, radiant glow over objects of devotion: crystals, curved branches, seashells, round black seeds, and small cups of water where colorful rose blossoms floated. The scent of frankincense hung in the air. At the end of Mira's bed, a black cat with white feet and lunar eyes let out a tiny sigh and stretched its legs.

"We have our own balcony that leads up to the roof through those doors. I sleep outside in summer but not this time of year." Mira rubbed her arms as she crossed the room and picked up a bundle of sticks from a basket in the corner, tossing them into the brazier. Then she took a seat on the floor to warm her back.

Hannah set her bag on the straw mattress, the lyre on the floor. She found a fine sleeveless white linen *khiton* with a braided sash on the pillow and stroked it, finding the fabric as smooth as water.

Mira smiled. "You can change, then we will go outside."

As they stepped into the garden, a bell high in the temple clanged, and all the priestesses paused, closing their eyes. Hannah watched as Mira and the others brought their hands together at their foreheads, and then lowered them to their hearts. The world slowed, stilled.

When Mira opened her eyes she explained that it was a meditation bell. The priestesses took turns sitting beside the bell in the temple attic, ringing it several times a day. If the bell rang twice, it signified a meal. If the bell rang three times, it was time to wake up or go to sleep.

Mira led Hannah out a south-facing archway erupting with wisteria and down a winding path to a labyrinth, its four quadrants lined with white stones. At its navel was a giant clamshell half buried in the ground, set there for offerings. Then they wandered up the hill to a secret cave carved in the rock, an elaborate fabric embroidered with falcons and snakes hung over the door. Mira explained with reverence that this was the moon hollow, a place where the women went to relax during their monthly blood when they were not expected to do chores or participate in temple rituals. It was a time when the priestesses recognized women were closest to the goddess, and so they were invited to create art for the temple if they felt so inspired.

Behind the Garden House and the chicken coup, a long arbor led back toward the temple. Just beyond it, Hannah noticed a small path that snaked down to the cliffs on the far side of the island.

"That path leads to the *tholos*." A spirited smile sprung into Mira's cheeks.

"The what?"

"The *tholos*. The temple without doors where we offer our dances. Ours was built of white marble as a replica of the one in Delfi, with grand Corinthian columns. When the ships pass by, we hide behind them so the sailors will not see us."

Dances. Hannah felt her throat tighten. Would she be expected to dance? She had never danced before, and she had a dreadful feeling she would dance miserably. "Perhaps I could just play music for the dancers instead."

"You play music?"

"Yes."

Mira eyed Hannah up and down: her limbs curved like an eagle feather and her thick lashes framed eyes the color of the deep sea. Mira pursed her lips, irritated that this new priestess had to be so beautiful, although *beautiful* was not the word she would choose. "Where are you from, Hannah? You speak with a coarse accent I do not recognize."

"I come from Sinai. And you?"

Mira looked off into the mist. "My father was a sailor. Mother Hathora says his ship sank in a storm and I was brought here by a flock of gulls."

"Gulls?" Hannah scoffed.

"Mother Hathora gives all the children here a story of where they came from. The truth is that the boatmen in Alexandria are paid to bring us, the unwanted babies from the brothels, but Mother believes that we need roots in order for our lives to have meaning. In a way she was right about me. I long to fly over the sea with broad wings that can carry me anywhere I want to go. When I look up into the sky I feel completely free. And this island, this temple is my nest. My heart always returns here."

So.

That evening, the priestesses gathered in the temple for a new-moon ritual. Hundreds of white candles burned on the altar, illuminating the wide room in a warm, peaceful glow. At the front of the temple, a large brass bowl rested on a dais before the altar of Isis: Isis, whose image was painted upon the reredos in the style of the Egyptians, down on one knee, her rainbow wings outstretched, her golden uraeus gleaming in the candlelight; Isis whose stone image holding her son, Horus, stood in the anteroom. Hannah found herself instantly captivated by this mother goddess, whose beauty was so soothing and strength so reassuring. But she also felt afraid, knowing her father would disapprove of her being in a strange temple before a goddess. He had raised her to believe in the Jewish God, the one God, *Yahweh*. Yet she wondered about Isis.

Before the altar, a beautiful glint of light caught Hannah's eye. On the floor were three large spheres resting in concentric circles at various syzygies. Upon the outermost circle sat a large silver sphere the size of a small child curled up in a ball. Next, and slightly larger than the first, was a sphere of beautiful hammered brass, its surface scintillating in the candlelight. The third sphere in the center was the smallest, the size of a round melon and of solid copper, its surface of mottled verdigris. "Mira," Hannah whispered, "What are those?"

Mira's lips spread into a reverent smile. "The Sacred Calendar. The large golden sphere there represents the sun. The silver one is the moon, and the copper one marks the beginnings and middles of the seasons. It is an ancient way of keeping time."

Hannah sat up on her heels to get a better view. The floor around the Sacred Calendar was exquisitely painted with the renderings of the twelve zodiac signs as well as other images of wheat, wine, fruit, and women praying and dancing. "Mother Hathora had the calendar created for us long before I came here. She is Egyptian, but studied as far as Britannia, where all the priestesses have sacred stone circles that keep time the way that this one does."

"A primitive Celestial Clock of Archimedes," whispered Hannah, thinking of Hypatia. Hannah felt indebted to Hypatia for the lyre, and so vowed she would use her time on the island for songwriting devoted to Hypatia's philosophy. That way she would have a new repertoire when she returned to Alexandria. She hated to think *if*. Although one reassurance was she would no longer face Tarek while on Pharos. He had suffered no punishment for what he had nearly done to her, no repercussions, but then, nor had she for what she had done to him. Alizar never spoke of any of it. Tarek left on a voyage to Cyrene to help Alizar retrieve several texts from the library there. Hannah thought of the others, Jemir, Leitah, though none so much as Gideon, gutted as she was by his rejection, and the shame at her false hopes for attaining his love. How simple she had been not to realize she had been just an opportunity for him to enjoy a night of lust. To think she had even indulged the thought that he would purchase her from Alizar, that she would be his wife. She had been nothing to him, and was left with the regret that as a slave she had no way to complain about it. At least the herbs had worked their magic in keeping her uterus empty. Leitah had helped her see to that.

The temple doors opened, and a hush fell over the room as an elegant woman with long silver hair pinned up in a topknot swept gracefully into the temple, her palms held in prayer before her heart.

Mother Hathora.

High on the dais, the High Priestess's piercing gaze paused to acknowledge every face, a peaceful smile pressed upon her lips. When her eyes fell on Hannah, Hannah felt speared straight through. She swallowed and returned the gaze as best she could.

Mother Hathora bowed and the priestesses all joined their palms in front of their hearts and bowed in return. Then Mother Hathora lifted the long handle of a brass bell and tapped the brim decisively with a wooden mallet. A simple, pure note rang out and began to grow louder, resonating in the stone walls of the temple and the bones of the women. Even after she lifted the mallet from the bell the note continued to pulse in the room. When it had dissipated, the women stood and chanted. Hannah watched them from where she sat.

"Goddess guide the path of my heart," they said in Greek with their hands in prayer at their hearts. Then they brought their palms up to their foreheads. "Goddess guide the path of my mind." Then they opened their arms out to the sides and circled their palms back to their hearts saying, "Goddess guide me to the source of light."

Then Mother Hathora sat down in a limestone throne chair behind the dais and invited a spider-limbed priestess called Celesta to lead the women in the invocation of the four directions. The priestesses chanted the positions of the sun, moon, and seasons in the Sacred Calendar. When they had finished, Mother Hathora stepped back to the dais, closing her eyes. Hannah admired how her long, pale-blue robes draped around her body, giving her a graceful definition that softened her otherwise angular features. Hannah had a difficult time placing her age until she saw the Mother's hands, fingers knotted at the knuckles like the roots of her old olive tree. As if she could hear Hannah's thoughts, Mother Hathora looked straight at her. "We have a new priestess in our midst this evening. Hannah, is it?" Hannah nodded in the affirmative. "Please stand, Hannah, and receive the blessing of our temple."

Hannah slowly came to her feet, nervous at having been singled out. Then the priestesses all turned their eyes toward her and chanted, "Welcome, child of the Goddess." Hannah felt a warmth rush into her heart, and she smiled in return.

"Thank you," said Mother Hathora, lifting her hand to indicate Hannah could sit. "You have come to our temple on a fortuitous evening on the night of the dark moon, when we gather to tell the story of our beloved goddess, Isis. May she live always in your heart. She is a wise and compassionate teacher. Learn to serve her, and you will be filled by her spirit."

Two priestesses swiftly walked to the dais and removed from beneath it an enormous codex bound in vellum—a book so large it required two women to lift it. They set it on a tall stone podium surrounded by a number of candles and turned the thick pages to somewhere in the center. The candlelight glowed on the pages of the book, on Mother Hathora's pale skin, and on the metal spheres of the Sacred Calendar. She placed one hand on the book and closed her eyes as a large silver moth fluttered around her head.

"It is the Great Book," whispered Mira.

There was a long, interminable silence before Mother Hathora spoke again. When she did, her voice acquired the cadence of reading. Hannah understood little of what was spoken, but she sat enraptured just the same.

When the story reached its end, Mother Hathora closed the Great Book and smiled. While she was reading, a soft rain had begun to wet the earth, the scent of damp soil and foliage wafting into the temple.

The priestesses then joined hands and said the evening blessing and silently departed through the door leading out into the garden.

Mira turned to Hannah. "Mother Hathora is expecting you in her study," she said, pointing to the courtyard and the steps that led upward. So Hannah turned away from the group of women who were walking beneath the arbor back to the Garden House and entered the little courtyard, thankful she had not eaten much at dinner since her stomach was now churning.

Beyond the fountain lay the stairs covered in thick tangles of bougainvillea. Hannah took a deep breath and began to ascend. Partway up, she wondered how an old woman could climb such steep stairs every day. When Hannah arrived at the top, she saw a small door that was left partially open, a soft light streaming through.

"Come in, Hannah," said a voice from behind the door.

Hannah entered and stood before Mother Hathora, who was seated cross-legged in the center of the room, indicating a cushion in front of her.

The small room was without ornament. A small straw bed in the corner was positioned beside an altar of beeswax candles that were arranged on the floor beneath the one window. A teapot perched on a stand with several earthenware cups stacked beside it, and a brazier glowed in the corner. Hannah sat on the cushion and folded her hands in her lap.

Mother Hathora looked her up and down, then she slid the sleeves of her robe up to her elbows. "You are a popular girl in Alexandria."

"Pardon?"

"I received two letters about you. Both of them hailed your talent."

"Two letters? Both for me? Are you certain?"

Mother Hathora gazed into Hannah's eyes, unsure if the girl was unworldly or simply naive. Another priestess in her place, slave or no, would have already boasted of her position in the high society of Alexandria. She reached beneath her cushion and withdrew the folded letters and set them before Hannah. "I received one from your master, Alizar, and another from Hypatia in the Great Library. Both letters spoke highly of your ability in music and indicated your education should continue in this vein. Is that what you wish?"

"It is."

"Very well," Mother Hathora said, her voice without any warmth of welcoming. "But I want you to know these letters will not grant you any special privileges here. We are all equal in this temple and in the eyes of the Goddess, do you understand?"

Hannah nodded.

Mother Hathora then listed Hannah's duties in the temple, describing the schedule and her classes. "You seem like a bright girl. I think you will do well here."

Hannah was about to respond, but then the High Priestess said, "Thank you, Hannah. That is all for now." Mother Hathora lifted one arm ceremoniously, indicating the door.

———

Hannah quickly made her way back to the Garden House feeling both reassured and a little unsettled by her time with the High Priestess. The other priestesses were gathered in the common room, some chatting together by the glowing brazier, others playing merles by candlelight or painting henna designs on their ankles. They spoke in hushed voices so as not to wake the younger children.

"Hannah," Mira waved. She was seated beside two girls who did not look up from their conversation. One had hair the color of autumn's richest red, and Hannah thought of Synesius's maps and the people he had described from Britannia and wondered how this girl had come to be so far from home. Gulls seemed unlikely.

Several of the women wanted to know about Hannah's life outside the temple, how she became a slave, and what languages she spoke, while the rest seemed content to ignore her presence, secretly sneaking glances at her when they thought she was unaware.

Hannah crawled into bed that night beneath a shaft of moonlight that spilled through the little rectangular window high in the wall, spreading a cool glow over the bedcovers. The day had gone as well as could be expected, and yet she felt even more imprisoned. The cold bronze collar at her throat choked her tears. This was not her home.

Home was a field without a roof, and the sound of goat bells tinkling in the afternoon as the black-faced sheep and sprightly lambs trotted across the rugged slopes, her father calling to her across the meadow. Home was a thousand stars trailing through the sky in late summer above the humped shoulders of Mount Sinai as the locusts whirred.

Home was far away, and never, never again.

18

The morning passed quickly with her new chores. After writing two short letters to say she arrived safely, one to Alizar and the other to Gideon, Hannah joined the redhead named Ursula to feed the chickens and carry wood to stoke the fire in the kitchens that would heat the breakfast porridge for the children.

Elder priestesses bent over the flowerbeds, talking as they clipped the dead leaves from the plants. One of them stood and walked past the window. She was a striking beauty with gentle eyes and straight blonde hair that fell around her face and down her back. Her rose-bud lips did not seal completely over her large front teeth, which made her look far too kissable for a woman devoted to a life of celibacy. Hannah watched her as she tossed grain to the chickens. She seemed perfectly poised and serene, at once of the world and beyond it. Hannah tried not to stare, but she had never seen such hair before. True, Hypatia's locks were golden, but this woman had hair the color of clouds. The priestess picked up a tall *hydria*, balanced it effortlessly on one shoulder and drifted to the other end of the yard to pour water on the herbs.

Mira appeared at Hannah's side, her arms full of dirty bowls. "Could you help me carry these into the kitchen?"

Hannah nodded, still watching the unnamed priestess lean over the water trough, supple as a willow branch, to set the pitcher on the ground. "Who is she, Mira? I do not remember seeing her yesterday."

Mira smiled. "Iris. She is the eldest among us. She lives in the temple loft, in the room above the bell."

Mira took the dishes from Hannah's arms, set them on the counter, and hurriedly drew her into a back corner of the kitchen. "You must promise not to share with anyone what I am about to tell you," she whispered. Hannah nodded. "We have it on the wind that Kolossofia Master Junkar has announced his death."

"Announced his death? What?" Hannah wrinkled her brow in confusion.

Mira pressed her finger to her lips. "It is still a secret," she whispered. "Master Junkar is one of the Nuapar masters. No one knows for certain, but if it is true, the Kolossofia coronation will take place soon. The coronations of the High Priestess of Isis and the Kolossofia only happen once every hundred years. I have always dreamed I would be there. It is so grand!"

Hannah nodded, not fully understanding. How could anyone announce their own death?

Mira pulled Hannah deeper into the corner, not wanting to risk her explanation being overheard. "The ritual is ancient and has very specific meanings. We do not know for certain if the rumor is true, but Mother Hathora will announce it soon if it is. How I long to be the bride of the sacred rite!" Mira squealed and then quieted herself.

"A bride?" Hannah whispered. "I thought the monks take vows of celibacy."

Mira smiled. "The rite is the highest honor a priestess can be given. Her name is remembered forever, written in the Great Book, the one Mother Hathora was reading from last night."

Hannah stiffened at the thought. She knew the Christian punishment for the rites of the pagans.

The meditation bell rang, and they performed the ritual gestures. Then it was time to go to the *tholos*.

As they wound their way down the trail, Hannah paused on the hilltop overlooking the sea. A husky voice several steps behind her said, "You must be Hannah."

Hannah turned around and politely introduced herself to a beautiful, round-hipped Egyptian woman who was smiling cheerfully. A significant golden hoop shone from the septum of her nose, and bangles ran down the length of both arms. As she spoke, her breasts heaved up and down. "My name is Su. I teach *Raks-sharqi*, the temple dance."

"A pleasure to meet you." Hannah returned the smile, admiring Su's jewelry. Hannah had noticed that it was the tribal people in Alexandria, the Egyptians and Bedouins and other pagans, who were the most heavily pierced and adorned. Bodily decorations were less popular among the Greek-speaking upper class who chose simple, though valuable, rings and necklaces.

From down the path came the sound of a drum and then the shrill ululation of a female voice. All the priestesses responded by cupping a hand over their lips and joining their voices.

The women gathered in the center of the *tholos*, putting on their finger cymbals beside a large trunk of colorful costumes and scarves of eastern silk.

Hannah donned a costume with Mira's help, one piece at a time. The cut of the blouse left her belly bare while the neckline scooped down between her breasts with ties that crisscrossed in the back. The entire costume was strung with beads that hung at specific positions for the emphasis of the dance. Su tied two gold tassels to her hips.

Hannah felt as foppish as a peacock, although she was by no means the most decorated of the women. Mira had spent two years beading her costume in the theme of the ocean with rows of little seashells and bright abalone chips strung to a belt that hung low on her hips. Many of the other girls had also embellished their costumes along a theme—fire, wind, trees, and birds like swans and peacocks were the most popular.

The dance lesson proved to be just as challenging as Hannah expected. Su had to keep reminding her to look up. "You cannot look at your hips, Hannah. You have to feel them."

There was so much to concentrate on simultaneously that Hannah found the moment she got one movement correct she forgot everything else. When she remembered to move her eyes, she forgot to circle her ribcage, or circled too quickly. When she remembered her ribcage she forgot to bend her knees. Then her arms were just flung out at crooked angles as she tried to consider where she was stepping. Once she stepped on Su's foot by mistake. Su just chuckled and pushed her back into the line of twirling priestesses.

After they paused for water, Su asked Mira if she would mind demonstrating the sword dance. Hannah learned from Ursula then that Mira had a special talent for balancing things on her head while she danced: swords, candles, bowls, and anything else she could find. "Mira was born a dancer. You will see," said Ursula.

The priestesses made a circle around Mira, and the doumbek slowed to a heartbeat. Su began to sing as a nearby priestess called Renenet played an Egyptian reed flute. Mira picked up a silver sword and set the blade on her head to find the exact point of balance before she let it go, and then she began to ripple her belly and slowly twirl her hands, using the bells on her ankles to bring emphasis to the beat, the sword floating in the air as Mira's anguine-like body undulated beneath it. She had a light smile on her lips and a way of flitting her eyes at precisely the perfect moment in the song to emphasize a word or a movement she was doing. She circled slowly, hypnotically swaying her hips from side to side, and then came down gently to her knees, shimmying her shoulders wildly as the sword remained perfectly still on her head to the delight of the other priestesses, who clapped and cheered. Then, with tremendous control, Mira dropped down to her elbows and began to roll all the way over from her belly to her back in a wide circle, again and again, without the sword so much as slipping. Hannah was spellbound, never imagining that such a thing was even possible. Then slowly, Mira made her way back up, one little movement at a time, until she was standing fully upright, snaking her body from side to side, her arms raised. Her amber eyes moved side to side like a cat's, never revealing too much. As Mira brought her hands to her heart, the drumbeat stopped, and Su lifted the sword from the top of her head.

So.

Hannah met the rest of her teachers in the afternoon, all of whom were priestesses at the House of Secrets. None treated her as a slave, but as an equal, since there were more than a few slaves in the temple, owing to the fact that many of their masters wanted to increase the value of their investment; one slave who could write was worth two who could not. Many of the subjects proved to be quite fascinating. From Daphne in a class on herbs and medicine, Hannah learned how to draw pain out of someone's body with her hands, how kava root tea relaxed the mind, and how raspberry leaves toned the uterus for childbirth. In astronomy, she learned the signs of the zodiac and their corresponding elements. There were a thousand things to take her mind from the pain of her father's death, of Gideon's rejection, and she was relieved to have so much to do.

After supper the following day, Mother Hathora called a special meeting in the temple for all the priestesses. Mira pressed her hands to her heart. "This is it," she said. "I can feel it. Praise the Goddess!"

Hannah had no idea how to respond.

Mira went on in her rapture. "Oh, Hannah, I have prayed all my life to dance for the Kolossofia coronation. I know I will be chosen as his bride. It is why I dance. It is my destiny."

Hannah looked around the temple, seeing that Mira was not the only one with such dreams, which were dancing in the eyes of every priestess in the temple.

"I find it difficult keeping secrets from you, especially as I train you to sharpen your intuition." Mother Hathora laughed. She stood at the dais, the altar of beeswax candles behind her casting a halo of golden light about her shoulders. "It seems I am telling you this evening what you already know. Kolossofia Master Junkar has announced his death."

Waves of gasps and sighs swept through the temple.

Mother Hathora called for silence. "The Coronation of the Kolossofia will come this Yule, the winter solstice. We have much to do. New robes must be sewn, music composed, and dances rehearsed. Elder priestesses, please take one of these young women under your wing as a younger sister. They will need your help in preparation, as they will not have time to do everything themselves. We have only two turns of the moon." Mother Hathora nodded and smiled, clearly delighted in the coming festivities. "That is all."

Outside, walking back down the path to the Garden House, the women could not contain themselves. They squealed and hugged and twirled circles in the orchard.

Hannah fell behind the other priestesses, not knowing where her place was. She felt excluded but not particularly disappointed. She hoped there would be a way to avoid participation in the ceremony, perhaps by offering to clean the temple that night. Hannah leaned her head against a cold pillar and watched the other women from a distance, her arms folded beneath her breasts. She had waited for return letters from Alizar and Gideon, but none had come. She felt forgotten.

"Hannah?" someone asked. Startled, Hannah unfolded her arms and looked around. There to her left stood the graceful woman Hannah had seen in the orchard that morning.

"Yes?"

"I heard you singing this morning," she said. "The song was beautiful. You have a heavenly voice. My name is Iris."

"Thank you." Hannah had awakened before dawn to slip into the garden to sing and had thought no one else awake.

"The ceremony is a great honor for us."

"Not for me," Hannah said.

"You will change your mind, I can assure you," Iris declared.

"But I have no talent in dance. Besides I am a slave. Surely we are not expected to participate."

"I will help you with your dancing," said Iris, her words falling like autumn leaves that spin as they catch the breeze. "And you are only a slave if you allow yourself to think it."

Hannah remembered the way that Iris had glided through the garden like a swan. How much she wanted to be able to move like that. "Thank you. Your words are very kind."

Iris smiled, her lips parting like pillowy clouds for the sun. "I see something in you that you do not even know is there. And besides, I love to sing, and you might teach me some of your songs."

Hannah nodded. "I would teach you."

"You will have to work hard, but I think you can succeed." Iris smiled, placing her hand on Hannah's back, behind her heart. "I will be your sister."

 19

Iris proved a worthy teacher. When Hannah could not execute the movement of the veil correctly, Iris would demonstrate with an effortless ease that came with years of practice. Again and again they rehearsed the dance until Iris could begin to see Hannah's natural grace emerge through her stumbling.

"Slow your steps. Good, now slow your breath. Use your eyes more. Yes, like that. Your thumb and middle finger should long for one another like two separated lovers. No, no. Let me show you." Then finally, "Good."

After the practice sessions were finished, often well into the night, Hannah and Iris would sit in the cool grass and sing together. Iris had a plain but lovely voice, and soon they were able to practice some of the Pythagorean harmonics, sometimes singing familiar songs, but more often simply improvising together.

As the weeks ushered the isle of Pharos ever closer to Yule, Iris could see that Hannah still fell far behind the rest of the priest-esses in her dancing. Iris insisted they meet every night instead of every other night so she could help Hannah work through her awkwardness, and sometimes they stayed in the *tholos* to prac-tice for hours after sunset. The rehearsing coupled with Hannah's regular workload proved exhausting. She struggled to stay awake in her afternoon classes and often collapsed on her bed in the evening without supper.

One moonless evening, Hannah and Iris met and worked on the movements as a cold rain burst down upon them and a flock of migrating white pelicans swept down from the sky and took refuge between the columns. The fatigued birds rested as the women pressed on well into the night. Hannah was learning the shimmy and would not rest until she got her hips and shoulders to swivel and dip. The rain poured down her cheeks and her chest, wetting her arms, her belly, her face. The costume clung like wet petals to her skin, and her breath fogged the air. Still she pressed on. The soles of her feet were bruised, and her low back ached, but she was confident she could find the movement in her body before it was time for bed.

Sometimes she imagined her father could watch her and that he would clap to the beat of the drum. Her father who would never see her free to marry or bear children. Hannah often thought of the past, of the night she was captured. It was hard to picture a future she wanted any part of now, so this would have to be enough.

Sometime deep in the night after their practice session had ended, Hannah found herself walking through the garden and then toward the temple. She tried the doors and found them unlocked. The anteroom of the temple, illuminated in candle-light, held an immense stone statue of the goddess Isis seated on a throne with her baby Horus on her lap, her lips curled into an almost imperceptible smile. Hannah brushed the smooth stone with her fingertips. The Egyptian statue was thousands of years old and had been brought to Pharos from the upper Nile. For a moment Hannah felt she should not be there at all, even though the temple was open to worship even in the night.

Hannah lit a joss stick before the beautiful goddess and let the words of the *Shema* wash over her, bringing her peace. She had longed to spend time alone. Overhead the pocked moon, white and round, bathed the world in white light. Her father had shown her the rabbit in the moon when she was a little girl, and when she asked him why God put a rabbit in the moon and not some other creature, he had replied, "Because the rabbit is the only animal that can keep a secret, and the moon has many secrets to keep." How she missed him.

So.

With her eyes closed, Hannah listened to the sound of the surf pounding the north shore of the island. She had dreamed of making love to Gideon, his dark, mischievous eyes, his kisses, the way the muscles of his back and arms rippled like a stallion as he moved inside her. The dream had pushed her to the climax of ecstasy, and she had awoken with a start. It seemed like so long ago, yet the dream made their time together seem so recent. She wondered how he was and where Alizar had sent him to conceal the latest shipment of manuscripts from the Great Library. She wished he would write to her but knew that he would not. He did not think of her, and so she urged herself not think of him—a strategy that only brought him to mind all the more urgently.

———

That evening the *tholos* was dark and quiet as Hannah approached. Iris was already there, setting candles at the base of the columns and lighting a frankincense joss stick from them. Mira was also there with Ursula, Daphne, and Hepsut.

"Hannah, I am glad you are here." Iris gave her a hug.

"Do you have any music for us?" asked Renenet as she fidgeted with a loose tassel on her hip.

Hannah closed her eyes and drifted back to a bright morning sitting beside Naomi where she had composed a new song that carried a sprightly rhythm. The melody was right there waiting for her.

The priestesses began to explore the movements that the song inspired in them. When Hannah finished and opened her eyes the women stopped dancing and broke out in joyful applause.

"Oh, Hannah, it is simply perfect!" Ursula clapped her hands, excited as a child.

"It is your most beautiful melody yet," said Iris, beaming with pride.

"What language are the lyrics?" asked Renenet. "I love the melody, but I would like to know the meaning."

"It is Aramaic, they—"

"Oh, I disagree completely," Mira interrupted. "I prefer not knowing the meaning. We do not want anything to take away from the beauty of the dance. The music should compliment, not distract."

As the priestesses fell into discussion, Hannah could tell that it was going to take hours to come to any definite decisions, and then more time to teach the other priestesses the dance, and still more time for practice. Yet, Yule was fast approaching. What she did not know was that the dance of the priestesses was simply one strand in a tapestry of an ornate ceremony that would take three days to complete. The priestesses were only to play a part on the last evening.

Hannah wondered when she would be able to speak to Mother Hathora about not participating. But they never had a moment alone together. At least the island was still free of Christians who had not yet made it their place to cross the harbor. But for how long?

So.

The weeks before the ceremony passed in a wink.

Dreading the night before her, Hannah chose a swath of peacock blue chiffon silk for her veil and began to sew tiny glass beads along the hem and corners in an Egyptian design, but she kept making mistakes and would have to pull out a day's worth of work and start the pattern anew.

Preparations for the ceremony consumed everyone in the temple. The most tedious and arduous of all the tasks, however, also proved to be the most enjoyable. The day before the ceremony, the priestesses filled an enormous tile bath beside the Garden House with water heated in large kettles over open flames. Since there was no wood on the island, a request was sent across the harbor for ten loads of firewood to be shipped from Alexandria. Hauling the firewood up the hill from the beach on their backs was a grueling process that took all the women and the older girls an entire day.

Hannah and Mira filled the bath every hour, draining the cold dirty water and then refilling it again with hot clean water boiled on the fire. The sky outside was cold and damp, so standing beside the fire was not such a terrible duty to have. The sunken tile bath in the garden was large enough for three priestesses at once, so they sang songs and washed each other's backs like mermaids in a warm sea. Even the youngest children delighted in the midwinter bathing ritual.

Finally, Yule drew near.

The angel, so near to earth, grew heavy with anticipation. The door had been promised. The warrior would come.

On the first night of the three-day Kolossofia coronation ceremony, with their own part still two days off, Mira and Hannah snuck away to the hill behind the moon hollow to watch the bonfire on the beach in front of the Temple of Poseidon.

Far off on the west side of the island, elder Master Junkar climbed to the top of a stack of wood and took a cross-legged seat to allow the flames consume his bones, his flesh. His spirit in exalted meditation, fearing nothing, took to the sky. Hannah squeezed Mira's hand as a fearsome wind picked up from the north, blowing wildly all through the night until sunrise brought a profound stillness to the island, revealing the wind's mischief in all the flowers and decorations strewn across the land.

So.

Two days later, during the short daylight hours of Yule, the priestesses rose early and prepared themselves meticulously for

the ceremony by making last minute alterations to their costumes
and plaiting their hair with flowers, rehearsing the steps for the
dances in their minds as they smeared sweet smelling amber
resin into their navels and painted their eyes, feet, and hands with
henna.

They were ready.

———————

The priestesses wound out the courtyard gate and down the side
of the hill, a snake of light, the *ching!ching!ching!* of shiny bangle
bracelets, anklets, earrings, and other adornments ringing in the
night. The air was cool and pleasant for the first night of winter,
but Hannah noticed a squall forming over the ocean. Occasionally
there was the boom of distant thunder and a flash of light across
the water. Hannah could taste the approach of rain in the air and
hoped that they would reach the other side of the island before the
storm.

As the veiled priestesses led by Mother Hathora reached the
north shore of the island, their bare feet sunk into the soft white
sand, cold and electric. All across the beach little wavelets spat
phosphorescent green sparks on the shore that flickered and
danced, then disappeared. Hannah marveled at the beauty. Before
them stood the Temple of Poseidon, its pale blue spire rising up
to heaven, bonfires lit all around its circumference, the scent of
roasted meat filling the air. The thumping of the little waves
seemed to grow louder as the priestesses approached, as if to
announce their arrival.

Up ahead, fifty or so men dressed in long black ceremonial
robes made two long rows to greet the priestesses on the beach,
men who, as they had been instructed, averted their eyes from the
faces of the women as they entered the temple. Hannah let her
eyes drift down to her painted feet and then flicker up to the enormous brass bowls of freshly slaughtered bull's blood set in offering

beside the temple doors, the dank metallic scent soaking the air. Torches leapt upward, smoke licking the sky as they passed.

The adytum of the Temple of Poseidon was surprisingly warm and beautifully decorated in long murals created by the monks to tell the story of the Nuapar legend. One radiant figure had been painted in lotus posture atop a funeral pyre, and Mira whispered to Hannah that he had to be Kalanos, the Indian mystic who founded the Nuapar. Beside him stood a tall, clean-shaven man reading a green tablet, whom Mira thought must be Alexander the Great. The ceiling had been painted meticulously in the Egyptian tradition to depict Nut, the goddess of the night sky. In truth, the ceiling had been painted over a century prior, but it had faded quite badly, so the monks had decided to retouch it for the ceremony.

The priestesses entered the grand hall of the temple and sat in the front row for the invocation ceremony, the monks filling the rest of the temple behind them. The energy in the room was charged with anticipation and the electrifying forbidden pleasure of breaking the customary separation between monks and priestesses. When Hannah lifted her eyes to the podium where a giant clam shell rested open, she was pleasantly surprised to see a familiar face looking out over the sea of monks and priestesses. Julian. The elegant monk she had met in Hypatia's study.

She inhaled sharply and looked away. Julian. Could he be the one they had come to dance for, the new Kolossofia Master? So this was *his* coronation ceremony. What had he said about completing the final rites? Perhaps his training had led to this moment. She traced his body with her eyes, taking in each detail. He looked more regal than when she had first seen him. His long black hair had been swept up into a topknot on the crown of his head, and his eyes were the same ocean green that she remembered. He wore a long black robe pinned at the shoulder, meticulously tied with the wide red sash. He looked utterly serene standing beside Master Savitur, whose robes were identical to Julian's except for two small details: Savitur wore a large star ruby ring on the middle finger of his left hand, and a thin white sash decorated with Egyptian amulets bound the center of his red waist sash.

"Welcome, daughters of Isis, to our temple for the crowning of Kolossofia master, Junkar. I am Master Savitur." The old man stood still as a cat. "Tonight we begin the coronation of our new master with three rituals. One, the conquest of his new name. Choosing his weapon, he must defeat me in a duel. Then if he lives," Savitur bowed to the priestesses, "*The Dance of Many Veils*. Our new master will be given his title and sealed with his chosen priestess in the lighthouse."

Sealed. Hannah shuddered. It made it sound as if the couple would be entombed together. She stole a glance down the row of priestesses to gauge their reactions, but they all sat perfectly serene, their kohl-lined eyes sparkling with excitement, each longing to be chosen.

Savitur bowed, and the monks and priestesses all bowed in return. Then Savitur bowed again, and his audience again returned his bow. Then Savitur bowed a third time and began to giggle. He was playing with them like a mischievous child.

"Come. To the Posidium," he said, and everyone rose and filed outside. They were led to a narrow amphitheatre that jutted up from the wide courtyard encircled by columns and invited to sit. Savitur strode to the center of the courtyard as a row of torches mysteriously lit behind him. From the other side of the courtyard Julian approached, his outer robes removed to reveal a sleeveless black *tunica*, his black Persian pants drawn at the ankles for freedom of movement, a quarterstaff in his strong hands. They faced one another and bowed again as a horn sounded from behind them.

"Have you chosen your weapon?" asked Savitur.

Julian nodded reverently. "Yes, Master Savitur," he said, twirling the long staff in his hands.

"Very good. This duel shall be won when one of us delivers the death blow." As Savitur spoke the words, his eyes glittered playfully in the light.

Hannah looked to Mira. Surely the men would not fight each other to the death? But Mira was engrossed in what was happening before her and did not return the glance.

There was a dramatic pause as two other monks approached with long black sashes draped across their hands. They bound the blindfolds snug over the men's eyes and then handed Savitur a staff of equal length to Julian's, iron spears on the tips.

Hannah felt unsure of how a duel would be fought between two blindfolded men. Surely there had to be some mistake.

Savitur and Julian bowed to each other one last time, and then the horn sounded. Julian raised his staff instinctively but made no move to attack. He let his breath extend to the blunt tips of the long staff as he invited his root energy in the base of his spine to ascend into his belly, his heart, the center of his forehead. The yoga techniques brought to Pharos by the mystic Kalanos from the caves of India had taught him how to redirect this powerful energy, and now his test had come.

Savitur lifted his staff smoothly, poised for the moment of first contact. Stillness enveloped the two men, as if no one else was present. Then Julian cut in and swung the first blow, but his staff whistled through the empty air. He swung twice more, but each time Savitur ducked or stepped back from the staff's reach as though he could see it perfectly.

Hannah was astonished. Beside her, Mira let out a little gasp.

Julian spun sideways and extended his staff, and this time the two staffs smacked. Sensing an opening, Julian advanced with formidable intensity that would have toppled any other opponent, but Savitur parried the blows effortlessly and then slunk back into the shadows and disappeared.

Julian crouched in the courtyard, turning slowly, waiting for Savitur's attack, using his other senses to hone in on his opponent. Suddenly Savitur sprang from above, his staff aimed at Julian's shoulder in a downward thrust, but Julian managed to roll and dodge the blow.

The two opponents circled each other slowly, as though walking on opposite sides of a wheel. Though Julian had trained for this moment extensively, he still did not know how he would succeed in besting his teacher. Savitur had the spring of a stag in his agile step and the severity and power of a tiger's deadly lunge in his blows. So far as Julian knew, no one had ever beaten him . . . or had they?

Perhaps sensing Julian's questioning thoughts, Savitur twirled his staff at a low angle to knock him off his feet. The staff nicked Julian's ankle, but he leapt out of the way, landing on his knees and then springing to his feet. He was only off balance for an instant, but the cleverness of his teacher fanned his hunger to win. Suddenly he burst in with a loud yell, and there was a blur of staffs as the two men fought and parried. Julian managed to back Savitur into a corner of the courtyard and smiled to himself, feeling the advantage, but then Savitur turned one end of his staff to the ground and vaulted to the rooftop.

There was a gasp from the monks and priestesses that muffled the sound of Savitur's gentle landing on the roof. Julian turned his head to one side, listening. Sensing that Savitur had leapt, he turned his own staff and followed him up to the roofline, losing his balance for a moment as he landed and then righting himself.

Savitur burst in immediately and went for low cuts to Julian's knees to try to knock him off balance. Then his head. Then his knees. The cuts came high low, high low, attempting to confuse his student. Julian leapt several times and then ducked to avoid a staff blow to his skull. The energy around the fighters began to whirl. The flash of staffs created circular patterns like flowers of light in the air. Julian focused on his breath while parrying and looking for openings. He took a blow to the shoulder that caught him off balance for a moment, but he responded by snatching Savitur's staff and giving it a yank to throw him. Savitur tumbled forward with the flow of the jolt, and then stood, quickly regaining his center.

Thunder crackled in the distance as the storm drew nearer. A roost of starlings in the palms beside the temple suddenly erupted into flight and swept in low over the rooftop, a black veil of wings. For a moment the fighters were concealed. When the birds passed, Julian struck for the elder Kolossofia master, but Savitur returned the trick and grabbed his staff and hurdled Julian off the roof. Julian spun a back flip and landed on his feet, but without a weapon.

Fight with a weapon and risk that it will be used against you, the voice echoed in Julian's mind. Then Savitur sprung down from the roof. He dashed forward and struck out with a flying kick, but Julian caught his heel and sent him spinning backward. Savitur flipped and landed on his feet, his agility never faltering.

Seeing the men fight, Hannah's fears of the Parabolani appearing at the ceremony evaporated. Apparently, what happened on the island of Pharos was of no interest to them, and if it was, surely these well-trained warriors were more than suited to fight and win. Why had they not entered Alexandria to fight the Christians before? Still, Hannah felt some relief knowing they stood as sentries to protect the Great Library. And Hypatia. Now she only wondered how the fight would ever end with two opponents so well matched. Mira apparently shared her thought, because she looked over at Hannah with questions in her golden eyes. Would they wait all night?

Though no one in the audience could perceive it, at that moment in the duel, both men engaged the mental powers for which the Kolossofia were known. Capable of projecting an image of himself into his opponent's mind, Savitur lunged forward and Julian parried the projection. He took a jab to his ribcage and doubled over, spreading his hands on the stone cobbles of the courtyard as his topknot came undone, his long black hair spilling down around his shoulders. Then Julian realized what was happening and set a cloak over his mind. Savitur circled him playfully, a light smile upon his lips.

Coming to his feet, Julian extended his senses beyond his body and felt for Savitur's presence. As he did so, a world began to open behind his eyelids as though he had just stepped through a door. Suddenly he could not just sense but actually *see* the entire courtyard with its lanterns lit, the monks and priestesses watching him. Savitur stood before him, smiling. Julian was so perplexed that he actually reached up to check his blindfold, but it was still secure.

There is no division between us now, Julian, your eyes are my eyes, your body my body. You must let die within you what would dim your vision, and when you do, you will find the open door. The voice of Savitur resonated in the hollows of Julian's mind.

From his depths a great rush of light flooded Julian's heart and filled the chasm there with ecstatic sensation. The energy consumed him, overwhelmed him. His whole body began to shake. He heard the words of the Emerald Tablet in his mind: *Join earth to heaven, heaven to earth . . . learn to live in both worlds equally.*

The meridians of his heart pulsing with renewed life, Julian swung his staff in a full circle and as it whistled past his ear, he swung full force at Savitur and the staff connected with his neck. There was a sickening crack, and the old master fell to the ground, his head at a twisted angle to his body.

Julian tugged his blindfold from his eyes, suddenly despondent. He knelt beside the body of Savitur, picking up his hand and pressing it to his cheek. What would happen now? Savitur had no successor.

But as Julian held his hand, the skin of the corpse began to glow and pulsate, and then finally there was a burst of light from within the chest cavity of the body, and then it was gone. The robe where Savitur had been lay empty and shapeless on the ground.

Julian sat up, confused. He looked around at the monks and priestesses. Then there was a gasp from the audience, but it was too late. Master Savitur stood above Julian with a staff and pierced him cleanly in the sternum. Julian crumpled forward and lay dead on the ground. Savitur raised the staff overhead, then set it down. The audience might have cheered, but they were now completely confused. Where had Savitur come from? Was this some magician's trick? Had he been standing in the shadows the entire time?

The enemy you must fight now is death. The words rang in Julian's mind, though he no longer knew where he was. *A true Kolossofia Master knows his immortality. Death does not exist.*

Julian floated a short length above his body, watching the scene unfold. He knew that the Kolossofia Masters sometimes dematerialized themselves bodily, but he had never encountered any text or teaching about the technique. As far as he knew, it was not achievable, till now.

Seconds lengthened into minutes. No one moved. The corpse of Julian lay on the ground to everyone around him. But in the ethers, Julian struggled to reclaim his body, his center, his light attempting to pour into a broken vessel. He called out to his teacher, but there was no inner answer. Above Julian, the full moon appeared from behind the clouds.

And then he knew.

Julian set his intention on the moon, recalling certain passages from the writings of Hermes Trismagistus. He willed himself to pass through the moon. He willed himself alive on the other side.

Suddenly the body of Julian began to shimmer and glow, and then there was another blinding flash, and it too was gone.

Every gasped and looked around.

Suddenly, Julian stood beside Savitur, alive and unharmed.

Savitur strode forward, removed his own blindfold, and placed his hand upon Julian's shoulder. "I take from you this name of Julian and bequeath to you your new name. From dawn tomorrow you will be known as Master Junkar, defender of peace. Now you understand that fighting only spawns more fighting. Anger, more anger. Hatred, more hatred. In your death you have found the greatest lesson, immortal life." Savitur helped Julian to his feet, and they bowed deeply to one another, eyes blossoming with kindness. Julian's heart had been purified, attaining the highest level of a warrior's mastery.

Chills swept through Hannah. She regretted that she would never be able to tell Synesius of that moment. Surely the monks had reason to keep their ceremonies a secret, but it seemed such a tragedy to keep it from Synesius, who would have rejoiced with his brother in his new title. But Mother Hathora had made them promise, giving their word to never speak of the rites.

Master Savitur crossed the courtyard to an urn set on a stone pillar. "These are the ashes of Master Junkar, who gave up his body. Julian, as his successor, do you accept the honor of carrying them to the far mountains of India to the sacred burial site?"

Julian nodded. "I do."

 **20**

In the dim temple archways, monks and priestesses held their breath, nervously anticipating the final rite in the coronation ceremony.

Savitur's commanding voice cut through the quiet temple. All eyes trained on him. "Tonight, in utmost reverence, we call upon the priestesses of Isis to perform for our new master *The Dance of Many Veils*, that one may be chosen as his bride of the sacred rite."

Savitur bowed and winked at Julian, who sat patiently on a silk cushion near the front of the temple, his shirt removed, his thick black hair braided like a rope down his back, a string of shining garnet beads resting against his smooth, tanned chest. Encircling him were the abundant offerings of the ceremony: moist breads and cakes on silver plates, glass vials of the finest Arabian oils, golden pitchers of milk, bowls filled with ruby pomegranate seeds, apples, dates, olives, berries, and shells, while rich Egyptian frankincense dusted the air with its sultry smoke. Julian sat, poised upon the edge of his cushion, awaiting the entrance of the priestesses while several monks behind him tested their musical instruments. One tuned a kanun while another fingered his flute, as beside him two others smacked their doumbeks with several loud slaps. There were pillows to be adjusted, drum skins to be tightened, strings to be changed, until finally, the monks were ready. With a nod from the kanun player, the drummers began to tap out a rhythm to invite the priestesses to enter.

Hannah shivered. She reminded herself that this was merely an hour, something she could fake her way through until they were able to leave. She thought of Gideon, wishing she could dance for him instead. The hours of the night had stretched longer and longer. She remembered her warm bed and longed to sleep. A yawn escaped her lips. Still, she must sing well, so she pinched her cheeks and took a breath.

Veiled and barefoot, *ching!ching!ching!ching!*, the priestesses streamed into the temple, their silken skin gleaming in the candlelight, kohl-lined eyes peering over the colorful veils that hid their faces. Some held candles in their palms while others kept the rhythm with delicate brass finger cymbals. Their arms swayed, bare and bangled, jewels in their navels glinting as they turned in the amber light, bodies undulating with the ease of swirling smoke.

The line of twenty-one priestesses approached the front of the temple and turned in a slow figure-eight formation before Julian, hips swinging playfully, eyes smiling flirtatiously, polished toenails flashing like cut gems from beneath the chimerical cloth of their costumes.

Hannah could scarcely believe she was participating in such a ritual. The excitement of the dance moved in her, yet she felt torn from her origins; whether or not she was Roman or Jew did not matter. She knew who she was, and she was the daughter of Kaleb of Sinai. She reminded herself that she could participate in the ceremony as an actor, as someone giving a marvelous performance, and this quieted her nerves.

Julian was hypnotized by the beauty before him, in awe of the women and their flexibility, their radiance. He wondered how he would ever choose from among them. He looked into their eyes. Languid, mysterious eyes. Some fluttered their eyelashes at him while some winked; others moved their eyes side to side like calm, Egyptian cats.

Hannah, at the very end of the line, concentrated on the flow of the steps she had practiced so many times. Every few measures, she had to remind herself not to hold her breath. Several times her toes caught the end of the veil of the priestess beside her, but fortunately, she managed not to trip. Her throat dry and hands trembling, she could not help but notice how Mira, directly in front of her, danced with effortless ease and flawless rhythm, not a single bead of sweat upon her golden brow, while Hannah could already feel the droplets trickling down her spine.

Hannah lifted her arms as the women spiraled into three circles, and then into one. When again they fell into rows, the priestesses ululated as the monks slapped the doumbeks to signal the end of the first dance. Hannah froze in position, as did the others, her chest rising and falling with breath. All she could hear was the throbbing of her heart in her temples. She wet her lips, tasting the moist salt with her tongue as her eyes flicked to Julian, who sat between the candles. He looked so peaceful, so at ease. She wondered how he planned to choose.

As the rhythm started up again, Hannah closed her eyes to center herself. At the music's invitation, she felt the song she had composed rise into her throat. She inhaled, and then parted her lips.

The instant she began to sing, Hannah felt a magical strength pour into her limbs.

The angel swooned.

Somehow, all Hannah's anxiety melted away, untangled like a net from her bones. Never had her voice responded so effortlessly, so intricately, to the strength she thrust into each note. Never had she felt her heart come alive within the music so fully. She closed her eyes in ecstasy and let the song carry her higher.

Julian sat up straighter. What haunting voice was this? His eyes searched the row of priestesses, but their veils concealed her lips from view. Where was she? He looked for her as they turned before him, but he could not decipher who was singing. Even when the priestesses split into three rows, and Hannah stood so near, he did not know for certain.

Listening carefully, Julian watched the three women he thought might be the singer and decided it was probably the small priestess with the elegant frame who moved so effortlessly, the one with the golden eyes. He smiled at her, feeling the possibility that billowed between them like a sail. She returned his smile with her eyes, batting her long lashes.

Mira.

Hannah smiled, relieved. This had been what they all predicted, Mira's destiny.

The dance continued, and the priestesses fanned into one long crescent to give each woman the opportunity to step forward for a solo performance. Julian watched them all in a respectful but half-interested manner. He was waiting to see the singer, the golden priestess at the end of the row.

As soon as Mira came forward, Hannah could not take her eyes away from her friend's jeweled figure. She had never seen Mira dance as beautifully and provocatively as she did that night, indisputably the most talented of them all. She arched her back and undulated her hips as her arms floated like weightless white snakes over her smooth, naked belly. Then she slowly tiptoed closer to Julian so that he might see the dip and curve of her shapely hips as she flirtatiously flicked the tassels that hung from the sides of her belt, letting him see the valley between the domes of her golden breasts. She held everyone in the temple spellbound.

Julian was captivated by Mira's movements, but as she approached, he listened. To his surprise, the melody seemed to be coming not from her, but from behind her. He leaned forward and listened again until he was convinced his ears were not deceiving him. No, this priestess was not the one with the angelic voice. She was not the one. He sat back, and his smile dimmed.

As Mira stepped back into the line and struck her final pose, Hannah swallowed hard. It was her turn. If only she had been allowed to remain behind and clean the temple. This was sure to be a disaster.

From within the music, Hannah lifted her eyes, dropped her shoulders, and let her long thin fingers float up to the sky. At last she felt herself relax into the shapes her body was making, letting the dance flow through her. The other priestesses watching were impressed with how far she had come in such a short time, though she still had a beginner's lack of articulation.

Julian closed his eyes. Here, undoubtedly, was the singer. True, she did not have the flamboyance of the other priestess with the golden eyes, but her movements were smooth, and the curve of her waist, the shining skin of her flat belly, her full breasts, he found as irresistible as her voice.

Hannah looked at Julian and then closed her eyes. But with her eyes closed, suddenly Hannah tripped on her veil and stumbled, sending gasps through the audience. She righted herself quickly and tried to find her place in the steps. Would the dreadful dance never end? She cursed beneath her veil and kept singing. Julian chuckled.

At the song's conclusion Hannah sustained the last note as long as her breath would last. In the silence that followed, her arms fell softly to her sides, and she opened her eyes and met Julian's intense gaze. Heat flashed through her body like the quick, trembling fingers of lightning.

Those dark blue eyes, the feline shape of them, he had seen them before, but he could not remember where. They seemed familiar. From that moment, Julian watched only the priestess with the azure veil, remembering the rapturous melody that poured from her throat like enchanted birdsong.

So.

The priestesses danced one final piece, a fast-paced rhythm with a happy turn. Hips swishing, wrists twisting, eyes smiling, they made a long line that brought the women close to where the new master sat upon his cushion so that he could smell their perfumed skin and be pleased by the way the light played upon the luscious curves of their young bodies.

They concluded with a deliberate crescendo: bangles, breasts, and tassels jiggling in a wild shimmy. Finally, the doumbek players struck the drumheads three times, and the dance ended. The priestesses gathered together swiftly, collarbones rising and falling as they caught their breath.

Savitur nodded to Julian from where he sat in the window of the temple. It was time to choose.

Julian rose gracefully to his feet and clasped his hands behind his back. He started at the far end of the line and walked slowly, deliberately, before the women.

Mother Hathora watched him from the rear of the temple, hands folded, eyebrows lifted. She had been predicting the girl he would choose.

As Julian swept down the line past the priestesses, Hannah held her breath and looked down. Beside her, Mira smiled beneath her veil and thrust her breasts forward to entice the new master one last time.

Julian looked into Mira's eyes and smiled, and then stepped past her, and took the fingers of the priestess beside her.

Hannah looked up.

Julian smiled and kissed her hand.

"I have made my selection," he said softly.

"And so the sacred rite begins." Savitur sprung down from the window with impossible ease, given his age, and strode over to where Hannah and Julian stood side by side.

Hannah could scarcely breathe. This could not be happening. Julian had chosen her? A silent cry of longing went out to Gideon from her heart, knowing this moment, this chance of fate, would sever their connection completely. She looked into the eyes of

Mother Hathora, the eyes of Master Savitur, and knew that she, a slave, could not refuse this gift. Julian's eyes met hers, and she remembered the man who had come to Hypatia's study that afternoon, the man she had longed to encounter again. Yes, even then this possibility had been there between them, silent and eventual. She could accept it.

Just beyond her, Mira trembled in fury, her fists clenched, and her eyes pierced Hannah with twin shafts of hatred.

So.

The elder master himself led the pair away from the temple, up a dune to a trail that snaked along the north shore of the island. They walked for ages until Hannah realized where they must be going.

The lighthouse.

Soon it loomed before them, and Hannah followed as they climbed the three hundred steps to the top, the stone cool on her feet. They entered the octagonal tower and climbed another flight of stairs, all the way to the temple at the top, crowned by the statue of Poseidon. On the level just beneath them, the mighty brass mirror cast its gleam across the sea. Hannah bowed and entered the temple high above the sea through a narrow crawl space on her knees. Julian followed her. Inside, the light of three whispering torches set at eye level softly illuminated the limestone walls of the round room. The tower had no windows except for one square in the east that let in the light of the full moon, much like those the Egyptians cut in the pyramids so the *ka* of the pharaoh might be free after his entombment.

When Hannah and Julian were both inside, two Nuapar monks stationed to guard the door pushed an enormous block of stone over the entrance with a slow scraping sound that continued ominously until the last wedge of light from the outside world had vanished.

Hannah swallowed, her throat tight and dry. Julian, though indisputably handsome, was not the man her heart longed for. She felt a familiar stab of regret, wishing she were elsewhere. Still, perhaps this would be an opportunity to heal her heart, if nothing else. Besides, it might not be unpleasant.

The room had been decorated for the ceremony with vivid bird-of-paradise flowers set in tall vases, their shadows dancing on the walls in the torchlight. On the earthen floor adjacent to the door rested a simple wool mattress blanketed with linen sheets, the skin of a tiger spread before it just as Mira had said. A brass hookah, an array of fruits, and an amphora of wine stood beside an offering of roasted meat from the slaughtered bull. The union of the sacred rite expected them to sample each and leave the rest for the gods.

Hannah trembled as she found her feet.

Julian turned toward her and, with a tender touch, raised one hand to her ear and loosened her veil, letting it fall.

He paused and regarded Hannah with a curious expression. "I remember you," he said. "We met the day I visited Lady Hypatia in her study."

Hannah nodded, still too nervous to speak.

Julian stepped back to admire the woman before him. "I had no idea you were a priestess of Isis. How beautiful you are," he said, "and you have the most heavenly voice. What is your name?"

"Hannah."

"Hannah, yes. My brother tutors you." Julian tasted the sweetness of her name on his tongue. "How did you come to be at the Temple of Isis?" As he spoke, his eyes flicked to her slave collar, but he said nothing.

"Alizar wanted me to continue my education." Hannah fingered her veil, knowing there was more she could not mention. "Synesius would have wanted to be here for your ceremony."

Julian lowered his head, his voice tinged with regret. "I asked Master Savitur to let my brother come, but Synesius is a Christian. There was no way to allow him to be here." Julian sighed. "Now I will never see him again."

"Why?"

Shadows brushed Julian's sharp cheekbones in the torchlight. "Tomorrow morning, to everyone who knew him, Julian is dead. There will even be a funeral for me, I mean, for *him*, on the north shore at sunset."

"But how can that be?"

"It is the tradition. I must cut all ties from my former life in order to best serve the Temple of Poseidon and the monks of the Nuapar as Kolossofia Master. My new name will be Junkar, same as the master who preceded me. It has been this way for centuries."

Hannah's eyes filled with compassion for Julian then, and for Synesius, who had on more than one occasion confessed to her how much he missed his brother. "How unfortunate for you, for you both."

Julian poured red wine from the amphora into a golden *rython,* then a splash of water, and handed it to Hannah. "My brother and I came to Alexandria together, did Synesius tell you? From Cyrene. When our parents died, my noble brother became a philosopher, and even went so far as the court of Constantinople to sway Emperor Arcadius to his ideas, though his favor was short lived. I became a fighter."

"A fighter?"

Julian smiled at Hannah, a tender smile of gratitude that she was interested in knowing the story of his life, realizing that this might be the last time he told it. "I was sponsored by a wealthy Greek patron who found opponents for me to fight. I was very successful, so he saw to it I had shoes and bread, and a dry loft to sleep in."

Hannah handed Julian the *rython*, so they might share.

Julian set it on his thigh as his chest rose with a thoughtful breath. The facts were so ugly he did not know how to share them in a way that would not offend a priestess, but he would try. "He was an angry man, my father. His fists often found our faces, especially my mother. He was a general of the Imperial Army, a drunkard, though he claimed lineage of Spartan kings. My mother, Alaya was her name, was a beautiful woman. She could not stand up to him. I was only a boy when he killed her by bringing down the blunt end of his sword on the side of her head. He suspected she was in love with another man. I had often insisted we should just run away, but then it was too late. My father died the following year when, drunk, he fell and his head struck the corner of a table in precisely the spot he hit my mother. Sy and I felt her spirit had vindicated itself and lifted his curse from our lives."

Hannah felt the welling up within her of all the injustices she had witnessed and endured, all of them cruel and unfair. "Alaya was your mother's name?"

"Yes."

"What a beautiful name."

Julian took a sip of wine, then gave her the *rython* they were drinking from. "And you, Hannah? How did you come to this island? Your accent is of the desert."

They sat cross-legged, facing one another on the tiger skin, relaxing into the space little by little as the awkwardness between them slowly dissolved with each sip of wine.

Hannah's fingers traced the bronze slave collar at her throat. "I came to Alexandria from Sinai."

"From Sinai? Is that where you learned to sing so beautifully?" Julian asked in Aramaic.

Hannah inhaled sharply, her heart warming. She had not heard the syllables of her language in many months, and he spoke eloquently and with a perfect accent. She answered him happily, and their conversation went on in her native tongue.

Hannah told him about her father and their goats and sheep, and the olive tree on the hill. She told him about the funny things she overheard in the shepherd's tents when they thought she was asleep. She told him things that she had never told anyone before, and it was liberating to let those secrets breathe in the tower where no one else could hear. But she did not tell him about the men and the road to Alexandria.

Julian listened intently as she spoke about her first impressions of Alexandria. As they spoke, the conversation wove between them like an invisible golden thread that slowly drew them closer.

Julian hung on her every word, leaning forward to hear more, and ask more questions.

Hannah blushed, continuing to speak: small memories, her childhood, moments she had forgotten until his playful questions sought them out. She found the ecstasy of the connection that flowed between them effortless, and for the first time in months, she forgot her persistent thoughts of Gideon entirely.

Eventually the storm that had been squatting on the horizon descended, and a slow, soaking rain began to wet the lighthouse. It might as well have been raining gold for the merchants in the city. Perhaps the drought would recede at last. Occasionally, a rumble of thunder overhead punctuated one of their sentences with a timing that indicated the gods might be eavesdropping. Together, they laughed.

Inside the tower, listening to the rain, Hannah traced the rim of the *rython* with one finger. There was something she had to know.

Julian could almost hear the whir of her thoughts, as though her mind was his own. "What is it?" he asked.

Her eyes darted to him, and then back to the *rython* as she nibbled her lower lip. "How did you choose?"

"How did I choose *you*, you mean?" Julian smiled, reclining back on one elbow. "It was your voice," he said. "I chose the priestess with the voice of a goddess."

Hannah felt a warm rush of blood flow into her cheeks as she released her sweetest smile.

Julian, realizing the opportunity, reached forward and touched his fingers to her knee. "Hannah, would you sing for me? Here. Just us."

"Here?" Hannah looked around.

"Why not?"

"Now?"

Julian smiled and lay back. "Yes."

She could not refuse. Smiling, he closed his eyes and listened to the way her voice lilted along, the way the rain blended into the melody. He never wanted to forget the sound of her voice. He tried to remember it in his bones so that he would always hear her singing in his heart, no matter how far apart the years took them. Sometimes perfection is offered only in a night, once.

When she finished and opened her eyes, Julian leaned forward, cupped her cheeks in his hand and kissed her lips with a gentleness that Hannah had never imagined a man could possess. Her eyes widened in surprise and then closed as she relaxed into the softness of his touch.

The angel watched intently. The warrior had come. The door would open. This was the promise.

Julian, no stranger to women before his time in the Temple of Poseidon, had never found such passion with a woman before. He kissed her bare shoulder, brushed his thumb along her cheek, suckled the sweet flesh beneath her ears.

Hannah felt herself melting beneath his touch, ripples of fire beneath her skin. Kisses became caresses. Caresses became questions. They explored each other like two nomads discovering a hidden landscape, savoring every curve, every canyon, every secret cavern. Julian rested his head on her belly. He loved how different her face looked from every angle. When she was smiling, when she was not. Eyes closed, eyes open. In profile her features looked almost fierce. But then from beneath they became delicate as a child's. He traced a finger across her full lips. "You are so beautiful, so clever. What a gift to spend this night with you."

They lay prone on the tiger skin, and Julian removed Hannah's ceremonial costume one piece at a time, encircling her navel with his tongue, drinking in the scent of her, his body quivering with desire. She felt the heat rise in her blood and for a moment thought of Gideon. Gideon, the man she truly yearned to feel inside her, but she brushed the thought away. Julian before her, tender and kind, Julian had breathed her back to life, a gift she would accept gladly. She arched her back and slid her hand to the front of his groin, finding it stiff, ready.

Not yet.

He delicately kissed her eyelids, her lips, the center of her palm, her soft round breasts, her nipples tensing under his tongue. She trembled beneath his hands like a wild forest creature. *Take me*, she willed to him. *I want this. This. With you. Here.*

The torchlight played on the curves of their bodies.

Their hair entangled, their legs entwined.

Even the moon could not tell them apart.

He threw off his clothing and raised her wrist to kiss it and then drew her on top of him so he could see her in the torchlight. Then he pulled her up to his face so she straddled him like a horse, and he kissed her sex.

Hannah cried out, entirely unfamiliar with this new pleasure. The waves of energy overtook her, and she felt her body release in the suspended joy of deep ecstasy.

As she fell on top of him in a rush of pleasure, he pushed his cock inside her, savoring the slowest motion. She moved above him effortlessly, a goddess brought to life. Hannah let herself go, forgetting all but their intricate dance. Slowly, so slowly, then with deliberate force, he took her from every angle, never satisfied even after releasing himself inside her again.

Hannah trembled, her spirit collected into a sphere of euphoria inside her and yet released the ecstasy far beyond her skin. She felt enlarged, yet only a tiny speck against the heavens.

Julian did not relent in his determination to pleasure her. She cried out, screamed his name, succumbed to the shock of a lover so talented, so remarkably suited to her.

The two drank of each other many times that night in the sacred marriage rite. The smoke of the torches carried the sounds of their lovemaking out into the rainstorm, offering their union to the gods. The scent of the sea filled their nostrils; luminous strands of moonlight and kelp tangled in their bones. The surf drummed against the staves of their ribs, swirled inside their navels. Gulls circled in the bright sky of their desire. Together, they washed up on the languid shores of love, tousled by wave after wave.

Neither slept.

Neither wanted to.

Dawn approached, and the sky through the tower window grew pale and faded as a worn kilim. Hannah, naked beneath the sheet, fell silent and turned on her side.

Julian brushed her hair away and kissed the back of her neck tenderly, wishing he could remove the terrible bronze collar from her throat. "What is it?"

"They will come for us," she said, realizing that their precious night, which had seemed so eternal, had waned into day.

"Hannah," he whispered, turning her to him, taking her chin tenderly between his fingertips. "I may be Master Junkar to all the world, but I will always be Julian to you. Never forget this. Promise me."

Hannah smiled as two tears slid down her cheeks. "I promise," she whispered.

Then he kissed her again, burying his hands in her hair, his nostrils flaring as he drank in the scent of her sweet skin. He wanted to memorize the feel of her, the taste of her, his affection for her. He turned her towards him, and they made love one final time in the ecstasy of what was soon to end, her tears anointing his body, his fingers interlaced with her own until her back arched in ecstasy, and she held her breath as he lost himself inside her. Then she collapsed on top of him, her heart pressed against his heart as he kissed her cheek, her hair, her fingertips.

She pushed the thoughts of the coming day from her mind, wanting the moment between them never to end. *Kairos*, he whispered, *the eternal*. She wanted to memorize the shape of his eyes, his shoulders, his cock. She wanted her body to remember the weight of his body, her nose to remember the scent of his breath, her tongue to remember the shape of his name.

This discovery was love, this. Love: a home between hearts. But this love was an impermanent treasure, soon to be scattered like ashes. What Hannah felt with Julian she knew she may never feel again, and the thought ached inside her, a new sorrow to bear.

He turned her over and took a sip of wine in his mouth and let her drink it from his parted lips, as if to silence her thoughts.

They had only one more hour.

It collapsed as though time did not exist.

Julian rose and collected a bowl of figs and then nestled his thighs against hers. He pulled her naked body to his, and she nibbled the sweet fruit.

When the figs were gone, Julian spoke. "Hannah, there is something I must give you now, and I want you to accept it."

Hannah, playfully suspicious, interlaced her fingers through his. "What is it?"

Julian smiled and held out his hand to reveal a gleaming emerald shard inscribed with mysterious letters. "I had a vision." He slipped the black cord over her head, and she touched the emerald shard that hung between her breasts. "What does it say?"

"It says '*Soul immortal beyond death, no fire can burn thee, no fate can change thy eternal truth.*' The shard will guide you as you travel to see the Pythia in Delfi. Use it to enhance your vision."

"Delfi? I have no such travel plans."

"She holds the Emerald Tablet, which you must bring back to Alexandria. You must make haste. Promise me, Hannah, for I must go on my quest to India."

"I cannot," she said, concerned. "Surely there must be some monk who can do what you ask."

"Why not?"

"I am a slave in Alizar's house. I was sent to this island to be educated as a priestess. I have no right to go on any quest."

"I will speak to Alizar. He is an old friend. I had a vision that you are the one to take this quest. He will support us."

Hannah opened her mouth, but he placed his finger gently on her lips. "Shhh," he said. "Do not speak. Do not think. Look into your heart and feel if what I ask is true. Then do as you are guided."

So.

No more could the angel feel the sky. The light had dimmed inside the door. Heavy as a stone, the angel plummeted into darkness.

When the first rays of sunlight streamed through the tiny window at the top of the temple, the sound of the stone door grated against their hearts.

They heard voices outside, calling.

Hannah donned her costume quickly, and Julian threw his robe over her shoulders. Beyond the white square of daylight behind the door, Mother Hathora waited. Master Savitur stood beside her. Hannah could see their leather sandals inside the patch of light.

The sacred marriage rite was complete.

Hannah looked back at Julian one final time, the last time she knew she might ever look on him. He was reclining on the bed, the rumpled sheet around his legs, propped up on his elbows. The smooth skin of his chest shone in the diffuse light, and a strand of black hair was caught in the corner of his mouth. His eyes glinted, the same luminous green as the emerald shard around her neck.

As she watched him, he sat up and leaned forward to catch her hand, pressing her fingertips to his lips. "I will never forget you, Hannah of Sinai," he whispered in a voice only she could hear. "Know this."

She pressed a smile to her lips. Then she brought his hand to her mouth, kissed each of his fingers, and slowly released it. There were words of love locked in her throat, but she dared not speak them lest she burst into tears. Besides, the look they shared said everything that words could not.

She had to let go.

Hannah took a deep breath and somehow forced herself to crouch beneath the door, crawl through the threshold, and face the blinding light of day that lay beyond. From the top of the lighthouse, she could see the entire city, the harbor where Alizar's ship rested, Lake Mareotis, and the desert far beyond. And in the north, the Mediterranean Sea, stretching into a limitless blue sky. Somewhere far beyond the horizon lay Crete.

Julian collapsed back on the bed, feeling the destiny that he had prayed for sweeping down on him like a swift blade.

He buried his face in the warm sheet where Hannah had been only a moment before, where he could still drink in the scent of her. As he stroked the empty bed, his hand came to rest on something sharp and cold.

He drew the strange object up into the light and found that he was holding the beautiful silver hairpin that had been nestled in her hair.

Her hair.

He pressed the silver peacock to his lips and dressed quickly, dropping the treasure into his pocket. She would have his name, and he would have this to remember her by.

Julian was dead.

 21

Hannah returned to the Temple of Isis in a daze, exhausted and unkempt, every last drop of energy sapped from her bones. Mother Hathora knowingly took Hannah to the moon hollow and told her to rest until she felt recovered.

The storm had passed and the sun returned, but the thin winter light held little warmth.

Hannah still yearned for Julian's touch, the sound of his voice, the way they had spoken so intimately. Her heart called out to him though she knew she should not let it. Julian was dead. Yet to her, to her he had been so alive, so powerfully alive.

For the first time then, she thought of Gideon, their night together a memory that had all but vanished inside this new feeling.

Mother Hathora brought Hannah the bitter herbs, and she drank and spat, and rested. The rite had waned. The mundane world and all its dull duties waited. On her bed there was a letter from Hypatia and one from Alizar. None from Gideon. Hannah sighed, the disappointment she had expected still a prick to her heart.

Returning to temple life proved to be a blessed distraction. There were chores to be done, lessons to learn, and meals to be prepared. Hannah worked with as much enthusiasm as she could muster, soothing her sadness with the cadence of repetitious tasks. If only everything could have returned to the way it was.

Hannah had assumed that the other priestesses would be interested in hearing about what had happened in the lighthouse. But this was not to be.

Her first encounter came during her morning chores with Ursula, the red-haired beauty. Ursula, who was usually quite garrulous, had nothing to say to Hannah. After several attempts to make conversation, Hannah fell silent and worked alongside the other priestess without so much as a word.

The dance lesson that morning only brought more of the same. Hannah was ignored by the others, save Su, who had a lovely smile for her and praise for her improvement. During the steps, the priestesses would not meet her eyes. Some even bumped into her purposely. Hannah was deeply hurt, though she veiled her feelings with pride.

The midday meal brought a slight change as an enthusiastic mob of younger girls thronged around her for anything she would share about the sacred rite in the tower. This brought a smile to Hannah's heart, though it dimmed quickly with a cold stare from Mira, who picked up her plate and departed in silence.

Later, Iris came to Hannah's table and pulled her aside. "I am so proud of you," she said, her lovely eyes shining. "I just wanted to tell you that I knew he would choose you. I just knew. How do you feel, are you well?"

Hannah lied. "Well enough."

Iris sighed. "I thought this could happen. They are envious."

"I did not expect it."

"We are human first, priestesses second. Wait a little while. Unfortunately, everyone knows about your position in the Great Library with Hypatia as well. It is a lot to swallow at once."

"But I am a slave! Many of you are free to be anything you like."

"Not anything. You know this. Women have no titles, own no land, hold no seats in the government except by birth."

Hannah's eyes darkened with disappointment.

So.

Several weeks later, a bitterly cold winter evening brought more of the same. In the temple during a recital ceremony, the priestesses were each selected to recall passages from the Great Book. They all but flayed her.

"Begin with the Hymn of Apollo, please." Renenet's sibilant tone had acquired a few icicles.

Hannah stood at the dais before the other priestesses, a sea of faces looking up at her. She found her throat was dry. She tried to swallow. "I am sorry, I . . . I am not familiar with the Hymn of Apollo."

"Fine," Renenet said. "Then recite for us the Song of Abraham."

There was a long silence during which Hannah could hear the slight settling of the stone walls.

"The Song of Abraham," Hannah began hesitantly, "I do not know it in its entirety, but—"

"Sit down then, Hannah," Celesta interrupted. "I am sure that Ursula can recite them for us." There were snickers from the front row.

Hannah paused, unsure of what was happening. As she looked around the temple, the priestesses refused to meet her eyes. She looked to Mira and Ursula, their heads bowed together, and then Hannah knew. They intended to stultify her, to punish her.

Hannah stepped down from the dais, humiliated. She walked slowly, purposefully, up the aisle of priestesses, looking into the eyes of the women to see who would look back. Su looked up. Iris smiled. All the others looked away.

Hannah kept walking.

In her room she pulled out the cold jar of ashes her father had given her. She turned it over in her hands, hugged it to her chest. It was all she had of family.

A light rap fell on the door.

Hannah stuffed the bundle behind her bed. "Come in."

"Hannah," said a little voice. It was Suhaila, the child. "Mother Hathora would like to see you."

Hannah climbed the steps to Mother Hathora's study. Amber light spilled out into the night from beneath the door. Hannah peeked in to see the High Priestess seated upon her meditation cushion in the center of the room, facing the altar with its many lit candles. The Great Book was open on her lap.

"Hannah. Come in." Mother Hathora closed the book and turned to face the door.

Hannah pulled her shawl a little tighter around her shoulders and sat down.

The candlelight danced in shadow over Mother Hathora's pale blue robes as she spoke. "I once chose Master Savitur in the sacred rite."

Hannah furrowed her brow. "How can that be? You chose him?"

"Did you not know the ceremony reverses itself when it is our time? It will again once I pass, and my successor will choose a monk for herself. Our names are here. Come and see," she opened the book and pointed to a timeworn page.

Hannah crept forward and peered over the High Priestess's shoulder. There in red ink was the swirl of her signature.

Mother Hathora smiled, remembering. "In this book, your spirit and his are eternally wed to one another. Nothing can change that. As first man and first woman, you complete one another. Like Isis and Osiris, Adam and Eve. You cannot lose him, you will see. His spirit is in everything."

So.

That evening, as she crawled into bed and blew out the candle, Hannah curled in a ball beneath the sheets, needled by the pain inside her. Mira lay with her back to the room, silent as a corpse. Neither priestess said a word. Finally, Hannah spoke. "Mira, I am sorry for what happened," she said. "I had no intention of things turning out this way."

Silence.

"Mira?"

A twisted voice responded in the darkness. "You had no intention? How could you even hope to understand what you stole from me, Hannah? I should never have trusted a *slave*."

Hannah cringed to hear her own name spoken so hatefully. "If you think it was so grand, and you wish you could have given your heart to a dead man, then you do not know the agony you wish for."

Silence.

Hannah sighed in defeat. She had never been capable of striking clever blows in an argument, and besides, she did not even wish it. "Mira," she paused. "You have been my most beloved friend." Hannah waited in the darkness for Mira to say something. When no words came, and Mira's breath took the slow cadence of sleep, Hannah turned on her back and lay awake with her hands folded over her chest. She had never lost a friend before. It was the most empty feeling in the world.

The next evening at supper, Hannah sat alone at the far end of one of the tables. Since it was not her turn in the kitchens, she waited patiently to be served. Suhaila came over and sat in her lap. Hannah kissed the little girl's head and hummed softly.

A moment later, Ursula appeared with two steaming bowls in her hands. She began to set them before each of the priestesses. Hannah smiled. A lamb stew. This would be nourishing. They seldom had lamb, and she craved meat now more than she realized. The scent reminded Hannah of her childhood.

Ursula set a bowl before Hannah, and Hannah waited for everyone to be served so that they could say a prayer and begin the meal. Once they each had a bowl, Hannah closed her eyes and brought her hands before her heart. They whispered the ancient Egyptian prayer of abundance. When Hannah opened her eyes, her stew was gone.

She sat up and looked around. Then there was a giggle from beneath the table. Suhaila had taken the bowl and was dipping her bread into the stew and eating ravenously, laughing playfully.

"Suhaila!" Hannah slid out from the bench and bent down to reach the little girl, but Suhaila pulled away from her farther under the table and continued to eat her portion.

"Fine then," said Hannah playfully. "I will go and get another."

Hannah went into the kitchen to fetch herself another bowl and found Mira stirring the pot. She did not bother to speak as words between them were as useless as torn clothes now. Mira went out into the dining hall, and Hannah scooped another portion of the stew.

When Hannah opened the door to the hall, it was to see little Suhaila writhing and convulsing on the ground.

Mira flew to the girl and picked her up in her arms. The child vomited a little, her eyes rolling into her head, and her limbs shook. Mira cried out, and kissed the child's cheek again and again, calling her name. The other priestesses stood around in shock.

Mira tried tipping the child's head to one side to clear her nose and mouth for breath. Then she looked up, seeing everyone just standing there. "Go and get Mother Hathora!" she shouted to Ursula and Renenet. "Go!"

Hannah squeezed her knees into her body and rocked, tears streaming down her cheeks unbidden. Why was this happening? The child had been so healthy. Seizures? Was she cursed?

Mira kissed the child's soft face and closed her eyes, then glanced up through the window to the belladonna tree where the pink trumpet blossoms twisted gently in the breeze.

In that moment, Hannah knew. The portion of stew Suhaila had eaten had been meant for her.

Mira had tried to poison her.

They held the funeral for Suhaila the next morning in the garden. Mira had been taken to a chamber beneath the temple that was usually used as storage. She was put there because the door locked from the outside, a prison cell. Mother Hathora had turned the lock herself. There had been no need for inquiry; Mira herself had openly confessed to everything when Suhaila died.

Hannah cried and cried, the tears streamed down her face and stuck hot in her throat, where they threatened to choke her with sorrow. Here this sweet little girl had died. A portion of belladonna that an adult may have been greatly sickened by was enough to kill a child.

Mother Hathora put her arm around Hannah's shoulder to console her. Hannah's entire body was wracked with deepening sobs that gurgled in her throat and made it feel as if she were drowning. "It is all my fault," she said.

"No," said Mother Hathora. "It is Mira's fault, and she will be sent to the brothels to become a whore. It is her fate."

Hannah nodded. Such a fate was shame to any priestess. It was a mark of dishonor as well as a miserable and short-lived existence. Older whores either became brothel owners or took their own lives. Only while she was young would she stand any chance to prosper, and she would always risk bearing a child, or numerous children, or succumbing to any number of diseases. Mira would never step foot on the island again but live her life as a servant to a bawd on the wharf, seeing as many men a night as would pay. Hannah did not hate her. There was no need. She knew that kind of pain intimately, and it would be hard for a woman as proud as Mira to endure.

So.

Before the sun came to Pharos the next day, a missive arrived from Alizar, summoning her. Hannah dressed warmly, picked up her satchel and her lyre, and snuck away. So Julian, or Master Junkar, had indeed paid him a visit. She felt ready to return to Alizar's, even if it meant facing Bishop Cyril's dogs. Anything would be better than the stark memory of Suhaila's death, the bed the child had slept in still warm.

But then there would be Tarek. Hannah must keep her knife sharp and her mind sharper still to deal with him. She could only hope he would not attempt to punish her. Perhaps a quest would be the answer, indeed, and the further away the better. Where was Delfi? In Greece?

Hannah slipped out of the Garden House before the ringing of the first bell. A thin perspiration of mist clung to the ground in little wisps. The cold was damp and pierced her to the bone.

As soon as she felt the little skiff shove off, Hannah's eyes swelled with tears. She watched regretfully as the blue dome of the Temple of Isis shrunk from view. Was it not just yesterday that she had taken the skiff in the other direction, to the shore of Pharos?

As the spire from the Temple of Poseidon came into view, Hannah's tears flowed freely and unwelcome sobs escaped her throat for Suhaila and for Julian. She thought of Julian's eyes, the way they had filled with love for her. Julian. Not dead, but just as lost.

I may be Junkar to all the world, but I will always be Julian to you.

Their love, like ashes scattered to the wind. And now in the library she would forever have Synesius to remind her of him, his face shaped by the same womb.

Before her, Hannah could see Alexandria, the many buildings on the wharf drifting into view.

She trailed her fingers in the cold sea, recalling the feeling of Julian's silky hair between her fingers. Her life suddenly felt like an empty shell washed upon the sand. Beautiful and hollow.

Her tears flowed into the sea, the source of all tears. As Hannah looked down into the cold grey water, she wished she had the courage to pitch herself overboard and end her life. At least then her pain would find an end.

Just then, beneath the dark water, a dark shape darted under the skiff. It reappeared beside Hannah, breaking the surface. A spray of mist, and the dolphin's blowhole opened and closed. Greek stories said that dolphins rescued drowning sailors by carrying them back to shore. Apollo rolled on his side and looked up at Hannah with one of his ancient eyes, smiling as if to reassure her. She smiled back at him, and he disappeared in the sea.

When the skiff slid next to the wharf, the harbor was already bustling with activity in the shadows of the towering palms. She made her way from the wharf down the narrow alley to Alizar's familiar green door with its peeling paint and shiny brass latch, feeling like a troublemaker yet again.

❧ 22

Alizar himself opened the door. He kissed Hannah's cheeks and opened the door wider so that she could step through.

"Thank you," said Hannah.

Alizar nodded. "Tell me, have you brought it with you?"

Hannah thought a moment, and then realized he must be speaking about the emerald shard around her neck. She slipped it out from her *himation* to show him.

"Excellent," said Alizar. "Orestes is beside himself with glee that we might obtain the Emerald Tablet. Hypatia sails for Greece as soon as the weather clears. She has an invitation from Zophocles of Athens to speak at the Odeum and the Library of Hadrian. I have convinced her to take you along."

Hannah followed Alizar through the atrium into the courtyard, where Aziz was lunging the grey stallion on a long rope in a circle. So she would travel to Greece. She wondered what Julian had said to him.

"So he came?"

"*Neh.* Master Junkar has told me of his vision, and I am eager to obtain it. We need the Emerald Tablet more than ever and the uprising it might inspire against the empire, the Christian extremists. It is the only way."

"Will you come with us?"

"No. I have business here."

Hannah nodded, as if in a dream. "When do we sail?"

Alizar placed his hands squarely upon her shoulders. "Five days. Come, Jemir has just baked a fresh loaf of sweet bread. You must be famished, and you will need strength for the journey."

Hannah's trip across the Mediterranean faced the deep winter, a time when even rugged ships seldom sailed. Alizar had lent his ship for the journey, but Gideon required considerable convincing to sail. Even though summer voyages were considerably more dangerous because they meant confrontation with innumerable pirates—the Greeks took to pirating the way the Alexandrians took to the beaches—Gideon knew that midwinter sailing would ensure a gamble with the weather gods. Poseidon willing, they must brave a straight shot across the Mediterranean against the fierce Etesian winds. To reach Athens they might be at sea for a month or more, whereas the return trip with the winds would take only ten to twelve days. And there may be storms and rogue waves. It was a risk Hannah was determined to take. If Alizar believed that obtaining the Emerald Tablet would protect and unite the pagans of the city and the whole of the Mediterranean she would do anything possible to see the quest to its end.

Alizar explained a few pieces of his plan. They must unite the western half of the empire against the east. With the tablet, the Gauls, Romans, and Celts may follow to take back the realm from the Christians, who were drawing more and more blood wherever they marched. With the Emerald Tablet, they stood a chance to overthrow the crown and place a pagan on the throne, reversing the Imperial edict against them all. It would be a war, to be sure, but perhaps one that would unite the empire in the end. The Christians needed to learn their place as a religion that must share the world with other religions and give up their grasp for seats in the government. The Emerald Tablet was the key, and this was the time to bring it from legend to the people.

Gideon and Alizar watched intently as the gulls left the beaches and soared out over the sea toward Malta and Sicily, an indication that they would have good weather for at least a week. The captain sent word to Hypatia. They would sail at dawn.

After a goat had been sacrificed and offerings for a safe voyage had been blessed and set on an altar in the adytum of the Caesarium in the Great Library, the women gathered on the docks. With her lyre tucked beneath her arm, Hannah strode out onto the wharf to meet Hypatia, who waited beside Alizar's massive ship where it was tethered to an immense stone ring on the quay. The *Vesta* was the largest ship in the harbor that day, at a length of forty-six-and-a-half meters, a width of seventeen meters, and a bilge thirteen meters deep that could hold up to seven hundred barrels of wine. Or, as it happened, over a thousand children. Captain Gideon explained to Hypatia that Alizar had purchased the ship from a Roman grain merchant who had taken immaculate care of it, re-sealed the hull with tar twice a year, then lined the bilge with lead. The ship's ribs and hull planks were expertly carved and fitted edge to edge so that the swelling of the wood would keep the ship watertight for over a century. Her three iron anchors took a crew of twelve men to drop and hoist.

"She is almost sixty years old, and in finer condition than all these lateen-rigged pieces of rubbish." Gideon patted the *Vesta* lovingly before walking the dock to check that the crew had scraped the hull clean of barnacles. He smiled with welcome at Hannah and kissed her cheeks.

Hannah stepped back in surprise. Had the ship captain missed her then? And did it even matter now? She decided she could not let it. A fickle man was a dangerous man in matters of the heart. Although she delighted at the return of his warmth, she inwardly rebuked herself and decided she would have to avoid him out of self-preservation. Who knew when his affection would wane to a chill again? She did not want to find out.

Fixed in fertile darkness, the angel slept.

So.

The *Vesta* bore many stories of her journeys on the sea. Hannah drank in the immense beauty of the ship, the way the shirtless sailors scurried up and down the skinny rat lines to ready the sails and check the yards, how the ornamental gilded goose at the stern curved like the tip of her lyre, the way the twin figures of Isis perched beneath the bowsprit gleamed in the sun. The *Vesta* was a mythical dream brought to life. But like her captain, she also bore her battle scars. A repair made to the port hull thirteen years earlier sealed a rupture that a Roman galley called the *Agamemnon* had made with its sharpened metal prow in an attempt to loot her and drown her crew. The entire deck had been rebuilt twice, the sails torn and shredded by so many storms that Gideon kept five spares down in the bilge. The *Vesta* was a ship that had learned from her mistakes and lived to cross the Mediterranean forty-nine times, a ship with the earth in her ballast, the sky in her sails.

Hypatia discussed the trip itinerary and port fees with Gideon. It seemed that for a man to leave Alexandria, the port fee would be two silver *siliqaue*. But since the city preferred not to send its women abroad, Hypatia and Hannah were faced with fees of twenty *siliquae* each. Hypatia paid the fees for both of them, and Hannah watched the precious bag of silver coins exchange hands in silent awe, wishing it could be used to buy her freedom instead.

Soon Gideon announced that the rigging had been secured, and the *Vesta* was ready to leave her slip. "If you are sailing with this ship, ladies," he yelled down to the dock, "you had best be aboard it."

The *Vesta* slipped out of the royal harbor with practiced ease and with far less fanfare than her previous voyage, past the three-tiered lighthouse with its gleaming statue of Poseidon at the crown and the tremendous statues of Ptolemy and his queen that stood at the harbor's mouth. She was not a ship to be kept away from the sea for long. Hannah stared at the lighthouse, remembering her night with Julian inside of it. How much time had passed? A turn of the moon? Not even. He may be on his way to India now.

Rushing along under full canvas, the women shouted from the bowsprit in delight as the dolphin of Alexandria's harbor, Apollo, caught a ride at the bow of the ship. The crewmen too cheered at the sight of the dolphin leaping and rolling in the bow waves, an omen of a safe voyage.

After a nap, Hannah awoke in the evening, lulled by the creaking of the wood and ropes all around her and the swaying of the deck. A white ship cat was curled on her legs, fast asleep. When she sat up, it opened a single steely blue eye and then leapt to the floor and vanished through a crack in the door.

Hannah rose quietly, disoriented and drowsy. Her fingers combed through her hair for the hairpin her father had given her, but then she remembered she had lost it. Her heart clenched at her own carelessness. It had been the last piece of him she had—a small thing, but one that meant so much. Now all that was left were her memories. And his grave.

Suddenly gripped by loneliness, she wondered where the others were, so she staggered out through the same door as the cat. While she slept, the sky had turned indigo with the first stars appearing; a persimmon slash was all that remained of the sun on the horizon. Hannah looked out to sea as the Egyptian and Greek flags above her snapped and fluttered. It was an altogether different world than she had imagined it would be, terrifying and enervating. The nearness of the deep ocean coupled with the sibilant wind brought to the forefront of Hannah's mind the memory of nearly drowning in the catacombs, and it was on this new terror she was dwelling when Gideon came up the stairs with a plate in his hand.

"Even goddesses require nourishment," he said, handing her the plate with a thick slice of olive bread slathered in honey, ringed with slices of white cheese and apple.

Hannah thanked Gideon formally and took the plate. "Where is Hypatia?"

Gideon pointed to the bow. "She has been there all afternoon making adjustments to her astrolabe. She is eager to check it now that the stars are appearing. Two whales surfaced alongside the ship an hour ago. We tried to wake you."

Hannah clutching the railing. "How terrifying."

"Not at all. Whales have the largest hearts of all creatures. A whale is just an enormous wet puppy, always happy to see a sailor. Are you all right?"

Hannah smiled dimly. "I am afraid I am not used to the sea." She did not want to mention how she could not swim, the terror of being pitched overboard.

"The first time I came to Alexandria from Epidavros, I was just a boy. I spent half the voyage bent over the rail. But it got easier every day we were on the water, and soon I was in love with the sea. We are very fortunate to have this weather—the swells are calm for this time of year. And would you believe that Apollo is still at the bow? He never leaves the harbor."

Hannah let her eyes glide out across the deck to where the virgin philosopher in her long grey *tribon* was tinkering with a round brass instrument in her hands while gesticulating seriously to one of the crew. Hannah was struck by how unusual this sight truly was: a proud woman at the bow of a ship, dressed as only men before her ever had been, explaining the changes she was making to one of the captain's most important navigational instruments so they might better understand the stars and how to chart their course. There was a divine luminescence about Hypatia that transcended ordinary beauty, ordinary femininity; she was a star fallen to earth, still pulsing with heaven's light. "What do you know of her, Gideon?" Hannah asked, resting her elbows on the rail. It was a question she would have preferred to ask Alizar, but it seemed that enough time had elapsed for she and Gideon to converse without awkwardness.

"Her life is glamorous and fatiguing, her inescapable responsibilities beyond what you or I could ever imagine. Her mother went mad, apparently, and had to be sent away when Hypatia was just a girl. Some say the woman took her own life a short time later or wasted away. Her father, Theon, raised her to be his successor. He was a stoic, a disciplined perfectionist, incredibly talented in his work as a mathematician. He created several important works of commentary on the *Almagest* and single-handedly opened the doors to Hypatia's destiny as headmistress of the library. But her own brilliant work kept her there."

Just then, Hypatia spotted Hannah and Gideon up on the deck and waved for them to come down so she could show them her progress on the astrolabe.

As the sky burst into stars, they gathered together beneath the sails to share a flagon of watered-down wine. Hypatia stood, leaning on a yard as she examined the sky with her astrolabe, while Hannah reclined on the midline of the deck where the rocking of the ship seemed to be less severe. The wind was cold but gentle for the season, the sky clear as a bowl of diamonds.

Hypatia explained to Hannah the stationary position of the pole star as relative to the Earth's axis while she made calibrations to discern the ship's latitude.

Unfamiliar with the language of stars, Hannah set to watching the dark sea. She knew the journey ahead would be long. She felt grateful for every day that would distance her from the feeling of Julian's embrace. She had thought seeing Gideon again would be painful, but she leaned into his company, content yet aloof, laughing at his jokes. The two men were so different: Gideon brash and fearless, Julian contemplative and considerate. Yet she loved them both, albeit differently, even if neither of them would ever lay claim to her heart. As a slave, she could not even expect it.

So.

The following morning, and every hour of every day thereafter, Hannah was wracked by seasickness, the nausea so severe
that she could not rise from the berth. The entire world rocked
and swayed and turned around her. Nowhere was there a stable
point on which to fix her eyes, and she could scarcely keep down
a scrap of food.

Even in her bunk, the sickness was so extreme that Hannah's
only relief came from sleep. And so the shepherd's daughter slept.
Hypatia felt terrible for her, as did Gideon. They tried every remedy any of them had ever heard of, to no avail. Hannah was simply
not of the constitution for ocean traveling—she was a shepherdess, the earth in her bones, the solid world her place. Hypatia reassured her that they would consult every doctor in Athens to find a
suitable cure for the return voyage. By the third week at sea, Hannah had lost both weight and energy. Gideon left the wheel to his
most able crewmen and sat beside Hannah while Hypatia stoically
read to her from Homer and Socrates.

As miserable as the seasickness was, Hannah felt secretly grateful that she could grieve for little Suhaila beneath the shroud of nausea without having to speak about her sorrow. So much loss. Her
father, Naomi, so many had died. As a child she never realized how
many she would lose, or would still. How many she had trusted, like
Mira, who would turn on her. There were the dead in the ground,
and the dead among the living whom she would never see again.

On the twenty-third day at sea, Gideon steered the ship past
several islands and into a glistening cerulean cove. He plunged
into the sea and swam with one of the large ropes around his waist
so he could secure them to a rock on the shore. Then he gave the
orders for the crew to drop anchor.

When they arrived on the beach in the early afternoon, Hannah sank to her knees and picked up handfuls of sand, joyous as
a child, laughing her relief, immediately cured of the misery of
ocean travel.

"Where are we?" asked Hypatia, knowing this was not the harbor at Piraeus south of Athens.

"Alizar's secondary residence, Harmonia," declared Gideon. "In Epidavros. We are picking up another passenger."

Beyond a thicket of rustling pine, they passed between two immense iron gates supported by stone pillars that bore the vineyard's symbol: two rearing griffins with a chalice set between them, its two halves joined when the gates were closed.

Four large spotted hounds came running to greet the travelers, braying loudly, and Hannah reached down to scratch their floppy ears and kiss their heads. Behind a stand of torulosa pine and across fields of orange groves lay the main house, a massive stone villa with two ladders leaning against it where three suntanned men were repairing the roof. They waved when they saw Gideon.

Peasant women bent beside twisted grape vines paused in their work to greet the travelers. A number of excited children followed them, chattering about how they were digging another well and insisting that they come to meet the new hound puppies. Hannah looked to Gideon with questions in her eyes, and Gideon pointed to a stand of huts between the pines and explained that the servants lived on the premises and tended the land. "My family's land is just beyond that hillock, very near the great temple of Asclepius. We have been the keepers of that land for generations. I met Alizar as a boy and trained beneath his previous captain in those years as his successor."

Before them sat the palatial house, which had been built over two hundred years earlier by the same man who planted the vineyard, Alizar's great-great uncle, Iannis. Each generation had constructed an additional wing, usually for a newly married son and his bride, and added another wine cellar beneath it. The entire main house covered nearly an acre of ground not including the guest quarters, with almost four hundred acres to the entire property. As they approached the main house, a young woman stepped out from the doorway to greet them. Her long black hair was bound on top of her head, and her skin shone like moonlight. In every way she looked as though she belonged in a palace instead of the countryside. Every urn ever painted through the ages had been embossed with her graceful silhouette.

"Sofia!" called Hypatia to the sloe-eyed woman who bounded out of the house and ran down the path to greet Hypatia in an enormous embrace.

Gideon leaned down to Hannah and whispered, "Alizar's daughter."

After brief introductions, Sofia invited the weary travelers inside for a sumptuous meal of grilled octopus and fish stew with oregano, potatoes, carrots, and onions in an egg-lemon broth. There were also wide plates of salted sardines and cured olives, grilled eggplant, and fresh bread. Hannah had never tasted a finer meal in all her life, and she was so relieved to be capable of actually digesting it.

Sofia proved to be every bit as hospitable as her father. She gave Hannah a tour of the house and expressed her enthusiasm about hearing her sing in Athens. While the two got to know one another, Gideon retreated to shower, and Hypatia indulged in the rare afternoon luxury of a nap.

In the late afternoon, Gideon found Hannah alone on the terrace. She seemed idle, so he suggested she accompany him on a walk to his land just to the south of Harmonia. They strolled between the rows of vines that were only just beginning to sprout the tiniest of green leaves and out into the old olive orchard that overlooked the sea. Gnarled tree trunks the color of otter pelts vanished into wreaths of delicate leaves that shimmered like thousands of fish strung in the air. Hannah held out her hand to touch the trees as they walked. They were like peaceful deities, the trees. How much history they must have seen. Hippocrates had once studied, dreamed, and taught beneath them. Perhaps even Socrates.

Gideon led her down to the cove, a blue tongue where porpoises mated and frolicked in the summer. Once there, Gideon skipped flat stones in the surf while Hannah stroked the cobbled skin of starfish in the tide pools. Several gulls hoping for scraps circled and settled on the sand.

Hannah collected beautiful bits of broken pottery that seemed strewn everywhere. "What are these?" she asked.

"The men come here to dive for octopus," said Gideon. "The shards are from all the octopus pots. They must break them to get the octopus out." As he spoke, Hannah imagined the timid, fleshy creatures that slipped into the safety of the jars only to be snatched out of the sea by the hands of hungry men. She reached down and picked up a large shard from a broken octopus jar and turned it over in her hands, feeling its sharp edges, its smooth concavity. A remnant of something beautiful. She fondled it as they walked.

Gideon pointed to the promontory ahead where a beautiful house stood on the hill and nodded to Hannah. This was his home. A single servant tarried in the garden. Gideon explained he would return the following day. "Can you find your way back?"

Hannah nodded.

He paused, smiled at her, and then departed. Hannah watched him a moment, and he turned and waved. Did he remember their night together as she did? Perhaps it was one of many such nights to him. She did not know. To her, their night together had opened a door in her heart to a profound love. But now she thought of Julian and realized she did not know what love was or where it could be found. Had she mistaken desire for love? She watched Gideon traverse the trail up the hill, growing smaller and then disappearing over the distant hill. Surely she knew what love was and what it was not. That night between them had been love, at least to her, but now it seemed that love would not stay still. Love seemed to slip away as she reached for it, changing its form like Proteus escaping the grasp of Menelaus. She reached for love and it was a lion, a serpent, now a leopard, a tree. Proteus, whose Homeric home was also Pharos, the island of the Nuapar. She shuddered to think how this shape-shifting god may be defining her journey, even now, with all she wanted held constantly out of reach: her freedom, a life to call her own, children with a man who would claim her heart. Whatever she reached for remained a mirage.

The next day Hypatia, Hannah, and Sofia ate lunch together overlooking the orchard on the sprawling portico. Afterward, Hannah and Sofia spent the rest of the day collecting lavender, twisting oranges from the trees, and kissing the hound puppies, tiny eyes sealed shut as they wriggled and suckled against their mother's belly, hungry mouths latched to swollen nipples.

"How did the vineyard come to be called Harmonia?" asked Hannah as she braided her long black hair in the sparse light of the winter sun.

"It was my mother's name," said Sofia, her voice delicate as falling snow. They leaned back on the stone benches of the small amphitheatre built in ancient days, overlooking the bay, dogs howling in the distance. "Everyone called her Mona except for my father, who thought it unforgivable to call a girl Mona when her name was really Harmonia, after the daughter of Aphrodite and Ares. I was seven when she died and we moved to Alexandria. This house always reminds me of her. I think her spirit is still here sometimes. It is why I returned here when my brother died, to be near her." Sofia smiled, her eyes far off in the sky. "I wish I could remember her better."

Hannah nodded. "My father passed away recently. Already I am forgetting his face."

"It is wonderful then that you have Gideon. He is one of the dearest souls to my heart."

Hannah looked shocked, then fingered her bronze slave collar and contained her expression. "I do not belong to him but to your father."

"Hannah, I have known Gideon all my life, and I have never seen him look at a woman the way he looks at you."

"Well, I have heard nothing of any intention he has to buy me."

"You are still a woman. What of your heart? Does he not excite you?"

Hannah thought of Julian, their sacred ritual together in the lighthouse, his tender touch, his kisses. She thought of Gideon, poised at the helm of Alizar's ship, then his hands on her breasts, his powerful desire that had claimed her till the dawn the night they had spent. Feelings for both men were still so alive within her, locked behind a door of memory she dare not enter. "As long as I am a slave, my heart will belong to no one," she said and changed the subject to ask with genuine interest of the kinds of olives that were grown on the property.

The evening was spent in music and dancing, wine, and merriment. Gideon played the doumbek and Hannah her lyre, and Sofia danced with Hypatia. There were songs and jokes and stories and laughter, and Hannah never remembered a night that made her so happy. When at last the moon went down, Sofia yawned, and Gideon stuck his finger in her mouth, which made everyone laugh.

"Come, we should all go to bed so we can get an early start in the morning. Hannah, Gideon, Sofia, good night to you." Hypatia stood and turned to go, taking half the light in the room with her.

Sofia rose and smiled at Hannah, leaving her alone in the room with Gideon, the candlelight playing on their faces, their skin. Whether it was the wine or the warmth in the fire, Hannah found herself smiling at Gideon, grateful to see him there, a faithful friend. He may be brash, but Alizar trusted him.

Gideon smiled at her, and placed his hand on her knee. She took another sip of wine, and did not move his hand, inwardly cornered by her own desire and fear of his capricious affection. Then he suddenly leaned forward, cupped her chin in his hand and kissed her on the lips, lingering there as if tasting the wine, his hand moving to her breast. She kissed him fully, desire rising in her, betraying her decision to avoid his advances. He slipped his hand between her legs, and she moaned, her back arching, and then he kissed her neck and pulled his tunic over her head.

He was naked, his cock in his hand, a soldier at full attention only for her.

Hannah saw it and quickly closed her legs, pulling away before he could climb on top of her. "No," she said. This night would not be another she would live to regret. She had been spurned by him once, and it would not, could not happen again. To invite that pain would make a fool of her, and she had endured that agony before. "Go back to your ship, captain," she said hotly as she drew her shawl around her body, leaving the room.

The words lit a fire in him. He paced the room and punched one of the pillows. Then he found his clothes and walked out into the night, a newfound admiration for her in his eyes.

The next morning before sunrise they sailed for the harbor of Piraeus with its temple to Athena of Sunium on the peak of the promontory. By noon they anchored in the mooring lines just off the coast and took an oar boat in.

Gideon hired a cart to carry them up the long road to Athens, which was guarded by high walls to keep out raiders. They passed the famous grave of Menander and a broad stone cenotaph of Euripides and by afternoon reached the fabled arches of the ancient city gates.

Athens.

As the donkey jerked the cart forward, Hannah marveled at the warm stone city set above a crystal sea. Forever in her mind she would see that first moment: the starkness of the stunning architecture and how it formed a regal backdrop for the simple merchants that passed by with their loads of hay and chickens, stone and cloth.

Athens offered change from all that was familiar.

Athens offered beauty as unselfishly as a child.

She was an undoubtedly feminine city, although she was a nest of contradictions much like the goddess Athena for which she was named: proud yet sensitive, beautiful yet untouchable.

The travelers enjoyed a light meal that evening in a local taverna run by a heavyset man with such thick dark hair that Hannah thought it looked as though a skunk had curled around his head, its tail hanging down beneath his chin to form a beard. He refilled the empty cups for his guests all through the night as he eavesdropped on their conversations.

The four sat together at a large wooden table beneath a curved window that looked out onto the street where a late winter rain wet the stone cobbles. They could hear chariots and horses clopping past as the drivers called out to friends or snarled at beggars with the animated joviality of the Greeks.

"Tomorrow afternoon we go to the Library of Hadrian in the Roman Agora and meet Zophocles," Hypatia announced. "That will give us the morning to visit the Akropolis."

"Lovely," said Sofia.

"When is your lecture?" Hannah asked, soaking a wedge of bread in a pool of olive oil in a green ceramic dish.

"The day after tomorrow, I believe," said Hypatia. As she spoke, the taverna owner brought bowls of six different kinds of olives to the table, lingered a moment to ask if they needed anything, and then rushed off to fetch their orders of spice-stewed lamb and cabbage rolls, the latter for Hypatia, who insisted on a purely vegetarian diet. "We should be well-rested by then. Zophocles is expecting an audience of nearly two thousand."

"Two thousand?" asked Hannah, her pupils expanding.

Hypatia winked. "They will love you just as we do."

❦ 23

Hannah felt more at ease in her new surroundings than she had expected she would. Athens was not only a beautiful city, but one accustomed to a wide variety of people walking the streets. It was a very safe city as well, full of parks and trees and pleasant little shrub brushes where tortoises hid for shade. There was an even sharper degree of classicism than in Alexandria, so some of the populace walked with airs of dignity that gave everyone on the street a view up both nostrils, while others walked in rags with a lilting sway in the hips that suggested there was nothing in life to be taken seriously, even poverty. Peasant women, followed by gaggles of enthusiastic children, sold smooth white eggs from woven baskets. Peasant men screamed at their donkeys when they were not screaming at their wives. Here and there, a pair of lovers would promenade around a corner, holding hands and laughing before disappearing into a taverna.

Gideon ventured off to visit friends, leaving the women to climb the declivitous hill from the Roman *agora* in the Plaka toward the Akropolis. Hannah noticed that the sparse sandy earth beneath her feet felt and looked familiar. Something about the color and angle of the hills that swept up from the harbor had the feel of Sinai. Even the same pines and olive trees that dotted the slopes of her childhood home stood stretching their limbs into the pale aquamarine sky above these mighty temples. This reassured Hannah and gave her a good feeling about her journey.

The women passed most of the morning marveling at the stone gods and goddesses of the Akropolis, then made their way back down the vast steps into the city toward the Library of Hadrian. Hypatia was making such haste that the other women could not keep up. "Hypatia!" Sofia called out, taking the hem of her *himation* in both hands to run. Hypatia did not look back. Pigeons on the steps scattered before her.

Hannah and Sofia caught up to her at the Gate of Athena Archegetis, a row of four ornate Doric columns of Pentelic marble in the west leading into the Roman Agora. "I have dreamed of seeing her all my life. The Horologion of Andronikos, designed by Andronikos of Kyrrhos, the Tower of the Winds. Come," said Hypatia. Like an excited child she took the hands of her friends and dashed across the cobbles toward the octagonal tower at the very heart of the Plaka.

Hypatia rushed them past the bronze statues of Hermes and Poseidon, and the lovely Athena of Parian marble, without a glance, the tower before her drawing her in. The women all but burst through the door. Inside the tower loomed a massive water clock twenty feet in height, measuring the hours of the day and night with water that poured down from a spring within the heart of the Akropolis. Smaller gears beside the clock turned to show the position of the planets and the stars.

"Why, it is a giant version of your Celestial Clock of Archimedes!" declared Hannah.

"Yes it is," said a jolly red-cheeked, round-bellied praetor strolling up to the where the women stood. He raised his hand to Hypatia with a smile. "You must be Hypatia of Alexandria. I am Zophocles. Welcome to Athens."

After introductions and a round of pleasant discourse, they began to plan the lecture at the library. Zophocles proved to be a true host. He wanted to ensure their every comfort, but his tongue snagged when he learned that Hannah would be singing. "Your

slave has a gift for song, then? How lucky you are. She is very valuable indeed."

Hypatia looked to Hannah, who lowered her eyes in shame.
She would never be seen as a woman, only as a slave in any land
she traveled.

"She is talented, you will see," declared Hypatia.

The women wound back through the Plaka streets that curved
beneath the hill of the Akropolis. Hannah paused beside a large
splashing fountain to catch her breath and take a sip of water. Hypatia
watched her in quiet concern. Hannah had not regained her energy
from the seasickness and seemed to be withering before them.
"Hannah, are you well?" Hypatia asked, taking a seat beside her.

Hannah nodded. "I am tired. The journey was harder on me
than I realized."

"You should go back to the inn and rest. Gather your strength
for this evening. Take the whole afternoon. I will have a meal
brought up for you."

"Thank you, Hypatia. I could use some time to practice."

"Practice can wait, Hannah. Rest."

So.

That evening Hypatia's lecture on the evolution of time keeping,
the water clock, and the Celestial Clock of Archimedes was received
with tremendous interest by the patrons of the Library of Hadrian.
A significant number of obsequious senators, philosophers, teachers, rhetors, and magistrates spilled into the Odeum till the crush
of bodies had filled every available space, and oxygen was in much
demand. All those present were eager to behold the Celestial Clock
of Archimedes. Hannah opened the lecture with her songs in the
wide hall decorated with gold leaf and acanthus designs carved
along the doors. She delighted in the marvelous acoustics of the
marble building. Her voice had evolved from a shepherd's flute into
a stunning and sophisticated instrument that enchanted everyone
who heard her. Hannah found the massive crowd warmer and less

intimidating than she imagined. Both she and Hypatia received enthusiastic standing ovations. Afterward, Hypatia was rushed by dozens of men, always men, who wanted to ask her questions about the clock, the Great Library of Alexandria, and her renowned father, Theon of Alexandria. Some challenged her, most fawned over her. Many asked to buy her beautiful slave.

Hannah took the opportunity to join Sofia and Gideon in the gardens where they could enjoy some fresh air and sip fine Athenian wine. Spring had come early to Greece. The already mild winter was departing rapidly to make room for the tightly bound buds of daffodils and irises that were eagerly pressing up through the soft soil. Sofia remarked on the scent of jasmine in the night air, and Hannah paused to drink it in, eyes closed, a smile lifting her eyes. Sofia adjusted the folds of her pale orange *himation*, repositioned the elegant brass *fibula*, and sat gracefully upon the step, leaning her back against a column with a tired sigh. Hannah strolled out onto the cobbles past the long rows of columns, each flanked by impressive marble statues of the Egyptian Ptolemies, and toward a small temple glowing in the lavender moonlight.

There were few guests outside. Most had remained inside to question Hypatia and banter with one another. Hannah relished the precious moments by herself. She wanted to memorize every blade of grass so that she could always remember precisely how the night had been. The lopsided moon seemed to turn an ear toward her, listening to her thoughts. She wondered who else was sitting under that moon. Perhaps Alizar and the rest of his household. Perhaps Julian. She wrapped an arm around a temple column and peered up at the sky with all the questions in her heart about this quest and where it would lead. Her third cup of wine, watered though it was, coursed through her veins and warmed her fingertips, erasing from her memory the requests of the men who wanted to buy her from Hypatia. The wine's gentle euphoria was relaxing and sweet. She could understand how people became lost to the urges of Dionysus. Why not enjoy another cup? Soon she was drunk on the intense Attic wine and singing to the plants in the garden.

"We should get her back to the inn," said Gideon.

"You take her," said Sofia. "I should stay with Hypatia, or else she will be cornered by her admirers till dawn. I will bring Hannah's lyre with me when we return. She needs a warm bath and some tea."

"It would be my pleasure, lady," said Gideon with a bow.

Hannah fell into his arms and wrapped her hands around his neck. "Where are you taking me?"

"To the inn."

"We should not be alone together," she said with a flirtatious grin. "Who knows what might happen."

"Wench," he snarled playfully. "Do not toy with me. I will put you to bed, and you can sleep this off. You are drunk."

But she did not answer because she fell asleep in his arms. Back at the inn, he carried her up the stairs to her bed and dropped her on the mattress from a height so that she woke up and cursed at him. He winked and shut the door. "Goodnight, lady."

So.

Hannah awoke the next morning, exhausted and embarrassed about her drunken reverie the night before. She did not even remember being escorted back to the inn. She found Sofia enjoying breakfast on the wide balcony overlooking the mountains in the northeast and the sea of flat red roofs that made up the vista of the city in the south.

Sofia was intermittently tossing breadcrumbs to a one-legged pigeon and stirring her tea with a tinkling spoon. When she heard Hannah's footsteps she looked up. "*Kalimera*," she said. "How did you sleep?"

"*Kalimera*, Sofia. Well enough. And you?" Hannah poured herself a cup of tea and sat back on the chair with her knees up in her chest, pulling her shift down over her bare feet. Her head pounded like a soldier's march.

"Very well."

Hannah stirred her tea and rubbed her temples. "Where is Hypatia?"

Sofia rolled her eyes. "She has received almost fifty invitations to dine with the praetors and magistrates of the city just since last night. Would you believe the sun has not even been up an hour, and she is already back at the library discussing the Almagest with some fawning mathematicians? She will never escape them. Such madness. It would be torture for me."

Hannah smiled, blinking back the brightness of the sun. "I see," she said, seeking shade in the chair next to hers. Several crows swooped past them overhead, squawking as they sailed in acrobatic circles toward the beach. It was a remarkable day. This would never do. She was confined by these ridiculous obligations and by her resurrected desire for Gideon. Hannah knew what she must do. This was just the window she needed. She excused herself from the table, saying that she wanted to meet Hypatia at the library. Sofia thought nothing of it.

It was evening before they realized that Hannah was gone. Gideon, who had been informed by Alizar of her quest, was the only one among them who knew where she may have gone.

"Delfi?" asked Hypatia with some offense, straightening a pleat in her *tribon*. "But we will have to take one of those dreadful ox carts, and I despise the way they bounce. Will you go and bring her back, Gideon?"

"It might be an adventure, lady."

"Adventures are for young boys," said Hypatia, frowning. "I have tea scheduled with three important magistrates and a senator tomorrow."

"You are coming with us," said Gideon, "even if I have to drag you behind the ox."

"Us?" asked Sofia.

24

That evening Hannah tethered the black gelding she had borrowed from the inn and camped beside a winding stream that curved around a grassy bank. Though life in a city could offer baths and books, conversation and convenience, its beds could never offer a view of the stars. There beneath the sprawling limbs of a tall stand of pine, a chill biting her ears, Hannah felt finally at ease. She listened in delight to the sound of the stream and the wind in the branches as she reviewed the map to Delfi she had procured from the Athens library and then snuffed out her candle.

While Hannah slept, Gideon and the other women searched for her on the road, the innkeeper having told them the color of the horse he had lent her.

The screech of an owl startled Hannah out of her sleep. She reluctantly opened her eyes to see the creature just overhead in a nearby tree, staring at her, its eyes two yellow lamps full of warning and mystery. Hannah shut her eyes again but only for an instant before another kind of sound split the night.

She sat bolt upright, drawing the knife from the sheath at her calf. There was a cart on the road. She could hear the snorting of the ox.

Hannah paused, waiting. Nothing else came for several minutes.

There was a sharp whinny from her horse and then raised voices. This could mean robbers, meaning to steal the horse. She would be stranded or worse. But then a woman screamed.

Hannah flew to her feet and scrambled up the bank to where her horse was tethered. The sight in the clearing gave her such a shock she could scarcely comprehend it.

There on the ground lay Sofia, her dark hair tangled, her face contorted, the body of an enormous man laying motionless in a deepening pool of blood beside her. Hypatia stood beside a boulder, a knife raised in her hand, her sleeves streaked with blood, her shadow in the moonlight stretching behind her like a long, dark road. Gideon kicked at the corpse, its bloody throat gaping open like a macabre purse. Sofia, pale and shuddering, drew her *klamys* around her; it was torn across the shoulder, revealing one of her pale breasts.

Hypatia crumpled to the ground on her knees as the soiled knife fell from her hand. Hannah rushed to her. "Heavens, what happened here?"

Gideon spoke. "We saw your horse by the road. When we got out, the ox driver tried to fox Sofia's coin purse. When he drew his knife on her, we had a bit of a tussle. Hypatia killed him in the struggle with his own knife. Well done, lady. I could not have killed him more cleanly myself." He nodded respectfully to Hypatia.

"Are you hurt?" Hypatia asked Sofia.

Sofia's lovely dark eyes filled with tears, and she wiped them away and found her feet. "I am fine," she said. "Look, we have found Hannah."

Hypatia did not respond. She buried her face in her fingers. The deed was done. Time would not run backward to undo it. Which act was the more condemnable, hers or the ox driver's? She had just killed a man. Murdered him. She felt a noxious shame, yet complete justification all at once. She had violated every principle she knew but had done it out of love.

Hannah lifted her eyes to see a white spirit sweep over the fire, but it was only the owl, returning to the night.

"We must bury the body," Hannah whispered, then cleared her throat. "There will be wolves."

Gideon agreed and set to emptying the man's pockets.

Sofia stared with contempt at the ox driver where he lay on the blood-soaked ground. "I do not want to touch that beast."

Hypatia's eyes were strangely empty and far away. "Hannah is right. There are wolves in these mountains."

It was a strange moment for them all, discussing the body with the detached calm of four senators voting on a new law. They finally decided that without a shovel there was no way to bury the body, and since the dead are twice as heavy as the living, they really had no choice but to throw it in the river.

By dawn they stood on the road as the night gradually paled beyond the rolling hills, their breath fogging the air.

"We will return to Athens at once," said Hypatia.

Hannah steadied herself. "Go on without me," she said. "Please."

Before Hypatia could speak, Gideon broke in. "You cannot go back to Athens and neither can we. Not if it means the Emerald Tablet of Hermes Trismagistus."

"You told them of my quest?"

Gideon nodded. "Your quest is ours now, lady."

So.

Hannah, riding the horse, led the others in the ox cart into a wide valley that wound north into the mountains. She hoped that Mount Parnassus would be visible by evening. Gideon unfolded the map, then rolled it up again. He agreed.

By night Hannah felled two rabbits with her slingshot, skinned them, and then roasted them over the fire. Roads would be more difficult, maybe even impassable as they entered the mountains beyond the foothills, so they ate well and slept near one another for warmth.

On their third morning out of Athens, a cold rain fell in veils across the green valley floor before them. They came to a fork on the next hill, one side slanting off to a ledge, the other opening to a stony eastern face. Here the road vanished in a landslide. There was only one choice. They freed the animals (knowing the beasts would run for home) and picked their way across the wide field of shifting boulders toward a dent in the far-off hillside that looked like a cave, the cold rain soaking them to the skin. They had to move slowly to avoid tipping the boulders and falling into the crevices below, risking broken ankles and cracked skulls in an instant of miscalculation.

"Let us have a song, shall we?" said Hypatia, looking to Hannah.

Hannah smiled. There was no better way to cast out their fears. So.

The sunrise on their fourth day brought clear skies as the fibrous clouds brought by the storm receded in the morning sunlight. They continued climbing west over the steep terrain above the sea, the green winter grasses emerging beneath the scraggly tufts of dry autumn brush underfoot. In the early afternoon, exhausted and somewhat discouraged, they passed through a windblown meadow where high overhead a murder of crows turned acrobatics in the air.

Hannah scouted from the top of the next hill where, beyond a thicket of pine, she emerged at the blustery narrow pass to a view of the entire northwest mountains and the sea. Hannah smiled as the wind swirled around her, pushing her this way and that. Before her stood the crumbling grey stone peak of Mount Parnassus, home of the nine Muses. In the folds of its verdant slope lay a miniature city of white marble, a mere glint against the sun.

Delfi.

Hannah took a deep breath and then rushed back to collect the others, her heart pounding for the thrill of spotting their journey's end. She even hugged Gideon, the first real warmth she had shown him. He kissed the top of her head. They were nearly there.

The climb down the ragged cliffs took ages; they traversed back and forth, constantly crumbling the stone. After the torrential rain, the soil was muddy and slick. Sofia, unused to such athletics, slipped on a wet leaf and shrieked, reaching out to a pile of stones to stop her fall. The stones gave way and crumbled down the hill, breaking open a nest of bees.

Sofia screeched and swatted hysterically at the bees until she finally found her feet again and took off down the path to flee the vicious assault, and she did not stop running until she came to an outcropping of boulders further down that concealed a spring encircled by a swath of tall pines. She flung herself into the water with a splash.

Hannah, Gideon, and Hypatia exchanged quick glances and pursued Sofia at a careful distance, not wanting to draw the bees. When they arrived at the spring out of breath from the chase, they found her in the shallow water, her wet black hair hung limp around her body. "Are they gone?" she whimpered.

Hannah looked around and nodded. "I think so."

The others stared at Sofia, and then, though they tried to contain themselves, began to giggle. "Sofia, your *himation*," said Hypatia, pointing.

Sofia looked down to see her dress and expensive Persian shawl dripping magenta dye all down her arms, chest, and legs, into the bright clear water.

Then Sofia too, began to laugh. She lifted the ends of her wilted shawl in her hands and began to howl until she found it difficult to breathe. Then, with a devilish look in her eye, she strode up to the bank, grabbed Hypatia's arm and pulled her in. Hypatia shrieked and landed in the water with a splash, leaving Gideon and Hannah on the bank. Then it was Hypatia's turn to pull Hannah into the water while Gideon cast off his *tunica* and jumped in before anyone could drag him.

After the fit of laughter passed, the travelers spread their wet clothes over the rocks and lay on their backs in the thin winter sun to dry off.

Hannah found a mound of clay beside the spring and gently applied it to Sofia's numerous welts. "I am dreadfully sorry, Sofia. For all of this."

"No, I must thank you," said Sofia. "I have always dreamed of an adventure like the one had by Odysseus. You have brought it to me, and I am forever grateful, whatever happens. For now, I am fully alive, and it is wonderful, truly." She turned and kissed Hannah, smiling at her new friend.

The sun crouched on the sea over the Bay of Corinth when they finally wandered into the deserted streets of the ruined city of Delfi. Everywhere the heads of marble gods severed from torsos lay smashed on the ground, scattered amongst the ruins. High on the slope, the tall columns of the *tholos* at the sanctuary of Athena Pronaia still stood, though the roof had been destroyed. The travelers walked up to the broad platform and leaned their cheeks against the cold slick stone as the sun sank into the sea.

"The gateway to Delfi," whispered Hypatia, crestfallen.

"What is left of it," said Sofia, equally dismayed.

Gideon nudged a stone with his boot, then lifted it to see he had found a finger from a statue of Apollo. It was all that was left of a fine statue that had stood for hundreds of years. He slipped it in the sinus pocket of his robe.

Hannah tried to imagine the Delfi that Synesius had described to her, the Delfi that had once been considered the navel of the world, the throne of the Earth Mother Gaia, and later Apollo. In her mind she saw Delfi resplendent, gleaming, full of honor, its streets teeming with young athletes parading to the stadium, officials lining up to pay their pious respects to the Pythia. There was nothing left of that place. Hannah ran her hand over a splintered marble block, her heart aching for the city as it had for the girl killed by the Christians in the *agora* of Alexandria. "It is just as Alizar said, only worse."

"I fear the Christians will not rest until they have destroyed our entire world," replied Hypatia. "Who are the real heretics of history?"

"Terrorists." Gideon spat on the ground.

There was no way to look on Delfi without feeling the magnitude of the loss. Hannah bent down and, on a broken column, placed an offering of tiny forget-me-nots she had plucked from the mountain flank.

In the dim twilight left to them, the foursome solemnly continued up the hill to the quiescent city and found what they presumed to be the outer wall of the Temple of Apollo, a large structure of massive girth supported by thirty or more columns too tremendous to topple, though they had been defiled by Christian zealots who had smeared them with ink and excrement, and smashed them with stones and anything else they could find to hurl. One narrow opening led into a garden maze where the mulberry trees unfurled the first leaves of spring. Above them stretched a mighty amphitheatre, what might have been a gymnasium, and several paths overgrown with weeds between the tall temples, some of which were merely damaged while others lay toppled upon themselves, the drums of the columns scattered across the field as if a giant child had knocked them down in play.

"That path must lead to the stadium," said Gideon, pointing up the slope.

But the small, intact temple just beneath the amphitheatre caught Hannah's eye. "Look there," she said.

The travelers whispered as they walked toward it, as though passing through a cemetery in the presence of the dead. "Do you suppose there is anyone here?" asked Sofia.

"It seems completely deserted," said Hannah as she took several quick steps to be nearer to Gideon and Hypatia.

"Emperor Theodosius had the city destroyed the year of my birth," said Hypatia bitterly. "But I understand that there are several women still in residence here, protectors of the oracle, hidden beneath the streets."

Only the radiant temple before them stood unaffected, a paladin of light. Perched above a sloping apron of twenty or more marble steps, twelve white Corinthian columns stood in support of a wide, triangular roof. As they came closer, they could see words carved above the eaves, in the center of the marble frontispiece.

"What does it say?" Hannah whispered.

Hypatia examined the letters in the fading light, although she knew them long before they met her eyes, for the saying had been renowned in philosophical circles for a thousand years. "*Gnothi Se Auton*," she whispered. "Know Thy Self."

The travelers paused at the base of temple for a long time as the evening grew darker and Jupiter appeared in the deep sky over the highest peak of the mountain.

Hannah pressed the door and found it open.

A narrow hall opened to a line of flickering torches—yes, someone was here, and rather recently. Gideon called out, and an old woman approached from far down the hall wearing a white *himation,* bordered with an elegant *meandros*, which flowed in long perfect pleats to the floor. She walked without making a sound. "*Kalispera*," she said with a warm smile. "I am Stella. Welcome to the Temple of Apollo." Her eyes flicked to their necks, subtly searching for necklaces, crosses, signs of whether these travelers could be trusted. "Have you come of your own will or by the will of another?"

Hannah moved to speak, but Hypatia stepped forward and placed her hand on Hannah's arm to silence her. She sensed there would be questions here, and she was perhaps more prepared than the others from years of study within her mystery school. Wrong answers, she knew, would get them turned away. "By both, grace. We have traveled from the land of Egypt and chose to follow the road that led us to this temple. But this quest was given to Hannah, our slave girl, by another, by a great leader."

"Great leader, hmmph." The crone folded her arms. "I suggest you camp beside the stream and depart in the morning."

"We have come for the Emerald Tablet of Hermes Trismagistus," blurted Hannah, seeing the crone turn away.

"We know of no such tablet. You have wasted your time."

"Please," said Hannah. "We are not Christians. We only want to see the Pythia and then be on our way."

"Where are your offerings? Your gold? Your silver?"

"We have no such offerings," said Hypatia. "Merely our hearts."

"And this," offered Hannah, holding up the emerald shard that hung from the cord between her breasts. "It was given to me by Master Junkar of the Nuapar. Do you recognize it?"

Stella frowned. The torches murmured in the darkening hall. Hannah noticed now that only ever other one had been lit—perhaps they were running low on oil. "Come."

The travelers shared glances of supreme relief and followed the old woman as she led them to several simple rooms furnished with washbasins and down beds. "You may sleep here tonight," she said. "I will have some supper brought to you. In the morning you must go to the sacred spring and wash and gather white narcissus as an offering to the Pythia. You may stay one night, and then you must go. Our city is no place for visitors now."

The Pythia. Synesius had told her the Pythia had once been of tremendous importance when the oracle belonged to Gaia, the earth mother, but was gradually replaced by the monks of Apollo when the oracle was rededicated to the Greek sun god. What role did the Pythia play now that the city lay in ruin? Hannah sat down to untangle her thoughts as her stomach grumbled.

Gideon threw his rucksack on one of the beds and fished through for a flagon, which he offered to the women. "Mead?"

Hannah grasped it and tossed her head back, then nearly spit it out. "This is dreadful stuff." Then she swilled more of the bitter liquid and handed the flagon back to Gideon.

Sofia relished the opportunity to remove her boots, her heels bloodied by the hike through the mountains.

Of all the travelers, Hypatia was the most refreshed by the simple yet civilized furnishings of the rooms. While the others sat by candlelight and discussed Hannah's quest, she zealously scrubbed her arms, hands, face, and feet, then curled up like a cat on the softest bed and fell fast asleep.

25

Hannah awoke the next morning to the flutter of shiny black wings in a patch of grey sky through the window. Ravens. As she propped herself up on her elbows she saw Hypatia was already awake, sitting at the window looking out, a portrait of contemplation.

"*Kalimera,*" said Hannah.

"*Kalimera.*" Hypatia was worlds away, her large eyes lost in the landscape.

In the pine the raven chortled and cawed. "My father says a raven at dawn is a good omen," Hannah said.

"We could use a good omen," said Hypatia without turning her head.

After a simple meal of olives and seed bread, the four travelers walked east to the site of the sacred Castalian spring.

"It is said the spring was formed where the hoof of Pegasus struck the earth," said Gideon.

"I can feel the divinity of this place," whispered Hannah. "Like in a synagogue."

"No, this land is of the Goddess," said Sofia.

Hannah thought of the Temple of Isis . . . something of what Sofia said rang true. The same profound feeling of peace pervaded that place as well. If this place was of the Goddess, would that mean that She was different than God, or equal to God? Or perhaps the great Goddess was a wife of God, or his mother? But then how could there be one God? These were questions for Alizar or a rabbi, Hannah decided.

As they passed through the pine forest, they could hear water trickling. Several paces later they found the small stream strewn with bushels of watercress and followed it to find two thrones carved into the mountain, a rectangular pool beneath them where a great blue heron waded stoically. The outer perimeter of the pool was a dried-up basin that had clearly once held quite a bit more water. The stone channel—out of which the water flowed—had been smoothed by what was once a great waterfall, now nearly dry. The heron ignored his visitors and continued stalking unsuspecting frogs, lifting his head to swallow them whole when he found them.

Hannah sat on the bank to pray before entering the water. So sad this ruin had once been ornate marble halls lined in gold, magnificent statuary set all around the entrances, and massive gardens filled with flowers brought as gifts to the Pythia from all over the Mediterranean, Persia, and Africa by kings and emperors: rare orchids, lilies, roses, and fragrant vines. What had happened to them? There was supposedly a temple in the east built to house all the treasures of statues, vases, precious stones, perfumes, and silks. But all the temples in the east lay in ruin. Why must the Christians plunder such a sacred place? Surely Spirit had its reasons, beyond what humans can know. When she finished praying, Hannah carefully removed and folded her clothes and entered the spring, which was hardly knee deep. The others did the same. Together they raised the water to their lips in cupped palms and drank of the cool spring. It was the purest water any of them had ever tasted, cold and sweet.

When they emerged and dressed, Hannah walked the wood in search of the goddess Persephone's flower, the tender narcissus.

"Here," said Sofia, pointing to a cluster of tiny white flowers shooting up between two rocks at the pool's perimeter. Hannah picked one, drawing the little blossoms up to her lips to inhale their divine fragrance. Such a small gift did not seem like enough.

She wished she had some wonderful treasure to offer the Pythia like the ones she had read about, a gold piece, Persian silk, something more than the quest for a legend.

"I am sure the Pythia considers all earnest requests, regardless of the expense of the offering," said Hypatia. "One of the Indian texts I encountered said that one humble tear offered to God is more precious than a thousand chests of gold."

"I hope so," said Hannah, "because we have nothing else."

Stella met them at the temple gate and led the travelers through the long corridors of the temple and into a large hall to wait.

The cloister was clean, sparsely decorated with vases and cracked sculptures set on marble pedestals before large arching windows that afforded a view of the now barren garden and a wedge of sky between two tall hills. Whatever this place once was, there was nothing of extravagance here now, no comforts however spare.

Stella looked to Gideon. "The Pythia will see you now."

"Thank you, though this quest is not mine, but hers." He extended his arm toward Hannah.

"Your slave will speak?"

Gideon said, "She is more than any slave. She will speak."

Stella paused. A look in her eyes said a woman speaking to the Pythia, much less a slave, was unusual though not unwelcome. "Very well."

Hannah looked back to the group one last time. They smiled at her encouragingly, even Hypatia who had never believed in oracles or omens, who—as the headmistress of the Great Library—viewed the world empirically, scientifically, looking to the evidence itself for answers. Though they each entertained hopes, Hypatia knew if what had happened to Delfi was any sign of what was to come in Alexandria, she did not need an oracle to speak any words of prophesy, or an Emerald Tablet. The city would fall, and the Great Library with it. Time was the enemy now.

Stella led Hannah through the back of the temple to an alcove where an ornamental rug concealed a secret door. "The Christians never found this one," she whispered as they stepped inside and descended a long flight of steps that took them below ground to another door. Stella nudged a loose stone in the wall and removed a brass key that unlocked this door. Clearly she did not find Hannah a threat, which helped Hannah relax.

Once inside, a long, ornate room opened to a dais where a veiled figure was seated on a tripod throne, perched above a fissure in the earth that leaked a cool and pleasant-smelling vapor. The oracle! Hannah felt her heart leap. At last her quest was at an end. Between her and the Pythia burned the eternal blue flame said to have remained lit for a thousand years, set in a wide copper bowl supported by a marble base inlaid with opals, abalone, and rose quartz. Completely covering the floor, and even stacked three high in places, were elegant rugs brought as gifts from Asia Minor and Persia, now threadbare in patches where the knees of thousands of noblemen over the centuries had knelt before the oracle. All around the seated Pythia, and in every corner of the room stood enormous crystals: glittering amethyst clusters as tall as children, phantom quartz points, mounds of cut emeralds and sapphires like glittering anthills set in golden bowls beside shimmering peacock feathers in tall painted pots. Frankincense burned in long smoky coils, filling the air. As Hannah looked around at the concealed treasure of the Temple of Apollo, she was overcome by the feeling that here in the inner chamber of the Pythia, beneath the surface of the earth, there was a pulse, a promising heartbeat still supporting life, even though the city lay in ruin.

"Gaia," said Stella. "Hannah of Alexandria."

Hannah stepped forward, her head bowed. "Respectful greetings. I come from the Temple of Isis in Egypt and have traveled on this quest at the behest of Master Junkar of the Kolossophia to see you before all is lost."

The Pythia laughed chimerically. "The Goddess will never die, dear girl. The Christians are not so powerful as that. Is that what frightens you?" The voice of a girl spilled from the veiled figure seated upon the dais, a sapphire gown of silk flowing all around her like the tide. She was merely a child.

Hannah looked up, surprised.

"You are the last. The last seeker who will come to Gaia, the oracle of Apollo, the sanctuary of the old wisdom. I have many things to tell you, and you must listen with your heart and promise to remember."

Hannah nodded and knelt upon the floor at the base of the dais. "I promise," she said. "But—"

"Good," said the oracle firmly. "Do not despair over Delfi. Anything that dies is reborn a thousand times. In this way, there is nothing that does not live forever.

"What blossoms must also wilt. What dies will be reborn. It is the way of life eternal, and the greatest secret the Earth possesses. All tides must flow in two directions; their source is what remains the same. But no matter how they ebb and flow, all seasons, all tides, all contraries are connected. Forever. It has always been this way: one extreme becoming the other in a never-ending spiral of birth, decay, rebirth."

"But everything will be lost," said Hannah. "This is why I was sent to ask you about the Emerald Tablet. It will unite the pagan people against the Christians. Our last hope."

"It is true that the teachings of the Goddess are disappearing. Her sons reject her. They do what every child must, or would remain with the parents forever." The oracle shifted her position slightly, an aura of blue light appearing around her veil. Her voice lilted happily. "But you, fair daughter of the desert, you have been chosen to bring a child into the world who will learn the sacred ways and carry them in its blood through the coming times of darkness. All will not be lost."

Hannah shifted on her heels. "What child? I came to ask of the tablet."

The Pythia smiled beneath her veil. "I know."

Hannah brought her hands to her belly in concern. Her moon-blood had not come in several weeks, but this was not unusual; she assumed the seasickness and loss of appetite had delayed it. Besides, she herself drank the bitter herbs from Mother Hathora after the sacred rite. There would be no child. Not now.

Hannah dared not ponder this strange prophesy any more deeply—she had been warned of the oracle's capricious ways. One thing could mean something entirely other in retrospect as many accounts had been written by those who sought the Pythia's predictions over the centuries. A "child" might not even mean a baby. Why, it could mean anything.

Hannah stepped forward, "Beloved Pythia, my quest."

"Yes," said the Pythia child, pointing. "Look there."

Hannah turned and took several paces toward a small wooden chest, its lid carved with the image of the winged sun disk, the uraeus of Isis. It was probably the most unadorned item in the room.

"Open it."

Hannah knelt and unlatched the chest, lifting the lid. Inside was a bundle of burgundy cloth. She withdrew it and held it to her breast, then closed the chest.

"Unwrap it."

Hannah set the bundle down on a kilim and slowly unbound it until she beheld the green crystal of the Emerald Tablet, a mossy glass so luminous it seemed alive, pulsing with energy and light, a curious script embossed on its surface. But when the last of the cloth fell away, it revealed a jagged edge where the tablet had been broken.

Hannah held it aloft in her naked hands in awe tainted by confusion. "The Emerald Tablet, but, this is only half of it? Where is the other half?" she said. It seemed so utterly terrible, the broken edge jagged and sharp. What did this mean? Was this what Julian had intended? Hannah pulled the shard from between her breasts and crouched to slip it into place. Yes, there. The shard fit against the broken edge perfectly, but where was the rest of the tablet?

The Pythia shifted on her tripod chair, hearing her thoughts. "Deep in the Egyptian desert in the Siwa Oasis lies the Oracle of Amun-Ra. There you will find the twin."

Hannah looked up. Surely the Pythia did not mean this. "The tablet was divided? Siwa? Is that even a real place? What does this mean?"

The Pythia laughed. "So you thought this was the end of your quest. No. It is the center."

"And if I refuse?"

"You have a choice, surely, but you know already what you will choose."

Hannah cradled the tablet like a babe to her breast. Was this the child the Pythia had meant? The child of the pagans who would lead them all home?

"Hannah, all through the generations of your blood, you must guard the secret of the Emerald Tablet. The world will be entirely different one day, perhaps open to its wisdom. People will soar through the sky in metal birds and communicate though tiny boxes. You cannot imagine what I have seen. The tablet's magic will be summoned again in that time, many centuries from our own."

"I will do as you ask," said Hannah, troubled but fervent.

The Pythia dropped her head forward. Sadness seeped from her bones into the room, as if what she had to say came from such finality she knew nothing could undo it. Even for such a young child, her burden seemed so heavy. When the girl on the throne lifted her head again, it was to speak the very last words of the Oracle of Delfi.

"Tell your people that the carven halls of Delfi have fallen in decay. Apollo will not come again to this prophesying bay. The talking stream is dry that hath so much to say."

Hannah drew her breath in sharply. The only sound in the room came from the fire in the basin.

The oracle froze like a statue, and Hannah knew at once she was expected to leave. She rebound the upper half of the Emerald Tablet in the linen cloth and placed it in the chest.

Her audience with the Pythia had ended.

———

The travelers returned to Athens by nightfall on a rickety cart given them by Stella, driven by Gideon, and pulled by a donkey, its shiny black eyes the size of bumblebees. Above them the dark sky rumbled, and two fat drops struck the backs of Hannah's hands. Gideon clucked to the donkey and smacked it on, eager to miss the rain, though they had to stop several times for sheep in the roads, the shepherds and their golden dogs never in a hurry to push the animals along.

The women gathered the blankets tightly around themselves and huddled together for warmth, taciturn and solemn. But none more so than Hannah, who felt at the bottom of the world with a whole new quest before her, and one that may be even more dangerous than the last.

Each traveler felt a deep, silent sorrow in the oracle's pronouncement. They did not dare to breathe as they neared that place in the road where the body of the ox driver, or what might be left of it, lay hidden in the river. How could they?

Hannah had been eager to show them the tablet. Each of them had held it, touched the face of it, felt the magic it contained, weak though palpable still. Triumph though this was, half an Emerald

Tablet was not the whole. The Siwa Oasis was a dangerous world away—whole armies had been lost, seventy thousand men, in search of it.

Hannah, with so much time in the cart, the simple chest containing the tablet beside her, found her mind unwittingly counting the weeks since she had bled. It was not impossible she was with child, but surely she would feel differently. Would there not be some sense of sharing her own body with another soul?

But then, the subtle thoughts worked their magic and drew her back to Julian. She wanted nothing more than to see him, to press her ear to his chest and hold him. Hannah watched the clouds in the sky, scrying for an answer. How she wanted to return to Pharos to find him. But Julian was dead, and Master Junkar was on his way to India. She was alone, entirely alone, and what if she was with child? Such a secret that would tarnish her reputation and leave her without a home, for even Alizar would surely reject her and cast her into the street.

There was one possibility if there was a child within her womb, one she knew was within her reach: she could seduce Gideon, make him think the child was his. But this was a deceit she wondered if she was even capable of. A lie like that takes a moment and then must be kept up for a lifetime. And what of the child? What of the truth? Her father would disapprove.

But then she did not have to keep the child, she knew. She could try more herbs or give it away, even to the Temple of Isis. But a child of the sacred marriage rite? This would be no ordinary child.

She admonished herself for thinking too far ahead. Her moonblood would come and all this concern would simply disappear, the next half of her quest ahead of her.

Hannah looked at the back of Gideon's head, his body jostled by the cart, and she traced the shape of his broad shoulders. Even from this distance she could still catch the musky scent of him and remember their night together. What did he feel for her now? To her their connection had been love's beginning; to him, perhaps the means to a quick if pleasurable end. But perhaps, just perhaps, lying with him one more time would quench her desire and answer the questions still left unanswered in her heart. Then she could know for sure if it was love, or merely lust, that had driven him. Just once more.

Hypatia also struggled within herself as with the finest adversary imaginable. She had murdered a man. *Murdered.* His blood had stained her hands. Every time she shut her eyes she saw it all again. How could she ever reconcile herself to what she had done? She felt ill a thousand times over. How could she face her students with such a treacherous secret to hide? She would have to cleanse herself somehow, perform twice as many austerities to atone for what she had done. Sofia rested her head in the Great Lady's lap, knowing she owed Hypatia her life.

Death for life, one for the other, the stranger for their friend.

But murder was unclean, for whatever reason. Murder was the greatest sin to any believer of any faith, even to a scientist.

As the cart waggled along, a wheel would strike a stone and unsettle them, and the women in the rear would look at one another, their eyes filled with concern. And so it was that the women became bonded to one another beyond what any of them had known or defined as friends. They were bound by the experiences they had shared, by death, the journey, the words of the oracle, the unfamiliar wilderness, as people are always more bonded to one another who have shared a bag of salt than a bag of sugar.

"I am going to speak to Alizar. I think you should live in the Great Library when we return," affirmed Hypatia, squeezing Hannah's hand as a white vein of lightning struck the distant mountains. "Synesius will continue to tutor you. I will see to it that you have a room with a view of the gardens." How she longed for the precious, safe walls of the Great Library, the only home she had ever known. Once they retuned to Athens, Hypatia decided, they would collect their things, and the *Vesta* would sail straight away, provided the weather would allow it.

Hannah nodded, unable to speak the words that were turning in her mind.

The damp stone streets of Athens lay shrouded in heavy-bellied clouds that hung low to the ground, mostly grey, ready to burst at the seams.

Hypatia returned to the library for the remaining weeks of the journey, not knowing if she would ever have the opportunity to cross the Mediterranean again. She bargained for manuscripts: Homer, Sophocles, Porphyry, Plato, Euripides in exchange for five Archimedes treatises, several Eratosthenes, a rare Galen. She made sure to fill as many urns as she could with scrolls before they sailed, her acquisitions priceless additions to the collection of the Great Library. She would keep the originals, make copies, and send them in the coming year.

Hannah performed for the audiences that Hypatia gathered. Sofia worked to secure the collections that Hypatia had requested. Gideon stocked the ship, swapped out one of the sails, and brought on an Athenian crew he had worked with before; some of the men had families in Alexandria they had longed to see for years and leapt at the opportunity.

One night Hannah visited the Athens apothecary in secret, exchanging a copper coin for the herbs she needed. She was certain now that the weeks since her last moonblood had been six or even seven.

"Start with a little," the apothecary had warned. "Then increase the dose night by night if your blood does not come. Do not be hasty. These herbs can rid you of the babe but also put you in the grave if you take too much."

Hannah returned to the inn and cooked them in the kitchen while the innkeeper went to feed the pigs and horses. She tasted the concoction, finding it vile, but then squeezed her nose and forced it down. Child of the sacred marriage rite or not, this was not a babe she desired. Even Mother Hathora had brought her the herbs previously, on the day after the ritual, so clearly it was expected that the night bear no fruit.

She waited by the fire, watching the flames in the hearth, her hands resting on her belly. The bread was fresh from the oven, the olives tart, and wine washed away the miserable aftertaste. She probed her belly, feeling nothing, waiting. How long?

Soon enough she felt the nausea consume her, the horrible twitch and spasm of her throat, and then she ran outside to wretch the putrid green herb juice into a rose bush. Then again. And again. When she felt empty, and her stomach calmed, she cupped her hands and drank fresh rain water from the horse trough. Then she went inside, entirely baffled as to whether the apothecary had given her the right mixture. She felt no cramps that might suggest her monthly courses. But still, there was time. She settled into a deep chair and closed her eyes, easing into the fire's warmth against her shins.

"Hello, maiden." Gideon swept in, giving her a start. He reclined in the chair beside her. His beard had grown, mostly covering the scar on his face. It was flecked with silver and suited him.

Gideon poured himself a cup of wine. Hannah offered him the water from another flagon to add to his wine, and he raised his palm to refuse it. He wanted strong drink tonight to fortify his veins. They would sail in the morning, and the weather looked bleak at best, disturbing at worst. He explained he had checked with a respected soothsayer, and the man had told him they best sail on the dark moon, which was tomorrow. Storms would persecute them across the Mediterranean if they waited.

"Gideon, I meant to ask you, what do you think I should tell Alizar?"

"Of Delfi? Tell him everything. He will consult with Master Savitur about the rest of the quest."

"You speak as if you know him."

"*Neh*. I trained with the Nuapar for several years when I came to Alexandria. I know Master Savitur and Master Junkar."

Hannah considered this. Did he mean the master Junkar who had died on the funeral pyre, or Julian, the new master? She blushed, not wanting to ask. "Surely you have something that needs your attention this night?"

"That ship is my wife. She has had enough of my attention for a lifetime. Tonight, wine and music are my pleasure. Tomorrow we face the open sea." He threw back the wine, poured himself another and topped her cup as well.

"You seem uneasy."

"Do I? Then perhaps a song, lady. For us."

He said *us*, though he and Hannah were the only people in the main room of the tavern. Even the innkeeper had gone to bed.

Hannah nodded and went to fetch her lyre. She was not ready for bed, besides. Her stomach groaned but not unpleasantly now. Perhaps the herbs were working their magic. She relieved her bladder in a chamber pot, checking with unfulfilled hope for the monthly crimson stain, and then returned to the fire.

Gideon shut his eyes and waved her to begin.

She tuned the lyre and then sat up straight with her back to the warm fire to sing one of the songs she had composed in her mind on the road from Delfi. She had not yet set it to music, but it leapt to life as though she had been playing it all her life.

Gideon applauded when she had finished. "Another, lady. Please."

Hannah assented, and her fingers found the taut strings. She closed her eyes and let the beauty of the music pour through her as Gideon refilled their cups of wine, adding the water to hers.

Then Hypatia stumbled in, the ringlets of her hair having sprung loose around her face. She joined them silently at the fire, drinking only the water, and then left in the middle of a song to find the stairs that led to her bedroom, clearly exhausted.

Gideon let his eyes flick to the door—he had originally intended to spend the night down in Piraeus at the wharf. He knew a bawd there with a new stock of girls he had been longing to taste since last he came through Athens, but now his attention had been arrested. He looked back to Hannah, who finished her song with a smile and set her lyre down beside her. Piraeus was far away besides, and here was a woman, a goddess before him.

Gideon knew what he wanted. He sprung to his feet and took Hannah's hand, then leaned down to kiss her. This woman. This woman he had not been able to push from his mind no matter how many others he had. He had wanted only her.

Hannah, her brow furrowed, set down her lyre and did not move to stand. "Gideon."

Gideon pulled her to her feet, the small of her back in one strong arm as though they were dancing. "Yes, it is my name."

Hannah took a step back, looked at her boots, the tips still wet from walking in the rain. She could feel the cold against her toes. "You will only spurn me again."

"Hannah, I do not want to frighten you, but there are storms ahead. Let me ask you, if this was your last night of this life, how would you want to spend it?"

Hannah sighed, not really hearing him. The wine moved in her blood, warmed her face, her fingertips. He cupped one hand around her breast as he kissed her neck, down to the scar that ran across her sternum from the slave trader's knife. "You are impetuous, Gideon." She did not want to relent, though she both wanted, and did not want, this.

"I know the dangers we face."

"You never answered my letter."

"I never answered your letter because I cannot write." Gideon laughed. "It was kind of you to send it. Hannah, let this night be ours as if it were our last."

He did not wait for her reply, but wrapped her legs around his waist and held her there by the backs of her thighs. She shrieked and wrapped her arms around his neck, wishing not to be so easily won, but the wine surged in her blood, analgesic, warm and sweet, making her forget her pain, the thoughts, all that came before. Perhaps she could have him one last time, and it did not have to go cold the way it had before. She had no expectations of him now. She could fortify her heart. This was purely desire, and she was yet a slave. One night would not breach her careful defense.

Feeling her surrender, he carried her all the way up the stairs to her bedroom and dropped her on the bed. She laughed, and he pressed a finger to her lips. "Shhh. We do not want to wake the others." He pulled his tunic over his head and untied the belt of her *himation*, which fell off her shoulders her waist. He stopped just to look at her, finding he could not see her with the moon dark, the sky covered in a blanket of clouds. He rose and lit a single candle and brought it to the table beside the bed.

Luminous beauty. She shone in the light.

He climbed on top of her, pinning her arms above her head. "Fight."

"What?" She was taken aback by this strange request.

"Fight me. Pretend." He kissed her passionately, and she squirmed beneath him, unable to free her arms. He held her firmly. She laughed.

"Oh, you dare laugh, do you?"

His tongue circled her nipple as his fingers found their way down past her navel, down and down to slip inside her, warm and wet. He stroked his cock with his other hand. Praise Zeus, how he had wanted this woman. He had not even realized it.

Hannah, enlivened by this playful exchange, found his fingers arousing more passion than she could contain. She kissed him hungrily, enlivened by her desire. She so wanted to forget Julian, to find a way to release him. Perhaps this was her answered prayer. When finally Gideon plunged inside of her, she climaxed in one swift streak of ecstasy that moved like lightning up her spine, her body convulsing in pleasure. He had to cover her mouth with his palm to muffle her cries.

They played his games until dawn, but always he held back, waiting, not wanting to release his seed, not yet. Finally she turned to her hands and knees, inviting him the way she had seen the horses and the goats mounting each other in the fields. He groaned in pleasure, moving inside her faster and faster until found he could no longer hold back. He cupped both hands around her perfect buttocks, and released himself as he collapsed on top of her, fully spent and instantly asleep. Hannah wriggled out from the weight of him and curled against his warm body, reassured by the heat of the man in the bed beside her. She blew out the candle and stroked the fur of his chest, listened to his breathing in the dark. He was not Julian, and this was not love, true. But she knew in her heart that she would never see Julian again. Their spiritual union had lasted one profound and perfect night, and in its place, Gideon's brute passion would suffice. Deep within her mind, a part of her still hoped he might make her his wife, although it was swiftly eaten away, eroded by the fear he did not love her. That he would take her body, bring her pleasure, and it meant nothing. But perhaps she could do the same.

They slept without dreams in the Inn of the White Raven, and then Hannah rose and packed her belongings, finding Gideon had already left to reach his ship. At dawn, the gentle storm struck, turning the sparkling cerulean sea to a dismal slate grey. The *Vesta* rocked and swayed gently in her slip as Alexandria's dolphin,

Apollo, circled slowly in the dimpled water, rising for breath just beyond the stern of the ship, ready to accompany them home.

Gideon felt eager to get underway to avoid further inclement weather in the crossing and suggested they stay the night in Harmonia before taking on the Mediterranean with her mighty swells.

As they carried their things up the dock, Hypatia looked over at Hannah and noticed how her cheeks began to pale. "Oh, Mother of Zeus, I forgot." Hypatia dropped her bags. "We must get some herbs for your seasickness. Gideon!" Hypatia yelled for the captain. "We must go to the apothecary. Is there one here in Piraeus? Do not sail without us."

Hypatia and Hannah trotted down the docks, asking where they might find the apothecary. An old woman with a black scarf drawn over her head lifted a gnarled finger and pointed down an alleyway.

In between the winding narrow passageways—on every doorstep—stood or crouched rough-looking women, once objects of beauty, their hair tangled and matted, their elegant clothing torn and soiled, their eyes dark as hollows in decayed logs. Some smoked. Others spat. Most just hunkered, keeping out of the rain. Seeing Hypatia and Hannah in fine clean clothes, a few of them called out rudely. Hypatia dropped her head and quickened her steps while Hannah allowed herself to glance at the broken women, the unwanted ones who had to leave the brothels because they had grown too old, too unkempt, born too many children, or been injured by some rough sailor. Mother Hathora had taught her that long ago prostitutes had held respected positions as servants of the Goddess in the temples of Greece and in the temples of Sumer, in a time long before these brothels. They were literate bards and poets, priestesses and politicians then. They served the Goddess called by many names: She who was the Queen of Heaven, Mistress of Earth and Sea. The women of the temples were worshipped then. What would happen to them now the art had fallen so?

Around the last corner, Hypatia looked up to find herself standing eye to eye with a shrunken woman who was about her own age, once a celebrated courtesan, though she looked infinitely older. Her scarred fingers curled around an *amphora* of wine, her eyes encircled by dark blue rings of impoverished sleep. When she saw Hypatia, she stared remorselessly.

Hypatia froze.

The two women locked eyes and neither looked away.

In the gaze of the whore, Hypatia could not move. She felt the hardened eyes staring straight through her soul as if to say, *I know what you have done.*

Hypatia tried to swallow, to look away, but she could not.

"Come, Hypatia." Hannah took Hypatia's arm. "Come."

Slowly, Hypatia turned, though she kept glancing back to see the steely eyes of the whore still fixed on her as if condemning her to death. Then the whore let out a stream of curses, louder and louder, faster and faster, the bitterness of the attack not subsiding until they turned a corner and then another.

Hypatia shuddered, stopped in the street. Finally, she began to cry. "She knows what I have done. She can see it. Murderer that I am. I am just as she is. No better."

Hannah took her friend by the shoulders firmly. "Had you not slit his throat, he would have robbed and killed us all. You must take pride in that."

Hypatia met Hannah's eyes with her own. "It has stained my soul," she whispered.

Hannah shook her head. "Your soul could never be tainted by justice."

Hypatia nodded, her eyes far away. No words could dispel what she already knew, the dark fate of karma sealed around her like a wax cell.

They found the front gate of the apothecary on the next street, which opened into a pristine courtyard where a statue was surrounded by moss and vines. "I will go in and talk to him," said Hannah, touching Hypatia's shoulder. "Wait here." Perhaps this apothecary knew better than the one in Athens. She could ask for herbs for both her needs, and it could go unnoticed.

Hypatia nodded, and then slowly circled the puddled court-yard. She stared at her feet without seeing anything, the hateful dark eyes of the prostitute staring up at her from the ground. *Murderer*, said the eyes. *Murderer*.

When Hypatia lifted her gaze, she was standing directly before the statue at the center of the herbalist's garden. He must have been a Christian, because it was the Virgin Mary, her arms open at her sides in acceptance and love, her expression full of compassion.

In that instant, Hypatia had a vision, a vision that consumed her like a divine fire. As she looked up at the statue, it was eclipsed by the living image of Mother Mary herself, an aura of light around her, her arms outstretched in devotion, in an offering of love. So much love. It wove threads of light through Hypatia's darkened heart. Tears slid down Hypatia's cheeks. In that moment, she understood that she was looking not at the mother of a baby boy named Jesus, but at the mother of Christ, of God, whose mother is the eternal Mother of the World.

Here shone Mary, virgin, untainted heart of radiance, eternally pure in body and soul. And she leaned down and placed her hand on the crown of Hypatia's head.

Hypatia wept and threw herself down to kiss the holy virgin's feet.

❦ 26

To welcome the travelers home and celebrate the return of his daughter to Alexandria, Alizar had Jemir prepare a feast in the courtyard. Hannah had been given the night to enjoy the party, not needing to return to her work till the morning. They sat together in the torchlight on the cushioned divans beneath the sprawling fig tree that had seen so many occasions come and go, toasting to the beauty of the evening. Nothing could have pleased Alizar more than to have his daughter home, and her so ebullient. Synesius and Sofia sat opposite Alizar discussing Synesius's latest book on dog breeding, hounds, mastiffs, dogs that flushed birds from low shrubs with short hair that did not matt. Gideon had not yet arrived. Tarek swept in from the street toting a young coquette who seemed enamored of his style, pausing to chat with the doctor, Philemon, and several of his students, two male, two female. Governor Orestes and his wife, Phoebe, stood beside the fountain in deep discussion with several of the library's magistrates. Hypatia had declined the invitation with apologies, as her work had need of her.

Tarek and his scantily clad guest settled in across from Hannah, joined by Phoebe and Orestes. Hannah felt a cold ripple of disgust at the sight of Tarek. She looked away, adjusting the straps of her *khiton*. She knew he would be no trouble in Alizar's presence, but still she wished he would fall off a cliff. She was just hours over her seasickness and felt the nausea striking her anew.

"Hannah? Do tell us of your travels. Was Hypatia well received in the library at Athens?" asked Phoebe, her green eyes thrown open in a perpetual expression of surprise. "We are all relieved you returned safely."

"As am I, and yes, she was." Hannah breathed a sigh of relief. It was a miracle their ocean crossing had not sunk them to the bottom of Poseidon's lair. The waves pummeled the ship, swamped the deck, and only subsided as they passed through the Cycladic islands. A welcome respite came as they dropped anchor on the eastern shore of Crete to assess any damages and take to the shore to stretch their legs. Hannah vomited as her feet touched the sand. There was not an herb under the stars that had worked on her seasickness. She would have preferred to remain stranded on Crete the rest of her life than take to the unsteady sea again.

Even as Hannah acknowledged to Alizar's guests the good fortune of a safe return to Egypt, she dreaded the desert before her, another dangerous leg of her quest. She knew then that she was equally bound. Bound to her destiny. Bound upon her quest. Hers was a life of slavery indeed. With a forced smile she described the library at Athens, the performances, the fawning politicians. It had been tremendous, of course.

"Where is Gideon?" asked Alizar.

Tarek interjected before anyone could reply, tearing a piece of chicken from the bone with his teeth. "Surely back with his whores."

As though hearing his name, Gideon strode up, settling onto the bench beside Hannah, his dark eyes lit like some kind of predator as he smiled broadly at Tarek, his white teeth flashing. "Good evening," he said.

"Where is the lovely maiden you had with you at our last party, Gideon?" Tarek asked.

Gideon chuckled. "No matter, Tarek. But you have found yourself an adoring muse." Gideon nodded to the sweet girl who unknowingly dragged her curls in the cup of wine she sipped.

The girl and the rest of the guests seated on the couches of the *triclinium* found this amusing, and laughter sparked in a circle.

As the dinner wore on, Jemir watched Hannah out of the corner of his eye with concern as she nudged the food around her plate but none of it toward her mouth. In truth, the pungent scents of the meal had completely overwhelmed her and extinguished her appetite. She fingered the raised grape pattern on her chalice nervously, thinking of the half of the Emerald Tablet in its wooden chest she had concealed in her bed in the stables. It had begun to influence her dreams, and she tossed and turned at night, unable to shake their torpor. She dreamed of battles long ago. Kings and queens with bones turned to dust in their graves. Even split in half, the tablet's magic was in no way dim.

Gideon took another swig of wine and concluded a joke he had been building as more laughter shook the table. He loved a feast.

Alizar and Gideon went on with their animated discussion as Hannah watched them. Though she was distracted by her own emotions, she could not help but notice this was the first time she had seen Alizar happy since Naomi had passed away, and it brought her comfort to see him so. Sofia's arrival had brought him back to life, and this meant a great deal to Hannah, as the love she had felt for her father lived on in the love she felt for Alizar.

"Synesius, what is this dreadful rumor we hear of you leaving us for Cyrene?" asked Alizar.

"Only eventually, brother. I am to be ordained as a bishop first, and then I shall make my way there." Synesius smiled and folded his hands in his lap. "I shall miss Hypatia, but we will write. She promises to keep me abreast of her teaching."

"This is tremendous news," said Alizar. "We will all feel your absence, especially Hypatia, I am sure. Why this sudden change of heart?"

"The best influence is had from within. Though I remain a gnostic, I feel perhaps as a bishop I might bring the church temperance. To teach as Jesus taught, with humility. I can only hope my presence in the orthodox church will sway them toward more civilized means of sharing the word of Christ."

Gideon nodded. "It is a noble undertaking, Sy. I wish you well."

"Here, here." Words came from around the table as cups lifted.

"Cyrene?" asked Sofia, her eyes aglow. "But how soon?"

"Oh, in several years time," said Synesius. "The clergy moves quite slowly with these things."

"Is Cyrene anywhere near Siwa?" asked Hannah, recognizing the opportunity to inquire after information that may serve her quest.

Tarek was delighted to interject an explanation for her, as he believed it would demonstrate his intelligence, an attribute he would expect her to praise regularly once he took her for a wife, for this was his newest aim, laying eyes on Hannah again. A slave wife would suit him perfectly. "Siwa is where the Oracle of Amun-Ra gave Alexander the Great the knowledge of his lineage as the son of Zeus. Most think that Alexander found the Emerald Tablet there in the tomb of Hermes. The oasis lies deep in the southern desert. Men that have gone in search of it have never returned. It is said that Cleopatra took the secret of its whereabouts to her grave." Seeing he had Hannah's attention, Tarek grinned widely in showmanship, pausing for effect. "Cyrene, however, is on the coast just five days by sea west of here. The current moves in our favor for travel."

"A Christian city supposedly cleansed of heretics like us. But who will your friends be, Synesius, the sparrows?" said Alizar. Laughter crowned the table.

Gideon speared a piece of chicken off Tarek's plate and gulped it down with a wink at Hannah. "I do hope we might have the pleasure of your voice this evening, nightingale."

Tarek sneered, unable to protest both Gideon's affection toward Hannah, and his little slight.

"Certainly, if it pleases Alizar and our other company." Hannah nodded politely.

Jemir gazed at her plate with the paling disappointment only a chef is capable of wielding. "You must eat something, *Kukla*. Some bread, Hannah. Here." He tore a piece of flatbread, slathered it generously in olive paste and anchovies and set it on her plate, but as soon as the scent of the fish reached her nose, Hannah's eyes grew wide and she stood up abruptly, apologized to Jemir, and walked inside.

Gideon followed her with his eyes, concerned.

Jemir left the table behind her to fetch the second course and found Hannah in the kitchen. He waved a drumstick at her and pushed it into her hands. "I am going to stand here until I see that go into your stomach."

Hannah let out a little laugh and nibbled on the meat. "I am sorry, Jemir, my stomach has not settled since the voyage."

"Well, you need food." Jemir set down a handful of empty platters and began to bustle around the kitchen. Then he paused. "I know. You should go and have a warm bath before coming down and singing for us. It will make you feel better."

Hannah smiled. "A lovely suggestion, Jemir, thank you." She rose and kissed his cheek.

There were only a handful of homes in Alexandria wealthy enough at that time to have their own private baths. Everyone else went to the public baths, most of which were scandalous scenes of incessant gossip, secret trysts, political bribery, and prostitution. Of course, certain bathhouses had reputations for being more of one variety than another. Some were frequented only by politicians while others boasted amenities for sailors. Others charged admission so that only the rich could afford them. There were nearly fifty bathhouses in Alexandria, which was a relatively small number compared to Antioch, a city that boasted over three hundred.

The bathing chamber in Alizar's home was a large stone-tiled room with a sunken tub in the floor that was filled with water from an enormous wood-heated pot in the kitchen. Hannah entered the bathroom and latched the door. The bath was a modern convenience Hannah relished, one she had never known growing up in the desert but had come swiftly to appreciate.

Hannah pulled a carved ivory handle at the edge of the tub attached to a string, and hot water spilled through the sluices into the tub. She watched as it filled and stirred the steaming water in circles with her foot as the level rose. Once she had undressed and slipped into the water, Hannah let out a long sigh. Alizar's bath was a place no troubles in the world could reach.

Hannah dipped her hand into a jar of crumbled soap powder and smoothed it over her shoulders, belly, and feet. Then she dunked herself in the tub and came up again to draw red henna through her hair before plaiting it into one long braid that hung down her back. Once clean, she let her body go limp to bask in the warm water. If she was really to go to the Oracle of Amun-Ra, she knew she must leave soon. But how?

She had listened to what Tarek said of Siwa, a place so deep in the desert that men who tried to find it never returned. It seemed unlikely she would find a caravan traveling there, much less convince them to take her along.

Her fingertips brushed her belly. She swallowed hard. She had taken the apothecary's herbs for three weeks, increasing the dosage as he had said each night until she could bear the bitter potion no more and dumped it over the side of the ship.

Now the truth had her in its talons.

Within her womb, the angel slept.

She was with child.

This child that had no intention of quitting her womb whatsoever. The irony. All the women visiting the apothecaries to try and conceive a child to no avail, and here she had one so easily that she could not afford the scandal of.

Still, her heart began to soften. A baby. There would be a baby to hold and to kiss and to fawn over. Would Alizar ever allow her to keep it? Perhaps she could strap it to her back as she did her chores. But what in the world of the rest of her quest? She knew she had to speak to Alizar. This would wait no longer.

Hannah cleaned her teeth and then climbed out and wrapped herself in a towel. Singing for the feast would be a wonderful distraction. She dried herself off and applied a dab of amber resin behind each ear and donned a clean sleeveless *himation* of light linen in a pale blue with a border of repeating *meandros*.

In the sitting room just off the stairs where everyone had gathered to hear her music, she settled on a cushion. Gideon brought her the lyre Hypatia had given her as a gift. Hannah touched her lips to the cool smooth wood and then ran her fingers over the strings to check their tune. She made several adjustments, and when she was satisfied, turned her attention to her audience. Gideon sat close enough to nudge her lyre with his knee if he chose.

"This is a Bedouin song I learned as a child while spying on their fires," she said, and her heart felt light again even playing the first several notes. Hannah began to sing the happy song, smiling at Sofia and Alizar. Synesius clapped his hands while Phoebe and Orestes stood up to dance, and seeing this, Gideon picked up a doumbek and began to slap out a rhythm with practiced ease.

Hannah smiled at him and his talent and went on playing the playful melody as she sang and smiled at everyone. When it ended, they each bowed to her and clapped in appreciation.

"Oh, let us have another!" said Sofia.

"Very well," said Hannah. She sang many more songs that evening, well into the night as her audience was unwilling to let her conclude. Hannah played song after song, finding that there was immense happiness in that night, more than any she had known since her father's death. Eventually she just let herself be swept away by the music and the festivity of Sofia's return, and Alizar's joy in it. So.

The party went on until birds could be heard twittering in the trees. Hannah stood at the door and enfolded Sofia in her arms. "I am so happy to know you," she whispered, and kissed Sofia's cheeks.

"Hannah, speak to my father. He will help you," whispered Sofia as she kissed Hannah's cheeks in return. Hannah nodded, and then Synesius took Sofia's arm and led her into the street.

Hannah felt her eyelids grow heavy now that the music had left her, and so she turned back into the house with a yawn. Her thoughts were trained on the bed laid out for her in the warm stable straw when a strong hand caught her elbow.

"Hannah," said Gideon, letting go her arm. He was standing so close that she felt his breath on her lips.

She smiled at him, pleased he had not decided to don his armor again after their night of passion in Athens.

His dark eyes found hers, searching her face, and then he opened his mouth as if he had more to say.

She dropped her gaze.

"Thank you for the music," he said.

"Indeed," said Hannah. "It was a wonderful party." For a moment she wondered if he might stay, take her in his arms, but he simply reached for her hand, kissed it, and strode down the alley toward the harbor.

Hannah shut the door and swept through the atrium toward the kitchen and the stables beyond, her poise undiminished even in fatigue.

"Hannah?" Alizar stepped before her.

"Yes, Alizar?"

"I should like to see you in my study."

Creases appeared in her brow. "Now?"

Alizar shook his head. "Get some sleep. Come in the afternoon. There is much to discuss."

Hannah nodded.

She left the hall and went out to the stables, where she passed several hours beside the Emerald Tablet, unable to sleep, then slipped in and out of dreams that were neither real nor unreal but in some ways even more full of feeling than she had ever known in life. She became a boar being chased on the hunt, then transformed into a horse, trying to outrun the same predator that was gaining on her. She darted this way and that, but there was no shaking him; she was attacked with a roar, the predator's claws raking her skin. She awoke with a jolt, breathless, and pulled her shift around her body and went to splash water from the fountain on her face. Then she went straight to Alizar's study, the wooden chest in her hands. He would know what to do. He would see they had to make haste to the Siwa Oasis.

Alizar reclined in his morning robe although it was now early afternoon, enjoying a bowl of hashish. "My dear," he began.

Hannah interrupted him. "I have brought what the Pythia gave me." Hannah took a step forward and set the chest on the worktable. She nibbled on her lower lip. "Look for yourself."

Alizar unwrapped the bundle and regarded the raised script of the tablet with fascination. He stroked the crystal and clucked with pleasure. When he pulled the cloth back completely, he saw the jagged break that Gideon had spoken of. "This alone will not be enough to aid Orestes. Now that Rome has fallen, the pagans would unite if we had the entire tablet. They want to appease the angered gods. But I fear without the other half we have nothing."

"I was told we must retrieve it from the oracle of Amun-Ra."

Alizar nodded. "I wondered if the Nuapar would be as careful as this when they concealed the tablet." He again glided his fingers over the strange, mystical lettering on the tablet.

"You knew the tablet was at Delfi?"

"Not knew. Hoped."

"What does it say?"

"It reads: 'Ascend from the earth to the heavens. Extract the lights from the heights and descend to the earth containing the power of the above and the below, for it is with the light of the lights. Therefore the darkness flees.' And there is more, but it will not help us without the rest of the tablet intact. You see, the script is already known by the Kolossofia, but the legend is that the script alone does not have any effect without the Emerald Tablet. That is why they sent it to be protected by the oracles—so that its magic could not be used for evil."

"What is its magic?" asked Hannah.

"The tablet promises to make its interpreter immortal," said Alizar. "And beyond that, as I said, the reappearance of the Emerald Tablet would unite all the remaining pagans against Christianity. But only if we can find the other half."

"Which is why Orestes wants it?"

"Of course."

Hannah nodded and looked away.

Alizar looked through her as if he could read her thoughts. "There is something you have not told me."

Hannah shook her head. "No, I have told you everything there is to tell."

Alizar put his face in front of hers so she would have to look at him. "If there is one thing I pride myself on, it is reading the odd mannerisms of women, and you have not been yourself since you returned from Athens. Hannah, you must know I usually find things out in time, and I have come to prefer knowing any ill-fortune in advance. What is wrong? Does it involve Hypatia? Did the Oracle of Delfi say more?"

She nodded and met his eyes. "Yes."

"I cannot help you if I do not know the full truth."

Hannah sighed and then lifted her eyes. "I am with child."

Alizar shook his head, clearly disappointed. "A man from Athens?"

Hannah cringed. "No. I believe it is the child of the Sacred Marriage rite of the Nuapar."

"You believe?"

"There is little room for doubt."

"Hermes, Zeus, and Apollo. Master Junkar's child?" Alizar groaned and tapped his pipe. "The library might end their investment in you when Hypatia finds out. They cannot have an unwed mother about. And I, well, I am in another predicament entirely having aligned myself with Hypatia and Orestes. Cyril watches what I eat, what letters I send, where I take a shit; it is exhausting." Alizar sank onto his workbench and spread his hands on the table, revealing the bronze prosthetic thumb he had created for himself, fitted to his hand with a leather glove.

"What should I do?" Hannah was trembling.

"Well, if what you say is true, then you should either give the child up to the Temple of Isis or accept Gideon's proposal."

Hannah lifted her eyes, stunned. "What proposal?"

It was Alizar's turn to look confused. "Why, last night he approached me to purchase you. I thought he would have spoken of it to you. It is a wonderful proposal, Hannah. Gideon is wealthy and he would treat you well. It is true he has a history of many women, as I am sure you will hear, but he has a good heart. Besides, I believe he has fallen in love with you."

Hannah stood up and crossed to the window, stunned, bitter. "Purchase me? In love with me? For how long, a week until he tires of me?" Buy her. Buy her? She wanted to spit. Julian would never want to purchase her. He would know love cannot be purchased nor sold.

"Consider it."

The heat of fury burned in Hannah's blood, scalding the tips of her ears. "Over what alternative? I am yours to dispose of, Alizar. Never mind that I am a shepherdess. That I was raised by a good and caring father, not born a slave. And what of the child? You think Gideon would want me like this? Or would he take me at a *bargain*?" She nearly spat the word.

"Hannah. Take some time to calm down. I think it would be wise I accept Gideon's offer, as Cyril is hunting for you still, and we are all in danger here. The Temple of Isis may even want the child. It would be the most sensible arrangement, besides. You could speak to Mother Hathora. Gideon is a proud and loyal man. Do you not find him handsome? He may even let you keep up your studies at the Great Library."

"Why, to increase my value?" said Hannah, feeling the full weight of her circumstances strike her down. Then she muttered, "I did find him handsome." But he was not Julian. He would never be Julian. And the quest for the Emerald Tablet was all she may ever have of Julian, once in her arms, now so very far away and lost to her. "Alizar, what then of the Emerald Tablet and the Oracle of Amun-Ra? I have not completed my quest given to me by Julian, eh, I mean Master Junkar."

Alizar coughed a plume of smoke and knocked his pipe on the edge of the table, letting the small cake of ashes fall to the floor. "Leave that to me. In your current state I hardly think it wise to take on such a trek as that. It is more than dangerous, Hannah; it could be deadly. But I have all my life longed to go to Siwa and found that a wife and young children always prevented me. Since I no longer have those responsibilities, here is my thought: I will go in your place, and you shall stay here until the child comes. That way your quest may yet be fulfilled by those more capable of it."

Hannah shook her head. "More capable? But I succeeded at Delfi. I want to go. This quest belongs to me," she said, tears filling her eyes, for she knew that if she had any sense at all she would listen to Alizar. She felt like a petulant child, suddenly, her entire fate decided by those larger than herself. "Please."

Alizar gently collected the tablet, rebound it in the cloth, and then crossed the room to procure a far sturdier chest of brass from the shelf than the one Hannah had delivered it in. Then he set the bundle inside as gently as a sleeping babe, closed the lid and secured a new iron lock to the hasp, tugging it with satisfaction to find it held fast. "As your master, I forbid it."

27

Alizar stood solitary on the ridge of a sand dune surveying the fading dark horizon of the southern desert, his head and shoulders bound in a white burnoose, only his stark blue eyes visible, like holes that led to the sky. The clues of the desert landscape were subtle. He sampled a pinch of sand from beside his feet and let the granules run through his fingertips to discern that the coming day would be warmer than the one that preceded it, if only slightly. A light wind fluttered the cloth of his *tunica* as he trudged down the face of the rippled dune. Behind him the sand lifted like sea spray, then settled.

The ocean and the desert were twins by birth, he felt. The sea whirled like a dervish beneath the stars while the desert undulated beneath the fingers of the wind. The dunes, like waves, changed shape with the currents. The ocean was a salty desert of unquenchable thirst, the rolling dry dunes, an endless sea of adamantine waves. Each landscape could be filled with unspeakable beauty one moment, deadly peril the next.

Alizar had no preference. He felt useful in the midst of any purposeful adventure no matter the landscape. He had prayed all his life to visit the fabled city of Siwa, and somewhere out beyond the endless sea of sand and parched earth, the oracle of Amun-Ra lay waiting for him.

What would Naomi say?

Behave your age.

And what would he say?

Never.

And then he would kiss her. How he longed to kiss her again.

Alizar scryed the sky for his wife's face—as if he expected to see her looking down on him—but of course, she was not there. He heard her laughing in his memory the day they were wed; he saw her hands lifting a cup to her lips. There was still time yet before he joined her in the other world. He had to make the most of it. He pushed on while the wind picked up again, swirling capriciously and then settling. His feet sunk in the coarse sand to his ankles with every step.

Beyond the dunes, a cave lay situated in an odd lump of hills shaped like the head of a camel. There the others waited for Alizar to return. In the end, he had chosen to bring Jemir, Gideon, and Tarek. None wanted to be excluded from the adventure. Tarek heard of the journey and immediately packed his belongings. Jemir scurried through the kitchen determining which pots would be the best to bring. "No cook, no food, no journey," he had said, adamantly. How could Alizar refuse? He accepted and went into the market to acquire three camels.

When Alizar was just a youth in the Nuapar and heard of the Emerald Tablet for the first time, he knew his destiny was tied to it, and only standing in his stables so many decades later packing for Siwa did he know why.

"The camels are ready." Gideon threw a coiled rope to Alizar and crossed the straw to Hannah. "When the moon has gone from dark to light and dark again I will return for you," he said. "Then you will be mine."

He drew her close and kissed her. He did not ask her what she wanted, and if he had, she no longer knew what to say. Was she insulted at his presumption or exuberant that he wanted her beside him? Both ways, she could still feel the bright wilderness of freedom now a memory leeched from her bones, all the wild fury of her womanhood locked in a tiny cage. It was not he that infuriated her but her own fate of being captured and sold. And sold again. Her future a mere transaction to the grave.

Alizar busied himself with balancing the bags on the camel, for he was unsure if she had told Gideon all there was to know when Alizar had agreed to sell her to his captain. He just hoped she would not do anything foolish. As if reading Alizar's thoughts, Hannah turned away and drew out the silken cord from between her breasts where the shard of the Emerald Tablet rested to kiss it.

Curse these men. This was her quest.

The party left at dawn's first light to travel the coast west and then push south.

So.

Hannah was discovered on the second night out of Alexandria. She had managed to hide herself between a bedroll and a grain bin on top of the larger camel. She was just small enough to curl herself into place and wait through the terrible heat until the night came, the jostling blistering her hips bones, her neck stiff and sore. Once she was sure the men slept, desperate to pee, she snuck out and relieved herself, then she rummaged until she found a piece of dried mutton she had brought in her haversack. Gideon surprised her with his knife at her throat. "Stop thief," he growled.

"Gideon," she turned slowly. "Lower your blade."

"Hannah? But how?"

"It is my quest to finish."

Gideon laughed, sheathing his knife. "Foolish woman. This quest is for men. You must go back home."

"What is it?" Alizar appeared beside Gideon, awake and irritated.

Hannah stepped forward, all the fight in her small body aroused to a pitch. "I am joining you. This is my quest for Master Junkar." She held up the shard of the Emerald Tablet. "He gave this to me, and I gave him my word."

Alizar closed his eyes. Opened them. She still stood before him. Not a dream then. *Humph.* "What do you think, Gideon?"

Hannah clenched her fists, thrust her chest forward. "I am as fit as any of you."

"She is fit. Though she may slow us."

"Have you told him?" Alizar asked Hannah, without letting Gideon answer his first question.

"Told me what?" asked Gideon.

"It is nothing. I am quite able, I assure you."

Alizar searched her face, her eyes in the thin starlight. Was she so determined that she would risk her own child? Her waist looked thin as parchment. Perhaps she had gotten rid of it then. Still, the issue would be for Gideon to address as her new master, whatever course fate had chosen.

"My vote is she may join us. Have we the rations?" Gideon smiled, amused.

"I packed mine with me," said Hannah. "In the camel bag."

"So be it." When Alizar finished admonishing his impetuous slave, he sat down and offered her a date. He knew he would not sleep again before the sun rose.

Hannah took the bowl, hunger ravaging her body. As she ate, she eyed Tarek who was sprawled behind the dying fire, asleep. She instinctively checked her knife affixed to her calf. She wished Tarek had not come along. For now she could live with her disgust, the proximity of her knife, and the protection of the other men. Eventually, she hoped she might be healed of the memory of that night entirely. But when she thought of this, she considered how that same dreadful night had led her to Gideon on the ship. How strange it was, she thought, that some circumstances enter our lives as gifts and leave as curses, while others enter as curses and leave us gifts.

The next day they turned inland from the coast and dropped south into the desert, waiting in a shallow cave for the noonday sun to pass. Gideon and Alizar poured over the half-dozen maps they had acquired from the Great Library, checking them against each other, Gideon utilizing his cartography skills to close the discrepancies. The others sat in a circle, sharing water and throwing back handfuls of almonds and dried figs. The cave was a welcome relief from the egregious sand that burrowed into every bodily orifice. They shared it with only one other inhabitant: a skeleton corpse that lay partially mummified by the desert, sprawled on its side, the jaw slightly agape as if its occupant had died in astonishment or perhaps uttering some final words of warning. Even the skin was perfectly preserved, tanned to a hide.

"Alizar, that thing sickens me. Why must we camp here?" Tarek pointed at the skeleton as he entered the cave, smacking noisily on a strip of dried fish.

Hannah laughed. "That from the boy who always takes the catacombs to the library."

Tarek stared at her, "Who are you calling *boy*, slave?"

"You shall not speak to her that way," Gideon growled.

"She is a slave."

"And you are a stinking turd," said Gideon, knocking Tarek on the side of the head.

"Why did we have to keep her with us?" whined Tarek.

Alizar set down the map in irritation. "Tarek, you begged me to join this caravan, and I was reluctant to let you, if you recall. I gave only one condition. Can you name it?"

Tarek's shoulders slumped forward and his eyes fell to the floor. "No whining."

"Yes, that sounds accurate. Now, make yourself useful and help Jemir with our supper. We will be finished in a moment."

Gideon and Alizar went on discussing the old maps, then walked out to measure their course against the path of the sun. They were not in agreement about their position. There were two mounds of rock that contained caves pictured on each of the maps, one due west of the other. Gideon seemed to think they were occupying the eastern outcropping, Alizar, the west. It was Gideon who surrendered to Alizar's way of thinking against his better judgment, but the discrepancy was only slight; in the end they would be merely half a day to the east of Siwa if Alizar's course was off. The maps had belonged to Cleopatra, who had made frequent treks to the oasis, so each man felt confident in their reliability, if only they knew which one would be the more so.

While they huddled around the fire that night discussing the adventure and the miles ahead, Jemir questioned Alizar about the Oracle of Amun-Ra. "What do we actually know of it, aside from legend?"

"Very little." Alizar smiled. That was the enchantment for him. No one from Alexandria had been to the oracle for hundreds of years—this factor alone had persuaded him to let Tarek join them, for Tarek's artistic talents would enable them to return to Alexandria with not just memories, but sketches. "Apparently, Cleopatra thought so highly of the anti-aging properties of the mineral baths that she took frequent trips from Alexandria. Still, I wonder how much of that is mere rumor."

"When was the last time anyone summoned the oracle?" asked Hannah.

Alizar leaned back on his elbows and stretched his legs. "I have no idea. The library shows no record of it. But the Oracle of Amun-Ra is ancient. It was named for the god Amun. This is the word we still use in most languages to close our prayers, as it heralds his protection and the sun of life: Amen. Perhaps Alexander was the last to summon the oracle. Do you know, Gideon?"

Gideon nodded. "We know of no other after him."

Hannah let her eyes trace Gideon's form beneath his dusty tunic. What kind of master would he make? Would he care for her or would he spurn her yet again? Still, she would never be his wife, merely his slave. She knew she would have to watch him frequent the brothels and sleep with his mistresses beneath their roof—a painful insult she was certain she could not endure. She longed to stay with Alizar, continue her studies in the Great Library, put the past behind her. But she carried the past in her belly, and it grew by the hour.

When Hannah let Gideon into her bed the night before the caravan departed, she had felt a mix of emotion from wanting to please him, to longing for Julian's embrace, to concern that Gideon would find out she was pregnant. Afterward, she had pulled the blanket over her hips, hiding her navel although there was nothing yet to hide.

"You are so beautiful," said Gideon. "Like a lioness." He turned her over, ready to take her again.

She smiled for the first time since their return voyage home, her desire for him restored to its former power inside her, burning like the eternal flame of Delfi. She knew that such a man as Gideon would never have wanted her if she had been ugly or misshapen. Her fate could be worse. Much worse, indeed. Alizar could have sent her to the brothels to whore beside Mira when he learned she was pregnant to earn back the price he paid for her. Hannah shuddered, and then Gideon kissed her and made her forget.

She knew she should tell him, but she was not ready. Not yet. So.

Alizar sat back beside the fire Jemir had created from camel dung and lit his pipe. He looked at Hannah and then to Gideon beside her. He wondered if he was not making a mistake in selling her. In the small cave, Gideon's presence was imposing, his massive chest broader than a bull's. Alizar knew how brash he could be. So much charisma should never be squeezed into one human being. Still, he reminded himself to find the time to tell Hannah that beneath Gideon's fearsome exterior was a man of refined spirit, as he had a passion for poetry and a gift for nursing sick plants in Alizar's herb garden whenever he came to visit. In truth, Alizar preferred Gideon's company to many of the aristocrats and philosophers of the Great Library, for he had retained his humanity.

"And how are things faring in the church of St. Alexander?" Gideon kicked Alizar's boot with his own. "You talked any sense into the bishop yet?"

"Currently, my impression of the church is that its clergy care a great deal more about preaching against supposed heretics and heathens than they do for instructing their flock to follow the example of Christ. Of late, Cyril's sermons resemble instructions on how to dispose of what he considers the filth of Alexandria: the scientists, mathematicians, philosophers; those bastions of sorcery and black magic, the Jews; the beggars. And us, of course."

This drew laughter.

"Do you think Cyril will actually follow through with the reconstruction of the Heptastadion bridge to Pharos?" asked Tarek. This was the latest news in Alexandria. No one could remember when or how the bridge that separated the two harbors had collapsed, although Hypatia surmised it had probably fallen during one of the city's many earthquakes some hundred years earlier. This had proved fortunate for the preservation of the Temples of Isis and Poseidon, although massive amounts of fuel for the lighthouse had to be shipped across the harbor on a barge, an expensive and laborious endeavor just to keep the light shining. Still, it was slightly less daunting than finding an architect the city could afford, as its economic seat in the empire had crashed since the drought had diminished Egypt's grain supply. There was simply nothing to export. Gone were the days of Caesar's prolific economy. Still, with the many generous donations from Constantinople and the treasury of Alexander the Great pouring into their church from the imperial coffers, the Christians could no doubt take on the expense of the bridge, which would give them access to the little isle, the last stronghold of pagans in the empire.

"Yes, I do." Alizar shook his head in a burdened way as though he had already considered the subject from every possible angle. "Cyril has control of the mob. They heed his every word. They would build him a bridge to heaven if he asked it of them."

The conversation then turned to talk of the Great Library, Hypatia's newest lecture series, and Sofia's apparent interest in Synesius. Alizar seemed outwardly pleased with the match, though he said little else. His answers were pithy, punctuated with yawns as he pulled off his boots and rubbed his swollen toes.

Soon talk died down and turned to preparing the camels for the hours of trekking ahead. Hannah sat and listened to the busy crackling of the fire and watched the stars. She could not stop herself from thinking of Julian, the night they had spent together, all that she wished she could confide in him now. Gideon . . . Julian. Her heart swung between them like a pendulum. The longing that blossomed in her heart for Julian continued to deepen, especially now, carrying his child. She wanted to see him again, to tell him. Her feelings would sound ridiculous, she knew, for they only had the one night, but it was so deeply true for her. A falling star punctuated her thought, for a moment the brightest, most startling light in the heavens, burning across half the sky before winking out above the black dunes. Perhaps that is what he was, she thought, saddened suddenly as the truth leaked into her reverie. He was the brightest point of light in her sky for a solitary night of love, outshining everyone and everything else, before disappearing forever. The unbidden tears fell faster than she could wipe them away.

Gideon snored beside her, content to dream. She would be his as soon as they returned to Alexandria. Alizar had agreed to it. He hoped she would be pleased, although he had some concerns for her inability to endure the sea that was his home. Perhaps he could keep her in a small apartment and always enjoy a woman to return home to. He had never had that kind of sanctuary before. It was appealing. He could enjoy his freedom and a woman, both. So.

Gideon stood at Alizar's shoulder, the two men equal in height as they trudged along the spine of a broad dune checking their location. "We cannot stay in Siwa. We must be certain we turn east within one week of arriving."

Alizar nodded. "The *Kahmsin* winds."

"You have experienced them?"

"No, but I hear they blow for fifty days across the southern desert."

"We have until mid-spring. Merely days."

Alizar nodded in agreement. "We best pick up the pace."

The caravan struck out over the dunes by day and camped at dusk within a small outcropping of boulders above a dry earthen sea bed speckled with shell fossils: ammonite, mussel, brachiopods. They had trampled the eras as they walked, shoved time in their sinus pockets in the shapes of tiny ancient creatures: circles, triangles, ovals. Little treasures.

Hannah slowed. She pretended it was to check the laces on her boots or to stop to urinate even when nothing came out. The truth was the child was sapping all her strength. A fatigue beyond anything she had ever known pulled at her every step as though her feet weighted her like anchors. *Tiredtiredtiredtired* was all she could think. So tired. Rest. She just wanted to sleep.

The next morning Gideon was the first to rise. He went for a quick walk along the salt flat beyond their camp to find a suitable place for them to cross. Then he reached into a fold in his dusty tunic and pulled out a single smooth, black pebble and dropped it on the ground. Since the records in the library said the journey to Siwa was expected to take ten to twelve days, Gideon had filled his pocket with twelve small stones, dropping one each morning as a method of keeping time in the desert, a landscape where time could be extremely deceptive, especially traversing the same rolling dunes or flat parched earth day after day. Eleven left.

When everyone was roused and packed, Hannah, dreading the tedious day of walking before them, realized they were missing someone she preferred would stay missing. "Where is Tarek?"

In the pale lavender light of morning, everyone set down their cups and scanned the surrounding area for the familiar figure of their friend.

Then, as if on cue, Tarek dashed out from behind the boulders in a frenzy, shrieking, slapping at his neck. "Ay! Get it off me!" he screeched. "Ayiiii!"

Alizar and Gideon rushed to his side. The desert was filled with deadly reasons why Tarek would be in such a state, snakebite being the worst.

"Tarek, calm yourself. What happened?" Gideon grasped Tarek by the shoulders.

"My neck."

Gideon looked on one side, then the other; he touched Tarek's skin, so smooth with youth. A red welt the size of a goat's nipple was already swelling up there.

Hannah touched Gideon's arm, stepping in beside him to examine the welt. "Did you see the creature?" she asked Tarek, who shook his head, no. "Where were you sleeping?"

Tarek pointed to an outcropping of jagged stone.

"Lie here. Do not move," Gideon said.

Alizar and Jemir searched Tarek's sleeping site. Hannah clamped both hands on Tarek's shoulders to hold him still as he writhed in pain.

Alizar and Jemir ran back from the boulders. "Black scorpion," said Alizar. "This long." He held his two index fingers apart the width of a baby's rattle.

"*Androctonus*," Jemir whispered in Greek.

"Man-killer," Gideon translated. He had been stung several times by scorpions in the desert, but with his thick Greek blood, had never reacted with more than a momentary dizziness. He could only hope that Tarek's Egyptian blood would respond as well.

"Alizar, kill the thing and bring it to me. Do not touch it. Jemir, have you any garlic?" Hannah moved to the fire.

"Yes." He fetched three cloves from a camel bag.

"Am I going to die?" Tarek asked.

"Hold still, Tarek," whispered Hannah. "I have seen enough death. As have we all. Grind it to a paste, please, Jemir."

A memory, Hannah's father Kaleb crouched beside the fire cooking the remedy, flashed in her mind. She had watched him in fascination, merely a child who should have been asleep in her bed. The rabbi's youngest son needed a healer. The boy was smaller still than she, and she carried him on her back when they played together. The nearest healer was a full three days ride, but Kaleb knew a shepherd's remedy for scorpion bite. The boy had lived. Now Hannah bent over the fire to cook the garlic, add the oil, mimicking his gestures, the recipe. A good part of her longed to spit in the medicine, though she restrained herself.

Alizar returned with the nasty black beast, tiny yet still viscerally terrifying, decapitated and held at arm's length by a spade like an offering to the god of death. "You are certain this will work?"

"Crush it between two stones, those will do," she pointed, "and hold it over the fire so the blood drops in the pan. Do not touch it." Hannah had disposed of any excess words, words that might gentle the fact she was giving orders, but the men trusted her medicinal skill and obeyed without complaint to save their friend.

Alizar smashed the creature between the flat stones with a sickening crunch of shell and innards as the viscous blue blood leaked and splattered.

"Just five drops, no more," Hannah warned. "The scorpion is immune to his own venom so the blood is a healing agent—if we are fortunate." Beneath the wooden spoon, the mash turned the color of vomit and smelled twice as noxious. Gideon thrust his nose inside his tunic and held Tarek still.

Hannah applied the poultice carefully, wrapping Tarek's neck in a clean bandage Alizar had brought in his kit. Tarek winced and moaned, then his eyelids drooped and he began to drool a foul white liquid. "You chose a dreadful place to be stung, Tarek," she remarked. "Hold still."

Alizar scanned the horizon. "We best get moving. The day is already ahead of us. Tarek can ride one of the camels." Alizar placed a hand on one knee to steady himself, then rose to his feet.

They continued through the heat of the day under the open sky where fibrous clouds receded upwards and disappeared in the heat like a magician's handkerchief trick. The caravan traversed a desolate landscape of flat, parched ground where they occasionally paused to enjoy the rare appearance of Cleopatra's stone cairns, still standing after hundreds of years, marking the way to the oasis. The edges of the pale blue sky and the striated blond earth bled together at the horizon in a fine wash of color that made each of the travelers feel that they were trapped in a vast and unchanging landscape without nearing their destination, or moving at all.

Hannah covered Tarek's welt every few hours with fresh poultice, then clay, and for those first hours of the morning it seemed that Tarek had fought off the worst of the venom and would be fine. But by noon he had fallen into a feverish swoon and tumbled head first off the camel Jemir was leading. He landed without waking. They then tugged Tarek behind the camel on a little sleigh made with one of the camel blankets. They had come too far from Alexandria to go back.

By nightfall they reached the edge of a crater pocket that backed up to still another ocean of rolling dunes. It would be a suitable place to camp for the night, so the men unburdened the two camels and staked them.

Tarek did not wake for two days. Alizar had seen such severe symptoms in the small children of the Bedouin but not in a boy of nineteen like Tarek. The sting's unfortunate location must have played a part in his reaction. Soon Tarek's fever was hotter than the sun at midday, and his pallor blanched like a dead fish.

"We must bury him," Gideon announced. Hannah nodded in agreement. Beneath the sands would be the only cool place in the day, though the temperatures dropped at night. They could insulate his body, help him regulate.

Alizar rummaged until he came up with several shovels from the camel bags, chiding himself. Praise Zeus, that morning he had wanted to push on and ignore the severity of the scorpion sting; he simply assumed the boy would rouse. Tarek could be foolish, petulant, but he loved him just the same. To have Tarek near him was the closest thing to having his son, Theon, alive. As Tarek lay on the cool ground, incoherent and weak, he realized that he had relied on the boy to be a bridge to his own child, a child already irretrievably lost years before. The third death. Alizar had almost forgotten his own prediction. A bolt of fear flashed through him. He had to prevent it.

Alizar chose a place where the ground seemed less densely packed and began to dig. The handle of the shovel snapped at once. He cursed as he carved and chipped the stubborn ground while Gideon and Jemir joined him. Eventually after they were drenched in sweat, they created a trench.

"The desert has afflicted him, and so the desert must heal him," said Hannah as they lay Tarek, limp as a sleeping cat, in the trench and covered him with the cool earth up to his chin.

Alizar would not leave the boy's side to eat or to sleep. Every hour or so he would tilt Tarek's head back and pour water between his parted lips, most of which spilled down his chin onto the ground. The others awoke intermittently to relieve Alizar but were always refused.

When morning arrived, Alizar cupped his palm to Tarek's forehead to find that it was cool, and the pulse of life was still in his neck.

When they pulled Tarek out of the ground, he was weak but coherent, retaining no memory of what had happened to him. But his recovery brought with it a new problem, namely that they had used up Tarek's ration of water for the trek in an effort to flush the poison from his body. There would be no more morning tea, no more stews. There was just enough to make it to Siwa if they were careful. If need be, they would collect their own urine to drink.

The days that followed led them over the steep shoulders of the dunes. Hannah found the walking exhausting in the unabating heat, as she was always sinking in the sand, climbing the faces of the dunes only to slide back. Gideon provided her with his arm for support whenever she needed it, and Hannah swallowed her pride and allowed him to help her. The child was fatiguing her, she knew, and she dared not tell him of it, not yet, not until the right moment. This babe was strong, stronger even than she, drawing life from her bones, wanting more, always more.

Tarek walked when he could, and rode one of the camels the rest of the time. The sting left him unusually taciturn, wearing a far-off expression as though he had traveled to the edge of a precipice and some part of him had not returned from that distant place. He answered any questions laconically, his eyes fixed elsewhere when he spoke.

So.

When Gideon had three pebbles left in his pocket, they came to a wide valley where the ruddy ground was covered in small white fossil shells as flat and round as rose petals. Alizar picked up a handful of them and thrust them in his pocket for Sofia back at home, who always loved such little treasures.

Then, as he was standing up, something else caught his eye beside his foot. A hint of blue buried in the ground. Alizar nudged the earth away from the object with his fingertips and freed it.

It was an image of Horus, imprinted on a faience pawn. Alizar presented it to Gideon and Hannah.

"A wonderful omen," said Gideon. "Let us hope the falcon god guides us."

"Isis," whispered Hannah. *Goddess guide the path of my heart, my mind, my feet.*

When the day came that Gideon had one stone left in his pocket, the wind pushed them back, blasting their cheeks with sand. By noon it was impossible to press ahead. The caravan made a tight circle as the windstorm flung sand in all directions. It was too wild to attempt to erect a tent, so they huddled between the camels and stacked the camel bags beside them, covering the little fort with blankets to keep out the sand, which was totally ineffective. In silence they passed the hours, focusing only on sipping tiny threads of breath from inside their burnooses, praying for a breath free of dust, coughing, trying to keep the water skins free of sand as they parched their dirty throats.

The storm did not subside till that night when, half buried, they pulled themselves from the sand. The caravan had made almost no progress that day. Profoundly relieved, they set up camp, and Jemir made fresh bread using a Bedouin technique by digging a hole in the sand. Hannah tugged off her boots to rub her aching feet, both heels bloody, several toenails blackened by the fact they fit her too snugly. God almighty, why had she insisted on this journey?

Gideon and Alizar continued to pour over the maps as Tarek trudged to the top of a dune and pulled out a roll of Pergamon parchment so he could draw. Hour by hour he angrily shredded the parchment in front of him until he had quite a good charcoal depiction of the landscape.

"Impressive," said Hannah, who had sought him out. There was something she wanted to discuss.

He glanced at her, continued drawing. The ink dried instantly in the desert air. "It was a good poultice. Thank you."

"You would do the same for me." Her tone held all the sarcasm she could wield.

He sniffed, wiped his nose on his sleeve, said nothing.

"You did not tell Alizar about the incident between us, did you?" she asked.

He knew instantly what she meant, how he had tried to rape her, and she had stabbed him. "I was drunk."

"You could have had me flayed for what I did to you. But you did not punish me. Why?" Hannah wanted to know if he was biding his time, waiting to strike at a later time.

"I do not know. It is past." Tarek swept the charcoal across his page, completing the dunes.

"Is it?"

"I hear Gideon will be your new master. I have tired of your trouble, besides."

"It seems to me now you owe me your life."

"As you have owed me yours." Tarek met her eyes. "The slave girl I bought who should have died, had Alizar not brought the doctor."

"Then we are square, Tarek." Hannah wanted to hear this from him, the words from his mouth, though she feared even words would never be enough from the capricious boy to whom honor meant nothing.

He nodded, irritated. "We are square, Hannah."

Hannah smiled, stood, dusted her hands on her *tunica*, her aim attained: an accord for her safety, the safety of the child. For now.

The next day, Gideon dropped the last stone from his pocket as they struck out over the sand, lifted as though the wind itself was breathing. By midday, they came to the end of the dunes and traversed a long salt flat hemmed in by hills of rounded rock that rose up from the eastern and southern horizons. There were no cairns, no signs of the oasis. Just the endless expanse of dry desert.

That night they camped on a plateau overlooking a wide, flat plain. "I think we are south of the oasis here." Gideon indicated the position on the map. Alizar squinted. "It is possible."

They decided that it might still be too soon to see the oasis, given the time they had lost during the windstorm and Tarek's recovery, so they walked for another day, and that evening they came to a ledge of caves and set up camp. Tarek checked their gear as the others gathered around a fire Jemir had made from camel dung. As they stretched their aching legs and backs, they chatted about their quest, and the discussion again led to Cyril.

"Someone should just kill him before it is too late," said Gideon with a comical smile on his face, a wineskin in one hand that he had been saving in his haversack till now. He passed the grape to Alizar, who chuckled and took a swig. While the men voiced their complaints about Cyril, Tarek crept up to the fire. He hung back behind a large boulder, listening.

"He just needs a woman to remind him of the flesh," offered Jemir, taking the wineskin from Alizar.

"What hag would touch him?" Gideon jested.

"Agreed," said Alizar.

Hannah slept with her head on Gideon's lap as he stroked her hair. She had impressed him on these journeys. He knew now not to underestimate her, though the desert seemed to be wearing on her. She looked exhausted day and night and had slowed her pace considerably. He woke her to eat, concerned. "You need to keep up your strength, woman."

She roused, took several bites, and fell instantly asleep again.

"He will never change," said Alizar picking up the thread of conversation. "We just have to find a way to endure his stupidity, I fear."

"He is a child," said Gideon.

Jemir shook his head and downed a swig. "I agree with Alizar. He will never change. He is a coward, the most fearsome kind of brute."

As the men tossed out their sardonic opinions, Tarek skulked away.

"Hey, what has been keeping you?" Gideon left the fire to empty his bladder and found Tarek leaning against one of the boulders.

"I have been checking the camels," said Tarek, his eyes steely and dark. He cleaned his nails with the point of a knife. "Did you think I could not hear you?"

"Hear us?" Gideon turned his back to piss off the ledge. "You mean discussing Cyril? I think the time has come to choose an assassin, myself."

"Why should I believe you?" Tarek snapped.

"What got you all hot, man?"

Tarek shrugged. Perhaps they were not discussing him after all.

Gideon shook himself and returned to the fire. The maps needed his attention. Time was short.

Over a week into their journey with still no sign of Siwa, the caravan ran out of water as they passed the last sheep bladder. By afternoon, they subsisted on the remainder of Gideon's liquor, which only brought on dehydration from the alcohol. By evening, they captured and drank their own urine.

Alizar knew they had three days left, at best. If they did not find Siwa soon, they would have to kill one of the camels.

Hannah watched as the men debated their options. Gideon and Alizar fell to arguing over the direction they were heading.

Jemir just dabbed his forehead with a dusty white cloth and stared off to the horizon while Tarek looked at the ground, waiting. Hannah had no energy left to even consider breaking up the argument, so she sat down on her heels and closed her eyes, listening to the rush of blood in her ears. She was so thirsty. Painfully thirsty. Tired. Painfully tired. Each step a monument of effort and agony.

She looked through her mind for something soothing—a thought, a prayer, anything—and an old melody appeared, one she had written as a child playing beside some stones in a stream, which she began to remember in threads that all wove back into one line, something about the sun and the sea and the silverfish, but the words did not matter.

As if in a trance, Hannah stood up and began to drift away from the rest of the caravan, her eyes closed, humming the melody.

Gideon stopped mid-sentence and thrust the map into Alizar's hands. "Hannah?" he called out, but she did not respond. She was sauntering like a dancer, eyes closed, humming dreamily, and he felt certain she was delirious.

Gideon moved to step in front of her to stop her, and Alizar's hand fell on his shoulder. "No," he said. "I think we should follow her."

"Follow her?" said Gideon, befuddled. "First you say we are to move south, now west after a delirious woman?"

Alizar nodded and called out. "Jemir, you and Tarek stay here. We will return."

Hannah went on as if she did not hear, the melody filling her as she moved, singing what lyrics she could remember. Threads of light danced all around her, like she swam underwater, not altogether unpleasant.

Alizar fell into step behind her with Gideon. "Let us see where she goes. She seems not delirious, but in a trance."

Gideon licked the painful blisters on his lips. "We are all going mad."

A glint against Hannah's chest caught her eye, and she looked down to see the shard of the tablet around her neck, glowing in the sunlight. Yes, Julian had said it would guide her. What else? Something else . . . she felt so thirsty she could not think. So tired. She could no longer command her own mind. Then it struck her. He had said to use it to enhance her vision. What if it was a real instruction, not just a metaphor of some kind?

She lifted the green glass, translucent save for the raised script, up to the sky and looked through it to behold a world awash with green. Hannah thought she saw a little demarcation in the green landscape. When she removed the shard from before her eyes, however, it was no longer there. Abruptly, she stopped and turned to Alizar.

"Alizar, look," she said, holding up the shard of the tablet. "Look through it."

Intrigued, he came forward and closed one eye to see through the shard. He gazed for a moment, then lifted his head and opened both eyes, then looked through the shard again. "I see a line," he said. "A facet in the shard, perhaps."

"Or perhaps not," said Hannah.

Alizar looked again. She was right. The shard illuminated a subtle world they could not see with their eyes. It had the magic of the Emerald Tablet, which guided them even here in the wasteland of heat and dust.

Alizar stopped Hannah and pointed. Then he lifted the shard again, lowered it, and conferred with her.

"What is it?" asked Gideon.

Hannah smiled at the men and lowered the shard to her chest. "A cliff. With a light beyond it."

Alizar and Gideon walked past her in silence to the edge of the tall cliff that overlooked a wide valley sprawling from east to west as far as the eye could see. The wind was surprisingly gentle, carrying a slight bit of moisture. Alizar licked his peeling lips and stared out over the endless expanse before him.

"Look. Look there!" Gideon raised his arm and pointed into the sky. Two black specks soared on an updraft, too far away to identify. The birds swung circles around the sun, then disappeared in the sky.

"And there," Alizar added enthusiastically, spotting the tiniest glint of light at the western end of the valley before the fiery sun. A reverent smile spread across his lips. Only water glistened in the desert. Or a mirage. But they prayed, prayed for water.

When they were all rejoined, Tarek found a steep trail carved by an ancient stream that descended the cliff. It took them most of the afternoon just to reach the valley floor. On the way down, the tallest of the two camels scraped the cliff and one of its canvas bags came untied, tumbling hundreds of feet into the valley below. They could hear it bouncing all the way down. The camel brayed loudly as if it was delighted to have discarded some of the load. The footing was loose, rocky, dangerous. The sole of one of Hannah's boots sprung apart at the toe as she struck a stone, and she fell into Gideon who turned and held her; she was inches from falling over the ledge. Picking their way down the slope was painfully slow but necessary. Their heads throbbed, bodies sucked dry of sweat in seconds.

On the valley floor the dusty bag was lying within plain sight. They tied it back on the camel and walked through a maze of rocky passages, twenty meters tall, the boulders twisted into tortured shapes. There was no vegetation whatsoever. One passage gave way to the next, and the next. By evening, there was no way to tell which direction they were walking, and they had yet to find a way out of the passages. Eventually, the stars shone overhead, and Alizar waited to see the direction of their movement before walking any farther.

Hannah succumbed to her fatigue. "Please, Alizar. I need to rest." He agreed, and they stopped to camp in a circle of stones.

At last, they slept.

As the first light of morning paled the sky, Alizar awoke to the sound of a raven cawing. "*Gebel Sekunder*," he whispered. And then he rose quickly and rallied the others. "In Alexander's journal he describes a place called *Gebel Sekunder* where the ravens took him and his men to Siwa. I think this is that place. Be perfectly quiet. If another passes, we must follow it."

Within the hour two more ravens passed, and they began to weave through the passageways that were wide enough for the camels to pass. By midday, the caravan stepped into the blinding sunlight of the valley floor.

Hannah and Jemir spotted five ravens circling high overhead, and so each of them, delirious with anticipation, drew upon their last reserves of energy to follow the birds. Gideon hoisted Hannah onto a camel to let her ride and rest.

In the late afternoon of the intense desert heat, the caravan stopped as they sighted, as if in a dream, the unmistakable paladin of an island of some kind within a shimmering lake. They shouted and cheered, throwing their hands up to the sky in gratitude.

So.

28

Exhausted, parched, and caked in grime and sweat, the men of the caravan ran full tilt to the edge of the enormous saline lake, ecstatic whoops of joy bursting from their throats as they tore off their clothes and plunged into the cool spring as Hannah waded in the shallows. Several white egrets took to the sky as flirtatious quail disappeared into nappy reed beds overshadowed by towering palms that rustled and swayed in the hot, dry breeze. The craggy trunks masked the small, thin faces of the children hiding at the water's edge.

Though they enjoyed the swim, what they really needed was a fresh spring. The saline water could not satisfy their thirst. Hannah drank several long sips and then spat it out.

It was Alizar's voice, rumbling like a storm cloud, that broke their reverie. He stood at the edge of the water surveying the surrounding landscape. When his eyes came to rest on a strange mountain beyond the lake, his hands fell to his sides in astonishment. "My word . . ."

"What is it?" Gideon sprung to his feet and threw on his *tunica* to join Alizar. As he eyed the mound, he too, could not believe his eyes. "By the gods of my father," he said.

"Impossible," said Jemir, his jowls hanging agape.

"It cannot be real," mused Tarek.

"What do you think it is?" asked Hannah.

"That, my dear—" said Alizar, tipping his head slowly in Hannah's direction without taking his eyes off the magical vista before him, "—is the city of Siwa."

It rose in the north straight out of the desert floor like a magnificent hive carved from one tremendous block of clay, the walls blending seamlessly into the rosy earth. And yet it was clear from the little windows and doors that speckled the exterior that this was no natural formation. The city of Siwa stood nearly as high as the lighthouse of Pharos, being stacked at least seven floors vertically, and spanning a length of about thirteen city blocks from one end to the other. Every little dwelling, shop, temple, and home was connected to the rest of the raised mound by winding narrow streets, tiny earthen bridges, and footholds sculpted into the walls for access to the higher levels. It was a living human honeycomb. And what was more, tiny particles of salt and limestone blown across the expansive desert had become embedded in the silt and mud used to construct the city, causing it to scintillate like a sanguineous ruby in the warm light of the sunset. The caravan gazed on it, spellbound.

They were drawn toward it, eyes raised, until they stumbled on a small spring, hidden in a stand of date palms. They dropped to their knees in exaltation as if praying to a deity, the deity of water, of life itself. Inhaling the water, splashing it on their faces, each at last slaked of a painful thirst.

It was Gideon who suggested they camp there, outside the city for the night, as the inhabitants might think them bandits if they arrived after sundown. Tarek was disappointed at this, but the others quickly agreed. They had no idea how their presence would be interpreted by the local people.

"Can I go spying?" Tarek asked Alizar, his voice crackling with excitement.

Alizar considered it, and then shook his head. "No. I think Gideon is right and we should wait till the morning."

"But the Siwans will see our campfire. They will know we are here," protested Tarek, chewing on a date.

"Then we make no fire tonight," said Alizar.

So.

The following morning, Hannah awakened in surprise to find that she was surrounded by bright, curious eyes belonging to dozens of dirty children who crouched all around her. She nudged Gideon, who roused with a groan and rubbed his eyes. It seemed to Hannah, fresh from dream, that these were not ordinary children at all, but otherworldly spirit children, some having hair and skin the color of the whitest sea foam, while others bore exotic traits of the nomadic desert tribes. A few had the golden skin, curved lips, and slanted foreheads of the Egyptian people, while others looked distinctly Nubian like Jemir, with black skin, almond eyes, and plump lips that quickly split into happy grins. One gamine little girl even had blue eyes paler than Hannah's.

Gideon quickly reasoned that Alexander the Great's army and presumably Cleopatra's and Caesar's attendants had contributed these Greek characteristics to the Siwan people, an interbreeding which had, over the last six hundred years or more, resulted in an abundance of albino and blue-eyed youngsters. Alizar, too, propped himself up on his elbows to admire the beautiful children. "Welcome to Siwa," he said.

The children began to squeal and chatter when the strangers awoke, calling back to unseen friends behind the palm trees to come and see. The caravan found they were further encircled by even more giggling children, who grabbed their hands and led them like prizes up the narrow path into the palatial city.

The men and Hannah were struck speechless, marveling at the stark interior of the raised city, which was strong as stone and intricately sculpted at every turn in rounded corners, narrow windows, and curved steps. The Siwan people had relatively few possessions, it seemed, as most of their baskets and pots were woven from palm fronds or formed from the same smooth clay as everything else. Items of the civilized world like spades and animal harnesses, they had probably acquired from trade with nomadic tribes like the Bedouin. The desert had literally baked everything they knew into permanent existence. With a little water they could dissolve a wall in a house to create a door, or in one day a family could add a room onto their dwelling for a newly married couple. Everywhere dusty goats hopped from ledge to ledge, braying constantly as they sat with their stubby legs curled beneath them on the highest roofs of the city. Occasionally, a solitary jeweled figure in long black and orange dress, her face hidden beneath a veil, would appear and then vanish into the labyrinth of the city.

Surprisingly, many of the Siwan people did not react to the presence of the caravan at all, but merely looked up, then went back to whatever they were doing: repairing walls, milking goats, carrying water, or brandishing sticks at overburdened donkeys. Others recognized the opportunity to make sales and rushed toward them with handfuls of brightly colored fruits and crude silver jewelry, jabbering in a language that sounded like the cacophony of birds to Hannah.

They walked on, turning their eyes in all directions as the children led them through the dusty streets that curved like the inside of a seashell. Alizar and Gideon, the two tallest men, were especially aware of how narrow the doors and passageways were and how low. The Siwan people were considerably smaller than the Greeks and quite used to crouching. The men felt like giants in their midst. Hannah, her thirst slaked at last, looked around herself in awe and delight, enjoying the way the stark landscape illuminated the atmosphere as if it had captured a thousand years of sunlight in stone. She eyed the fruits, ruby red, pale green, and longed to taste that flesh after so many days of salted meat and nuts.

As they continued through the labyrinth of the city—climbing steps, crossing bridges, and turning down curving narrow passages flanked by high steep walls—still more children flocked to the caravan leading Hannah and the others towards some unspoken destination deep in the heart of the magical city that smelled of salt and strawberries.

At the end of a long winding passage where laundry hung from long sticks jutting from the walls overhead, the children climbed a set of steep stairs that ran diagonally along the edge of a tall wall. At the top of the narrow steps sat a plump little opening that could hardly be called a door. They each had to enter on their knees, and even then it was a squeeze. Hannah crouched low and ducked her head.

On the other side, once her eyes adjusted to the dim light, she could see that they were in a small square anteroom with lofty ceilings. The sound of flies buzzing in their ears, they all sat shoulder to shoulder as the children crawled over them to sit between their feet or against their broad shoulders, examining their nostrils and beards, fingernails and freckles. An adolescent boy with legs as thin as a grasshopper's that jutted from beneath his dusty loincloth clutched a staff and called through another doorway to someone behind the walls. Remarkably, Hannah felt no fear at all, only nervous excitement. However, beside her, Gideon shifted on his haunches and whispered to the others, "Trust no one."

A few moments passed, and then a stooped, formally clad elder appeared in the hollow of a small open passage that led out of the room. He wore long robes the color of sand decorated with black stripes, and for a moment Hannah thought perhaps he might be a scribe, until she noticed that one of the man's long black sleeves concealed a withered hand. As he came closer, Hannah saw that this was not his only misfortune. Both his eyes were capped by snowy cataracts, a condition that she had seen many times among the elder shepherds of Sinai, which afflicted many desert dwellers due to the harsh conditions of the climate. The old hierophant sensed the strangers before him and smiled politely, taking a seat in front of them, swatting the flies away.

"Welcome, Welcome. Omar-the-Goat, I am," said the elder in broken Egyptian. Then he coughed violently and spat on the floor. Tarek looked at Gideon, who looked at Alizar, who looked back at Jemir, who looked at Hannah. No one knew quite what to do, but since Tarek and Alizar were the only two among them who spoke Egyptian, they responded by introducing themselves, and then Alizar explained where they were from.

This pleased the old man who laughed, coughed, spat, and then said cheerfully, "The dung of your people has not been smelled here for a thousand years! Delighted you we."

"Is he the king?" Gideon leaned in toward Alizar.

"No," whispered Alizar. "A magician or possibly a priest. I suspect he seldom has visitors. It could be the first time in half a century he has even spoken to outsiders."

The priest nodded his head, as though he understood. Then he said, "Fruit we have for you, our guests." Then he whispered to the crouching boy with the staff who leapt to his feet and rushed off, returning with a tray of the most beautiful food any of them had seen in weeks. There were perfect white grapes, blood oranges, dates, figs, glassy plums, and a sweet red fruit that Hannah had never seen before that looked exactly like a tomato.

When they had eaten the feast and praised the food to their host, Alizar opened his palm and rained silver coins on the straw mat before them. "We would like to consult the Oracle of Amun-Ra," he said. "Can you take us there?"

Omar-the-Goat pressed his lips together and cast his limp gaze down to the floor for a long time. "No oracle," he said.

"No oracle?" asked Alizar.

"No oracle," said the old priest, scooping up the coins with his good hand as though he could see them perfectly, dropping them into the leather satchel at his hip. "No, no, no oracle today. Come tomorrow."

Alizar began to protest, but Omar-the-Goat shook his head and resolutely held up the palm of his hand. "Tomorrow, tomorrow," he said, and then he shooed the men and children out of the room as though they were chickens.

So.

The next nine days played out in precisely the same manner. Every morning the caravan would awaken to the flaming desert sun and the round, peaceful eyes of the children watching them sleep. The children would then rush them into the city to see the blind old priest who would feed them fresh fruit and announce happily when they inquired about the Oracle of Amun-Ra, "Tomorrow."

"What should we do, Alizar?" asked Gideon. "The *Kahmsin* winds are approaching. If we do not leave soon, I fear we will be stranded here."

Alizar poked at the campfire with a stick, and a spray of sparks flew up and vanished in between the constellations. "The full moon approaches. I believe this is why he is making us wait."

"What if I go exploring the cliffs to the north of the city? I have seen people up there," said Tarek, "and dwellings."

"No, I think we should be patient," said Alizar. "If by the full moon he does not agree to take us to the oracle, then I permit you to explore, Tarek."

Tarek let out a sigh but did not argue.

On the morning of the full moon, the caravan gathered at the mouth of the city and followed the children to see Omar-the-Goat. Right away, the routine shifted. Alizar smiled a knowing smile at the others as the children proceeded to lead them, not up the stairs like before, but behind the little town of Aghurmi and up a steep slope where a row of little huts stood huddled together like doves on a short branch. Eventually they came to a wide vista overlooking the entire valley where a large rectangular temple made of the same ruddy clay as everything else rose up impressively. Its twenty or so columns of red granite ornamented with intricate hieroglyphic carvings depicted stories of fishing, hunting as well as scenes of prayer and feasting. A mammoth granite obelisk taller than any in Alexandria stood in the courtyard beside a shimmering spring just as Alexander the Great had described in his journals.

"*Omm Beyda*," whispered Alizar.

The Temple of Amun-Ra.

The children scattered and disappeared with whoops of excitement, leaving the caravan outside the temple to wait in the growing heat of the day. At first they stood and paced eagerly, but as time wore on they realized that an immediate audience with the oracle was not in store. Tarek took out a sheet of parchment and a sprig of charcoal he had sharpened on a stone and began to take impressions of the carvings. Hannah and Alizar opted to recline against the shade of the wall and chat while Gideon and Jemir played several rounds of tipstone, a game where two opponents used alabaster balls rolled at a distance toward a triangular configuration of twenty rectangular stones, ten white and ten black, in attempts to tip the opponent's stones while leaving their own upright. Tarek remained reticent, seated on the wide cliff overlooking the palace of the king and queen with its four sprawling courtyards and tremendous statues set at specific intervals to catch the sunlight, statues that according to legend would speak at certain times of day.

"Do you imagine we will be going home soon, Alizar?" Hannah's eyes looked hollow and dim. In the last several days, her optimistic curiosity had been replaced with deepening concern.

Alizar placed a hand on her shoulder. "Do not worry, Hannah. We will be back even before the moon turns another cycle. You will see."

"If you say so."

Alizar lowered his voice. "Are you well?"

Hannah nodded. "Tired. The pain of my past haunts me. I see the faces of the dead: my father, Suhaila, the girl in the market, the ox driver on the road. How is it you remain so elevated after all you have been through, Alizar? You have lost a son and two wives, yet you seem so full of faith in the future."

Alizar closed his eyes against the sun. "Hannah," he began slowly, "as a shepherd you have within you a sense of the natural world and its forces that the people of Alexandria cannot even imagine. In this way, you have something even greater than faith because you have an understanding of your place in the family of things, whereas I cling to my cumbersome instruments and my incomplete maps, always unsure. My faith in the future, if you can call it that, stems from knowing that whatever trial I face is my teacher. Resistance takes energy, you see. Better to just surrender to the greater forces that brought us this birth." Alizar licked his rough lips and looked up at the sky, running a hand through his matted hair. "At my age, Hannah, I have seen that even my mistakes were the right path, so I do not worry so much about making them anymore. But I do make an effort to keep some fuel in the lantern, so to speak. You must laugh in the face of adversity. In the end, humor is the greatest weapon against the pain. The dead are gone. One day we will join them, every one of us. It is the way of things." Alizar touched Hannah's shoulder to reassure her.

Hannah smiled weakly, looking out over the sea of palm trees dancing in the scorching breeze, and then she turned back to Alizar. There was a question she had been meaning to ask him. "In the time I have lived in your home, Alizar, I have seen you come and go from many different churches and synagogues. But what god do you pray to?"

Alizar smiled and stretched his arms overhead as Jemir scored three tips in his game and howled in victory, his elbows thrust out in a quirky chicken dance. "Why, I pray to them all, Hannah," he said.

Hannah made a face. "You cannot pray to them all," she said flatly.

"Oh, but I do," said Alizar, a playful look in his eyes. "You see, the one God, the Great I Am of Moses, is a radiant mystery, like a light that is too bright to look upon. And so we interpret that light through colored glass, a bit like the dome in the Great Library. Each color is a name we give it: Yahweh, Ahura Mazda, Krishna, Isis, Poseidon, Demeter, Elohim, Shakti, Shekinah. It is as though we can only describe that much greatness by naming it in part. By definition, I think God, or Goddess, must be beyond our intellectual sciences, and even religions, the same way geometry is beyond what a fish can ever comprehend."

Hannah folded her arms. "If what you say is true, then for the Egyptians, Seth and Osiris would be the same, but that cannot be, as one is evil and one is good."

Alizar smiled. "You are right. Osiris and Seth are as opposite as day and night. But day and night have something subtle in common, do they not?"

"They have nothing in common."

"But they do. Day and night are events of the sky. Now the sun. Now the stars. Now the moonlight. They sky does not say, 'Oh, the sun is leaving and I cannot abide the night's return. I think I shall just be day from now on.' So when I say I pray to all the gods, I do. They are each a necessary aspect of the formless God."

"So you are a pagan, then?"

"You ask me if I am pagan, I say yes. You ask me if I am Christian, I say yes. You ask me to which religion I adhere, I answer that I adhere to any religion that has love as its foundation, truth as its windows, faith as its door. Anything less is drawing lines in the sand. How should we decide where to draw those lines? I draw one here, you draw one there. We erect cities, and we defend the lines, and many innocent people die. For what? For God? God has no boundaries. God knows no separation. We are the ones who imagine separation. For us, Hannah, there is leaving God in birth, and there is returning to God in death, and in between there is only this breath. Whatever the religious interpretation, I believe it is the breath of the Goddess of life itself."

"Are you not afraid of the Parabolani?"

"I have no fear of the Parabolani or the bishop. If they kill me, they will kill only a man." Alizar smiled, quite satisfied with himself.

The angel within Hannah's womb turned, listening.

"Thank you, Alizar. Your words give me courage." Hannah smiled as a flock of gold songbirds swooped over her head.

Alizar walked to the ledge, thinking to himself how all his life he had been one of those loquacious little fifes jabbering on and on about things that no one else bothered to consider. For a moment, he felt an ache of longing in his heart for the privacy of his tower, where the muse permitted him endless hours of uninterrupted contemplation and creation. This was something that Alizar had never been able to reconcile: when high in his tower, creating and inventing, he longed for adventure and the world; and when out in the world, he pined for his little tower and the universes it contained. He was nothing to himself if not this endless wheel of contradictions.

As the sun approached its zenith in the sky, the otiose caravan sought shade around the temple to escape the blaring heat. Without much else to do, they fell asleep. Late in the afternoon they awakened from their naps to devour the remainder of Jemir's bannocks. As they argued about how long to keep waiting, a tall Egyptian in ceremonial regalia appeared beneath a slim archway in the outer wall. "The Oracle of Amun-Ra will see you now," he said with a formal nod.

Hannah was the first to fly to her feet.

The stoic Egyptian led them through a high-walled courtyard and a narrow tunnel and into the first hall of the temple. It was a spectacle that no one could have imagined. Inside, the large rectangular limestone temple was supported by six massive columns set at even intervals around the room, and at one end, a gurgling spring bubbled cool water into a wide stone basin. "*Fons Solis,*" whispered Alizar, quoting again from Alexander's journal. "The Fountain of the Sun. It feeds fresh water to the entire city."

Seven steps led up through a tremendous archway carved of pale stone covered in hieroglyphs. Tarek translated the words set in stone above the steps. "Look down, not towards the step above, lest ye become proud." Beyond the inscription stood the second hall, where high overhead, the body of the celestial goddess Nut stretched across the entire ceiling, her arms and feet reaching from one wall to the other, her mouth swallowing the sun. The columns, walls, and even floor had also been painted with colorful Egyptian murals, most of which depicted the god Amun-Ra interacting with his worshippers. But a few indicated the tasks of every day life. Women held blue lotus flowers before their naked bellies as men fished from small lateens encircled by crocodiles. Vertical lines of hieroglyphs bridged the images. Alizar instructed Tarek to make several quick sketches, hoping their host would afford them the time to linger a moment.

A sight at the end of the temple caught Hannah's eye. There, beyond the swirling smoke of the thick incense, sat a long golden barge on a raised dais. Hannah looked up to the wall and noticed an identical barge in miniature captained by Amun-Ra and supported by twenty devotees, the weight of it set upon the shoulders of the god's willing devotees. She pointed it out to Gideon, and as she did, she realized it was the first time she had thought to share something with him without wishing he was Julian. Her hand went to her belly. She would have to tell him of the child. She had wanted to tell him every day, but there was always some interruption. In truth, she might have overcome these, but she feared he would reject her, and she had come to rely on him and appreciate his support. There were so many obstacles before them, it seemed unkind to add another.

While they marveled at the visual treasures of the temple, a door on the far side opened, and a flood of Siwans rushed in and found seats along the wall. Apparently the oracle required an audience. Alizar chuckled to himself at the vanity of the gods. The populace of Siwa was surprisingly quiet and reverent for such a large group, taking seats on the floor behind the columns to leave the center of the temple open as a playing field. When it seemed that everyone in the entire oasis was present, the temple door closed, and out from behind one of the columns stepped Omar-the-Goat clad in full-length white ceremonial robes. On his head he wore a pair of gilded ram's horns, richly ornamented with emeralds and other precious stones, which curved around his narrow face and shoulders. He carried a long staff in his good hand, not dissimilar to the caduceus of Hermes, and approached them guided by two bare-chested young boys who led him forward by the elbows.

Alizar gestured for the others to keep silent and stepped forward to address the ceremonial hierophant.

Silence. Alizar and Omar-the-Goat bowed to each other respectfully. The remoteness of the oracle had made it all the more appealing to consult, but now, looking into the tired face of an old man, Alizar hoped they had not made the trek in vain. He held out a heavy black obsidian jar to Omar-the-Goat.

Hannah held her breath.

Omar-the-Goat unscrewed the lid, dipped a finger into the jar, and withdrew it covered in a viscous amber liquid.

Hannah smiled. Honey.

The priest accepted the gift and bowed.

When Alizar finally stepped back, there was an uproar of chatter, and then preparations for the ceremony began. The complex rituals alone lasted well into the night, for there were offerings to be made, goats to be slaughtered, joss sticks to be burned, precise rules to be followed.

Everyone was tired of sitting by the time the actual ceremony began. Their knees and low backs ached. Their bellies growled. Only Alizar and Gideon seemed unaffected by the demands of their bodies; the Nuapar were known for their ability to wait, poised like cats in alert stillness until the moment of attack.

Deep into the night, a long line of two dozen bare-chested men strode out from behind the walls in long white skirts and stood beside the golden barge, which had been hung with votive cups of silver and oasis fruits.

Then there was a commotion.

A regal woman of Egyptian descent appeared dressed in long striped robes of white and gold, her bare arms covered in bangles, her striking eyes belonging more to a falcon than a woman. Hannah gasped at her beauty and evident power, completely overcome with awe.

Alizar bowed, and the others followed.

"I am Queen Khamissa of Siwa," said the woman. "Who addresses us?" Her eyes scanned the men before her. Alizar nodded to Hannah, who stepped forward.

Hannah knelt and bowed before the queen. "We have been sent by the Pythia at the Oracle of Delfi, and from Kolossofia Master Junkar on the island of Pharos in Alexandria, to collect the Emerald Tablet. We already possess the one broken half. Without the other, our city is falling into ruin."

The queen nodded. "We remember the gift given long ago by the oracle of Amun-Ra to Alexander, son of Zeus. But you say it is broken? How?"

Hannah lifted her head. "We do not know, we were only told to seek the other half of the tablet here."

The queen grew very still. "I have no knowledge of it." She turned to Alizar. "Is this your question for the Oracle of Amun-Ra?"

"Let the girl pose it," he said.

The Queen nodded.

Hannah cleared her throat, pleased she had been given permission to fulfill her quest. "In humility, I address the Oracle of Amun-Ra to hear my words. Our people and traditions are threatened by the growing power of the Christians. We have come in desperate times to beseech the oracle of the ancient god Amun-Ra to give us the location of the lost half of the Emerald Tablet."

In the light of several hundred flickering candles, the queen and the hierophant, Omar-the-Goat, nodded. Then she stepped aside and he lifted his arms. The men behind him removed his long robes, revealing a white kilt beneath; his arms, chest and ankles were bare except for several large ornamental gold cuffs. Around his neck hung the perennial ankh strung on a dozen strands of rare turquoise beads.

Omar-the-Goat stared straight ahead, his empty white gaze never faltering as the devotees hoisted him up onto their shoulders and passed him into the barge. Then they took their places beside the gleaming golden boat and lifted it onto their shoulders. They spun to face the center of the temple, and then the hierophant began to recite a long list of prayers and invocations as the men who held the barge remained stiff in their places.

Then slowly, the hierophant rose to his feet, the golden ram horn headdress casting massive twin spiral shadows on the wall behind the barge. There was a gasp in the crowd as the people hid their eyes.

Each member of Alizar's caravan knew the story: Alexander the Great had visited the Oracle of Amun-Ra, and the god had told him that he was the son of Zeus. When he returned from Siwa, he had coins minted with an image of his profile crowned in laurel leaves. He went on to conquer more territory than any general that came before, all in his early twenties. Some said that the oracle also predicted his death, which came shortly thereafter. The oracle had led Alexander to believe he was a god, and soon after the decree, he left the earth, immortalized as the most powerful youth ever to rule the empire. What had he seen in the temple of Amun-Ra? What had possessed him so powerfully after the ceremony that turned him from mortal man to immortal god?

Alizar stood patiently, his hands clasped before him as the golden barge began to sway. Omar-the-Goat, the last ceremonial hierophant of two thousand years, began to shudder and shake until his eyes closed, rolling back in his head. When his eyes opened again he was visibly, if only energetically, transformed. The old man was gone, his body occupied by the presence of the god, Amun-Ra. Whether he was acting, or the transformation was truly complete, the power that now emanated from his eyes was terrifying. The man-turned-god gestured demurely to the men, and slowly the barge began its journey.

Hannah watched the unfolding scene in awe.

Accompanied by twelve singing girls wielding incense trays, Amun-Ra, perched proudly in the golden barge, ordered it onward as though they were crossing a mighty ocean, but then the god would capriciously lift an arm, bark several commands, and the entire entourage would change direction as though caught in the current of some invisible stream.

Hannah could not discern the meaning of the barge's meandering. At one end of the temple stood two black pillars, a scene of darkness stretching between them. There was not a single candle flame, not even a window to let in the light, for between the pillars of darkness stretched oblivion, an eternal absence of life, the undeniable pull of death's inescapable gravity. Hannah watched as the barge of the god wandered toward and then away from these two pillars, while at the other end of the temple stood quite another possibility. There between two gold pillars lay fruits piled on fruits, glittering coins and endless staves of light bursting from the tips of dancing flames tied to cylinders of melting candle wax.

There sat eight of the most beautiful children in the village, side by side, their faces framed by halos of golden light. But the golden barge of the god approached these pillars time and time again, only to recede from them.

This suspenseful dance of Amun-Ra went on and on, directionless but purposeful, as the god chanted the forward motion of the barge. Amun-Ra, like most oracles, was not quick to grant mortals the jewels of his sight. Alizar knew that gods of oracles were often tricksters, playful divas who both loved and served the humans who called them, teasing them endlessly with obscure advice. He prayed that Hannah's sincerity would weigh favorably.

The night wore on for hours with the god coming no closer to a pronouncement. Hannah grew weary with the game, and ever so hungry, the child in her belly pleading for sustenance. But then, the god marched with conviction toward the columns of light. Everyone sat up. Suddenly the entire temple was awake. Alizar did not even bother to wipe the sweat that poured from his brow.

But just as he neared the pillars of light, coming within inches of this hopeful decree, Amun-Ra turned fully around in his seat, lifted his staff, and ordered the men to march across the temple.

The crowd sighed as if watching a sporting event. Some of the children had fallen asleep in the arms of their parents. It seemed an answer would never be reached.

Responding to this new direction, the men turned, stooping slightly forward as they walked, perhaps as unsure as everyone else if the god would again change his mind.

But this time, the barge did not stop.

Hannah held her breath. Gideon squeezed her hand.

The god shouted his command, and as the men knelt down, the bottom of the wooden barge scraped against the stone floor.

Queen Khamissa of Siwa stepped forward and stood beside the barge. "An answer has been given."

Hannah shuddered. The barge rested in between the pillars of death. What could this mean? Terror seized her. They would fail now, it was evident.

The Siwan people groaned and all filed out of the temple.

Clearly, the ceremony was over. The men stepped away from the barge, and led Omar-the-Goat to stand before Hannah.

"But, where is it?" asked Hannah, searching around the temple with her eyes, confused.

"The time of the tablet has not yet come," he said. "There will be great death. Great destruction. But the tablet you will have, though it will not help you."

Hannah inhaled sharply. "Where is it?"

Omar-the-Goat smiled. "You have the answer you need."

Alizar examined the room, the people, the queen ... there could be meaning anywhere. He approached the golden barge and peered inside. It was empty.

The caravan split up, searching the temple. Jemir searched the foyer, Alizar the lower level, Gideon the upper.

Hannah remained where she was, walking the length of the temple until she paused before the golden barge where she remembered the shard of the Emerald Tablet around her neck. She held it up before her eyes, and scanned the room. Surely it would reveal something here, but the room just blurred into a green fog.

In the direction the barge was pointed, between the twin black pillars, stood a tiny window slat, precisely the size of the shard when held up vertically to her eyes. She approached it. Outside stood the remarkable obelisk of Siwa.

But there, just beneath it, a clear black rectangle. Could it be a door? She lowered the shard and saw nothing, then lifted it and saw the shape appear again.

She looked back at the vast temple and the nose of the barge pointed straight at her. What if the golden barge of Amun-Ra had been set here to indicate the tiny window, not the twin pillars of death at all?

Hannah gasped as three fiery gusts of wind blew into the temple. In an instant she remembered where they were. Outside, the first light of day illuminated the vast Egyptian desert as plumes of sand swept across the horizon.

They would have to leave immediately to escape the *Kahmsin* winds.

29

"It is inside the obelisk," said Hannah. "I am sure of it."

They all stopped at the edge of the courtyard, taking turns to look through the shard.

"We must move quickly," said Alizar, eager to pack their belongings and begin the journey home.

They walked down a set of stone steps to the base of the enormous obelisk, its hieroglyphs slightly eroded by centuries of wind but still deep enough to see and to touch. Hannah marveled.

They each walked the perimeter until they met at the side that faced the temple.

"It should be here," said Hannah. She held up the shard, and it glowed in the sunlight.

"Yes, I see it!" proclaimed Tarek. Here is the line that would mark the door.

"We need tools," said Jemir.

"And another month," said Gideon.

"Perhaps not," said Alizar.

"But the door will not have been opened for over six hundred years," said Tarek.

"What if the Siwans have kept it in use?" asked Hannah.

"We must ask Omar-the-Goat or Queen Khamissa. Tarek will you please go find someone?" Alizar said.

Hannah felt along the stone outline of the door—it was small, as if for a dog. "Wait, there is an indentation here. Gideon, is there one on the other side?"

He felt along the slit. "Yes."

"Like handles," said Hannah.

"The stone must weigh as much as an elephant, though," said Gideon. "We could not hope to move it, not without help."

So.

The entire oasis was delighted to step in and take hold of the ropes they rigged to two iron hooks they attached to the stone. The nautical hooks, acquired somewhere on the coast more than likely, were often used to repair the buildings of the city, hoisting supplies in the air. Though they were rusted, they were still strong.

The stone groaned and creaked, and then slid forward in slow motion. Everyone cheered and kept pulling.

Soon there was an opening large enough to squeeze through, and Hannah knelt down to enter. Alizar followed her with a torch.

"What if we have found the lost tomb of Alexander the Great?" said Alizar, hoping for a magnificent sarcophagus.

The room may have been a tomb, but the torchlight revealed it was entirely empty now. Not even a mural on the walls adorned it.

Hannah walked all through the small rectangular room, as it was just tall enough for her to stand. Gideon, Jemir, Alizar, and Tarek each walked the length of the tomb, and they could not find anything that would indicate the Emerald Tablet.

"It is not here," said Hannah. "We came in vain."

Tarek started to speak but then stumbled on an uneven stone in the floor. Gideon knelt down on the ground and brushed his hand across the ground. "Perhaps not in vain," he said. "Alizar, your torch."

Alizar knelt down beside him. The two men blew at the thick layer of dust and wiped it away with the lengths of their burnooses. Once the dust had been cleared, Hannah could see a limestone block with hieroglyphs carved along one edge, slightly raised in the floor, not something of interest to a grave robber.

Gideon sat down on the floor and pushed at it with the heel of his boots. "I felt it shift."

Hannah, Jemir, Tarek, and Alizar wedged their feet on adjacent sides of the stone cover to slide it open with the force of their legs.

Tarek read the inscription. "The hieroglyphs indicate this tomb is guarded by Seth. To trespass here will bring his wrath."

"Surely you are not as superstitious as all that," said Gideon.

"I agree with him," announced Jemir. "I feel this place is cursed."

"Then we should leave an offering before we move it," said Alizar. "For the god Seth."

"What do we have left?" asked Gideon.

"Almost nothing," said Alizar.

Hannah emptied her haversack of the fossil shells she had been collecting on the journey. "What of these?"

"They will have to do," said Alizar.

Hannah arranged them in a crescent, and whispered several words of prayer. Then she returned to her seat, feet in place.

With several great pushes, teeth clenched, they managed to move the lid aside to reveal a gaping hole in the floor.

There in the center, Alizar's torch illuminated a wooden chest with the winged sun disk painted over the lid. Hannah recognized it as identical to the one from Delfi. "It is here!" she called out. "We have found it!"

Gideon sprung the hasp, and Hannah reached inside and removed an identical burgundy linen bundle painted with glyphs of protection. She carefully unwrapped it to reveal the upper half of the Emerald Tablet of Hermes Trismagistus, resplendent in the torchlight. She fit the shard to it on the broken edge, and it fit there as well. They had all the pieces now. This one here and the one hidden in Alizar's tower, locked in the brass chest he had created for it.

Hannah stumbled outside, leaving Alizar to carry the chest. The moon had risen. The night pulsed around her with the hum of insects and frogs. Outside it smelled of pond water and clean linen. She staggered toward a patch of moonlight and sat down, breathing heavily, the shard at her neck became virescent, glowing like a sidereal beacon. She took it off, coiled the cord in her palm.

Gideon went to her. "Hannah? What is wrong?"

"It is nothing."

"Perhaps Seth was not satisfied with her offering," suggested Tarek.

"Tarek, shut up!" said Gideon.

Insulted, Tarek flew at him, attempting to land a punch.

Gideon stood up and with one swift punch to the gut, Tarek fell to his knees unable to breathe.

"Now get lost," declared Gideon.

Tarek found his feet and disappeared into the reeds, following Jemir who went to pack the camels for the trip home.

Hannah slumped over, her hands clutching her belly. Gideon caught her before her head struck the ground. "What is wrong, woman?"

Alizar stood over them. Hannah implored him with her eyes not to speak her secret. "Exhaustion," he said. "Come. We must carry her."

Hannah pressed the emerald shard into Gideon's hand. He took it, lifted the cord over his head. She nodded, satisfied.

The angel collapsed in discomfort as the edges of the crushing darkness spread inward. No sky to escape into. No light. No light.

As they trekked across the valley floor, the hot breath of the deadly wind began its attack, first in short bursts and then in blasts. Hannah's belly felt taut and hunger gnawed at her so constantly as to be a constant irritation. She felt terrified of the return journey, her intuition screaming at her for joining them in the first place.

"We cannot go north to the sea," said Gideon. "But if we travel east to the Nile, we might outpace it."

Alizar agreed. It would add a week or more to their return trip home, but at the Nile, there would be water. They could perhaps find a ship to carry them down to the Mediterranean.

Hannah road the camel, and the men trudged across the broad dunes as the flurries whistled all around them, whipping the fabric of their *tunicas*. Sand stung their skin from every possible direction. Having narrowly missed the window of departure in Siwa, Gideon explained the best option for their survival was that they might reach the Valley of Cheetahs in the east.

The sky darkened in a thick spray of sand, blocking out the sun. They tied ropes around their waists to stay together in the wicked gales. Their maps were useless. Even Alizar's lodestone spun and spun with no indication of direction. Gideon attempted to shield Hannah with his body, walking directly before her. She tired quickly as much from fear as physical exertion, the journey depleting all her strength. She regretted her previous naivety. Why had she been so convinced that she should be the one to carry out the quest, and with child? Alizar, too, hung his head. The only choice before them was to keep walking, step by step, slipping, falling back, gaining ground so slowly.

After six days of poor sleep and endless traveling, they were becoming less and less hopeful of ever escaping the desert. Near nightfall they entered a narrow canyon where the fierce wind became capricious, spiraling around them, teasing them mercilessly, pelting them with sand and small pebbles until their cheeks bled. They huddled together in between the camels and wrapped a canvas tent around the bodies of the beasts in order to break the wind. There, in a cramped little pocket of relative calm, they slept fitfully, their bellies cramped from the mixture of salted meat and fruit, their muscles aching, their hopes dwindling.

The low growl started in the distance and then grew closer. Hannah's eyes flew open. "What is that? Is that the wind?"

"Shhh." Gideon clamped his hand over her mouth.

In the pitch blackness, the caravan waited, and the camels groaned uneasily. The wind had calmed. This was something else. Alizar lit a torch and swung it in a wide circle but a gust of wind snuffed it out as the eyes of hungry animals flashed beyond the sand hill. "We found the Valley of Cheetahs," he said.

Hannah whispered the shard's inscription for strength. *Soul immortal beyond death, no fire can burn thee, no fate can change thy eternal truth.*

After an hour of interminable terror, the cats showed themselves. Two large males accompanied by a juvenile. "Alizar?" whispered Hannah, her voice quavering in fear.

"Stay calm. We will use our knives if attacked."

"It is likely they will take one of the camels," whispered Gideon.

"Yes, if we are lucky that is all they will take," said Alizar.

The first attack came swiftly. Hannah screamed. The massive claws of the young cheetah split the canvas where they hid between the camels, and the beast's belly met with an upward thrust of Gideon's knife. He jerked his knife sideways, and the cat fell dead beside them, though it had managed a considerable slash across Gideon's shoulder with its claws.

The second attack came shortly thereafter: hungered by the scent of blood, the two adult animals joined forces to bring down the smaller camel. There was nothing they could do to save it. The camel brayed and blood spurted from its throat as the group clamored to pull themselves away from the dying beast, leaving it to the cheetahs that emerged in the darkness: six, then seven, then nine.

They had been fortunate, indeed.

The next morning the stars faded into blue sky that emerged flawless, without a cloud. The winds had subsided, if only for a brief time. Alizar sprung to his feet and began to assess their losses as Hannah bandaged Gideon's shoulder while he did some quick calculations and set them back on course. Jemir skinned the dead cheetah. Nearly half their supplies had to be left in the desert as they secured only the most vital elements to the remaining camel. Hannah would have to walk, as her weight would be too much for the beast. They set out to the east with the sun burning in their eyes, and somewhere in the distance, the Nile River.

The river in Egypt. Hannah's father had promised her this was where they would go. Now, if they survived, she would reach it. She closed her eyes and asked her father to lead them there. She was shaken from the attack of the cheetahs and weakened. Yet she prayed they would find their way. *Abba, help us, guide us to the river.*

Whether by prayers or the hand of fortune, the *Kahmsin* winds subsided as they crossed another canyon. Gideon knew patches of this route, as he had traveled the region before to bury a *pythos* full of manuscripts in the desert for Alizar. He knew where to find water and wild yams, and like a true captain, followed his nose to water.

At a small oasis, Gideon struck up a conversation with a tribe of friendly Bedouin, and the caravan was led east to the Nile thanks to several coins from Alizar's purse.

Hannah grew reticent, fatigue stealing all her strength.

Though the beautiful river offered a new array of vegetation and wildlife, it brought only mild relief as their travels continued on. Hannah was able to bring down several ducks with her shepherd's sling. The Bedouin offered fresh milk and tasty seed bread. They ate well again, and no one was more thankful than Hannah to have a full belly. Gideon squinted at her watching her fill a plate as high as his own, a tiny woman half his weight. She continued to earn his respect.

Once on the Nile, they were introduced by the Bedouin to a group of Egyptian tradesmen traveling to the sea, and the caravan was welcomed on board the little skiffs that made their way downstream. When the tradesmen commented on the beauty of the cheetah skin, Alizar was happy to gift it in thanks.

As the sun slipped from the horizon, Hannah was met by a vision from her dreams: the Pyramids of the Giza plateau rose up from the desert as the skiff drifted slowly past, illuminated from behind by the setting sun as a flock of ibis floated past. Entranced, Hannah could not tear her eyes away. Gideon settled beside her and slid his arms around her to view the citadels of light, pyramids shielded by the geometry of heaven.

Yes, this was Egypt, after all.

So.

Come first light, they sailed from Memphis to the coast and struck out on foot the rest of the way to Alexandria. This proved a monumental task for Hannah, whose feet were so sore and bloody that she could no longer feel them. The sand had ground all the skin from her toes and heels. She stopped to empty her boots again and to urinate. But there, in the sand was the unmistakenable glint of red, of blood. Just enough to give her a start. Then she felt her belly cramp. So, all this way, and now she would lose the babe. The child she had longed to be rid of, that now her heart desperately wanted to keep. She had to stop walking. She had to rest.

Alizar sat beside her beneath the shade of a palm. "Are you well enough to continue, Hannah?"

Tears streamed from her eyes. She wiped them with her fingertips and lay down on her side in the dust. "I will lose it."

"I will have to tell the others."

"No," said Hannah. "Please. I am just so tired. Can I rest? I need only an hour of sleep."

Alizar cocked his head to Gideon who appeared at his side. "If we are to continue on today, we must make room on the camel for Hannah."

Gideon chewed on his lips. "Impossible."

"Then we must carry her."

Gideon nodded and hoisted her easily. They would not stop now.

The desire of reaching home sustained the men. Each considered the food they most wanted to taste.

"Roasted lamb," said Jemir, licking his lips.

"Honey cakes," said Tarek.

"Wine," said Gideon.

"A bath," declared Alizar, uncharacteristically giddy, "and a smoke."

"Julian," whispered Hannah under her breath, letting her hand reach for the shard of the tablet, forgetting she had given it to Gideon for safe keeping. Gideon shifted her from his arms to his back, the wound from the cheetah's claws screaming with his every step.

By the time they saw the outline of the walls of Alexandria etched against the sky, no one had the energy to pick up the pace. Even the camel groaned. By early evening they entered Alizar's courtyard, exhausted, caked in dust and grime, yet still eager to unite the two halves of the tablet.

Alizar threw the camel rope over a rail and rushed into his house to announce his return before going to the Great Library to summon the doctor and the midwife.

But something struck him internally. His home was silent. Too silent. Where were his hounds?

Alizar cupped his hands beside his mouth and called them. Silence.

At once his heart began to race.

He gave a familiar whistle, praying.

Nothing.

He ran up the back steps from the stable through the courtyard, and that was when he heard it. A whimper. Somewhere in the stones. He hunted through the yard until he found his two hounds beside the cistern, one with its throat slit, dull red fur squirming with maggots beneath the cloud of carnivorous flies, the other dog still alive, though barely, whimpering in pain. Alizar stopped, struck through. Then he bent and carried the living dog away from the dead.

Alizar set his hound on a pillow in the kitchen and waited for it to take a drink before he ran through the house and the gardens, knowing, just knowing in his gut, that disaster had struck. Jemir and Tarek followed Alizar while Gideon took Hannah to wash and rest.

The men found Leitah slumped at the door to Alizar's tower, the lock broken, her breath nearly gone from her body. Jemir cried out and clutched Leitah to his breast. "No! Not my angel."

"Leitah, speak, you must tell us what happened," Alizar pleaded with the mute girl. "Praise Zeus, I wish that you would speak."

With a last strained effort, Leitah looked up at them, her eyes wet with blood that ran from her crown. "Orestes," she said in a thin, faltering voice so unaccustomed to speech. "The library."

As the breath left Leitah's lips, a scroll marked with the bishop's seal fell from her fingers and rolled through the open door. Her spirit departed while her body lay in Jemir's arms.

Beyond her, Alizar's tower lay in ruin: his work of decades lost, the scrolls and codices shredded, the pots smashed to dust. She had died trying to prevent the Parabolani from entering, that much was clear.

Alizar swept through the tower. There was much, so much that could never be replaced, but the tablet, that he had to be certain was still safe. He rushed toward the second pillar to the wood panel set in the wall, the fake front to his safe room. It had been cracked by an axe, the room behind it as empty as dreamless sleep. The brass chest containing the half of the Emerald Tablet that Hannah had procured at Delfi was gone.

So.

Gideon stayed with Hannah, whose breath grew thinner by the hour.

Alizar had to follow Leitah's last words before he could do more. Without having so much as changed his clothes, he took a horse to the Great Library. Synesius met him in the Great Hall.

"Synesius, what has happened?"

Synesius bent his head and joined his fingertips. This would be hard news to deliver, especially to Alizar. He took a breath.

Alizar lunged forward. "Synesius, I must know!"

Synesius exhaled and met Alizar's intense gaze. "Orestes was stoned."

An arrow of anger flashed though Alizar's heart. "Curse them."

They walked swiftly through the Great Hall of the library, not even bothering to quiet their voices as they passed beneath the glass cupola.

"He is alive?"

Synesius nodded. "Yes, but the wounds are deep. He may not wake."

Alizar quickened his steps. "And Phoebe?"

"She is with him now."

Alizar clenched his fists. Cyril had gone too far with this unforgivable religious politics of his. "What incited this stoning?"

"Orestes refused the Pentateuch when Cyril offered it to him to kiss. They stood in the *agora*, Cyril having invited him there to make peace. The priests were ready with their stones. They knew Orestes would refuse."

"Do we have the men responsible?"

Synesius nodded. "A young priest named Ammonius threw the stone that struck his head. He was arrested and imprisoned yesterday evening. The council convenes to decide a punishment this evening."

"I do hope they consider castration," growled Alizar.

They hurried through the Caesarium gardens, passing beside Cleopatra's crypt then beneath the *peripatos* that led to the long hall that functioned as a medical facility for both research and treatment.

At the door, Alizar swiftly unwound the tattered burnoose that covered his neck and shoulders, spilling sand and desert dust.

Once inside, Synesius led Alizar down a colonnade and up a flight of stone steps to a door wedged between two tall pillars, where a female figure was slumped, her arms wrapped around her slim waist.

Hypatia looked up. "Oh, Alizar."

Alizar's anger toward Cyril instantly melted as he folded Hypatia into his arms, pressing her tiny body to his chest. "Be brave, Great Lady," he whispered as he kissed the top of her head. "Be brave."

She sobbed against his chest, wetting the cloth. "Why Orestes?" she asked again and again through her tears. Her precious friend. Her confidant. Her devoted student.

Though he wanted to console her, Alizar knew his time was short, and so he pulled away and swept Hypatia's golden curls back from her forehead. "I must see him," he said. She nodded and leaned against the pillar.

Orestes lay on a cot in the center of the floor, the last remaining staves of sunlight falling across his bare, bruised shoulders. Phoebe knelt beside him, pressing the back of his hand to her cheek. When she saw Alizar, she stood up and hugged him wordlessly and then knelt back down beside her husband. Orestes lay motionless, eyes closed, his forehead and left eye bandaged with strips of linen. His chest and shoulders were cut and scratched; another bandage encircled his ribcage. The sheets were pulled down low over his hips to let the wounds breathe.

As Alizar took in this tragic vision of his beloved friend, Philemon, the doctor, appeared. He was a shrewd little man, having short stubby arms with elbows that never straightened completely. When he saw Alizar he gave a disinterested nod of greeting.

"Philemon," Alizar nodded in return.

"This is a medical ward, Alizar," Philemon chided him, elbows akimbo. "You come here, you need to *wash*."

Alizar ignored the doctor's strange obsession with cleanliness. "How bad is he?"

"If you wash," said Philemon, regarding Alizar's grimy appearance in disgust, "you can help me change the patient's bandages."

Alizar inhaled sharply. "How long will it take?"

Philemon frowned. "You have a dinner to attend? Dressed like that?"

Alizar shook his head. "Our caravan has returned. My slave, Hannah, needs you, as does my captain, Gideon. When we are done here."

Philemon nodded, and they went to work.

———

Later in the night, Alizar emerged from the ward where the praetorian prefect of Egypt lay in a coma, his head split from the temple to the crown to the white skull where the stones had struck him, his left eye crushed and useless. Philemon, who tended to cluck his tongue as he examined his patients, thought it unlikely that he would survive the night. He packed his bag and set out to Alizar's home.

"Alizar?"

The alchemist turned his head.

"Please walk with me," Hypatia said.

The doctor nodded, and Alizar let him go on ahead.

The Great Lady had composed herself a little since their meeting in the hall several hours earlier, having changed into a *tribon* of pure white and bound her hair high up on her head in a topknot. But her eyes were still wet and pained. "I am thankful you have returned from the desert safely," she said.

He nodded, thinking it best not to tell her about the Emerald Tablet, especially now that they only had the half of it. "The Parabolani were at my home. I can stay only a moment," he said.

Hypatia bowed her head. "Understood."

They walked arm-in-arm to the top of the garden and sat on the stairs of the amphitheatre that overlooked the harbor, the lighthouse glowing like a beacon of promise against the night.

"I fear our precious city is cursed," Hypatia said.

"All the more reason for our continued diligence," said Alizar. A long pause followed his words, bringing with it the sound of the waves lapping the seawall.

Hypatia lifted her eyes. "The council has ruled unanimously. Ammonius will be executed tomorrow morning."

Alizar folded his hands. It was good news, but it did not seem to matter. Nothing seemed to matter. Leitah's death, the third of his prophesy, was a terrible blow. And now this.

"Cyril has grown in his audacity," said Hypatia quietly. "We must appease him somehow before he destroys all of us."

"Perhaps we should just give him what he wants," said Alizar, his words tumbled together in a heap. All he could see behind his eyes was Leitah, slumped in Jemir's arms, the flies that circled his precious hound, Orestes's cracked skull, all the light disappearing from the room.

"The Celestial Clock of Archimedes? Has the desert stripped you of your senses? If we give it to him he will not stop there, and you know it. The entire library may fall in the name of his God.

Think of the scrolls that would perish. You are even more aware than I of how much the world would lose."

"He has written you as well?"

"Of course," said Hypatia, a glimmer in her eyes.

Alizar took notice and sat up. "You have an idea," he said. "Speak."

"I have taken a new interest in Christianity," she announced. "I am working on a treatise about the Virgin Mary that I believe will have immense influence."

Alizar laughed heartily. "You mean you expect Cyril to read it? Nonsense. Put it out of your mind."

Hypatia let her eyes drift across the harbor to Pharos. "They began constructing the Heptastadion bridge, Alizar, in the weeks since you have been away. We could not stop them. Pharos will fall next."

"They found an architect?" Alizar had thought it would take more time.

"Empress Pulcheria has personally commissioned it in the name of the emperor. Imperial spies told her that Pharos concealed the last of the pagans, and she wants them brought into the Christian faith by any means. Or her court does. They have plans to erect a church on the southern shore. Beside the Temple of Poseidon or on top of its ashes," said Hypatia, her disbelief outweighing her disappointment.

Alizar inhaled sharply. "How many texts are there in the library remaining to be copied?"

Hypatia laughed. "We will never save them all." She slid her hand under the crook of Alizar's elbow. "You have been like a father to me all these years. I am thankful you returned safely."

"As am I," said Alizar.

Hypatia squeezed his arm. "Tell me, in how many locations have you hidden the manuscripts?"

Alizar counted on his fingers. Malta, Nag Hammadi, Antioch, Crete, Ephesus, Cyprus, Cappodocia, Epidavros, and in the forbidden caves of Macedonia. "Nine," he said.

"Have you finished the maps?"

"No, not yet."

"How will you conceal them? It is of utmost importance the maps last the centuries should anything happen to the Great Library."

"I am working on it. Hypatia, I must go."

"Of course. Certainly."

They bade each other a swift goodnight.

Alizar rushed to find his horse, his mind a flurry of thoughts. With Orestes indisposed, Hypatia was now Cyril's final threat to power. Alizar knew he must make a plan to protect her at once.

30

Hannah listened to the tinkling sound of goat bells, pleasant and timeless, familiar and soothing, and in that moment between sleeping and waking she believed she was in her childhood pasture with her father in Sinai. She could hear him cooking over the fire, clinking spoons and pots, rummaging in his leather sacks beneath the acacia trees. But as she roused, Sinai faded, and her eyes opened to Naomi's bedroom, Gideon asleep in the chair beside her.

"Gideon?"

"Praise Zeus, Hannah. Are you awake?" He lifted a cup of cool water to her blistered lips.

"How long was I asleep?"

"Through the night. Part of the day before that."

Hannah's eyes absorbed the room as she sorted through her confusion of not remembering how she came to be there. There was Naomi's cedar chest, the diaphanous white curtains drifting away from the balcony door, the stack of parchment tied with red string on the table, letters from Naomi's sister. "Where is Alizar?"

"He returned with the doctor then went out again."

"Gideon," Hannah sat up, sensing something. "Why is the house so quiet?"

"Hannah, the house was . . . the Parabolani were here. Leitah is dead."

"Leitah?"

Gideon nodded. He believed that hard truths were best shared quickly.

"How?" Hannah wiped her tears with her fingers and leaned back in bed as Gideon explained.

"Then we also lost the tablet from Delfi?"

"*Neh.*"

Hannah fell silent, shocked, horrified.

"Poor Orestes. And Hypatia. How is Jemir?"

Gideon gave her his handkerchief. "It will take time."

Hannah's tears fell like a rainstorm. She could have drowned everything in the room. Gideon left and returned with fresh yogurt and lemon. She pushed it away.

"You must eat, Hannah," he ventured. "For our child."

"Alizar told you?" she asked, her face streaked with dust and rivers of water. She still had not bathed after the desert.

"The midwife, when she came." Gideon held out the yogurt.

"I still have it?" Hannah was awed, relieved and concerned all at once. She could feel a rag between her legs, set there carefully. "But the blood."

"You must rest, she said. Until you are well. Then she will come again. But it is possible you will remain in bed for the rest of it."

"You are not angry?"

"Why would I be angry? I will see to it we have all we need."

Hannah clutched a pillow to her belly. "What did the midwife say?"

"You are fatigued. The heat, the trek, you should not have joined us. But you lived, and the babe has a strong heartbeat. Like his father." Gideon grinned.

So he thought the child was his. Of course he did. Now she saw the glint in his eyes and understood what the thick sleep had prevented her from hearing. He was happy at the prospect of fatherhood.

Hannah accepted the yogurt, tried to think. This new hunger was unlike any she had ever known. It eclipsed her mind completely with a desperate, insatiable, and commanding instinct to eat. The yogurt disappeared instantly. Her thoughts were a blur, completely out of reach. She had no idea what to say in the shame of deceiving him. Yet for all the death, the misfortune of losing the tablet, she still had the child by some miracle. There was no other word for it: miracle. She tried to think and thinking eluded her. Gideon brought chicken, cabbage, raisins, grilled octopus. Hannah ate every last bite.

Finally, he rose to depart. "I should see about the *Vesta*. But I will return for supper."

"Gideon?" Hannah chewed on her lips, the skin peeling away like parchment. "You still intend this transaction with Alizar?"

"More than ever before," he said with pride. "You may be a slave, but I am to be a father. I will see to it you both have all you need. That is my duty."

"Then I must speak," she said. "Please, sit."

If anything, the truth would be a gift, a lifted burden, and a way of somehow putting the past behind her, behind both of them. "This babe—still in my womb by some miracle—I believe is the child of the sacred marriage rite of the Nuapar. I was wrong in not telling you sooner. I am sorry."

Gideon recoiled, stunned. He shook himself free of her hands, and turned his back, pacing to the window. "Are you certain?"

"Mostly certain."

"Mostly." He grunted his disgust. "Whose then?"

"Master Junkar. I was chosen. It was the coronation." She wanted to say *not my fault*, but she would not apologize for the night she had spent and all it meant to her, especially after Gideon himself had spurned her.

"Julian."

Hannah nodded, her stomach churning like a pit of vipers. "You know him?"

"I know him. Or I did." Gideon clutched the edges of the table. He wore a clean black *khiton*, his shoulder freshly dressed from the doctor's visit, his sword sharpened and slung at his hip. "No matter now."

"Gideon, I . . ." Her voice trickled out as little more than a whisper.

"If you feel you can make a statement that does not merely mock my manhood I should like to hear it. Otherwise, I am finished here."

"I could give the child to the Temple of Isis." Hannah swallowed the words, knowing that she could never follow through with it. But if it was the only choice left to her, maybe then it would be better for the both of them.

Gideon turned around, his dark eyes piercing her. "Is that what you wish?"

Hannah looked down at her belly to where the warrior child still clung to life in her womb. She looked up. "No, but it would be better than the brothel."

Gideon clenched his jaw, still angry, a master of fury. He kicked the chair across the room and it shattered against the wall. "The brothel. *Neh*, I have half the mind to send you there myself. But your heart cannot be bought or sold."

"Gideon, why are you saying this? What my heart wishes matters to no one. I am a slave who can read, nearly write, and sing. I speak Greek and Aramaic. I am told I am pretty. That is the sum total of my value. You and Alizar either have a deal or you do not. Where will you send me?"

Gideon stood over her. "Do you love him?"

"Why do you speak of love?" A desperation rose in her voice that she could not conceal.

"Tell me the truth, woman."

Hannah speared him with her eyes, blue and piercing as the cold north sea. "I have known one great love in my life for a man who sacrificed his entire world for me. When we were separated, I knew a grief deeper than I ever imagined possible. When we were reunited, my heart soared to a height in the sky higher than any eagle has ever seen. That man was my father."

"You lie."

"How can you say such a thing?" Hannah recoiled.

"You do not think of Julian? Not even as his child grows inside you?"

Hannah never imagined a man's jealousy could extend so far. "Gideon, what does it matter? It is true I think of Julian, yes. But that night fades in my mind even as I long for it. Master Junkar is wed to an entire order of men who require his guidance. You say you knew him, so you also know that Julian is dead to all who knew him, even to his own brother, Synesius. Also to me." As she spoke the words she knew they were true.

Gideon sat on the bed beside her and met her eyes. "If what you say is true, I will accept this child."

Hannah's lower lip trembled, and she squinted through the tears that would not cease falling. This was a surprise. "You are a generous man." She forced the words out of her mouth.

"Beauty is common, Hannah. Any woman can be beautiful. But you. You have the heart of a lioness. I need you." He lifted her fingers and kissed them.

I need you. Hannah felt her heart disappearing inside her chest like the clouds in the desert heat, dissolving into despair, confusion, loss. In the place of love, would *need* ever be enough? Or was it need that birthed a truer love, a love more resolute and lasting? She no longer knew or truly cared. Once she had longed for a husband, a love, a family. That dream had died a thousand deaths already.

Gideon cleared his throat. "If I had a friend who confessed to me he said such things to a woman, I would laugh at him and tell him to come to his senses. How wrong I would be. For these are my senses, and I have lived an entire life without them." He kissed her neck.

Lioness. Need. Heart of a lioness. Hannah's mind replayed his words. She knew she should feel grateful, relieved, happy even that he planned to keep her. Her fingers brushed her slave collar. It had burrowed into her skin on the journey, bruised and cut her, searing metal against her skin that cooked her like a lamb; it would never be part of her, always this alien thing that prevented her from remembering who she was, who she had been before. "Thank you," she said, wishing that she meant it more.

Outside, a peacock screamed, and a cat in heat responded with a yowl as if the two creatures might somehow alleviate their mutual desire.

"This has been my dream. You have been part of it. As a boy in Epidavros I longed for the sea spray in my face, adventure, and the touch of a beautiful woman."

"Women." Hannah corrected him.

"Women," he laughed.

Hannah's lips spread into a smirk, her dark blue eyes shining like lotus flowers in the twilight. The smile faded abruptly, though, for there in the door was Alizar, looking haggard and grave.

"Gideon, come. Ammonius, the priest who stoned Orestes, will be dead within the hour. We must protect Hypatia. It is time to pay another visit to Cyril."

Hannah protested. "No, no good can come of it."

"Hannah," said Alizar resolutely, "pray to Hecate that this crossroads knows her benevolent favor."

Hannah and Gideon shared a glance, and then Gideon rose and followed Alizar as Hannah clung to the pillow in terror, knowing in her heart she might never see them alive again.

31

"I said I was not to be disturbed," barked Cyril, jolted from his desk where he was furiously composing a letter. Ink spilled across the wood in a thin dribble that bled to the floor where half a dozen crumpled balls of parchment lay scattered like dead mice.

The priest at the door, his face speckled with pockmarks, nodded curtly and stepped out.

Cyril set his stylus against the page as the door burst open, and Alizar and Gideon stepped into the room.

Cyril did not even look up. "There is a contest on, Alizar, and I suggest before you speak you strongly consider your position, for I have within my possession the evidence of your treason."

"My position, if you call it that, is on the side of men and peace," Alizar growled. "While you are on the side of your own ambition."

Cyril pushed his chair back and met Alizar's eyes with his own fierce gaze, and for a moment there was a flicker of fear deep within them, and then it was gone. "I am on the side of God, pagan. I suggest you explain why you have burst into my church before I kill you myself as I should have done long ago."

"You know why we are here," said Gideon, his hand resting on the hilt of his sword.

Cyril smiled. "Ah yes, perhaps for these." He gestured across the room to the *pythos* filled with documents stolen from Alizar's tower. "Confiscated by the empire. To be burned, I am afraid, as they are not in accord with the teachings of Jesus Christ our Lord."

Alizar chose his words carefully, trying to suppress his rage. "I come here in the name of peace in Alexandria to speak to you about this massacring crusade you are on. Your Eminence, I have lived in Alexandria since before your father was born. We are a city of tolerance for all religions, views, and people. If you cut this city from her roots she will whither and die, and you will rule a necropolis. Orestes is no threat to you now. Hypatia is a figurehead in the library with no real power."

"What do you want, Alizar? You tire me."

"I want an accord of peace in the city. And I want my chest."

"Guards!" Cyril rose.

Gideon and Alizar pressed the desk, guided by instincts honed from years of trained fighting, that Cyril was indeed resting at a point of weakness where, if pushed, he may break. Alizar drew his sword. "I demand you cease your campaigns against both Orestes and Hypatia," he said. "At once. I want an ordinance of peace drawn up. There shall be no more bloodshed." Then Alizar set his sword on Cyril's desk for effect.

"I have nothing to gain from deals with pagan heathens."

Alizar would not relent. "For every stone you throw, one comes back to strike you. Eye for an eye, is it? Surely you see that clearly today. As you know I respect the Christian faith but do not respect any action that punishes the innocent. Children have died. Women. It is preposterous, and it must end. It can end. Right here. We can draw the treaty together."

Alizar grabbed a sheet of Pergamon parchment and set it before Cyril with a stylus.

"Seize them!" Declared Cyril.

Five enormous armed guards, priests of Nitria with skin as black as river stones, entered the room, swords drawn.

Cyril continued, pushing the parchment aside. "I would see this city cleansed of sorcery and black magic and traitors against God to make peace for those who live under Christ's teachings.

And you lay a sword before me and speak of peace? What do you know of peace?"

"Infinitely more than you," said Gideon, his eyes searching the room for Alizar's brass chest, the one that contained the tablet from Delfi. He did not see it. Cyril would need a blacksmith to open that chest. Merely thousands of blacksmiths in the city. But Gideon was sure the Church of St. Alexander had its own blacksmith, maybe even here.

Cyril laughed. "You see, Alizar, there is no need for a treaty of peace. God's will *is* peace, and *I* am his instrument. Seize them," he said calmly to the Nitrian guards.

Alizar grabbed his sword, and Gideon unsheathed his. The men stood back to back, swords raised.

"Your friends will die, Alizar, and you will watch them die, but not by my hand. No. By the hand of their own evil faith. For vengeance is mine, saith the Lord."

The duel was short, as both Gideon and Alizar were fatigued from the long journey, and the priests of Nitria, armored and rested, moved with the instinctual grace of animals. Alizar had only seen such fine fighting from the Nuapar. These priests were of another breed entirely: Christian soldiers. Alizar and Gideon were both captured after merely scratching their opponents. They were forced to their knees, sword points at their throats.

"Kill us, then," growled Alizar.

"Oh no, I will not kill either of you, not today," said Cyril. "God's greater plan." Cyril stood over Gideon. "Set this captain free, but burn his ship." Then he stood over Alizar. "I think you should watch the fate that the prefect Orestes and his whore Hypatia have chosen for themselves. From your own private seat." Cyril turned back to his desk and considered one more thing. "And I will find your slave."

32

Hannah shifted uncomfortably on the cushion before Mother Hathora. It had taken all her strength to come to the island, but her purpose was urgent: she wanted Nuapar protection for Alizar's house and for the child. She had bathed and slid her arms through the pale blue *khiton*. A dab of amber to each wrist.

Jemir and Tarek had stayed behind to build the funeral pyre for Leitah. The funeral ceremony would take place as soon as everyone returned. Precious Leitah. Alizar had been right; there had been a third death, a death none had expected.

Hannah's face was drawn, dark half moons beneath her eyes, unable to conceal her exhaustion, and then her disappointment, indignant. "You mean to say that the Nuapar would only protect a male child? If I bore a daughter, they would not even raise a brow?"

Mother Hathora nodded. "A girl would not come under their protection, no, but she would be welcome here, of course. It is something I have always wished to change in the Great Book."

Hannah felt a surge of fire web through her veins. "Perhaps now would be an ideal time to consider it."

Mother Hathora caressed the codex before her. "Ancient traditions have deep roots that must be honored. The Great Book was written by the First Master."

"But if this child within me is a girl, then I should like to see her live to write her own philosophies and mathematical formulas, and claim her own spiritual path, equal to any man's."

Mother Hathora smiled. "He was right to choose you. I knew he would, you know. The Goddess invests her power in certain women. I do not know why some and not others. She invests in them her greatest strength: the ability to awaken others to truth."

"So unless I have a boy, there is no hope for protection for us? My birth is yet many moons away . . ."

"I apologize, Hannah. But I am thankful that you came, and I know this child within you has a special destiny, regardless."

Hannah clenched her fists. "Where is equality? Justice? Alizar risks his life for you, for all of us. As have I in finding the Emerald Tablet. And now the Christians are building their bridge to Pharos. Do you realize what will happen when it is finished? Do you? Where will your sacred tradition be then? I have seen the Parabolani with my own eyes. I know what they do. Please, at least speak with Master Savitur."

"He will feel as I do."

"How do you know unless you speak to him?"

"The Nuapar do not interfere with the way of men, of history."

"I am asking for protection, not interference. This is the child of the sacred marriage rite."

Mother Hathora pursed her lips. "This is why I gave you the herbs. There should not have been a child."

"But it grows within me even now. Even after all the herbs I have taken. Surely that is a sign of something."

"You may give the baby to our temple, if you like. Even without a patron. I would sponsor it myself."

"That is your offer?" Hannah stood up, insulted. "No, I will keep it."

"As you wish."

––––––––––––

It was dark when Hannah returned to Alizar's, emotionally fatigued from the journey to Pharos and all the other adversities she had faced. She longed to sleep. She thought only of sleep. Sofia met her in the atrium on the other side of the little green door, wringing her hands, her eyes red and puffy, her face streaked with tears, her hair a tangled mess.

Hannah was struck through with fear. "Sofia?"

Sofia began to cry. Gideon appeared in the doorway, out of breath, and embraced Hannah.

Hannah gasped, knowing in her bones what had happened. "No. No. Where is Alizar?"

"They have him," he said solemnly.

"He is not dead?" Hannah found the arm of a small bench with her fingers and lowered herself onto the cushion. "Sofia, I am grateful you are here." She reached out to her friend, and they held one another.

"Not dead. Not yet," said Gideon. "I must make haste to the harbor before Cyril's men reach the ship." Gideon held a wide stance, one hand on the hilt of his sword, the blue veins in his temples throbbing visibly.

Hannah rested her head in her hands. "What of Leitah? We cannot just leave."

"They will come," whispered Sofia. "We have very little time. Jemir can stay. He will meet us."

Tarek appeared at the door scratching the back of his head like a nervous monkey. "The barge is ready."

Gideon nodded to Tarek and then went upstairs with Hannah and grabbed several articles of clothing and stuffed them into a black leather satchel at his feet. "Hannah, are you well enough?"

"I shall have to be," she said.

Gideon leaned toward her and pulled a cord down over her head. "You need this," he said. Her hand brushed the emerald shard around her neck once again, grateful to see it.

"Cyril is looking for you, even now. We must go to the Great Library."

"What of the tablet?"

"Cyril will need a blacksmith to open the lock. That is my task. I have spies searching the city already. A brass chest with a weighty lock will be easily identified."

"And the half we still have?"

Gideon patted his rucksack. "Taking it with us, of course."

Downstairs, Jemir met them outside the kitchen. Sofia pressed a key into his hand. "Lock up the house, Jemir, and admit no one. I will send guards. Once they discover the house is empty, they will depart."

"But Leitah," said Hannah. "It is not right."

"I will see to her," said Jemir. "Speak your prayers to God. Leitah will hear them. She is with Him now."

Hannah turned to Gideon, yet more tears in her eyes. "What good could possibly have come of going to see Cyril?"

Just then, voices erupted, strong and harsh, beyond the walls of the courtyard.

"Come!" Gideon took Hannah's hand as a commotion began in the street outside the house. "Jemir, lock every door! Let no one enter here."

Tarek slid the key out from under his *tunica* and fiddled with the lock to the door of the catacombs as a loud bang fell on the front door, followed by another.

"Hurry, Tarek," whispered Hannah, taking Sofia's hand.

The lock sprung under Tarek's hand, and they rushed down the stairs while Jemir shut the door from the inside and re-hinged the lock.

Gideon helped Hannah down the steps one at a time.

"What of Alizar?" said Hannah.

"I know," said Gideon. "I will get him out."

"Why would Cyril imprison him?" asked Tarek, hopping onto the barge behind Sofia and steadying it with his pole. Something lacking in Tarek's tone Hannah found suspicious. Where was his concern, his empathy?

Gideon untied the ropes, and they shoved off through the catacombs. "Cyril has the manuscripts Alizar was copying. He declared it an act of treason, but I fully expect the city's council will free him, especially after what happened to Orestes."

When they arrived at the Great Library, Tarek turned back to Alizar's to help Jemir while Hannah, Sofia, and Gideon continued on together. They found Hypatia in the garden, having just come from where Orestes lay in the medical ward. She looked upset.

"What is it, Great Lady?" asked Gideon.

Hypatia shook her head. "Clearly you have news. Tell me. Then I will share with you mine."

"Alizar has been imprisoned by Cyril."

"But why, Gideon? Why would he go to see Cyril when he knew no good could possibly come of it?" Hypatia began to cry. She sat on a bench and put her face in her hands.

Gideon stood as still as a soldier. "To make peace."

Hypatia shook her head, not even listening. "Phoebe took her life today."

Hannah inhaled sharply, remembering Orestes's wife, the jealous wife who had not wanted her husband to buy Hannah from Alizar. "How?"

"She hung herself." Hypatia dabbed at her eyes with the hem of her white robe. "Orestes is near death. She could not bear to watch him die."

"You will be next if you do not listen to me," said Gideon.

"I am not in danger as long as I live in the library. And if I die in the name of defending the truth, so be it. I know Alizar was angry over what happened to Orestes, but it is unlike him to come so unraveled."

"He wanted to speak his mind before Cyril to prevent further unrest." By further unrest he meant violence against Hypatia, but he could not bring himself to say it. "And besides, we need both halves of the Emerald Tablet."

"Further unrest," said Hypatia, her face splitting with new pain. "But I do not dangle the meat in front of the tiger. What of the Emerald Tablet in Siwa?"

"We have it," said Gideon.

"The other half was lost when the Parabolani raided my father's house," said Sofia.

"It does not matter then," said Hypatia. "It cannot help us now."

Sofia helped Hypatia to her feet, and they all walked together along the path with its little footbridges over the reflecting pools guarded by enormous sphinxes, until finally they stood beside the crypt of Cleopatra. Creeping vines covered it completely so that the door was no longer visible.

"The Parabolani can be easily overtaken by the Nuapar," said Gideon. "I know we could get Alizar out. If I can convince them to help me."

Hypatia shook her head. "Oh Goddess, if only Orestes was well. At this moment we need his seniority in the council. No. I will have to appeal to the senate and see if we can get him pardoned. If not by them, then by the empress herself. Alizar's vineyard provides the wine for the royal palaces at Constantinople, and if what has happened here might affect the quality of the grape in their cups, I am certain it can be made a priority." Hypatia looked to Hannah and Gideon. "You look fatigued. Come with me and we will find you a room here in the library, both of you, until this passes. The library is perfectly safe, as the Main Gates are kept locked and guarded by Nuapar. No one can breach these high walls. You made the right decision coming here."

Gideon bowed his head. "With all due respect, Great Lady, there is not time. I must secure Alizar's ship, and then I will go to Pharos and speak with Master Savitur. He will know what we can do. Please care for Hannah until I return." Then Gideon turned to Hannah. "Stay here in the library where you will be safe, and do not go beyond these walls. Get some rest."

Sofia nodded in agreement. "Come stay with me in my room."

Hannah lifted her chin to Gideon. "Please find me when you return," she said. "Please return."

Gideon placed a hand on her shoulder and then bent to kiss her. "I will return. Keep this safe." He placed his rucksack containing the Emerald Tablet from Siwa in her arms and walked swiftly down the path toward the harbor.

Hannah watched Gideon slip out of sight and bowed her head, completely exhausted. She could not even remember the list of reasons why, there were so many added each hour.

"I will have Alizar back in time for grape harvest," said Hypatia. "Do not worry for him, Hannah. Rest here and gather your strength. The Great Library is your home now."

PART 3

The Great Library

(415 C.E.)

33

Alizar sat on a flat grey stone, his elbows folded across his bent knees, head down, shoulders burdened with regret. A shaft of light from the window fell across his back where his *tunica* was torn, and an empty wooden bowl sat beside him, cracked through the center like a ripe melon split open in the sun. These were all the room contained, and had contained, for years.

From time to time he stood, walked the five paces to the window, looked out, and then walked the five paces back to the stone where he always sat. So many emotions had moved through him, so much pain and sorrow. Yet gradually, it had all emptied into stillness, dreary and vast as a winter sky in his heart.

During the first week of his imprisonment, even in spite of his painful wounds from the beating he took from the priests of Nitria, Alizar was hopeful, knowing that Hypatia would enter an appeal with the council. He simply waited. But the full moon had dimmed countless times. A blow to his ribs healed badly, leaving him with a wheeze that never went away. Bowls of bread and grain had been slipped through the small hole in his door once a day and then removed. No guards came to see about him.

Hope became rage. Alizar stormed the tower, screaming profanities out the narrow windows to the world below him. Occasionally someone would look up, then go back to the chore at hand. His fury was fully unleashed for every injustice he had witnessed at the hands of the bishop, from the exile of the Jews and Orestes's injuries, to the loss of the manuscripts, the Emer-

ald Tablet, and his own imprisonment. But he had grown tired
of the shouting after several weeks and fell silent. His thoughts of
revenge gradually faded, as he knew where revenge led, always to
more violence and never to its end.

Grief followed. For a time Alizar did not stand or stretch, or
even lift his head. He missed Sofia and longed to hear of her life
and the years he had missed. And he wanted to know of Orestes,
learn the hour when his friend had died, and what words had
been spoken at the funeral service. What flowers had been chosen
to wreath the dais? What poem? And his business, the vines, so
many shipments . . . could his servants manage them alone for so
long? There was no use in wanting to know.

Alizar came to accept the ignominy and ceased hoping.

Some years into his imprisonment in the tower, a line of large
black ants found their way in from a hole in the floor where he
was expected to defecate. He awoke in the night to the sensation
of being bitten in every spot imaginable, his eyelids, scrotum, belly
and neck all aflame from the little welts. So the next morning, he
waged war on the ants, killing them as they arose from the stench
pit, smashing them with the heel of his palm. But at night when he
slept, they returned to sting his lips, his ears, his thighs.

After interminable weeks of war with the ants, Alizar sat
and meditated on his actions. Here they were sharing a world,
albeit a small stone one, and he was attacking them, and so they
were returning his zealous crusades with their own deft retali-
ation. In some ways, the ants reminded him of the rampaging
thoughts in his mind that he could not control, each of which
stung his pride, or his heart, or his hope. When he blamed Cyril,
he became sullen and withdrawn. When he blamed himself, he
felt the same effect on his psyche. If he fell into self-pity and
remorse, his spirits sunk, and his heart burned and troubled him
endlessly after he ate.

"There is a lesson here for me," he said one morning to the ants, clutching the thin woolen blanket that had been slipped through the hole in the door with his food, a much-treasured new possession in the cold winter tower that was once a prison of heat in the summer months. "You are trying to teach me about my thoughts," he said to them, sitting cross-legged before the shit hole as they marched in erratic, aimless circles before him. "Perhaps if I observe my mind more closely, I will learn to handle the thoughts that sting," he said. And so he sat diligently beside the ants, watching his thoughts for many hours. He ceased killing them, although there had been a remarkably large satisfaction in the tiny crunching sound their bodies had made as he crushed them, and he missed the game of their deaths and how it had passed so many hours of imprisonment.

The ants also gradually ceased their attacks on him. He began to feed them whatever precious breadcrumbs were left over from his supper, and they in turn left him alone. And feeding the ants, to his surprise, became an activity he relished far more than killing them. He also appreciated how such tiny beings expressed the intelligence of recognizing his change in attitude toward them enough, in turn, to change their attitudes toward him. The ants became to Alizar intimately cherished friends in so many hours of solitude. He spoke to them in long monologues, pretending they were the many friends he had known throughout his life and could not speak to now.

But as the months grew colder, the ants retired to the garden and ceased to come. For many days, Alizar missed them, his tiny companions.

Some weeks later, a crow with only one foot alighted on the window somewhat crookedly, and Alizar sat perfectly still, hoping the bird would stay. But upon seeing him, the glossy bird departed, cawing loudly. Alizar went to the window and set a curl of crust from his bread where the crow had been, and whistled three times. The following day, the crow returned, and then the following, and each day thereafter, always when he whistled the same two notes: low-high-low.

Alizar came to call the sententious bird "Caesar"—not after the Roman emperor, but after his favorite pharaoh hound killed by the Parabolani. Eventually, Caesar would take the crust from Alizar's fingers and sit in the window by the hour. Alizar would ask him all that had happened in the city that day and imagine the bird's responses, playing them out in his mind. But one day the crow did not return, and Alizar whistled and waited beside the window from dawn to dusk. The crow never returned. What Alizar never knew was that his beloved bird had grown exceedingly familiar with human companionship and had flown over the necropolis where some boys played among the crypts. It had landed on a nearby obelisk that marked a grave, and one of the boys hit it with a smooth stone from his sling, and the crow had fallen to the ground, red blood soaking the black glossy feathers as the boys laughed and clapped each other on the back, never realizing they had murdered a lonely prisoner's only friend.

Alizar thought of Casear with longing as he sat on his stone for most of the day, his heart plagued by loneliness. It was then that a new visitor arrived.

"Regret is a dangerous companion," said the voice.

Alizar did not even look up. "Yes, so it is said."

"I tried to warn you," said the voice, coming nearer.

"Yes. You did," said Alizar. "I was wrong to not heed your warning." He spoke without looking up. He had long been speaking to the many voices that drifted into his small stone world, and so this one was no different.

"Not wrong," said the voice.

Alizar lifted his head and peered sideways at the shimmering figure of Master Savitur illuminating the room, the particles of his body dancing like dust motes, and a smile lifted his lips. He was so unpracticed at smiling that he felt he was discovering the gesture for the first time. "So you have come," said Alizar, his voice deadened as a drum skin soaked in the rain.

Savitur settled on the floor beside Alizar and stretched his legs as though they had both been imprisoned together for years. "You look as if you should already be drawing flies," he said. "But I like the length of your beard."

Alizar chuckled, stroking his beard. "Yes, I suppose it may be back in fashion." He waited then for the vision to fade, for Savitur to simply disappear, but he did not. Instead, his body became all the more flesh, even exuding heat upon the stone where he sat. Alizar waited for his old master to say something more, and so when he did not, he ventured a conversation. "Tell me, how is the world?"

Savitur smiled. "The world is within you, where it has always been."

"I had thought there would be an appeal of Cyril's actions in the senate, but I suppose I am not as important as I imagined myself to be." Alizar laughed unconvincingly, as if he were an inexperienced actor practicing laughter. "Naomi would have prevented me from going out with Gideon that morning, you know. She was my wise restraint. Without her, look where I have fallen."

"He is not dead," said Savitur, his eyes glinting like coins in the bottom of a well.

Alizar wrinkled his brow in an effort to understand. "Not dead? Who?"

"Orestes."

"But I saw his wounds. How could anyone have survived?"

"He lives," said Savitur.

"How many years has it been?"

Savitur remained silent.

Feeling a burst of new life, Alizar harnessed the opportunity to learn more of what had been happening in Alexandria, since he had not yet given himself over to the temptation to think Savitur's appearance was merely the imagined apparition of an imprisoned madman.

"And Sofia? Have you seen my daughter?"

"She is married to Synesius, and with child. They are waiting for your release for the full celebration, I understand."

Alizar smiled again, little pools welling at the bottom of his eyes. "Is that so?"

Savitur nodded.

Alizar gazed out the window, longing to see her heart-shaped face, summoning it with the strength of his heart's memory until it floated before him, and he could almost touch her soft black hair.

Savitur let Alizar sit with his thoughts; a long time passed before he spoke again. He responded to each of Alizar's questions respectfully, as though the information were nourishment for a starving man. Eventually, Alizar was satiated, and thankful, and sitting in a whole new world of knowing that let him feel again connected to those he loved.

Savitur stood then, as if ready to depart. "The city has called a meeting on Antirrhodus next week. All the council members and magistrates will be there."

Alizar shook his head to dispel the settling flies that always came that time of day, drawn to the lumps of shit in the hole. "Is that so? Then it must be Lent. They always meet at this time. Then this is my third year. I think they have forgotten I am here." Alizar stood and accidentally kicked the empty wooden bowl across the room where it hit the stone wall and clattered to the floor. "Why bring me this news? What of it? Has Hypatia managed to bring me a pardon?"

Savitur said nothing, eyes full of firelight.

Alizar pursued the fading figure of his master across the room. "What of it? Savitur?" But the particles faded, snatching away the last remaining light from the room in a quick flash that left a footprint of emptiness behind, cold and silent.

Alizar strode to the north window that overlooked the little island of Antirrhodus in the harbor where the royal palace still stood, mostly unused except for the city's political affairs, the perimeter scintillating with torches in the darkness. What would the meeting of the council bring? Alizar dared, for the first time in years, hope for his release.

And so he walked to the east window and let his gaze fall across the red rooftops toward his own beloved tower where he had enjoyed so many hours of reverie. If there was a light within it, he would see it, but it was dark, as it had been whenever he looked at it. He pulled the dirty, fraying blanket around his shoulders, wishing Savitur had stayed to bring him more news. There were so many unanswered questions.

Alas.

Alizar had learned to live with them all.

34

Hannah stroked Gideon's hand. "So you will be there?"

"Have I ever missed one of your performances?" Gideon rolled his eyes playfully and pulled his hand free so that he could prop himself up on his elbows, digging his toes into the cool sand as the church bells rang over the city, calling the hour at the day's end. Hannah lifted her finger to trace the dark scar that ran down his cheek from the edge of his eye to where it tapered off at his jaw. "How did this happen?"

Gideon closed his eyes. "It was a long time ago."

"And?"

"There was a pirate called Ares I fought for my first ship, the *Artemis*. He came for gold, and he took it. It is how I lost my ship and came to sail for Alizar." Gideon took a swig of water and wiped his beard. Alizar. His friend long imprisoned. Two attempts to rescue him had failed. He must try again.

"What is it?" asked Hannah.

"Nothing. I think of the *Vesta*, of Alizar. The wrongs I must right."

Hannah stroked his hands. She understood. Gideon had been too late to save the *Vesta* and had watched her inferno from the docks, furious, maddened with grief at his failures. He spoke day and night of his plans to get Alizar out of the church tower, but there were always guards, more guards. The Nuapar would not help him.

Gideon shifted in the sand so he could hold her. "Let me ask you in return, then. What about this scar here?" His fingers traced her breast. He had never asked her, and she had never offered.

Hannah's fingers brushed her sternum and found the spot there where the skin had healed, smooth as the inside of a conch shell. "It is how I came to Alexandria, to Alizar's house."

Gideon touched her hand, sensing she felt uncomfortable. "You do not have to tell me."

But before she could speak, a familiar cry pierced the air.

Hannah instinctively swept the seashore with her eyes. Then she quickly stood up, her heart beginning to pound.

"Mama?" said a little voice behind her.

Hannah laughed with relief. "Alaya, you scared me. Why did you cry?"

The little girl twisted a toe into the sand and fluttered her eyelashes, a talent for flirtation she had practiced since birth. "I hurt my knee, see?" She pointed at nothing.

Gideon smiled and then suddenly grabbed Alaya by the hands. "I think it is your turn for a spinning!" he said, as he began to turn circles while Alaya shrieked and giggled happily. Then he stopped, flipped Alaya backwards onto the sand, and tickled her. Alaya shrieked with glee, and Gideon growled like a terrible lion and pretended to haul Alaya off to his cave in the direction of the waves, her little feet kicking against the sand.

Hannah closed her eyes and shook her head in disbelief at the passing of time. How was it that Alaya was already so big? So much had happened in the years since her birth, and yet time had rocked to a stop for most of them since Alizar had been imprisoned. Whenever Hannah went to visit Jemir, Tarek, Sofia, and Synesius, she saw that Alizar's household managed to function without him as though he was still there, much like the organs of a body during sleep.

Things in the Great Library, however, seemed to be changing at a more significant pace. Since Orestes's recovery, Hypatia had disbanded her public lecture platform to focus her attention on the core group of students that had been with her for the bulk of her career, formalizing the esoteric teachings of Platonism for them as she interpreted it within her mystery school. She became selective about whom she taught or saw socially, even foregoing walks in the city, preferring the company of the library's elite and the quiet hours of her own study where she could meditate, write, and practice yoga. This meant that Hannah was not performing as often, and so she became entirely devoted to cataloguing music. Through the many hours of the day, she sat inventing a musical language that could be used to notate the songs and melodies she knew and that others brought to her. Often she walked through Alexandria with a notepad and a stylus to sit beside the fountains where the women sang and told their stories so that she could find a way to re-create them later on back at the library. It was tedious work, and often she found that her notations were still too unrefined to capture the songs she encountered. The sailor songs on the wharf, however, were occasionally simple enough that her basic notation would do, and so after many weeks of work, when she found she could reproduce even a few lines from a song, she was ecstatic. But more often than not, there were many frustrating hours of time lost and notes still too unclear to reproduce. Hannah began to wonder if Hypatia had known what a Sisyphean task a music scholar would endure.

During those weeks when frustration was her only companion, Hannah sometimes fantasized about her freedom and how she would have a tent in the hawker's bazaar to sell jewelry: beaded necklaces, anklets, hair adornments, and other things she made herself, maybe even giving palm readings. Perhaps as the women of the bazaar became acquainted with her fine taste, Hannah's little business would grow. She could acquire rare

Indian silks for veils and headdresses and stitch lovely designs with dangling glass beads along the fine gossamer fabrics. In her mind she would create glorious costumes for dance that the women haggled over endlessly. But back in the library, Hannah bent over dozens of scrolls with her lyre, attempting to make sense of a language that simply did not lend itself well to being captured on paper.

How could she notate emotion? Notes were simple, as were lyrics, but emotion was something she began to feel more and more would never find an expression in words or symbols. She began to wonder if perhaps it would even be better that way. The notation would leave the interpretation up to the musician, and so in that way the songs would be the same yet always re-invent themselves. Hannah often worked well into the night, seated on the balcony of her upstairs bedroom overlooking the Caesarium gardens, attempting to make some sense of all her scribble.

Sometimes Gideon came to sit with her, but more and more often as she spoke, his eyes leaned toward the sea, and it was clear he had not been listening. At first she had minded this constant longing that had separated him from her after Alizar's ship was burned. But quite soon she found peace with it, as it left room for longings of her own. Gideon was a captain, and captains needed ships.

Hannah smiled, watching her daughter and Gideon playing on the beach. He had been out riding with friends who were visiting from Cyprus the day her daughter was born, spiraling from her womb into the world. She had danced naked in the room through her early labor, her belly full as the harvest moon, turning her hips, her wrists, listening intently to the drum the midwife played to call the child into the world. Eventually, she had settled on the blankets on the floor, satisfied that the birth would be in the company of women. Then the pain began in earnest, and she had to find a way through it.

The angel had found flesh. The doorway had been promised. The warrior had come. Now she would know the heaviness of earth, the beauty of sky and sea. Waiting had transformed to this.

Creases of regret had appeared around Gideon's mouth when he found that he had missed the birth, but he was willing to hold the baby, which was more than most fathers.

Then there had been the issue of ownership. Always an unspoken subject, Hannah's child would also be a slave. She had not been able to give Alaya up to the Temple of Isis to become a priestess. Better a child have a mother, she thought, better a mother in chains than an orphan anywhere. Sometimes she wondered if she was wrong. But her love was so strong it dictated only togetherness, as love will do. What with Alizar still in prison, Gideon had yet to pay him the coin. Hannah belonged to Alizar. She wondered if the transaction would ever be completed between them but did not seek to disturb those waters. Slavery was slavery. Men were men. She counted her blessings and no longer wished for more. In Alizar's absence, Gideon generously sponsored her time in the library and stayed with her most nights. Most.

As Hannah watched her daughter at play on the sand, she marveled at the differences between them. Where Hannah had always perceived herself as shy and reserved, Alaya had no inhibitions whatsoever. She constantly entertained anyone who would watch her, singing little songs that she made up or dancing with one of the veils Hannah created, flirtatiously batting her long dark lashes in a way that no one had needed to teach her. She had a natural capacity for theatrics and mimicry, always pretending to be outrageous personalities: the empress of an island in the sun, a healer with magical potions to cure snakebite, and goddesses like Isis and Aphrodite. Her impersonation of Jemir had been so accurate, lifting one eyebrow in his characteristic manner with her arms folded over a pillow she had stuffed under her shirt to be his belly, that Jemir and Tarek had nearly pissed themselves they laughed so hard the first time they saw it.

"Mama, can I go in the water?" Alaya wrapped her sandy arms around Hannah's neck, pressing her cheek to her mother's.

"No, love. We are going home now."

Alaya dashed off to chase the sand plovers that skittered at the water's edge as Hannah collected their things. Alaya had stepped out of the womb with a passion for the sea. Every time Hannah looked at her, she saw that passion mirrored back to her in Alaya's enormous eyes, chimerical eyes that danced like waves on the surface of the sea on a clear day. They were more colorful than Julian's, and even larger than her own, always looking into the world with a sparkle of joy. Just after Alaya was born, Hannah had caressed her baby's hands and feet and the soft down on the crown of her head, finding all the little details of her daughter. Alaya had Julian's golden skin, her own wide brow and pouty lips, and though it was impossible, her grandfather Kaleb's dented chin.

Gideon had embraced the girl even though he knew the child was not his, and so she called Gideon her "Pappo," a name she invented for him all on her own, a name he treasured hearing more than any other word.

Alaya had only asked about her Abba, her father, once. Hannah had been planning for years what she would say if that day came. But in the moment, all her carefully rehearsed answers had evaporated.

They had just awakened, and Hannah was stroking the long curls back from her daughter's dolphin forehead when Alaya had turned to look into her mother's eyes and asked sweetly, "Mama, is Pappo my Abba?"

Hannah took a beat to reply. "No. Gideon is your Pappo. Your Pappo who loves you."

"But my Abba?" asked the little girl, understanding far more than what seemed possible at her age.

"Your Abba is in India," said Hannah, which was true as far as she knew.

Alaya sat up. "India?"

This led to endless questioning about what was India and where was India and could they go there, and why not?

So.

To pacify her daughter's sudden interest in the mystical country in the east, Hannah had searched the Great Library for any texts or maps that had been procured from India. She found very little, however, as they were all under lock and key for fear of Cyril's threats. So she went to Synesius with her conundrum, and he had brought down a codex out of his personal collection and presented it to Alaya with pride. It was a book with pictures of the Hindu gods painted in ink surrounded by whimsical Sanskrit lettering, presumably prayers, which no one could interpret. But the pictures were more than enough to satisfy Alaya's imagination: Ganesha the great elephant riding on the back of a rat; Krishna with his flute flirtatiously calling to his gopis; Vishnu reclining upon his serpent bed in the milky cosmos; Hanuman leaping to Ceylon to rescue princess Sita from the demon king, Ravana.

Alaya had hugged the book to her heart and danced with the codex of colorful pictures all around the Main Hall. It had been the perfect gift.

From that day forward, Alaya impersonated the postures and expressions of the gods and goddesses in the book. She created her own *mudras* and begged her mother to make headdresses for her that were precisely like the ones in the pictures. Following the gift of the codex, Alaya also began to expand her repertoire of impersonations to include the expressions on statues around the city. She practiced Athena's majestic smile, always pouting when it made the adults around her laugh, and Isis's triumphant posture down on one knee with her wings outstretched.

"I want to be a goddess one day, like you," Alaya had whispered to her mother late one evening when Hannah was carrying her to bed.

Hannah kissed her daughter's shoulder. "Then you will be," she said, her heart flooding its banks with love, thinking of how the time had come to also take Alaya to the synagogue, so she would know her grandfather and her heritage.

Alaya had emerged from the womb head-first with the caul still wrapped around her tiny body, the sign of a fortunate life. When the midwife had cleaned the baby and handed her to her mother, she had exclaimed, "She has fallen from heaven to your arms!"

With tears of joy, Hannah had kissed her child for the first time and gazed into her oceanic eyes.

"What will you call her?" Gideon had asked later, his clothing still crusted in dust from riding through the reed beds that day.

Hannah had planned to name the baby "Iris" after her friend from Pharos who had been so kind. But looking down upon her, the name seemed not to fit. Instantly a new name came to her unbidden, one she had forgotten until that moment. And so she had chosen the name that had belonged to Julian's mother, the name he had whispered to her in the tower that first night of winter: Alaya. Her daughter would have at least one piece of her true father, if only in a name.

Hannah, Gideon, and Alaya strolled from the beach up Canopic Way, forgetting for a blissful hour that there had ever been anything to be frightened of in the city. The Parabolani had not been seen about in a year while Cyril had been traveling to Ephesus, Pergamon, and Constantinople to establish his name in the Christian hierarchy of bishops. Some of the Jews even resettled in the old quarter, daring to reclaim their homes and businesses.

Hannah caught sight of the copper sundial above the fountain and stopped, checking the time. They had tarried at the beach a bit longer than she had thought, but there was still an hour before she was expected back.

Gideon looked suddenly pensive, a rare expression for him. He reached inside his belt and untied his bag of coin.

"What are you doing?" Hannah asked.

"I must use the latrine," he said. "There are nothing but pirates and thieves on this side of town. Hold these for me."

Hannah felt the heavy bag of coins drop into her hand. It was a great sum of money. She looked into his eyes, confused. He had never done this before.

"I will meet you on the steps of the Tabularium," he said, characteristically terse, transferring Alaya to her arms. Then he turned and sauntered down the alley to the men's public latrine.

Whatever did he want to go to the Tabularium for? That place was nothing but records of lands transferred, and birth and death, and the names of criminals. Still, she would go. Hannah slid the bag of coins into her belt and quickened her steps toward the Tabularium.

The fastest way would be through the fish market on the wharf, so Hannah cut through the cobbled alleys behind the knoll of the Serapeum that wound around the hill much like the Plaka of Athens. She shifted Alaya to her back so they could move more quickly over the multitude of worn white marble steps that wound up and down the hill beneath the overgrown red bougainvillea.

As they came out into the *agora* from behind a large pillar, Hannah could see the steps of the Tabularium on the other side, and the row of people waiting their turn to register some birth or death with the scribe there. But then she heard a voice, and her feet turned to stone, a memory more powerful than death gripping her bones.

"Mama?"

"Shush," Hannah closed her eyes and listened to the voice of the man calling out across the crowd: deep, powerful, and raspy with too much wine. There was that lilt, an intoxication of power, and beneath it an untrustworthy wavering of tone that shifted every breath, like sand in the desert. Yes, it had to be him.

She took a tiny step forward so she could peer between the branches of the bougainvillea bush overcome with a pink effusion of blossoms. And then she saw the man she would have known anywhere in the world, his two friends beside him, men who years before had come into her father's field and kidnapped her while she slept. They stood with their faces turned away beside a wooden box where a young dark-haired girl stood positioned before a mildly interested crowd, wrists bound before her, head low.

A slave auction.

Hannah crouched and took Alaya's hand, creeping through the bougainvillea to find a way through the crowd without being seen.

"Bad men," said Alaya, repeating the term her mother used for the Parabolani.

"Yes," whispered Hannah, terribly anxious her daughter might give them away, her body seized by a debilitating fear that made it hard to move, to think. "Bad men, Alaya. We must be very quiet."

Alaya lifted a finger to her lips, "Shush."

Hannah looked back every two steps to see the slave traders. One counted coins into a box. One stood beside the girl. One moved among the crowd, raising the hand of the highest bidder while stealthily pick-pocketing the rest of the engrossed onlookers. Hannah had always thought of them as one man, oddly. In truth they were probably brothers, and so looked alike. But it was more than that for Hannah. In her mind, she had seen their faces and voices blend during the days on the road, and during the hours they pinned her down and forced themselves upon her. They were one man with black eyes like two empty holes in the ground. But here, suddenly, the men were very real, and brought like demons out from the corners of her mind where she had pushed them away for so long.

The man at the front was not even dark-haired like she remembered, but nearly grey, where his brothers were both dark-skinned and dark-haired, beards slick with oil. He called out to someone in the crowd and pointed, raising the girl's bound arms over her head like dead fish. Hannah cringed.

Had she been alone, she might have challenged them. Had it been years ago, before she came to understand the power of men, she might have called out and tried to save the girl. But now, all she thought of was her daughter's safety and of moving through the crowd unseen. Still, she felt the rage burn in her blood, searing with desire for revenge. For here were the men who had killed her father. Here were the men who had stolen her life, her freedom.

As she neared the edge of the crowd, she stopped and picked up Alaya and swung her up to her back again. The highest bidder was before her, a tall thin man in a brown *tunica* with merry eyes. Here, three steps away, stood this young girl's fate. Would he be kind to her? Would he give her clean clothes to wear and fill her belly with bread? Would he rape her every night as she cried before he slept at her side and snored like a beast? Would he work her in the kitchens beside other women he had purchased, stolen from a dead shepherd's arms in the darkness of night?

She had thought often in that first year how fortunate she had been to come into Alizar's house of all houses. Tarek, fool though he was, had saved her life by allowing Alizar to fetch the doctor when he first brought her home. And Alizar was a kind master. She knew it could have been far, far worse, bad as it was.

One of the traders came to the tall man standing before Hannah and raised his arm to indicate he was the highest bidder. As he did so, he met Hannah's eyes, and she held it with a powerful stare like a tigress emerging from the trees.

For a long time, they stared at one another in recognition. Hate for hate. He saw the rage in Hannah's eyes and the bronze collar at her neck, and his eyes challenged her.

Come on, young thing.

Nothing has changed since that day.

You were so easy to destroy.

So easy.

Hannah stealthily withdrew her knife from the hilt at her calf, her fingers tightening around the bone handle as Alaya buried her face in her mother's hair and began to cry. But as Hannah stood poised before the trader, another power moved into her, overtaking her limbs.

Hannah raised her voice. For the first time in her life, she heard a power she did not know she possessed spill out of her throat. "Whatever he is bidding I will pay it twice," she said.

The slave trader met her eyes.

She stood firm.

He ignored her until she reached into her pocket and withdrew Gideon's bag of coins. Seeing it, the raider lowered the man's arm and walked toward her.

"Go and stand in the bushes, Alaya," whispered Hannah. "Run!" She lowered Alaya, who ran as fast as she could to the bougainvillea shrubs along the wall where she crouched down and watched, terrified.

Hannah trembled as the brute came to stand beside her, so close she could smell the stench of his unwashed *tunica*. She rooted herself on her heels and breathed deeply, summoning her strength. He locked eyes with her and slowly reached for her arm.

But Hannah met him with fierceness that spoke of death, and he did not dare take another step toward her. She shook the purse and held it higher. The entire crowd fell silent and turned to watch her, the only woman in Alexandria in seven hundred years to ever bid upon a slave girl. "You will bring that girl to me," she said in her loudest voice, "and then you will leave this city. You will return to where you came from and never, never take another girl from her father. Do you understand me? Or so help me, you will die in your sleep with your throat slit, every one of you." A low rumble like an animal sound left her throat.

The traders glared at her and then laughed. The fair-haired man beside the girl pushed her forward from the wooden platform, and the crowd parted to let her walk to where Hannah stood, her eyes fearful and timid as Hannah's had once been, her head low.

The man before her reached for the bag of coins, and she saw in his other hand a concealed knife. She swept the coins back, but he brought his knife up before her, waving it. "I remember you," he snarled. "Stupid Jewish whore. I remember your tight little cunny." He narrowed his eyes, taunting her. "And how you screamed for more."

In an instant, Hannah swung her own knife into view and faced off with him. "Shut your mouth."

He laughed. "Give us the coins, slave, and you can keep your curses," he said. Around them the crowd formed a circle, shifting uneasily.

Hannah held her knife firm. "Give me the girl," she said.

"The coins first." The man grasped the girl by the scruff, then threw her to the ground.

Alaya watched from the bushes, too terrified to move. "Mama!"

Hannah and the trader circled the girl, knives raised.

"How did you get the money, slave?" the man growled. "Did you steal it? Do you know the penalty for stealing?"

"It is my husband's money," Hannah lied. "Lower your weapon."

"Everyone knows slaves have no husbands," said the man. "Thief." And in one quick movement he lunged for her, grabbing her by the arm and turning her around. He held his knife to her throat, leaving her unable to use hers on him. "You dare to threaten me," he growled. "Let me tell you what I will do," he whispered to her through clenched teeth as she squirmed. "I will kill you as the thief you are, and I will take your coins and the girl.

And then I will take that pretty little daughter of yours hiding in the trees and find her a new home. What do you say?"

"I say you will rot in Hades," said Gideon, his own knife drawn against the man's neck with a firm hold. "Now let her go."

The man snarled and shoved Hannah to the ground, but he was no untrained fighter. He wrested free of Gideon's grip and spun around, his own knife flung out to meet Gideon's throat, but then, suddenly he crumbled instead, and behind him, Hannah pulled her knife from his back.

Alaya screamed as the man fell to the ground. The crowd shifted uneasily but stayed right where they were, thrilled to observe the unfolding drama. "You will never touch another woman again," she said through clenched teeth, and then she spat on him. On the ground the man's body twitched and then fell still, looking instantly smaller in death than in life.

Immediately, the grey-haired man that stood at the auction block lifted his sword and lunged into the crowd with a scream of fury. He came straight for Hannah who took halting steps backward. But Gideon was quicker. He shoved her out of the way saying, "Get up to the steps. Go!" as his sword met the slaver's gut, and the man dropped to his knees. As Gideon wrenched his blade out, an old woman with a dark red shawl the color of dried blood began to scream out, "Murderer! Murderer! Thieves!"

Hannah swiftly bent down and took the hands of the slaver's girl on the ground. Then they fled toward the bougainvillea bush, the weeping girl hanging from Hannah's hand, kissing her fingers.

Hannah called out for Alaya, but her daughter was not in the bushes. She called again, and still her child did not come.

Then before her appeared the third slaver, holding Alaya by the hair, a knife at her small smooth throat. Hannah screamed as suddenly he toppled backwards, a knife having flown through the air and plunged straight through his left eye, spraying blood across his face and hair. He fist released Alaya, and he fell back-

ward into the dust. Then Gideon strode forward, kicked the man
on his back, and retrieved his knife with one yank. He wiped it on
his black *tunica*, and then went to Hannah.

Hannah trembled in Gideon's arms, clutching Alaya to her, the
slave girl beside her. "They will imprison us now," Hannah whispered. "We have killed three men."

Gideon kissed her forehead. "Those men will meet their fate in
Hades. It is done." Then he called out to the crowd, "No funerals
for these bastards! Toss their bodies out the city gates to the desert
dogs." The crowd closed in around the slavers, eager to relieve
them of any wealth they concealed before discarding them like
rubbish over the wall.

Pigeons cooed and scattered as Gideon led Hannah, Alaya,
and the pretty Nubian girl up the steps to the Tabularium. Hannah clutched Alaya tightly. The slave girl wept silently and dried
her eyes without a word.

"Give me the coins," demanded Gideon, his hand outstretched.

Hannah pulled the heavy leather pouch out from under her
belt and handed it to him, her fingers trembling.

He took it. "And this girl? Who is she?"

Hannah cleared her throat, looked at the girl, her skin glistening like polished ebony. "The same as me."

"Have mercy," said the girl. "Please." She spoke only Nubian
and had probably been transported weeks away from her village.

Gideon turned away gruffly, leaving Hannah standing with Alaya
beside the slave girl. Then he cut to the front of the queue where the
scribe was receiving the people, and he threw the heavy bag of coins
on the table before the small, bald Roman man wearing a formal red
palla. "This is for the freedom of my wife and her friend," he said.
"Pay half these coins to the house of Alizar." And then he called the
women forward. "Tell the man your names, and it is done."

The women spoke one at a time, first Hannah, and then the
girl, whose name was Oni. The scribe eyed them suspiciously

and then wrote several brisk, jagged letters on his scroll. Then he set down his stylus and spilled Gideon's gold *solidi* into his hand to count them. After the Roman was satisfied, he nodded to the gruff soldier behind him. The soldier raised a hand and called the women forward to a blacksmith's stall. The same blacksmith appeared whom Hannah had encountered her first day in Alexandria. He turned her around, lifted her hair, and with the snap of metal in his clamp in one quick instant, it was done.

The collar fell, and Hannah was free.

Hannah walked with Gideon to the library, each saying nothing. When they reached the steps, Hannah looked at him, her eyes searching his face. She did not have the courage to ask the question in her heart.

Gideon kissed her cheek. "Those men will never trouble us again."

Hannah stroked her strangely bare throat. "I thought I was strong enough to confront them. I was wrong. Alaya could have been killed. I have no idea what possessed me. I, I—"

Gideon pressed his finger to her lips. "Hannah, if I wanted a wife as strong as a centurion, I would marry a man," he said. Then he kissed her, and she melted into him. His bones became her fortress, his breath her house of the divine.

"Thank you," she whispered, tears springing free of her eyes. "For my freedom. It would be an honor to be your wife."

Gideon smiled and kissed the top of Alaya's head. "*Neh*. Now you should both go inside and change your *khitons*."

A little while later, Hannah glided down from her room holding Alaya in one arm and her lyre in the other. Alaya was whimpering, still confused and frightened from the events earlier that day, and did not want to relinquish her mother's hand. She set Alaya down beside a large column at the edge of the garden.

"Alaya," Hannah whispered, gently sitting on her ankles to avoid brushing the ground with the beaded hem of her fine garment. "I am going to sing for Hypatia's lecture, and I want you to wait for me in the garden with Sofia."

Alaya scowled. "I want to come."

Hannah placed her hands on her daughter's shoulders and leaned forward to kiss her forehead gently. "Not tonight, *Kukla*. I promise I will see you after. Play with Sofia."

Sofia approached them, her belly swollen with her first child. Hannah whispered something to her and kissed her cheeks.

Reluctantly, Alaya took Sofia's hand and watched over her shoulder as her mother vanished into the Great Hall of the library.

Sofia smiled. "Shall we visit the butterflies?"

Alaya looked up at Sofia then back to the door her mother had slipped through. "I want Mama and Pappo," she whined.

"Afterward," said Sofia, stroking the top of Alaya's head.

The Caesarium garden was lit by torches set at intervals on marble pillars around the pond, creating warm pools of golden light all along the path. The evening was dreadfully hot without any promise of a breeze. Sofia and Alaya paraded around the rim of the garden, visiting the sleeping butterflies and making up songs as they went.

"I want the turtles," said Alaya, tugging Sofia's hand.

Sofia yawned. "Turtles it is."

Alaya let go and ran along the path to the little footbridge over the stream. "Where are they?" she called back.

"Maybe they are sleeping," offered Sofia.

Alaya trotted across the bridge and over to the edge of the pond. No turtles.

She looked back at Sofia, who had settled on a bench to rest. "I find them!" Alaya called out. A kingfisher swept up to a palm from his perch beside the reflecting pool, squawking his irritation at the child's disturbance.

"Just stay where I can see you."

Alaya turned back to the pond and got down on her hands and knees and began to search under the bushes and along the banks for where the turtles might be hiding. The torchlight created beautiful designs in the path that made Alaya think of tiger stripes, and so she decided to pretend she was a mother tiger in search of her cubs.

Sofia watched the rustling bushes and yawned again. The evening was deliriously warm, and she had not slept well in many nights. She brought her hands to her belly to feel the baby, and, without meaning to, she let her head rock forward and dozed off.

Alaya hummed happily to herself as she wandered through the bushes. On a smooth stone platform beside the pond slept three turtles. She rushed over to them only to discover that they were just stones set beside the water, but on the other side of the reflecting pool beneath the papyrus she saw two round shapes that she was certain must be turtles.

Alaya turned, ran back to the path and circled the pool, following the light of the torches. She ran as fast as she could to the place where she thought the turtles would be, but the path circled, and she ended up at the steps leading into the Mouseion. Recognizing her mistake, Alaya turned back toward the pond and ran headlong into a tall pair of legs, falling to the ground.

A man dressed in long black robes helped her to her feet, his waist bound in a red and white sash. His eyes shone like the stories she had heard her mother tell of the Emerald Tablet.

"Hello, little one," said the man, laughing, bending low. His appearance was altogether elegant: long black hair swept back from his face and bound at the nape of his neck, a stride like a lion's. His gentle voice lent him such nobility that Alaya thought he might be a pharaoh.

Alaya stepped back. "You know the turtles?"

"I saw three turtles back along the path," said the man, "beside the pool."

Alaya rolled her eyes. "Those were rocks."

"Where is your mother?" asked the man. He sounded appropriately concerned.

"Inside. I am with Sofia."

The stranger smiled, his eyes gleaming. "Will you allow me to accompany you?"

Alaya looked up at him and batted her lashes flirtatiously.

"What is your name?"

"It is a secret."

"A secret? I like secrets."

Alaya nodded and scurried down the path. Then from behind a bush she growled at the stranger. "I am a mother tiger."

"Ah, a tigress," said the man. "There are many tigers in India."

"India!" Alaya squealed coming out from behind the bushes. "My Abba is in India."

The man looked at Alaya quizzically.

"Alaya!" Sofia's urgent call swept across the reflecting pool. "Alaya!"

The stranger's eyes glowed magically, then dimmed. He looked down at the little girl beside him. "Your name is Alaya?" he asked her, his voice tinged with deeper interest.

"Yes."

"And where is your mother?" asked the elegant stranger.

Alaya sprinted down the path. "Singing with Hypatia!"

The stranger lifted himself to his full height and listened. Above the raga of insects pulsing in the sultry heat he could just make out the sound of a beautiful and somewhat familiar voice.

Intrigued, the yogi soundlessly swept down the path and paused outside the Great Hall of the library. There, framed by the window, sat Hannah, her fingers dancing over the strings of a lyre, the rich garnet beads along her *himation* scintillating like captured fireflies above her bosom, her full lips parting for the sweet notes of the melody, a dew of perspiration across her brow.

The stranger inhaled sharply and turned his back to the window. He measured the years in his mind, then he quickened his steps back to the gardens to find the little girl.

As he approached, he saw the child on the path holding hands with her ward. Alaya looked back over her shoulder and said, "See, there he is."

The stranger stepped forward and apologized to Sofia, who wore a look of surprise and intrigue.

"Please," he said. "Allow me to introduce myself. I am Master Junkar."

Sofia smiled, knowing who he was from her father's stories. "A pleasure, Master Junkar," she whispered, bowing her head in reverence.

"Junkar," Alaya repeated the stranger's name to him.

"Yes," he said tenderly. "And your name is Alaya." He bent down on one knee.

"How old are you, Alaya?" he asked.

Alaya held up two fingers. "Three."

Junkar closed his eyes and counted in his mind. "Come closer to me," he said.

Sofia nodded, and Alaya let go of her hand and went to him fearlessly.

He looked at her carefully and lifted one hand as though to touch her cheek, and then withdrew it. "You are every bit as beautiful as your mother," he said, not wanting to frighten her. Then he reached over his neck and pulled from under his robe a long string of polished sandalwood beads with a smooth red tassel. "I want to give these to you, Alaya. May I?"

Alaya eyed the beads suspiciously and poked them with one finger.

"They are from India," he said as he lifted them over his head and placed them around her neck.

Hearing the magic word, Alaya's lips spread into a smile. "India? For me?" she asked sweetly, fingering the beads.

"India. For you," said Master Junkar, his dark hair slipping free from the tie at the nape of his neck as he leaned forward to kiss her hand. In that moment, not blood, but love flowed through his veins.

Alaya nodded, clutching the beads.

The stranger rose to his feet. "Remember my name, Alaya. I am Master Junkar," he said. "And if you ever need me, I want you to call for me." He waited for a moment, to see that she understood. Then, overcome by so much unfamiliar feeling, he nodded to Sofia and swiftly left the garden.

Sofia bent down and picked Alaya up in her arms, though it was hard with her tummy. She perched the girl on her hip.

Alaya tugged at the beads around her neck. "Smell," she said.

Sofia leaned forward and let her nose brush the beads, inhaling the sweet aroma of the pungent sandalwood.

They circled the garden and sang songs until Hannah called. The moon hung in the western sky like an angelic fingernail. Hannah took Alaya in her arms and thanked Sofia for looking after her, then began to chatter about the audience and the energy in the hall and how one of the strings of her lyre had snapped right in the middle of the most important song, and how happy Jemir had been to see Hypatia.

Sofia's lips parted, about to speak, but then Hannah noticed the beads around her daughter's neck. "Alaya, where did you get these?"

"India," announced Alaya, kicking against her mother's legs to be set down.

Hannah let Alaya slide from her arms and looked to Sofia. "What does she mean?"

Sofia paused and inhaled deeply. She wanted to choose her words carefully.

But before Sofia could speak, Hannah's eyes flicked around the garden as if sensing something. She took in the emptiness and the magical glow of the torches as a feeling of warm knowing spread through her bones. Then she looked back into Sofia's eyes. "He was here."

Sofia nodded.

"Is he gone?" Hannah asked in a faint whisper.

"*Neh.*"

"Did he speak to you?"

"Briefly."

"And Alaya?"

"He found her in the garden when I was sitting by the pond, Hannah. I—" Sofia's voice faltered. "I am so sorry. I fell asleep."

Hannah did not even hear her. Was she really to believe that Julian had returned from India and found his daughter in the garden? But if the Kolossofia were such yogis, then surely he already knew of her. "What did he say?" Hannah reached forward to take Alaya's hand.

Sofia recounted his words and how he had given Alaya the beads.

Hannah's heart fluttered, awakened from an ancient sleep. But why would he not come to see her? She let her eyes scan the garden again, but it was empty.

"Mama, I am sleepy," said Alaya, leaning against her mother's leg.

Hannah gathered her daughter into her arms, the door to her heart drawing shut. If she allowed herself to hope, even for an instant, the dark disappointment that she had worked to free herself from would resurface, and she had no desire to put Alaya through the pain of losing a father she had never even known, a man who had abandoned them both. And what of Gideon? Gideon, who had purchased her freedom, who wanted to make her his wife. No, she must not think on Julian again. It was better for all of them.

"Come Alaya, it is time for bed," Hannah said abruptly. Then she thanked Sofia and turned away. This was all too much for one day. Hannah wanted only to sleep knowing her daughter was safe and that she had her freedom at last.

Alaya waved to Sofia from over her mother's shoulder with one hand, the other still clutching the stranger's sandalwood beads.

 35

A gentle knock fell on the door of Hypatia's study. She let out an irritated sigh, set down her stylus, lifted the parchment from her desk, and blew. The latest innovation in ink of lampblack gum and water seemed to take an eternity to dry.

"My lady?" The voice of the servant girl called softly from behind the door.

"Yes, come in," said Hypatia, her attention still on her work.

The girl entered with a tray that held a bowl of unspiced barley and a pot of tea. Hypatia did not look up. "Set it there."

The girl hesitated. The table already held four trays of empty teapots beside bowls of untouched food that she had brought over the past few days. There was no more room for another tray. She looked back to Hypatia, her eyes asking what she should do.

"Clear them," said Hypatia, more curtly than she intended. "And please send for a messenger."

The girl nodded and began to stack the trays.

Hypatia bent her head and went back to her writing. She worked steadily for several more minutes until another knock fell on the door. She answered without looking up. "Come." When the person she presumed to be the messenger entered she began giving orders. "I want this manuscript delivered promptly to the Church of St. Alexander. It is to be seen by no one but the bishop, do you understand?"

"Perfectly," said the figure, chuckling.

Hypatia looked up in surprise. "Good heavens, Orestes, what are you doing here? I thought you were the messenger I sent for."

"Perhaps I am," he said, taking a seat on the chair in front of Hypatia's desk and setting his cane beside him, a heavy codex cradled in his lap.

"Here, let me help you," said Hypatia, rushing to his side, but he shook her off.

"I am not dead yet."

She apologized and sat before him, attentive, as her favorite student had never come to visit her study, even in the years before he was attacked. The manuscript on his lap looked intriguing, but she would wait for him to offer more about it.

He looked around her study, seeing that the rumors were true. The entire room was in disarray. Pages of geometric equations once tacked to the wall had been blown down by the wind that rushed in from the open window, strewn around the floor, fluttering like so many dying fish. Hypatia's desk was overflowing with scrolls containing astronomical data, parchments that documented the library's annual accounting, and numerous smaller codices that held Hypatia's lecture notes that had been transcribed for her over the years. If there was any order to the chaotic mess, it was completely unapparent.

Hypatia brushed a wisp of greying hair back from her forehead with her ink-stained fingers, leaving a black smudge over one eyebrow. She looked exhausted. Her cheeks were sunken from loss of appetite, making her eyes appear even larger, but her skin had a glow of health that was derived perhaps more from meditation than her abstemious diet. Orestes, unlike most of Hypatia's staff, was unconcerned. He knew that when inspiration comes, it is best to flow with it, for the suffering that the body endures in the presence of that holy gift cannot equal the excruciating inner turmoil of a creative mind abandoned by the muse.

"You have finished it, then?"

Hypatia shoved the manuscript across the desk in his direction. "See for yourself."

Orestes leaned forward and took the pages in his hands. The title on the first page read: *Mary, Mother of God.* He scanned through the stack, letting his eyes glance over the pages. It was a small treatise, perhaps fifty pages altogether, unlike most of Hypatia's work, which tended to be extremely long-winded. "Will you sign it?"

Hypatia shook her head. "I am not decided."

"But it bears the seal of the library," Orestes protested. "Cyril will certainly guess who sent it."

"Perhaps," Hypatia said. "I only seek to open him to the possibility that the Christians and our Great Library are not an incompatible alliance. And besides, I am waiting for Alizar's pardon. I am certain it will come now that you are well and can influence the votes."

Orestes raised one eyebrow and set the manuscript back on the desk, impressed. "I must admit it is worth a try. Here, I have something for you, actually. It is by our old friend Augustine of Hippo." He reached out to hand her the heavy codex bound in dark vellum.

She turned the codex in her hands. "Augustine? Have you seen him?" Orestes nodded. "*The City of God: Against the Pagans.* What is it?" she asked, filled with ominous dread.

"You know better than anyone how the people felt after Rome fell."

"That the fall of Rome was a punishment for abandoning the Roman gods. What does this have to do with Augustine?"

"Augustine has left the teachings of Plotinus for Christianity. His treatise is powerful, Hypatia."

"He has always been imbued with the spirit. I am not surprised he found Christ."

"Augustine writes that the City of God will ultimately triumph, even after all our wonders crumble, and we ourselves."

"His eyes are fixed on heaven, then?"

Orestes nodded. "Yes. His manuscript is lauded around the empire. It is an important one to add to the stacks."

"I will read it at once." Hypatia set the manuscript down and regarded Orestes. She had not forgiven the bishop for what the Parabolani had done to her friend. Though his stuttering had improved over the years, Orestes was still half-blind. It had been a cruel way to gain the favor of the populace, and sadly, it had worked. The people began to view Orestes as weak. The emperor had even appointed a new praetorian prefect, though he allowed Orestes to retain his title of governor. Orestes, however, seemed quite at ease with his losses. The injury had slowed his mind and his speech, but this annoyed his friends far more than it bothered him. For the first time in his life he felt at peace, studying philosophy and taking long walks on the beach. His grief over Phoebe's death was behind him, but he had chosen never to remarry.

Orestes let his eyes sweep out the window and across the harbor to the island of Pharos. The Christians had almost completed their new church on the west shore. Through his one good eye he could see the white lime-washed walls glowing in the winter sunlight. They had completed the restored Heptastadion bridge across the harbor just before the previous year's flood, and begun shipping jungle hardwoods to Alexandria from the upper Nile to complete the church, harvesting what stones they needed from the fallen Serapeum. "You know, it is more beautiful than I expected it would be. I have to give them that," he said.

Hypatia scowled. "With the empire's purse at their disposal, how could it not be beautiful? They could have built an entire city for what he allotted. No church should ever be wed to government. Our freedoms will become extinct."

Orestes's face fell, his singular eye, black as the iron sea, moistening. "Indeed."

Hypatia lifted a cup of cold tea to her lips and took a sip.

"Have you considered my offer?" Orestes asked, bringing the subject around to the reason for his visit.

Hypatia leaned back in her chair. "No, I must refuse," she said, feeling a little guilty.

"You need a bodyguard. Cyril has returned to the city."

"No." Hypatia's chariot was the last pleasure that she allowed herself. Since the trip to Greece, she had given greater consideration to the austerities that Plotinus had recommended in his writings. Though she had long ago ceased eating meat, she had now given up milk, cheese, and eggs, rarely even seasoning her simple meals; she had given up drinking wine entirely and no longer slept on a mattress, but lay on the hard floor without a pillow. She had been attempting to purify her soul of all bodily associations and had come to despise the workings of her womb, only to be delighted that with her strict new regiments, her monthly blood had ceased altogether. Her mounting obsession with purification had prompted her to discard her grey philosopher's *tribon* in favor of an ivory one, a fashion that many of her students were now adopting. Orestes wondered if she was not taking things a bit to the extreme, but what could he do? It was Hypatia's nature. She seemed to be the living embodiment of Plotinus's philosophy, and her students adored her even if she offended the masses with her eccentricity.

"Hypatia," he pleaded. "You must be more careful."

"Orestes, you worry in vain. Things are precisely as we need them to be. Cyril will read my manuscript, and his thoughts toward the library will change. Christ's mother will offer us an opening into the hearts of the Christians; I have seen it in my visions. An alliance will be possible. I am certain of it."

"You are playing with fire, my dear," Orestes warned. "Am I not enough of an omen for you?" He slowly stood from the settee and took three slow steps across the room, dragging one leg, and lifted the Celestial Clock of Archimedes from Hypatia's desk. "Let me take it," he said.

"Take it?"

"Yes. If anything were to happen. We must conceal it outside of Egypt."

"But Orestes, you must think the library will not stand. Alizar has convinced you."

"You must trust me, Hypatia. I have only your interests in mind. We are the last bastion, and the empire will not stand with us if the Christians turn against the library."

Hypatia stroked the instrument in Orestes's hands with affection. "Will you put it on a ship?"

"I know a certain priest in Greece who would be an ideal guardian. He is a friend of Synesius."

"A Christian?"

"A trustworthy fellow."

Hypatia sighed with frustration. "If you must."

Orestes set the instrument in its fitted brass case, a covering that would travel with it for the next thousand years. "We will give it to Gideon to carry. He has confided to me that he longs for the sea, and he is working to acquire a new ship for Alizar's release. This would be a good opportunity. I have a magnificent ship that I confiscated from a pirate. I think I will give it to him."

Hypatia nodded. "Now you must leave me to my work. I have a public lecture in three days."

Orestes's remaining eyebrow shot up, the other side of his face covered by a bandage worn so as to not frighten people with the discomfiting scar where his eye and brow had been. "Why a public lecture all of a sudden?"

Hypatia smiled. "Lent."

Orestes was now thoroughly confused. "Since when do you observe a Christian holiday?"

Hypatia did not answer him directly. "I am speaking about the Virgin."

Orestes shrugged. "You are divinely mad, you know. A shame I am not Alizar. He is the only one capable of restraining you."

Hypatia smiled, unaffected. Then she picked up her stylus. "So you will attend?"

"I would like to, but I have the meeting of the city council on Antirrhodus and Alizar's pardon to address."

"Of course. Then come afterward with good news."

"I will." Orestes turned back at the door. "Take the Nuapar guards with you in precaution, Hypatia."

Hypatia nodded, unconcerned.

36

"I cannot find it," said Hannah, desperate. "I kept it here, hidden inside the wall." She paced the short length of her room on the second floor of the library.

Gideon helped her search. They tore apart the room. Orestes had asked him to move the Emerald Tablet from Amun-Ra out of the Great Library to a secret hiding place until the halves could be united publicly in a few days.

This was unfortunate timing, as Orestes had his men tear apart the Church of St. Alexander while Cyril was away, and he found the brass chest with the half of the Emerald Tablet from Delfi in the church treasury, strangely unopened. Orestes had opened the lock himself to see the tablet and slept more deeply since he had. With the pagan people united, they could rise up against the Christians. The people just needed a sign, an omen that they could prevail. This was that omen.

"You are certain it was here?" Gideon clasped Hannah's shoulders.

"You yourself created the hidden compartment in the wall."

"Who else knows of its existence here, Hannah?"

"Myself, you, Hypatia, Orestes. Not even Alizar knew where this half of the tablet was kept. I had given up dreaming we might ever unite it. This seems impossible. I cannot believe it is gone."

"Someone knew."

"What are you accusing me of?"

Gideon sat on the bed. "Nothing, Hannah. If it is not here, someone has it. Someone who knew it was here. Was there ever any sign of the room in disarray?"

Hannah kicked an old boot across the floor, sat at the tiny desk chair, and stared out the window at the gardens. "Never. I keep the room immaculate. Had anyone searched it, I would have known."

"Then someone came, and knew what he was looking for, and where to find it."

"Yes, but when?"

"When was the last time you saw the tablet?"

"I check it each month on the full moon. So, several weeks ago now. You?"

"I checked less often than you. I have been absorbed in fitting the new ship."

"It has not been out of our hands for long."

"Someone knew the timing. They may even have known that Orestes found the other half of the tablet in the church."

Hannah turned a wooden ball in her hands, one of Alaya's toys. "Synesius will return with Alaya soon."

"Hannah, it must be someone we know," said Gideon, the certainty gripping his soul.

"Someone we know? But who?" Then Hannah knew. She knew the one person she did not trust who was capable of such deceit. "Tarek."

"Go to Sofia. Search his room at Alizar's. I will find Tarek and make him speak."

Hannah rushed to Alizar's. Alaya had begged to go with her, but she thought it best to let her daughter stay with Synesius a while longer. She found Sofia in the upstairs bedroom, seated on the settee, sipping coffee.

"Hannah, so good to see you. What brings you here so early in the morning?"

"Sofia, do you have a key to Tarek's room?" Hannah knelt beside her friend.

"Whatever for?"

Hannah took Sofia's hands. "I believe he has betrayed us, betrayed Alizar. Do you trust me?"

Sofia nodded. "Tarek stayed at the brothels last night. He has a new girl there so he has not yet returned. Come with me."

When they opened the door, they found Tarek's room to be in complete disarray, clothes were strewn about, and dirty plates and cups were stacked on every available surface.

"What are we looking for?" asked Sofia.

"The Emerald Tablet, the half from Siwa."

They searched until Sofia found the hollow in the bedpost. She shoved the bedclothes to the floor and called Hannah over. "Listen." Sofia knocked to reveal the hollow sound in the wood.

Hannah's hands felt along the bedpost until they found the ornate carving of the falcon at the top to be loose. She twisted it and it came away. Sofia reached inside the post and withdrew a roll of documents. They replaced the post and retreated to Sofia's bedroom, where they locked the door.

They spread the documents out on the bed, and almost immediately Sofia found the cause for Hannah's intuitive notion. These were forged documents naming Tarek as Alizar's adopted son, heir to the entire estate. They had been notarized by scribes at the Tabularium and by bishop Cyril himself.

"This can mean only one thing," said Hannah.

"Tarek has betrayed us all." Sofia stood, her thoughts racing, the full expanse of the issue now realized. But as she crossed the room, a warm liquid trickled down the inside of her leg. "Praise Zeus," she said. "It is probably nothing, but would you call the midwife, Hannah?"

Hannah said, "Let me check you first."

Sofia agreed and tugged her gown up to her belly. It had been so helpful to have Hannah near, who had already experienced all these strange pregnancy ailments.

Hannah looked at the fluid. "No blood, but mucus. The babe will come soon. I will call her at once."

———————

Hypatia rode her chariot to the public lecture hall as evening settled in Alexandria like a dove on her roost. There had been no rain all month, and the air was cool and dusty, reminding her of the years of the long drought. Hypatia's horse snorted and pawed the ground. She patted the mare's silky white shoulder and turned to climb the steps. Orestes would have been infuriated with her to find out that she had ridden to the lecture hall unaccompanied. But Orestes would not be in the audience tonight till later; he had gone to the meeting of the Alexandrian senate on the island of Antirrhodus in the middle of the harbor. The city's politicians, bishop, magistrates, senators, and prefects would be occupied for most of the evening, and they had required the presence of most of the Nuapar guards as anonymous death threats had been sent. Hypatia wondered if anyone would even attend her lecture. She had taken the liberty of distributing pamphlets the previous week but doubted that they were even glanced at, as the people were awaiting several political decisions and appointments that would change the city if they passed. Hannah had suggested she cancel the lecture, but Hypatia had made up her mind to deliver her speech. "The people need this message now more than ever," she had insisted, forgetting that in five years she had not had a single discussion with a human being outside the Great Library. "People want bread, not philosophy," Alizar had said to her once. She had dismissed his thought with a wave of her hand and a laugh, incapable of imagining how anyone could possibly live without intellectual and spiritual sustenance.

Once inside, Hypatia was delighted to discover that the lecture hall was already nearly full of faces. They turned to look at her as she entered, recognizing the city's famed thinker by her elegant ivory robes and long, curling blonde hair pinned on top of her head. As she stepped up to the dais, several people whispered and hissed.

"Devil's concubine," someone said.

"Witch," said another.

Hypatia coolly dismissed the words as though she did not hear them. Her thoughts burned bright as newborn suns in her mind, suffusing all else. Once she shared her vision, the people would forgo their judgments. Eager to sway the crowd, she quickly thanked everyone for coming and began her lecture.

She began by illustrating the ideals of purity and virginity as embodied by the Virgin Mary. Her words were infused with love. For the first half of her lecture, she held the audience's attention easily. However, as her speech turned toward philosophy, things changed quickly.

What Hypatia did not realize was that most of the people in the audience had not come to hear her speak but only to lay eyes on the elite lady whom their bishop had taught them was in allegiance with the devil. Most of them had lived in Alexandria all their lives and had never seen Hypatia. They supposed that her purity was a demon's disguise of black magic.

". . . For the truth is that Christ can be found within each one of us. His birth demonstrates a metaphorical birth into a spiritual life through the purified heart." Hypatia's voice became emphatic. "You see, Mary was not merely the mother of the man we call Jesus, but the mother of Emmanuel, God with us, Christ everlasting. She came to show us that Christ is not separate from us. He was sent to teach us by example. When the mind, through contemplation, fasting, and focus upon eternal concepts, has been cleansed, then the Self is made pure, and Christ through each of our hearts can be born again on the Earth, and we too can live close to God." Hypatia paused. Although gnostic teachings had gone out of fashion in Alexandria the century before, she was eager to restore them.

"Heretic!" A man at the back of the lecture hall stood up and pointed angrily at Hypatia.

"Sorceress!" screamed another.

"Black magic!"

Hypatia tipped her head, confused. Had they not heard her words? She had just delivered the essence of the Christian faith. Could they not recognize the truth for what it was? Eager to make herself clear, Hypatia began again, her smile dimming slightly.

"You mistake me. What I mean to profess is how each of us can become purified in our own lives. Each of us can become Christlike, not Christ himself. He was an example to us. We do not have to simply worship his teaching. Jesus himself told us 'Greater works than these shall ye do.'" Hypatia opened her mouth to go on, but a stout, middle-aged man in the front row rose angrily to his feet and shouted at her.

"How dare you speak of Christ, you pagan whore!" Then he turned to the audience behind him. "This witch speaks the devil's words! We should not be blinded by her clever tongue!"

The audience stirred uneasily.

Then there was a loud bang in the foyer as the doors to the lecture hall were thrown open. The torches that stood in the back of the hall blew sideways in the sudden gust of wind as twenty priests in black robes swept into the room: the Parabolani, followed by priests of Nitria who had come from the southern desert at Cyril's behest. As they walked down the isles, they unsheathed their swords and raised them like silver crosses to the night.

Hypatia watched as the men streamed down the aisles, led by Cyril's interpreter, Peter the Reader. "Seize the witch!" he yelled, and the crowd sprung to their feet.

Hypatia, having never known a moment of doubt in herself or her teaching in all the occasions she had stood before an audience, backed away from the dais slowly, seized by newfound terror, her eyes growing wide as she recognized her mistake.

All thoughts except one vanished from Hypatia's mind immediately.

Flee.

———

Sofia clung tightly to Hannah's hand, who smoothed Sofia's hair back from her damp forehead with the other. "Breathe deeply," she said as Sofia clenched her teeth and groaned.

The midwife worked calmly. "We are very close now."

Sofia's labor had gone on throughout the entire day and into the evening. Hannah had not realized until now how easily Alaya's birth had been by comparison. Sofia's pelvis was so narrow, and the baby's head so large, that her efforts to push the child from her womb were thus far ineffective.

The midwife sighed and wiped her forehead with the back of her sleeve. "Rest a moment, Sofia," she said. "Take a breath."

Sofia nodded, the pain so great that her lips quivered uncontrollably. She looked up at Hannah fearfully from where she was squatting on the floor beside the window in Alizar's tower, where she had decided to birth the child. Hannah squeezed her hand. "Be brave. The baby is almost here."

The midwife bent down and rummaged through her bag. She carefully withdrew a short silver knife and concealed it inside her sleeve so that Sofia would not see. If necessary, she would cut the mother to free the baby. But not yet. These births where the child was turned with its spine against the mother's spine never went as well as the others. She did not want anyone to be alarmed just yet.

Sofia closed her eyes and whispered a prayer of strength to the Goddess. "Be with me now, Mother. Be with me now, Isis and Artemis."

"The child wants to be born, dear one. Push now," said the midwife.

Sofia drew energy up from the earth and dug her fingernails into her kneecaps, and the baby's head appeared between her legs, a mess of black hair on its head.

Two more pushes and the shoulders came one at a time, and then the babe was free. The midwife caught the child, covered in blood and fluid, and placed him on his mother's chest. "A boy." She cleaned the baby swiftly and offered to swaddle him in a blanket.

Where fear and intensity had dwelt only moments before blossomed peace. Sofia smiled at Hannah weakly, the joy in her eyes turning to tears of relief and love as she kissed her baby and stroked his soft skin.

Hannah bent down and touched his tiny fingernails, remembering the deep love she had felt when she had seen Alaya for the first time. Thinking of her daughter, she looked out the window. Now that the baby was here, healthy and hungry, Hannah realized how tired she felt. Her stomach grumbled noisily. How long had it been since she had eaten anything? They could send for Synesius now, and he could bring Alaya. The thought was comforting. Then Hannah looked down between Sofia's legs and saw the pool of blood on the sheet. She pulled the midwife aside and whispered.

The midwife shook her head and pulled several herbs from her bag. Then she began to press on Sofia's womb.

The blood kept coming.

Outside, darkness swept over the city as street lamps were snuffed out.

At that moment Gideon burst into the room with news of the meeting of the council on Antirrhodus, though it was still underway. Alizar had not been pardoned, Orestes had lost his debate with Cyril, and more Christians had been appointed seats in the council.

"It is a boy, Gideon," whispered Sofia proudly. "Will you send for my husband, for Synesius?"

"My congratulations, Sofia," he said, though his mind was still clearly elsewhere.

"I have decided to name him after my father, did I tell you?" Sofia said, her voice growing weaker. "We will call him Ali." Sofia reached over and brushed the baby's cheek lovingly with the back of her hand.

The midwife waved at Hannah and Gideon to take their conversation elsewhere as she worked. "The herbs will take effect. Do not disturb her now."

Hannah took Gideon's hand and led him back into the stacks of scrolls and shelves where Alizar kept his ancient books so they might speak privately. "We found falsified documents naming Tarek as Alizar's heir. Did you find Tarek?"

He looked to the door. "No. But in the *agora* I encountered a boy called Ignus that Orestes sent to the Christian church years ago to spy for us. He says that he is certain Cyril has the Emerald Tablet, or at least the piece from Siwa. He overheard a discussion between the bishop and Peter about it, that it has been concealed beneath the altar stone."

Hannah nodded. "Tarek must have traded the tablet for the documents he wanted. Such irony that Cyril had the other half all along and never knew."

"There are no doubt men who can be bribed in the Tabularium who would falsify documents for the bishop."

"Gideon, we must get the other half. The Emerald Tablet is our only hope."

Gideon smiled and kissed her. "We shall. I must go. There is something that can wait no longer."

Hannah flung her arms around his neck. "Go with God. I must stay here with Sofia and help the midwife."

Hypatia flew down the dais to the back stairs of the hall. At the bottom, she tried the door handles and flung her body against the latch only to find them bolted shut from the outside. She looked around herself, hearing the footsteps of the mob approaching.

A light at the end of a passageway caught her attention. She ran toward it and found a small glass window set above the street. Being merely ornamental, it had no latch, no way of opening.

Hypatia's eyes fell on a small statue of John the Apostle that had been placed in a niche in the wall. She grabbed it and threw it through the window with a crash. Then she hoisted herself up onto the ledge as the swarm of bodies spilled around the corner of the passageway.

"Do not let her get away!"

"Seize the witch!"

Hands clawed at Hypatia's feet, and the leather ties on her sandals snapped. Someone else snagged a corner of her robes as she fell the short distance through the window into the street, tearing them to the waist.

Hypatia landed on her hands in the broken glass and rolled before coming to her feet. As swiftly as she could, she raced to her chariot and took the reins in her bloody fingers.

"*Hyaaaa!*" she screamed, smacking the reins on her horse's neck. The mob streamed out of the lecture hall, followed by the Parabolani.

"She is headed to the library," said one of the priests. "We will never get through the gates."

"Then it is time to use this," growled Peter, drawing a scroll from his robes like a sword.

It was a map of the catacombs.

———————

Jemir was the first to hear the commotion. He was polishing the handle of a long spoon in the downstairs of the kitchen, humming a song to himself, so happy for the new baby, when a sudden uproar in the alleyway behind the stable caught his attention. He set down the rag and walked outside to the gate when a group of men ran past.

"What is happening?" Jemir called out.

A teenage boy spun around and without breaking his stride yelled back, "The Great Library is on fire!"

Jemir lifted his gaze to see the black smoke smudging out the stars; an instant later, the unmistakable scent of cedar reached his nostrils.

In a panic, he let out a stream of curses and ran as fast as he could into the house, flying to the tower as fast as his tubby legs could carry him. "Hannah! Come quickly!"

"What is it?" asked Hannah.

"Where is Gideon? Where is Alaya? And Synesius?" asked Jemir, his eyes filled with terror.

"Gideon has just left, and Alaya is in the library with Sy. Why Jemir? What has happened?"

But before he could respond, the criers on the street began to scream the news.

The library, the Great Library is on fire.

Hannah sprung for her little knife and laced it to her calf, then ran downstairs to the stable.

Jemir caught her arm in the kitchen. "Hannah, the Parabolani will be everywhere."

"I must find my child." Hannah whipped around and lunged for the door.

Jemir blocked it.

She faced him, her eyes two sharpened daggers.

"Let me go instead, Hannah," said Jemir quickly. "If I do not return within the hour, then you do what you must."

"No," said Hannah, her voice shaking but firm. "Someone must stay here and help the midwife."

The door flew open then as Tarek burst into the room from the courtyard, hurtling Jemir forward. "If the fires reach the tower, Jemir, set the horses loose in the street and you, Hannah, and Sofia take the Gate of the Moon to Lake Mareotis. No wait," Tarek changed his mind abruptly. "Do not pass through the Christian quarter. Go down to the west beach instead. Do you understand?"

"Sofia's baby has come, Tarek. She cannot be moved. There is too much blood."

Tarek shook his head. "We must evacuate."

Jemir nodded.

Hannah reached for the door.

"Stop, where are you going?" said Tarek, taking her arm.

"I must get my daughter, Tarek," said Hannah, wresting her arm free.

"Please, *Kukla*, let me go," insisted Jemir.

But Hannah embraced him and kissed his cheek firmly. "Stay alive," she whispered, and she flew down the steps to the stable.

37

The little voice called like a songbird in his mind from the deepest reaches of Master Junkar's meditation. His eyes flew open as his spirit rushed back into his body, aware again of the small room where Master Savitur sat cross-legged before him.

Instantly, he sprang to his feet.

Savitur narrowed his gaze as his thoughts streamed into Junkar's mind.

Do not interfere. It is the way.

Junkar paused, his predicament apparent to him.

Savitur, I must go. Come with me.

Savitur shook his head.

Junkar protested. *She is our responsibility, Savitur. We cannot abandon her.* He could see the flames encircling the child he had met in the garden. His child. He had to hurry.

We cannot interfere. Savitur folded his arms over his chest. *You know as well as I the consequences. It is our place to influence, not to interfere.*

Junkar shook his head. He had denied himself the love of a woman. He had denied himself the love of his own child. Now his position denied him the right to go to that child in need of him when he was capable of helping her? He lashed out at Savitur angrily. *Have you any heart at all? You and I alone can protect the child of the Sacred Marriage rite. It is our duty to protect her. What are we masters of if we do not use the powers we are given in times of need?*

Savitur pressed his lips together, the only sign that he was deep in thought. Alas, the final decision was not his to make. Junkar found his tongue, leaving the thought realm they shared. "I must go."

Savitur shut his eyes. He had prayed earnestly that the child would be born a boy. Things would have been entirely different then. The Great Book did not offer any words of instruction for a girl. "Do only what you must," he said. "But know your emotions have overtaken you. Julian lives within you still."

Junkar dropped his eyes, confused. His practices had removed him from the ordinary world to such a degree that he lived most of the time in a state of consciousness full of light and emptiness. From that perspective, no tragedy existed, and no loss could permeate his mind. In that world he was both wholly present and wholly detached, perceiving the physical world as a delightful illusion, charmed by both its trials and terrors. As Junkar, the entire world was a laughable extravagance, and so his heart remained always detached and illuminated in yogic peace.

But Savitur was right. Julian the man still lived inside him. It had been Julian who had fled the garden that night after seeing Hannah behind the window in the library. It had been Julian who had given Alaya the sandalwood beads and left with a heavy heart, unable to tell his daughter who he was.

So.

Do not hesitate, he told himself, just go. But he did hesitate. He looked back at the disappointment in Master Savitur's eyes, and his spirit shrank like a shadow in the sunlight. There must be another way, he reasoned. *This is not interference, Savitur. We are bound by the Great Book to protect the child.*

Savitur exhaled, opening his eyes. "The Great Book binds us to protect only a boy. A girl child born to the priestess of the Sacred Marriage is of no consequence to us. The child is entirely within the charge of her mother and the High Priestess of Isis. Go to them and let them decide what to do."

Junkar shook his head. There was no time.

Then, out of habit, his hand brushed the pocket fold in his robes where Hannah's hairpin rested. This was not a choice he wanted to make.

Savitur could see the two men inside of the one, battling. He knew that in the end, one of them would have to integrate the other.

Taking the hairpin in his fingers, Julian thought of Hannah and how over the years his memory of her had remained a sacred treasure. He had made a promise to her child. *Their* child. In that instant, his love for his daughter held more honor than any name he might be called. Silently he apologized to his master, both the one before him and the one whose ashes he had scattered in the mountains of a faraway land.

His heart was still too impure, too human to be a great one such as these.

Julian swept out of the room, unable to bear looking back.

He slipped down the hall toward the workshops and snatched a plain brown robe from a hook by the door. Then he burst into the weapons closet and pulled down a fourth sword after testing the edges of another three and dashed down to the beach toward a lateen-rigged skiff. He had to hurry. The smoke was rising into the night. He could see the mighty translucent flames licking at the buildings along the wharf, and the fire had already spread to the sails and masts of the tallest ships. High on the hill the Nuapar monks chanted into the night, their prayers ascending and mingling with the smoke. No one saw him go.

Hannah dashed through Alizar's courtyard in her bare feet; there was no time to look for her shoes. She rushed into the stable and threw open one of the stall doors. Behind it, Alizar's prize dappled grey stallion stood in a shaft of moonlight. The gentle Arabian horse lowered his head in greeting. Hannah lifted the bridle from the wall and touched the stallion's soft muzzle, whispering to him as she pulled the leather bridle over his ears. "I need you to be brave," she said. "I need you to be fast and fearless. I have to get my daughter, do you understand?" The stallion rubbed his face against Hannah's shoulder. She grabbed his mane and in one swift kick threw a leg over his back, righted herself, and took up the reins.

They galloped straight out of the stall and leapt clear of the gate that led out to the street. The stallion landed easily and spun on his hocks to enter the sea of frightened people all racing toward the beach.

The fire moved quickly—just one hour before, the city of Alexandria slept peacefully beneath the stars. Now a frantic chaos swept the streets. Mothers clutching children to their breasts rushed to safety. Camels, goats, chickens, and donkeys were freed and left to find their own way through the chaos. Hannah could see the flames rising high over the city in the direction of the harbor and hear the roar in her ears above the screams of the people.

She plunged her bare heels into the stallion's warm body, and they soared toward the west end of Canopic Way. Once at the beach they could run all the way to the harbor.

The stallion, the waves at his knees, gave Hannah the magnificence of all his strength, surging through the surf. At the edge of the sea, the dancing flames were reflected in the water. Every time a wave rose, the mirrored surface presented the picture of the burning city. Hannah leaned forward and let the reins fall slack as the stallion's ears flattened to his neck. There was only the sound of his breath, the movement of his massive warm shoulders, the feeling of the cold seawater licking at her toes, and the powerful roar of the fire growing nearer as the waves surged around them.

Once Hannah reached the harbor, the wind shifted and blew the fire in the direction of the desert, into the city. Many of the ships were already burning, their masts collapsing, their fiery sails snapping in the wind in the beautiful passion of destruction.

Hannah found the harbor consumed by fire as she neared, the heat of the flames impenetrable. She brought the stallion to a halt, and as she looked up at the library, her heart seized. Though the glass cupola was, miraculously, still standing, and the Great Hall looked intact, the entire east wing that housed the librarians was completely consumed in flames. Her little room, all her possessions, already lost. She could only pray Alaya and Synesius had gotten out. The people at the water's edge looked up in fascination and horror, holding one another.

There was no time to think. Hannah turned the stallion around and urged him on. They would have to go in through the zoological park. The gates there would probably be let open for the animals.

Sure enough, Hannah was right. In the fish market, she passed zebra and ostrich on the street nearing the rear entrance to the library. A man at the gate waved her to turn back and even began to shut the gate to stop the mad woman riding bareback toward the fire. But the stallion leapt the gate fearlessly and cantered into the Caesarium garden where the librarians were gathering.

Hannah reined the stallion through the masses of people, calling for her daughter. She spotted several friends, but Synesius was not among them.

"Where is Alaya?" she pleaded. "My daughter. Alaya. Where is Alaya? Synesius? Have you seen them?"

One of the men looked up at her, the side of his head bloody. "The Parabolani and the mob have destroyed everything," he said.

"Where is Alaya?" Hannah screamed at him. "Where is my daughter?"

He shook his head.

Then another librarian, squatting on the ground beside a dead peacock, looked up. He recognized Hannah from Hypatia's lectures. "Hypatia," he stammered. "Synesius went back to help her. They pulled her from her chariot. There were too many of them." He dropped his head.

"Where is Hypatia?" Hannah asked desperately.

The man looked up. "The mathematics stacks."

Hannah dismounted swiftly and pulled the bridle from the stallion's head, smacking his shoulder to send him off. Freed, the stallion rushed toward the gate and out into the street.

Hannah looked up at the scene before her. The sound of the fire was deafening. It shook the ground and filled the sky. Occasionally a loud crash was followed by a crackle as a wall collapsed. Directly in front of her, the door into the Great Hall was still clear. The fire was not yet upon it.

There was still time.

Hannah's eyes darted from side to side. As long as the glass cupola stood, she had a feeling she could risk going inside. She had to try.

The librarian squatting on the ground grabbed Hannah's elbow, his eyes foreboding. "No."

"My daughter is in there," Hannah wrested her arm free.

"Do not let the Parabolani see you," he pleaded. "We have lost so many already."

Hannah swallowed hard, her heart pounding audibly in her ears.

She looked to the Great Hall, pulled her *klamys* tightly around her body, and pushed her way through the mass of bodies to the doors, calling Alaya's name and checking every face that emerged for Synesius or her daughter.

———

As Julian's skiff crossed the harbor, a floating piece of flaming debris from one of the ships blew into his sail, and it caught flame. With no other choice, he dove over the side and swam in the direction of the library. He moved in slow motion as each stroke through the black seawater seemed to bring him no closer, the heavy sword weighing him down. Arm over arm he stroked toward the docks until finally he could pull himself up on the wharf.

Crouching, he paused for three breaths to regain his strength, then sprung to his feet dripping wet and raced across the crumbling wharf toward a window in the west wing of the Great Library.

It was open.

Julian hoisted himself up and landed on his feet inside, the smoke rushing into his lungs. He coughed and drew his robe across his face. This level of the library was still relatively intact, but elsewhere waves of blue and orange flames climbed the walls and devoured the staircases. Papyrus scrolls like flaming birds swirled and plunged through the air. The fire spiraled around the stone doorways like hungry serpents encircling the trunks of massive trees.

The heat pushed Julian down to his knees as the blaze shook the building all around him, but the fire itself was not yet upon him. He stayed low and swiftly made his way through the narrow library passageways, presuming that anyone who was still in the structure had to either be here in the west wing or the basement. With the meeting of the council on Antirrhodus, Julian knew that the Nuapar who had been guarding the library had mostly been called to protect Orestes and the other magistrates who would be meeting there. He hoped Hypatia still had a few men with her. He knew the Nuapar would protect her.

Then the little hairs on the back of Julian's neck prickled to attention and he instantly knew he was no longer alone. In keen awareness, Julian let his attackers approach and then swiftly drew his sword and turned.

Three Parabolani stood before him, their eyes wild with bloodshed, their strong hands brandishing freshly stained swords. With cries of battle they leapt on him, only to be disappointed that he slipped between their advances like water through open fingers.

They had not even a moment to realize what was happening as he spun upon them. The first priest fell with his throat slit, the second collapsed with Julian's sword impaled in his gut. The third advanced on Julian with a cry, but he stepped aside, grabbed the priest's wrist, and turned his own sword upon him with an accuracy Achilles would have envied. The priest fell dead, his eyes wide open, unaware that life had even left him.

Julian stood on the man's shoulder and pulled his sword free of the body. As he reached a staircase leading to levels both above and beneath him, he paused and shut his eyes, calling out to Alaya in his mind.

He chose to descend the stairs and proceed through the trembling halls, listening intently, but he heard nothing save the din of the fire approaching nearer.

Around a corner that led toward the lecture hall, a little cry reached his ears. He closed his eyes and paused to listen.

Then it came again. A child's cry. His eyes flew open.

"Alaya!" Julian raced down the long stone hall, descended a flight of steps and then another, to a dead end.

He had to backtrack and try again, calling out as he ran.

He flew through another passage and met seven men at its end. These were no Parabolani; they were hardened priests Julian knew from the stories told to him by Master Savitur. These enormous men with skin the color of a moonless night were the priests of Nitria, from a Christian monastery deep in the southern desert where the men trained as warriors. They stood seven feet tall, their chests wide as warhorses.

The priests plunged ahead, determined to kill and not be killed. Armed with shields, swords, and short knives, they raised their weapons for blood.

Julian had trained all his life for a moment such as this one. He slowed his perception of time and watched the men race toward him. With precision he ducked and spun to face them, impaling two priests, their bodies falling to the ground. The others spun and attacked.

These fit priests were the only men that remained in Egypt trained in the lineage of Roman soldiers and possessing both exceeding strategic and tactical skill. If Cyril had called them, by the hundreds they would have responded. The library was bound to be full of them. If he was too late, there had already been a massacre. The librarians kept no weapons at hand, and they would not even know how to use them if they had.

The priests raised their swords and attacked Julian. But in that instant, he remembered his initiation and the abilities that had come to him in the hour of his duel. He closed his eyes, and as the swords of the priests plunged into his body, he disappeared. The priests looked around in confusion.

Julian found himself projected several passageways beyond the narrow hall, somewhere near Hypatia's study. The winding staircase before him led to an underground room that held the reference codices for the philosophy stacks. As he flew into the room, a little figure in the corner looked up.

It was Alaya, crouched in a ball clutching her knees, crying. When she saw Julian, her eyes brightened, but she did not move. There was another figure beside her on the floor, collapsed.

"Master Junkar," she said, her little voice quavering.

Julian raced toward her. "I heard you," he said, sweeping her up in his arms.

"Synesius." Alaya reached toward the figure on the ground. "The bad men hurt him."

Julian looked down to see his brother lying on the floor. He quickly bent down and touched Sy's throat. His pulse was weak, but he was still alive, though unconscious.

Alaya whimpered, her tiny arms clinging to Julian's neck.

Mother of Zeus, how could he carry both of them?

He sheathed his sword.

"Alaya, hold on. Do not let go," Julian said as he shifted her so that she could ride on his back. Then he bent down, took his brother in his arms, and stood. There was a realization then that his brother's wine-colored robes were soaked. At first he thought it was dye, the same color as the robes. And then he saw the blood run onto his arms. Then he knew. The wound was near his ribs, but there was no time to assess it. He had to get them out immediately, or the fire would be on them and close their path outside.

"That way!" Alaya pointed at an open doorway.

Julian walked as swiftly as he could, crouched low through a long passageway until it came out beside a stairway leading up. The smoke was thicker here, stinging his eyes, burning the back of his throat. "Hold on, Alaya."

They were beneath the Great Hall.

Julian could hear the roar of the fire behind the walls, and his ears became uncomfortably hot. He climbed the stairs two at a time and stopped, the dust, the burning papyrus, and the thick metallic scent of blood reaching his nostrils.

There before them lay the tragic battle scene.

"Alaya, shut your eyes," he commanded as Alaya screamed and buried her head in his shoulder. Hundreds of bodies lay scattered all around the room, dismembered, unrecognizable, the carnage of the Parabolani and the priests of Nitria. Blood soaked the floor in pools of entrails, brains, and shards of tile and glass. Here an arm, there a hand, an ear. No faces recognizable, not one body left whole. The wine-red robes of the librarians lay scattered about the room like fallen spirits, among them the robes of several Nuapar monks, and black robes of the Parabolani. Julian noticed there were ordinary *tunicas* here as well, mostly men. So a Christian mob had joined the siege. Those in the library had been clearly outnumbered by the Christians. Through a window beyond the corpses, Julian could see the shimmering pools of the Caesarium gardens.

They were almost outside.

He raced across the floor, slipping in a pool of blood and then righting himself. Alaya opened her eyes and she began to cry.

"You are dreaming, Alaya," commanded Julian, his breath short. "You are going to wake up in your mother's arms, and all of this will be gone. Shut your eyes tightly and keep them shut."

She obeyed.

Julian picked his way through the bodies and burning scrolls. As he came around another corner, his foot crashed through the floor, and he fell to his elbows, dropping Synesius as Alaya shrieked. A searing pain flashed through Julian's leg, and he clenched his teeth, bearing down on it. As swiftly as he could, he freed his ankle and scrambled to his feet. His boot had been sliced open, the leather flapping. He tried to walk forward, but his ankle wobbled beneath him, unable to take the extra weight.

"Dear brother, I will return for you," Julian said as he laid Synesius against a wall just outside the Great Hall. He would have to get Alaya to safety first.

Limping, Julian swept Alaya into his arms and rushed through the Great Hall as the flames consumed the eastern wall.

As he stepped through the doors, they were met by the crush of warm bodies and the cool air from outside that flooded their stinging lungs. Julian hobbled as fast as his legs could carry him toward one of Cleopatra's Needles, the stone obelisk rising above him into the night like a promise that something would survive this night.

"Stay here, Alaya," he said, setting her down gently.

"I want Mama," Alaya cried. "Mama! Do not leave me!"

"I have to go back for Synesius," Julian said, stroking Alaya's hair back from her cheek, but as the words left his lips, there was a deafening crash as the glass cupola above the Great Hall came down, shattering into a million pieces.

There was no way to go back inside.

Julian dropped to his knees and swept Alaya into his arms, tears sliding down his cheeks.

His brother was gone.

Hannah wound her way through the west wing of the library, calling for Alaya, for Synesius. When the glass cupola fell, the ground beneath Hannah's feet trembled with the force of an earthquake. She grabbed the nearest wall to steady herself, and suddenly a rush of hot wind blew in from behind her. This was nothing like the heat of the desert wind, but a searing plume of smoke and ash.

The library had become an open furnace.

Hungry flames spread through the structure in search of fuel. There was no way for Hannah to go back the way she came.

She pressed the hem of her *himation* to her nose as she ran through the empty passage before her toward the lower stacks. The bones of the building around her trembled, caving in with enormous crashes that shook the air and the floor. The heat was becoming far too great, even on this side of the library. Her body was quaking with fear, but it did not matter. She would not leave the library without her daughter.

Hannah looked down to see the shard of the Emerald Tablet glowing. She touched it and remembered its inscription: *Soul immortal beyond death, no fire can burn thee, no fate can change thy eternal truth.* "God be with me," she whispered, reciting the inscription as she drew on strength deeper than she had ever known, and turned and faced the flames.

Hannah reached with her mind into the heart of the fire, concentrating on her daughter. All around the room where she was standing, the blue flames soared across the walls like vertical ocean waves.

Hannah's eyes flew open, knowing what she must do. Her father had long ago told her the story of Shadrach, Meshach, and Abednego, the three Jews who had been thrown to the fiery furnace to die. But the angel of the Lord had been with them. They had danced through the flames. Hannah centered herself and closed her eyes, clutching the emerald shard around her neck. And she walked through the wall of fire. Around her the flames leapt at her, but she moved through them unharmed, only her hair and clothing singed. When she opened her eyes, the fire was behind her. She ran down a flight of steps as one of the stacks collapsed around her and came out in a passage with a door at one end that led to the zoological park. Behind it was a tunnel that Alaya loved to play in. At the other end it opened into the butterfly enclosure.

Of course!

Alaya would have gone to her favorite sanctuary. Hannah tried the door. But as she did, she heard a clashing of swords in the passage behind her.

Then Peter, Cyril's reader, emerged from the passage, wiping his bloodied sword on his robes. He had not seen her.

Hannah looked around herself for a weapon and, without thinking, yanked the shard of the Emerald Tablet from her neck. Using the leather strap as a sling, she flung it with a shepherd's practiced ease. As though he were a rabbit, as though he were a quail and not the messenger of death itself.

The shard struck Peter at the base of the throat, piercing him, but not deeply, not enough. There was only one way. Hannah shoved him to the floor and wrested his sword from his hand. It was so heavy—she had never held a sword before, and it felt awkward, unwieldy, fat, too large. Peter rolled toward the wall, and

Hannah hoisted the sword and gathered her nerve. One of them would die, she knew. He found his way to his hands and knees and began to crawl toward her. If she let him live, he would continue to hunt her, her daughter. This she must do. She clenched her jaw and speared him in the back till the tip of the sword touched the floor. He collapsed, and his blood pooled on the floor in a widening circle as his eyes turned to stone.

Hannah tugged the emerald shard from his flesh. The relief of seeing Peter dead was something she did not have time to indulge.

When she came out beneath the Great Hall, she paused and looked toward the mathematics stacks, where she saw a body lying against the wall, surrounded by flaming codices toppled from the shelves in the dark hall behind it.

Hannah dashed over to the figure on the ground.

Synesius.

He opened his eyes and looked up at her, smiling weakly and then shutting them again.

"Sy!" Hannah screamed for joy and threw her arms around him.

He groaned in pain.

"Alaya, where is Alaya?" she asked, but he was too weak to reply.

Then Hannah looked at her hands, her arms, covered in blood. Not hers, not Peter's. Then she looked down at Synesius's body and saw the laceration over his chest, the edge of one stark white rib jutting from beneath his bloody robe.

Hannah clenched her eyes shut, her hands shaking. "We must go," she said as a wall behind them gave way, and a surge of heat from the flames burst into the room.

Hannah pulled Synesius's arms over his head and dragged him as best she could, the heat of the fire on their heels. She was such a small woman, it was a marvelous feat, but not one she would remember so.

When they reached the door at the other end, Hannah shoved, but it was sealed.

"Oh, please open," she whispered, inhaling sharply as her fingers fumbled. Then she kicked with one foot, hard, and again, until it slammed open.

They emerged into the cold, smoky darkness to find that the nets had been thrown off of the butterfly enclosure to free them. But even the gardens were burning now, Cleopatra's crypt a raft of flames.

"Alaya!" Hannah coughed desperately, tugging Synesius on. "Alaya!"

Panic seized her. There was no reply.

"Alaya!" Hannah screamed. "Where is my baby? Alaya! Alaya!"

The entire library and harbor were aflame. Ashes fluttered through the air like grey butterflies. Most of the people had already fled to the beach. A few brave souls remained behind to help rescue the wounded. Anyone else left in the library at that point was gone. The smell of the dead, the blood, the burned corpses mixed in the air with the smoke and the burning wood, as if there would be an enormous macabre meal served somewhere after the fire died.

Out of the darkness, a haggard old man with a long grey beard rushed headlong down the path toward Hannah and Synesius, his sword drawn. Hannah recoiled, then looked into his eyes, recognized him. "Alizar?"

He stopped instantly. "Hannah, praise Zeus, you are all right!" He threw his arms around her.

Hannah sighed. "Are we dead, then?"

"No," said Alizar. "Let me help you." He crouched to carry Synesius and hoist him over one shoulder.

"How?"

"Gideon freed me from the tower. The church was deserted."

Hannah's eyes glazed. "Have you seen Alaya, Alizar? Have you seen her?"

Alizar swallowed hard. His eyes looked to the gardens. Gideon had concealed the half of the Emerald Tablet they had procured from the Church of St. Alexander in Cleopatra's crypt when they heard Hypatia was in danger. But Synesius, Hannah, Alaya. Which was the more valuable to him?

Alizar steeled himself and turned away from the Great Library, from the loss of Hypatia, the Emerald Tablet, all he had worked for. No, he must serve the living. "Alaya must be at the beach with the others. Come." Hannah nearly collapsed as Alizar put one of his arms around her, the smoke so deep in her lungs. She let him guide them to the beach, where together they searched the sea of people for her daughter. But Alaya was nowhere to be found.

Hannah lifted her eyes to look at the roaring inferno that had just that day been the Great Library of Alexandria. Friends and strangers all around her did the same, watching their entire lives go up in flames. She could not speak. A pain seized her that was so enormous, her body could not even contain it. It was not just her life but all of history disappearing. It was her friends, her colleagues, every diligent soul, and lifetimes of work, all lost.

Gideon found them on the beach, his head low. Hannah collapsed in tears as he held her, his arms wrapped around her to keep her from breaking free. Though she struggled and screamed at him hysterically to let her go, he held tight. He was not going to let her go, not for anything, not while the fire raged on.

There was no feeling of time passing for any of them that night, as if eternity cloaked the city in one endless, inescapable moment. Hannah could feel the cool moist sand beneath her body, Gideon's strong, warm arms holding her, the tight constricting pain in her chest as she coughed. She could hear the sound of people talking, wailing all around her. It hardly seemed real. Philemon came to look at Synesius. She could see his lips moving as he inspected the gash and bound a cloth around Synesius's chest after sewing him shut. He shook his head from side to side and clucked his tongue. He was such a dour doctor, always believing the worst.

Shadows and silhouettes mingled on the sand. Someone said that half the city was on fire. People stood around in shock, unsure of what to do. A few smoked. A few wailed. A few paced and paced and paced. Others sat in a stupor. Bodies of loved ones were dragged to the beach and piled in front of the surf so that corpses could be recognized by their families.

Alaya, oh, Alaya.

Tears poured down Hannah's cheeks as she sobbed helplessly, screaming at Gideon to do something, but what could he do? He was as useless as she.

Pages and pages of the world's irreplaceable knowledge fluttered through the sky over their heads. Severed scrolls rained down upon the people on the beach. Sentences trailed off at charred edges. Meaning burned to ash. Was this a mathematical formula? This a play from Sophocles? This one of Homer's epics? It did not matter, not now.

Hannah could not breathe. Sobs choked her throat. Rage burned in her blood. Her lungs ached terribly. She pressed her eyes closed against the pain, against the atrocity, the impossibility. Had she not dreamed this moment? A million birds, their wings on fire, flailing on the wind. The night before the slave traders came to Sinai, she had seen it all with no way of knowing what she had seen.

People came to see who was alive.

Even the kind-eyed Nubian girl they had rescued in the market found her and came to sit beside her, stroking her hair. Hannah did not even know she was there. She called out for her child. How would she survive this night? How could she think of living without Alaya? How could the gods be so heartless and cruel as this? There was no choice: if Alaya did not live, neither would

Hannah. That she knew. She would not want to know a world without her daughter in it.

Then, from somewhere in the back of her mind Hannah thought she heard Alaya's voice. Her eyes flew open, thinking she was imagining it. She looked at Gideon. His eyes were wide. He had heard it, too.

"Alaya?" Hannah called out, cupping her hands around her mouth as she flew to her feet.

"Alaya!" Gideon yelled.

Alizar joined them then, and Tarek. They stood on the beach in a solemn line, calling out.

Hannah looked around desperately in all directions.

Then the crowd parted, and in a stranger's arms, her child appeared.

"Alaya!" Hannah screamed, running toward her daughter, her aching feet slipping in the sand.

Those ten steps toward her child were the longest strides of her entire life. A city that had erupted in chaos as the pillars of Alexandria crumbled and an impossible night of loss all fell into the background.

Her baby was safe.

Alaya was alive.

Hannah swept her child into her arms and clutched her so tightly that neither could breathe.

Hannah rocked from side to side, whispering words of gratitude and love to Alaya through lips wet with tears, kissing her hair, her fingers, her cheeks. A long time passed before her eyes slowly opened to see the man standing before her, the familiar man who had rescued her child from the flames.

Julian.

38

Hannah lifted her heavy eyelids to look at the morning star, her body exhausted from lack of sleep, her mind as empty as a bowl. She stared at the sky, mostly in disbelief that the heavens had not vanished overnight. It seemed wrong, somehow, that Venus showed her lovely white face while the embers of death still smoldered in the pit of what had been the Great Library.

Synesius died that morning on the beach. His last words were for Sofia, who, by some miracle herbs of the midwife, had lived even after she lost so much blood. The babe would have his mother, but not his father. Hannah felt grateful Synesius was conscious long enough to learn he had a son. Then in an instant he was gone, along with so many other friends.

"Stars winkle, planets glow, Mama," announced Alaya, who awakened in her mother's arms. "Pappo told me."

Hannah kissed her daughter's forehead and whispered, "Go back to sleep, Alaya."

In years to come, that moment was the only thing Hannah remembered of the days that followed the burning of the Great Library. Sometimes sparse fragments would float into her mind: the charred stone rubble that had fallen on the beach, the way the chartaceous ash dusted the rooftops like grey snow, the empty eyes of the people, the cows and goats wandering aimlessly through the streets beside an occasional ostrich or hyena. An eerie silence spread itself across the city like a blanket, unifying everyone beneath.

Stars winkle, planets glow.

Bells all over the city clanged without ceasing.

Hypatia of Alexandria, the Virgin of Serapis, was dead.

On the day of the Great Lady's funeral, Hannah sat wedged between Sofia and Gideon in front of a tremendous marble sarcophagus covered with bunches of flowers piled so high that they spilled in colorful waterfalls down the platform. The library was now an empty tomb of knowledge, a skeleton of bones without a heart, for that heart had been savagely torn to shreds by the hateful hands of the Parabolani and the mob.

As Orestes took the dais and attempted bravely to deliver the eulogy, Alizar bowed his head to hide the tears that burned in his eyes. How could this have happened?

Beloved Hypatia. Hers had been a life of devotion. He tried not to think how much she would have accomplished in the years stolen from her, as she had not yet reached her fortieth birthday.

Alizar went over the events of that night a thousand times in his mind, imagining what he could have done differently and how if they had just gotten there earlier he could have stopped it. When Gideon had rescued him, they searched the church for the half of the Emerald Tablet from Siwa and found it hidden below the altar bound in a simple linen cloth just as their spy had said. They thought it best to take it to the Great Library. But when they arrived, they found the door from the catacombs mysteriously unlocked and the barges that had carried the Parabolani scattered about the landing.

How had Cyril's men found the secret entrance? The number of people who knew the labyrinth of the catacombs Alizar could count on one hand. His only thought was perfidy. But who would betray Hypatia?

Try as he might, nothing could erase the horrific scene from his mind. The mob, the mounted priests of Nitria and the Parabolani, like voracious wolves, had not left even one recognizable scrap of Hypatia's body. They had flayed her alive. And then the fire had taken the rest. Before them now her sarcophagus stood empty, save for a handful of ashes.

But it was the secret of the fire that Alizar would carry to his grave and his part in it. The moment replayed in his mind a thousand times as the sickening guilt spread through his veins. Attacked from the rear by three priests of Nitria, Alizar had spun and unsheathed his sword in defense. The first man he ran through. The second priest, armed with a Roman sword, nearly took off Alizar's head. But Alizar had stepped aside and grabbed a nearby torch, thrusting it into the priest's bloodthirsty eyes. But the reeling priest had dropped to the floor in a pool of oil and blood, his body instantly ablaze. A pile of nearby scrolls caught fire. The third horseman of Nitria spun and fled as Alizar removed his *klamys*, desperate to put out the flames. But the fire had engulfed it, too.

In the end, over three hundred librarians, five hundred staff, and a thousand others lay dead in the Great Library, their bodies consumed by the flames. Elsewhere in the city, thousands more had lost their homes as the fire spread. The Nuapar guards that remained in the library had been completely outnumbered, though they fought with valor. Even Cleopatra's crypt had fallen in the flames, taking the Emerald Tablet with it. Now Hypatia was dead, and Alizar did not know how he would live with what he had done. Cyril had gotten the library and its heart, both.

The morning after the library had burned, some Christians had taken to the streets to celebrate their victory; after all, the pagan whore was dead, and the stain of the devil had been erased from history. But many of the Christian families did not approve of the atrocity and stood at the edges of the funeral, ashamed of their bishop, regretful of all that was lost. Alizar feared the Christian scribes of the Tabularium would conceal the destruction all the same, for now there were no other scribes left in the city. The Christians would write the story however they pleased, or perhaps they would simply erase it from history. Hypatia's name would be lost in whispers within a generation. Alizar vowed that he would do everything in his power to keep it alive.

What had been lost in the fire was totally irreplaceable, Alizar knew better than anyone, and every lost scroll impaled him on the axis of his own compunction: all of Synesius's work on the unsung gospels, the history of the Egyptian dynasties and how the pyramids had been constructed, the origin of alchemy and the writings of Hermes Trismagistus, innumerable medical codices and diagrams, mathematical and astronomical calculations from the most brilliant minds of the last five centuries, philosophical writings, plays, lists of herbal remedies, star charts, zoological and medical findings, the complete works, journals, and private collections of Aeschylus, Homer, Plato, Aristotle, Archimedes, Theon, Eratosthenes, Apuleius, Plotinus, and Hypatia. In the future, the world would never know the scope of what had been lost, irreplaceably lost.

There was so much more that Alizar had yet to copy, yet he knew he could never have saved it all. Although he had known that the Great Library's destruction was imminent, given what had happened to the other libraries around the Mediterranean over the last fifty years, nothing could have ever convinced Alizar he would play a part in the scope of the tragedy: Hypatia's murder, the loss of librarians and friends he had worked beside for over thirty years, the ashes, the endless ashes. Alizar wished he had died with them now that he was left in the fabric of a world torn to shreds, gaping holes where friends once stood. There was no word Alizar knew that could even begin to encompass or express that kind of pain.

Alizar looked back to the dais where Orestes was stuttering, his speech the worse for his grief. As the governor began to list

Hypatia's accomplishments, tears welled up in his throat, and he had to pause. In between the silences he apologized repeatedly, attempting to collect himself.

"Beloved Hypatia, how the halls of our hearts will always remember your beauty and wisdom. Muse, inspiration, teacher, philosopher, you instructed your pupils through your example, showing us the way to freedom. Now we will always remember you as united with that divine truth you so loved and served. Your death has been your wedding day to God." Orestes clutched the podium with both hands, his knuckles turning white. Noble Orestes, once praetorian prefect of Egypt, the most powerful man in all of North Africa, felt as helpless as a child. He lifted the scroll before him, but the tears in his one eye blurred his vision so he had to go on without his notes.

Alaya reached up and wiped her mother's tears with her fingers and hugged her. It hardly seemed real that Hypatia was gone. Hannah somehow expected her to turn up at her own funeral, laughing at the extravagance she had spent an entire lifetime avoiding.

Orestes looked down to collect himself, and when he looked up again, the startled expression on his face betrayed him. The mourners turned their heads to see what had caught his attention and witnessed the bishop's chariot approaching in a cloud of dust.

Bishop Cyril.

Seeing the chariot, Alizar clenched his jaw, stood to his full height, and walked swiftly toward it with only one thought in his mind. *How dare he.*

As Cyril stepped out of the box, Alizar greeted him with his sword raised. "Leave this gathering at once," he growled. "Let our people mourn in peace."

Cyril narrowed his eyes, realizing Alizar had escaped from the prison cell, none too pleased. Eyes turned on them, interrupting the eulogy. Cyril tapped his staff on the stone cobbles. "Stand aside, old man. I have come to pay my respects to the Great Lady of Alexandria. The mourners here expect to hear words of divine consolation from their bishop."

The light of truth burned in Alizar's eyes like a white fire. He spoke quietly, but forcefully, his words meant only for Cyril's ears. "Be well warned that the eyes of heaven have witnessed what you have done, Cyril. Every man, woman and child seated here knows your part in this lie, and you should be ashamed in the face of your Christ." Alizar spat in Cyril's face.

Cyril's cheeks flushed red, and he quivered with rage as he clenched his fists beneath his robes, but he said nothing.

Alizar stepped forward, the point of his sword now pressed to Cyril's belly. "Curse you and be gone from here. Let these people grieve in peace."

Cyril stepped backwards, tripping on the heel of his boot.

Alizar let his eyes speak of death, and stepped forward again.

Without a word, Cyril climbed into his chariot box and rode away.

Alizar sheathed his sword and returned to the mourners, still angry, but satisfied that he had defended Hypatia's name and her memory, even if he had not been able to defend her life.

One by one, Hypatia's students, friends and followers walked up the steps to kiss the cold marble sarcophagus that bore her name. Hannah stepped forward carrying Alaya. "Bless you, Great Lady, my beloved friend," Hannah whispered as her lips brushed the stone. "God keep you now."

39

Some weeks after Hypatia's funeral, Alizar, who had been clois-tered in the walls of his tower, was jolted from his grief by more upsetting news.

"It is true. Orestes has the half of the Emerald Tablet from Delfi. He found your brass chest intact in Cyril's treasury. Incred-ible the bishop did not know what it was or try to open it. But the half from Siwa, Alizar," Gideon swallowed hard. "I have searched to no avail. Nothing remains of it."

"I see. It is not your fault. But Gideon, how did that half of the tablet end up in the Church of St. Alexander in the first place? We knew Cyril had the other half, the one from Delfi. But how did he come by the one from Siwa?"

"It was stolen from Hannah's room in the Great Library."

"Do we know by whom?" Alizar paced the room. He was the one who told Gideon to hide the half of the tablet beneath the altar stone in Cleopatra's crypt when they went to help Hypatia. The crypt, which had burned with the rest of the library. He had sent Gideon to search the rubble for it since, and every day the captain returned empty handed.

"I am sorry to be the one to tell you," said Gideon, setting the small iron key on the table.

Alizar touched his key, a new pain in his eyes. The sweet hound puppy at his feet—a gift from Orestes—grunted in sleep, the tiny feet twitching, hunting rabbits. He took the key in his hands, turned it over in his hand, the hand fitted with the leather harness for his prosthetic brass thumb.

Gideon bowed his head. "A whore called Mira confessed it all when she learned that Hypatia had been killed. Apparently she was once a priestess in the Temple of Isis. She insisted that she was merely following Tarek's instructions when she gave it to the Parabolani. He paid her handsomely. And then there are these." Gideon reached beneath his *klamys* and produced the forged documents bearing the bishop's seal that declared Tarek the sole heir of Alizar's estate.

Alizar looked over the scrolls and nodded somberly. The Parabolani had everything they needed to enter the Great Library when they pursued Hypatia, but no one knew how. Alizar heard Gideon's explanation and then repeated it in disbelief. "You think Tarek stole the tablet from Hannah's room? That he sold it to Cyril for my estate?"

"He was the only one who knew where it would be or have access to it. I am sorry."

"You are simply doing what a true friend would do," he said. "I thank you."

Gideon paused at the tower door. "My loyalty is always to you, Alizar. Is there more I can do?"

Alizar propped his elbows on his knees and dropped his head into his hands. "No, there is nothing," he said, but then, as Gideon turned to leave, Alizar called to him, realizing that the sooner he dealt with this mess, the better. "No, wait. Send for Tarek."

Gideon nodded and left the room.

Tarek appeared in the doorway some hours later and stepped inside cautiously. "Gideon said you wanted to see me?"

Alizar lifted his head and Tarek saw the disappointment in his eyes.

"Tell me the truth, Tarek," said Alizar, holding up the iron key, his voice like raked gravel with grief.

Tarek's eyes opened wide. Alizar held the key to the Great Library entrance in the catacombs—the same key embossed with the seal of Alizar's house. He stammered as a few weak words escaped his lips.

"The truth!" Alizar demanded as his fist came down on the table, shaking the stone, several of the scrolls rolling to the floor.

Tarek recoiled. "I gave the key to a whore I favor. It was only for a tryst, just for a night, and—"

"Enough!" said Alizar. Then he shoved the bench back from the table and walked to the east window to look out, his eyes falling upon the blackened gash in the ground where the Great Library had been. It might as well have been his heart. "So you gave her the key and the map of the catacombs. She then sold them to the Parabolani at a very good price I understand. When questioned, she insisted that she got that idea from you. Did you benefit from this transaction?"

Tarek's head fell forward. "You have always hated me."

Alizar spun around. "Hated you? *Hated* you, Tarek? How far does your blindness reach, boy? Even after my son's death I took you in, I fed you and gave you a position in my house that is the envy of every orphan in this city. When my own family insisted that you played a part in my son's death, I pardoned you. Was I wrong to do that, Tarek? Tell me the truth. *The truth!* Or is the truth so malleable to you that it changes every time you think on it?"

Tarek did not look up.

"I ask you again, did you benefit from this transaction?"

"I gave them to her," Tarek whimpered. "That much is true. But she is the one who sold them. I arranged a tryst, just for us, for one night. I, I wanted to meet her in the Caesarium gardens, and, and—" Tarek stumbled over his words. "I never thought . . ."

"You never thought," repeated Alizar, his voice aseptic and cold, the words falling like dislodged icicles. "But it does not matter now, does it? Even if you are lying to me, what is done is done." Alizar took a deep breath and let his gaze drift back out to the empty harbor. He knew the ring of truth. Tarek's words lacked it entirely.

"That is not fair," said Tarek. "Hypatia herself risked her own life by giving a public lecture against the advice of everyone who knew her, including Orestes. And you want to make me responsible for what happened."

Alizar stood over the boy. "Not fair?"

"You are just looking for someone to blame."

Alizar took a deep breath and closed his eyes. "Sit down, Tarek, before I kill you myself."

Tarek sat.

"Let me explain the true function of an apology. It is not to admit guilt or to accept blame. An apology is to connect yourself to the pain of others, and in feeling their pain, experience remorse for the part you played in creating it. An apology releases pain. Creates room for forgiveness. Yes, I am very angry to learn what you have done, but I am even more infuriated to see that you seem to have no conscience about it."

"That is not true," said Tarek.

Alizar waited.

"I am sorry."

Alizar sighed. It was words, empty words spoken merely to prevent punishment. "Do these belong to you?" He shoved the scrolls across the table. Tarek recognized them immediately, and he looked up to the ceiling, his eyes unable to meet Alizar's. "What are you going to do to me?"

"I am not interested in punishing you. In fact, I am not interested in you. I will do now what I should have done years ago. All the while I have been in prison you have lived here without working, without practicing any skill except spending my money and waiting for me to die so you could steal my entire estate from my daughter. True, she is a woman, but I do plan for her, and my grandson, to inherit. I know you traded Cyril the Emerald Tablet we procured from Siwa for these forged documents."

"The tablet was a useless stone."

Alizar held out his hand. "Give me your keys, Tarek."

"My keys?" Tarek asked as his hand brushed the keys that hung at his chest beneath his *tunica*.

"Give them to me, or may Kronos devour your soul."

Tarek removed the string of keys from around his neck and coiled it in Alizar's open palm.

"Now get out."

Tarek looked around helplessly. "Get out? But, but where will I go? What will happen to me?"

Alizar did not look up. "That is your business now."

Tarek swallowed audibly as he realized that Alizar was serious. "But I am sorry," he said. "I am sorry for what happened. Surely you realize that."

"I realize that your apology comes because you do not find my decision agreeable to you, and you would like to alter it. And I am deeply disappointed that you feel nothing for anyone other than yourself, Tarek." Alizar turned his back and set his hands on the window ledge. "You are not my son."

"But I do not know what to do," Tarek whimpered.

Alizar put his hand on the hilt of his sword to emphasize his seriousness. "An extraordinary gift. Use it wisely. Now, get out of my house. And should you ever return, I will run you through in the name of Zeus."

Tarek slowly backed out of the room and fled down the steps.

Alizar waited until he heard the footsteps on the stairs, and then he paced the room.

How could it have come to this?

But then Alizar remembered his grandson asleep downstairs, a little infant completely unaware of the broken world beyond his mother's breast, and a grandfather's smile of pride flickered briefly across his lips.

40

The day of the spring equinox, beneath the shade of the sprawling fig tree in Alizar's courtyard, the women of the house gathered to drink in the fresh air, even if the spring they had hoped for was still shrouded in a grey gown of marine mist. The courtyard fountain sang musically, spouting a stream of water into the limpid pool of lotus flowers and golden fish while unseen larks and finches twittered in the newly leafed high branches of the fig tree. The delicious scent of fresh grass and fruit blossoms filled the air. Hannah stood by the courtyard gate, tickling the muzzle of the grey stallion while Alaya splashed her feet in the fountain. Sofia, relaxing on a divan in the shade, sewed the finishing touches on a pair of tiny satin slippers for baby Ali, asleep in her arms.

Hannah kissed the stallion's nose and walked across the courtyard to sit on the low wall beside her lyre. As her fingers traced the delicate curve of the instrument she let out a sigh of gratitude-tinged sorrow that she had loaned it to Sofia at Alizar's the week before the fire. It was the only piece of Hypatia she had left. Alizar had announced that morning that they he would sail for Athens within the month. He would return to Greece permanently so that he could attend to the vineyards in Harmonia. He had invited Gideon and Hannah to join him and the rest of his staff. The harbor at Epidavros would be deep enough for the new ship given to him by Orestes, which Gideon had named the *Persephone*. There was so much in Alexandria that Hannah was not ready to leave behind, yet those things were all mostly memories now. Alizar had already sold his vineyard beside Lake Mareotis, and though the price he received was fair, it was far lower than he might have gotten in the years before the drought. Hannah felt reluctant to go, but then there was also Alaya to consider. Hannah wanted to spare her daughter any further loss of friends. They had already lost their home, all their clothes and possessions burned in the fire. Thankfully, Alizar had been kind enough to take them all in. His house had never been so crowded as Hannah, Alaya, Gideon, and Sofia had all taken up residence. Alaya seemed to adore the attention, but she often asked for Hypatia. Hannah had to admit that a life in Alexandria would be miserable for her daughter without friends and family. Besides, Gideon's family had land in Greece. They were also her family now, and she looked forward to meeting the many aunts, uncles, and Gideon's parents and siblings (an older sister and brother). Hannah watched Alaya playing in the fountain and smiled. Soon it would be time to teach her about the rhythm of the moon and the seasons. How she would have loved to show her daughter the old olive tree on the hill in Sinai where she had tended the sheep and the goats in her father's pasture, where as a child she had come to befriend the moon. She wished Alaya could see the ewes giving birth in the soft green pastures of spring and taste the clear water of the streams that ran down the rocky crags of the mountain.

There was so much to consider, and time was so short.

Hannah took the lyre in her arms and began to play softly, humming one of the melodies she had written for Naomi years ago, if only to still the nuisance of the flies.

The music woke little Ali, who began to cry. Sofia sleepily parted the fabric of her *himation* and brought his mouth to her breast so he could suckle her nipple and be soothed. Then she yawned and stretched her legs. Poor Sofia had not fully smiled since Synesius had died. Her beauty was a relic of vanished happiness.

As Hannah finished the song, Sofia readjusted the babe in her arms and kissed his fingers. "Has anyone seen my father?"

"He is still hermetically sealed in his tower," said Hannah, gesturing up at the roof. "What do you suppose he is doing?"

"Who knows?" said Sofia. "He has not opened the door but twice since Hypatia's funeral."

"He is making a chow-ice," Alaya announced.

"A chalice?" asked the women.

"Alaya, what do you mean?" asked Hannah. "Is this another one of your stories about India?"

"He is making it for the em-por. He told me." Alaya looked over her shoulder at her mother while dangling her toes in the fountain. She had been the only one to enter Alizar's workshop in the tower, so no one could verify if she was in fact telling the truth.

"Are you sure, Alaya?" asked Hannah.

"Yes, Mama."

So.

The whole story unraveled that evening when the household sat down to eat, and a loud, official-sounding knock rattled the green door at the front of the house.

"It is an imperial messenger," said Jemir, returning to the room.

Sofia dabbed the corners of her mouth and frowned. "I will see him." She passed her babe to Hannah.

After a few moments she returned from the entryway with an elegant parchment letter bearing the royal seal of the Imperial Court. "It is from Emperor Theodosius the Second," she said, so full of disbelief that it sounded as if her words were made of pure air.

Alaya bounced on Gideon's lap. "Open it! Open it!"

"I cannot do that, Alaya," said Sofia. "It is for my father."

Everyone at the table exchanged curious looks as Sofia leaned the letter against a candelabra, the imperial gold seal gleaming in the candlelight. The missive was so beautiful that no one dared to speak. They all simply stared at it as if it would open itself.

That was when Alizar appeared in the doorway, his hound pup beside him, already loyal as a shadow in good light. "I heard we had a messenger," he said, as if he had been there all along.

Everyone looked up in surprise.

"A letter from the em-por," announced Alaya.

"Thank you, Alaya," he said as he strode up to the table and lifted the parchment. He turned the large letter over in his hands to examine the seal. "Ah, so it is. Well, shall we read it?"

Heads bobbed emphatically around the table.

Alizar smiled playfully, delighted to be keeping everyone in such suspense. He purposefully drew out the moment, slowly slitting the seal with a butter knife and then clearing his throat several times before reading.

His Majesty Emperor Theodosius II has granted your request
for audience and anticipates your arrival in Constantinople
upon the seventh month of Julius in the year of our Lord, 416.
A slip in the royal harbor has been arranged for your ship,
and a court guard will accompany you to the palace for your
much anticipated presentation.

The document was signed by a eunuch named Lysippus, the personal correspondent of the royal court.

The dining table erupted with questions.

Alizar smiled and said, "Perhaps you would like to see for yourselves. Come up to the tower after supper." Alizar exited dramatically, his long blue robes swishing in the hall like a rustle of papyrus reeds along the Nile.

Leaving their plates still laden with food on the table, everyone rose and followed him.

Alaya led the train up the stairs to the large wooden door marked by the caduceus.

It was open.

Alizar was seated at his worktable, smiling when they arrived. They entered singly through the door, first Alaya and Hannah, then Gideon, Jemir, and Sofia.

The sight they beheld stunned them all.

There in the center of Alizar's worktable stood an enormous chalice of impeccable workmanship: a gleaming bowl carved from one solid piece of lapis lazuli, the stem formed of two serpents intertwined around the trunk of a massive tree with gnarled roots that formed a heavy base to support the significant weight of the chalice. Serpentine branches cradled the lapis bowl that glowed like the blue canopy of the evening sky, tiny golden flecks speckling its rim like stars, while lovely whorls of white swirled between them like clouds traversing the heavens.

No one could speak.

The chalice seemed brought to earth from the dreamy realm of the gods, as nothing so beautiful could possibly have been created by mortal hands.

Everyone gathered around the table to get a closer look. Alaya bounced until Gideon lifted her up in his arms to see it. Hannah looked on in awe, as the chalice was large enough that Sofia's baby could be laid within it with still enough room for the swaddling blanket. Sofia, who was secretly disappointed that her father could have kept such an enormous secret from her, was the only one brave enough to touch it as she gently glided one finger along the glossy lip of the chalice where the gilded letters of a Latin inscription read: *ut supra ut infra, ut infra ut supra.* Hannah recognized the alchemist's riddle from a stanza in the Emerald Tablet. A wise thinker would be led to the secret the chalice contained. Sofia caressed the stone thoughtfully. "How on earth did you . . . I mean . . . *did* you make this, Papa?" She looked to her father, who seemed quite pleased with himself.

"An alchemist never divulges his secrets," he said with a wink. "I will tell you, though, that the Chalice of Sofia, as I have named it, serves a very special purpose. Behold." Alizar leaned forward and cradled the chalice in his arms, gently turning it upside-down on the table. Then he placed both hands on the large gold base and gave a mighty twist, and much to everyone's surprise, it began to turn.

With several more twists, the base came free of the stem, revealing it to be hollow. Alizar reached the fingers of one hand into the brass stem and pulled out two small papyrus scrolls that he handed to Gideon to unroll.

Gideon passed Alaya to Hannah and then slowly unrolled the scrolls and spread them on the table for everyone to see, fixing the corners with several small stones.

"Look, a map, Mama," said Alaya. "And a bird."

The second of the two scrolls bore an etching of the ibis-headed god Thoth at the fore and looked like a set of laws, as they were numbered.

"Yes, my love," said Hannah as she stroked her daughter's hair.

"Gideon?" said Alizar, inviting him to explain.

"It must be the map of all the places we have hidden the manuscripts from the Great Library," said Gideon thoughtfully as he traced the contours of the map with one finger. "Cyprus, Crete, Nag Hammadi, Malta, Antioch, Patmos, Delfi, Cappodocia . . . it is all here." He looked up at Alizar, who nodded that he was correct.

"Every document we saved from the library has been sealed in clay jars and buried in the ground in these locations. This is one of two maps that I made to reveal them," Alizar explained.

"Where is the other one?" asked Sofia.

"I will take it to Harmonia and have it walled into the hearth," announced Alizar. "It was my final promise to Hypatia."

"And this one you will give to the emperor?" asked Hannah.

Alizar smiled, so happy. "Yes, to Emperor Theodosius the Second and his sister, Pulcheria."

"That *is* madness," said Gideon. "Well done."

"But what is this other scroll?" asked Hannah, stroking the etching of Thoth.

"It is the etching Tarek made of the Emerald Tablet, of both halves," declared Alizar.

Hannah wanted to ask him to translate it for her but then thought again. The magical script was perfect as it was, unknown to her. She did not need every mystery revealed. This one could live in her heart, exactly as it was.

Alizar smiled as if he read her thoughts.

"Will you be telling the young emperor what the chalice conceals?" asked Jemir.

Alizar licked his lips, as though the decision had been a hard one for him. "The chalice and its secret will be safest in the royal palace until one day, many years from now, I assume, someone discovers what it contains." Then Alizar rolled up the maps and the etching of the Emerald Tablet and tucked them back into the stem, twisting the base to seal it.

"Astonishing," said Sofia.

"Unbelievable, really," said Gideon.

"And you made the chalice yourself?" asked Hannah, revisiting Sofia's earlier question.

Alizar did not answer, but smiled the artist's loving smile for his creation as he righted the chalice on the table. "The *Persephone* will sail for Greece at the month's end," he said, "and then from Athens to Constantinople."

Sofia nodded. "I am proud of you, Papa," she said.

Hannah took Alaya from Gideon and propped her on her hip.

"Have you decided if you will be coming with us?" asked Sofia of Hannah, reaching to take her son in her arms as he began to fuss for her breast.

Hannah passed the babe to Sofia, then looked at Gideon.

"We have not yet discussed our plans," said Hannah.

"Oh? I expected you and Gideon would sail with us," said Alizar. "Orestes has also requested we carry the Celestial Clock of Archimedes to Greece."

Hannah eyed Gideon. "Why do I not know of this?"

The others in the room looked away as the tension grew, as if turning their heads would make them less present.

Gideon uncrossed his arms, squared his shoulders, and walked to the door without a backward glance. His steps echoed loudly on the stairs as if etching his feelings in footprints.

Hannah looked through the door after him. "Gideon?"

41

Hannah paced the wharf, her grey woolen shawl pulled tightly around her body, her fingers nervously twiddling the sleeves. "Gideon, please come down and speak to me."

Gideon leaned over the bow, busy untangling a line. "Our ship sails at dawn tomorrow, Hannah. I am sorry. I do not have time for talk." He smiled at her and kicked a flying fish off the bow and into the water with a plunk. An osprey perched on the rigging instantly spied the opportunity and swept down to grasp the fish in its talons, returning to the mast to devour the prize in triumph.

Hannah groaned, frustrated. Why would he not speak to her? "But Gideon," she called up to the ship. "Please, just for a moment."

Again his face appeared over the edge, his dark eyes even darker, his tone as dead as the fish in the osprey's claws. "No. Go home to Alizar. And to Julian."

Hannah let out a guttural howl. "I have not seen Julian, Master Junkar, since the night of the fire, Gideon. You know that as well as I. Just come down and speak to me." Hannah tipped her chin toward him. "You are to be my husband. Please!"

Gideon secured the untangled manila line to a hook on the deck with three swift turns and threw the length overboard. "But you will see him," he said.

"If you will not speak to me then I am coming up." Hannah strode down the dock to the gangplank. But as she neared it, Gideon appeared, and drew the long board up onto the deck. "It is in need of repair. I would not want a lady to be injured," he said.

Hannah shook her head and rolled her eyes. As if he expected her to believe such nonsense. "Gideon, this is childish of you, and rude."

"Go back to Alizar's, Hannah," said Gideon flatly. "This ship sails at dawn. If you want to discuss matters, then you are welcome to be aboard it. If not, with my apologies, I have work to finish." And he turned his back to her and called out to one of his crew.

Hannah waited for a long time there, alone on the dock with the fog drifting in wisps around her body, the cold seeping through her bones. Then she turned and walked all the way back to Alizar's with her fists clenched, angry at Gideon's unfounded jealousy.

Without a thought to where she was going, Hannah climbed the stairs to Alizar's tower where the others had been and stopped at the closed door. She let her fist float in the air above the caduceus, and then she lowered it and turned away, and walked halfway down the steps. Then she turned and walked up again. Then down.

Up.

Down.

Then up.

Here her journey had begun. Here at the steps, sweeping. Here where she had discovered Alizar's wife, Naomi, pale and asleep behind the door.

Downstairs the baby wailed as if just awakening, and Hannah could hear Sofia croon to him. Voices of love.

Hannah turned back to the door, and this time she let her knuckles graze the wood.

"Come," said Alizar.

Hannah pushed the door and stepped inside. "Alizar, I am sorry to disturb you," Hannah began, but she lifted her head to see that no one was in the room. Strange. She was certain she had heard him.

That was when she noticed that the stairs to the roof had been lowered, a square patch of sky at the top.

Of course, the roof.

Hannah lifted the edge of her lavender *himation* embroidered with a lotus hem and ran up the stairs, beginning her speech again. "Alizar, I am sorry to disturb you, but I just wanted—" Her breath fell short at the last word she uttered, for there before her, framed by the orange disk of the sun, stood Alizar and another man she would have known anywhere.

Julian.

Alizar nodded to her, his eyes full of some deep, unnamed pain. Before Hannah could fully understand why, he excused himself. "I was just telling Master Junkar that there is a scroll downstairs that I want him to look at. I will go see if I can find it." He bowed his head and swept past her.

Hannah looked back at him, then to Julian.

He took three steps toward her to close the distance between them so they could hear each other over the wind that whipped against their clothes.

"It is good to see you again," he said.

"I did not realize you were here," said Hannah, her voice coming out colder than she intended. So Gideon had been right, he had come.

Julian sighed. Why was she not happy to see him? He reached forward to take her hand, leading her to the west parapet where the sun crouched on the horizon like a golden hen on her nest. There, Hannah withdrew her hand and pulled her shawl tighter around her body, her eyes full of concern but shielded by her brow.

"Hannah," Julian began, his deep green eyes lit so that she could see the flecks of gold that spun within them, the same little flecks she knew so well in her daughter's eyes. Their daughter. Unsettled, she looked away.

Julian sighed. "Have you not heard?"

Hannah straightened. "Heard?"

Julian closed his eyes. "The Parabolani also invaded Pharos."

Hannah stiffened and drew in a sharp breath. "What happened?"

Julian gently squeezed her arm to comfort and brace her. "The temples were all destroyed."

Hannah froze, her heart breaking anew. "But the monks? The priestesses?"

"A few escaped."

"But where did they go?"

"I do not know. We will attempt to live our tradition in secret wherever we can rebuild."

"And the priestesses in the Temple of Isis?"

"The Parabolani struck there first with their torches. I am so sorry."

Hannah shook her head, disbelieving. "But surely some made it out."

Julian took a breath and met her eyes. "None that we know of."

Hannah set her hands on the wall, bracing herself, suddenly flooded with a new despair. Mother Hathora, Iris, the little children, all lost? Could this be? "Why have we not heard this?"

"I came to inform Alizar just now."

"So that is why he looked so grave. But why did you not send another? Do you not belong with Master Savitur?"

Julian sighed. "The man and the master war within me. The man had to see you again."

Hannah closed her eyes and turned away, shaking her head.

Julian stepped forward. "What is it?"

"Gideon was right." Hannah swallowed against the tears that wanted to break free. She hated how she cried so easily.

Julian looked confused and waited for her to continue.

Hannah looked back to him. "Julian, Gideon is to be my husband."

Julian leaned against the parapet. "Is it what you want?"

"*Neh*. I am carrying his child. Gideon gifted me my freedom."

"You love him, then?"

Hannah inhaled the light of the sun, finally certain. "Yes."

He turned to go.

"No, please," Hannah reached for his arm. "You must know I have thought of you so often through the years. Gideon has been generous to me, yes. But it is not his eyes I see when Alaya looks at me."

Julian smiled. "She is my daughter, I know. I knew in the garden."

"*Neh*," said Hannah. "She is."

Julian thought for a moment, then reached into his pocket and held out to her the little silver treasure. "I have kept it, selfishly. You should have it."

Hannah smiled, instantly lifted. "My hairpin," she said, her voice quavering as she took it from his open palm. "My father gave it to me." She pressed the peacock to her lips, and ran her finger along the glossy silver feathers. "I thought I had lost it."

"Not lost," said Julian, his voice tinged with sadness. "Never lost."

"How did you know?" Hannah looked up into his eyes as she snuggled the hairpin back in her hair. "How did you know Alaya was yours?"

Julian smiled. His smile of light. The sun would be envious if it knew. "When I met her in the garden she told me her name, the same as my mother's, and I calculated the years since the marriage rite of my coronation. Then looking at her, I saw your face, and I knew."

Hannah nodded, her eyes drifting off beyond the city walls over her shoulder to the harbor in the west. To the harbor where

Gideon was preparing Alizar's ship. The line of the anchor might have tangled in her bones, for she felt pulled by the bond that had been forged between them over the years, in comfort and in trust.

Julian felt her thoughts. "I should not have come," he said. "I can see it was unfair to indulge myself this way."

"No," she said. "No, I am grateful you did." She touched his hand, and then she withdrew her fingers, warm from his skin. "It feels like such a long time ago. I had to fulfill the quest you gave me, pregnant with the child. Looking back, I am amazed that she lived. Daughter of a warrior. You were right, the shard of the tablet protected us." Hannah removed the necklace and coiled it in his hands. "That quest made me who I am," she said, closing his fingers over the shard. "I am sorry I failed."

"You did not fail," said Julian, surprised. "The Emerald Tablet was secured by Alizar in the crypt of Cleopatra the night the library burned."

Hannah interrupted. "Yes, but Alizar said the crypt was destroyed. And that was only the half of it, besides. Now the tablet can never be rejoined."

"No, Hannah. Master Savitur retrieved the half that Gideon hid in Cleopatra's crypt. Orestes entrusted us with the second half from Delfi. Now with the shard, the Emerald Tablet can be restored to its full magic, and hidden until the time is right."

"But the Great Library has fallen. The Christians are stronger than ever before. We have lost everything."

"You did not fail, Hannah, but succeeded magnificently. And we thank you. The time of the Emerald Tablet has not yet come. Trust the fabric of the universe that holds us all together in the face of so much loss. Spirit is greater, even than the breath in your chest. There is always a greater plan, always. Trust."

Hannah felt stunned at this news. The fall of the temples on Pharos. That the tablet itself was safe, restored. Alizar's etching would not be all that remained in the world of its magic. There was yet more mystery to the tablet than she had ever envisioned. So her quest had not been for naught in the end. Without Julian standing before her, she would never have known.

Julian smiled at her, the beautiful goddess from his dreams. She was more beautiful than the images his mind had conjured of her. He was grateful to see her one last time and knew the rightness of that decision in his heart.

Feeling their time was drawing to a close, Hannah took Julian's hands. "I want you to know I am forever indebted to you for rescuing Alaya from the fire. I do not know how to tell you how grateful I am, how grateful we all are. Master Junkar."

Julian nodded. "It was my honor."

Hannah scanned the horizon, searching that swift hard line at the edge of the world for words, then looked back to him, her eyes welling with tears.

Julian turned and set his palms on the parapet, more touched than he remembered by her beauty, her spirit. "I never expected this."

"Nor I," said Hannah, remembering their hours in the lighthouse together like it was only moments ago.

"I must go." Julian turned to her then, and took her in his arms and pressed his lips to hers, kissing her deeply, knowing it was all they would ever have.

"Forgive me," he said, stroking her cheek.

Hannah smiled. "Where will you go?"

"I will join Master Savitur and the remaining Nuapar monks in the Celtic Isles. We have a Roman fortress there built long ago. If it has survived the years, we will reclaim it."

"Will we never see you again?"

"You will see me."

Hannah nodded, allowing herself to look into his eyes until, unable to restrain herself, she kissed him one last time, her whole body trembling. Julian lifted her in his arms as the years between them scattered like ashes, the sun warming their faces.

"I will always be inside you," Julian promised.

"You always have been." Hannah said clutching him, drinking in the scent of his robe for the last time, her tears wetting the thin cotton.

"May I say goodbye to Alaya?"

Hannah nodded and pulled away. "Yes. She would like that."

And they descended the steps to Alizar's tower together, their fingers touching until the last stair when they each gave a squeeze, and let go.

❦ 42

"... And do not disturb me," Cyril said wryly.

The young priest whom Cyril was addressing ducked his head out of the room and left the bishop to his morning bath. As Cyril removed his night cap and set it on a nearby table, he chuckled to himself. Victory had come so easily it had actually surprised him. Word arrived that morning that Orestes had departed from Alexandria for Constantinople, and so with Hypatia gone as well, Alexandria had at last been cleansed of heretics. Cyril looked down at the codex in his hands that had arrived from the Great Library several days earlier and laughed. He did not actually plan to read the leaves. His Eminence had far better uses for the writings of heathens.

Cyril waddled over to his chamber pot, parted his robes, and took a seat. But as he waited for his morning release, much to his disappointment, he was met with the familiar curse of constipation. Though he grunted and groaned and clenched his jaw with a mighty force, nothing would budge his reluctant bowels. Not wanting to rise from the chamber pot to enter his bath without having relieved himself, and for lack of something better to do, Cyril angrily fanned himself with the pages of the manuscript. After a few drawn out minutes, his curiosity finally got the better of him, and he began to read with the thought that the pagan drivel would be, at least, entertaining if little else. He searched the leaves for the author's signature, but it had been left unsigned, so

Cyril flipped back to the front page, ignoring the title of the treatise completely.

He merely glanced through it at first, but found that, much to his dismay, with every page he became only more drawn into the arguments presented, arguments that struck him as an intelligent discourse of the most current heated debate within the church: the question as to whether the Virgin Mary was the mother of Jesus the man, or Jesus the son of God. The consideration was that if she were merely the mother of Jesus the man, the Virgin Mary would find her place in the background of the church's religious pantheon with perhaps only a few mentions of her contribution to Christianity. However, if it stood to reason that Mary was the mother of Christ, then this placed her at the pinnacle of honor in the Christian faith. Mother Mary would then be considered the mother of God, a title that no merely mortal woman could take on.

Cyril had not yet taken a position on the matter, but he realized that the coming debates in Ephesus would decide the matter and thereby alter the course of Christianity, and he longed to participate with an erudite speech prepared to impress.

So.

As he read the manuscript he found himself held in its powerful sway as whoever had written it had considered the matter extensively and proffered a valid and unique argument that was not to be overlooked. Cyril was struck by the terse poignancy of the pen, for the ideas it put forward were philosophically sound and so eloquent as to stir in him more than a dollop of envy.

As he reached the last page, Cyril let his eyes linger on the parchment. Suddenly he knew who must have sent it. It had to be Hypatia. Anyone else from the library would have signed such a brilliant treatise. But she would have known that had her mark appeared he would have sent the pages to the rubbish heap behind the church. Cyril snorted. He wanted to be disgusted and angry, and for a moment he considered shoving the whole manuscript in the chamber pot. But for some reason he could not bring himself to do it. Something had come over him as he read the treatise that unnerved him greatly, though he did not know what it was.

Cyril's hands began to shake.

Then he flipped the manuscript open and read the treatise in its entirety once again. This time, when he reached the last page, the bishop of Alexandria could scarcely breathe. He rolled the parchment into a tight cylinder and flung the manuscript onto the floor, dropping his head into his hands. He was certain, though he did not know how, that Hypatia had written the manuscript, and what was far, far worse, was that it was brilliant, and not only was it brilliant, it was original and precisely the logic he was looking for. If only he had considered the ideas it postulated himself.

"Tarek!" he called.

The boy appeared in the doorway, his head bowed.

Cyril thrust the document towards him. "Have this copied at once."

Tarek nodded and backed out of the room.

As he left, a dreadful knot rose in Cyril's throat. He licked his lips and squeezed his eyes shut; a feeling as sickening to the senses as a cat's pungent urine washed over him.

Then something altogether frightening and magnificent occurred that had never happened to the bishop in his entire adult life. Try though he did to repress it, a stubby little tear sprouted out the corner of Cyril's eye, followed by another, and still another, his armor pierced through.

Cyril wept.

He wept tears of regret while sitting on the chamber pot, his face in his hands, as a different perspective of his tirade against the library and its headmistress flooded his mind, just as Hypatia had presumed it would.

Cyril had easily convinced himself that he was not responsible for the tragic event. After all, he was at a meeting of the Alexandrian council on Antirrhodus when the Great Library had burned, and he had never raised a hand to the Great Lady himself. But slumbering deep within was the truth, the truth that all his ranting against Hypatia, his instructions to the Parabolani and the priests of Nitria, and his repeated sermons about the evils of paganism had been what murdered her.

A terrible guilt settled on Cyril as he sashed his robes and slipped on his sandals. He left his bath still steaming as he flew out the door and down the steps to the church. The sentry stationed at his door looked up at him in confusion as he passed. "Is everything all right, Your Eminence?"

Cyril did not even look back to respond, nor did he slow his steps until he reached the central nave of the church of St. Alexander. He paused at the last pew then slowly strode down to the altar where the tremendous wooden crucifix rose up from a rugged grey stone.

Bowing his head, Cyril joined his trembling hands together in prayer before his heart and dropped to his knees as the tears of repentance slid down his cheeks.

Forgive me.

Christ.

Forgive me.

The church that morning was still and empty, save for a bat crouching in the hollow rafters, so there was no one present to witness the bishop's unusual transformation as he wept.

In the years that followed, however, rumors and conjecture spread from Constantinople all the way to Gibraltar about what had happened to Bishop Cyril of Alexandria, for he was suddenly obsessed with the concept that the Virgin Mary was the mother of God, and an ingenious manuscript that he had authored was circulating among the clergy. No one knew, of course, that Cyril had simply signed his own name to Hypatia's work and sent it to the boy emperor's sister, Pulcheria, for support, which he received in great measure.

Though he never again spoke Hypatia's name, Cyril had the statue of the Virgin Mary with the Christ child seated upon her lap, which had stood for seventy years in the square of Alexandria, moved to the gardens of the Church of St. Alexander so that he could look out of his window and remember, perhaps not Hypatia herself, but the profound awakening that her writing had inspired in him.

43

"Alaya, come," Hannah held out her hand.

Alaya did not move, her pudgy little arms wrapped as far around the fig tree in the courtyard as they could reach.

Hannah waited impatiently, running a hand through her daughter's silky hair. "We have to go, Alaya."

"Shhh, Mama," said the girl, pressing her ear to the trunk.

Hannah went to pry her daughter's fingers from the knobby bark then stopped and sat on her heels instead. "What are you doing?" she whispered.

Alaya smiled. "Listening."

Hannah tipped her head. "To the tree?"

Alaya nodded emphatically.

Hannah squatted again. "Everyone is leaving, Alaya. Not just us. Alizar, Sofia, and—"

"And Jemir? And Baby Ali?"

"And Jemir, and Baby Ali. We are all leaving the city. It is not safe here for us."

"And Pappo?"

Hannah closed her eyes.

And Pappo.

Alaya nodded and let her hands fall away from the fig tree, a child's willingness still so alive in her eyes. Hannah shifted her haversack on her shoulder and took Alaya in her arms. There were yet two more bags at her feet, one concealing the lyre, and a woolen satchel that swung as though it held significant weight. "Come," she said, "We have to hurry now."

Alaya fingered her mother's necklace. "Will Master Junkar be there?"

Hannah took a deep breath. "No."

"Is he my Abba?"

"Yes. He is. But he has an important job to do. You will see him again one day."

Alaya nodded and rested her head on her mother's shoulder.

Above them, an angel circled and settled in the eaves of the sky, content to descend. A door had opened. The warrior had come. The light had promised it.

Together they walked together for what Hannah knew might be the last time through the cobbled streets of Alexandria in the thin morning light, past the merchants setting up their shops, until they reached the harbor. So much had happened here. Although a thin thread of nostalgia wrapped itself around her heart, Hannah longed to leave it all behind her. To take the beauty and leave the pain. To take the memories of beloved friends, and let the rest be. She quickened her steps. There was one stop they had to make, to her father's grave in the necropolis.

Hannah took Alaya's hand, and they plucked flowers from Alizar's garden.

His grave rested beneath a beautiful olive tree. As it should be, thought Hannah. "Abba. I love you. I promise I will return one day to honor you again." They placed the offering of lilies and wildflowers on the earth.

"Come, Alaya, the ship will sail soon."

They ran to the harbor.

Not the ship with the red sails bound for Cyprus.

No.

Not the small lateen-rigged skiff bound for the Upper Nile.

There.

Hannah let Alaya down, and she flounced across the last remaining dock in the city to a dark figure bent over beside a line, inspecting something. "Pappo!"

Gideon looked up, and the little girl flung herself into his arms. He closed his eyes and pressed her heart to his, feeling her warm breath on his neck. For a long time he cradled her, kissed her, and then stood up, letting her take his hand.

Hannah approached the tall sailor dressed in a sleeveless black *tunica*, his tanned shoulders gleaming, his onyx eyes shining. "Do you have room for two more?" she asked, squinting back the rising sun behind him. He looked so handsome and strong. Instantly, she felt grateful to be near him again.

Gideon searched her face.

Hannah swallowed, knowing she must speak. "You were right," she said. "He did come."

"And?" said Gideon.

"Master Junkar belongs with the Nuapar, Gideon. And we belong with you. All three of us." Her hands brushed her belly, and she smiled.

Gideon smiled then, triumphantly, and swept her in his arms, swinging her around and around as Alaya stepped back, giggling and shouting with glee. He kissed her belly and Alaya's cheeks.

"Then we sail at once!" he said and all but floated with them to the deck. "Come," he said.

So.

Hannah ran her fingers along the smooth wooden rail, Alaya beside her clutching her leg as the giant ship glided across the harbor as the sun peeked one eye over the world. Hannah could almost feel her father smiling beside her. She ran her fingers through her daughter's hair. There were things she could never undo. Hypatia was lost. The library was a ruin. The Temple of Isis was gone. But this. This she could protect.

Once the ship was underway, waves lapping the hull, Gideon came to stand beside her at the stern, his hands on her hips, looking back on what would be a clear spring day for the inhabitants of Alexandria. The outline of the city was inscribed upon the shore of Egypt as if etched in ivory, her lighthouse standing serene as if it might stand for all time. "I have something for you."

"For me?" asked Hannah.

Gideon nodded. "Yes, from the Temple of Isis."

Hannah felt her breath catch in her throat. "What? But how could that be?"

Gideon nodded toward a trunk fastened to the deck. Hannah knelt before it and unlatched it; as she lifted the heavy lid with a creak, her eyes fell on the Great Book. She pulled it out and held it in her arms, smelling the pages. Her fingers traced the edges of the codex, and then she replaced it carefully and closed the lid of the *armaria*, questions in her eyes.

Gideon smiled. "It was saved from the burning temple by a priestess. She heard we were leaving for Greece and asked me to give it to you."

Hannah embraced him. "Thank you, Gideon. You are my strength in this life." Then her eyes went wide in disbelief.

Iris stood before her, smiling.

"Iris?" Hannah said.

The two women embraced, ecstatic. They laughed, hugged, laughed, touched each other's faces, held hands, and smiled. "This is wonderful," declared Hannah, although it would become more wonderful still.

"Alizar has allowed me to join you," Iris said, as Alizar strode to her side, slipping one hand beneath her ribs.

Hannah realized their intimacy. "You kept this secret from me?" asked Hannah, teasing him.

"I did. Iris came to my house many times to deliver manuscripts for Hypatia over the years." Alizar kissed Iris's cheek. "After all that has happened, I decided she belongs beside me."

Hannah laughed. It was the first real laugh from her throat in weeks and felt unfamiliar and yet, miraculous and welcome.

So.

Hannah returned to Gideon at the stern. "It is the most wonderful gift to see her again. Better than any ancient book."

Gideon kissed Hannah's forehead and caressed her belly, pointing as Alexandria's dolphin leapt above the harbor in the wake. "There is one more thing," he said, and he unclasped the gold medallion from around his neck. "When we reach the shores of Epidavros, and the arms of my mother and father, we need a wedding." He held out his treasure, the *solidus* coin stamped with the image of the rearing lion, and she lifted her hair so he could fasten it around her neck.

Hannah touched the beautiful lion, meeting his eyes with a smile. "It will be an honor to be your wife, Gideon."

"We will marry in the olive grove beside the sea. By a rabbi if you like."

Beside the sea. Hannah nodded thoughtfully. She knew what she must do.

She untied the heavy satchel at her hip, reached inside it, and withdrew the white alabaster jar her father had given her.

"What is it?" asked Gideon.

Alaya, too, lifted her eyes in interest.

Hannah's lips trembled with sorrow, her thoughts drifting back in time. "It is the fields of Sinai and my father's herd. It is the parents I never knew. It is my father's laughter. And it is an ancient olive tree that once stood in a sunlit pasture. It is the drought that killed so many." She looked at him, her eyes full of pain, the pain of release. "And it is the Great Library of Alexandria, and Hypatia, Naomi, Synesius, and Leitah: all those I loved so dearly and miss so horribly."

Gideon waited.

Alaya, too.

Hannah clenched her teeth as she forced the lid to turn.

Once.

Twice.

She smiled then, feeling the weight of it in her hands. The weight she had carried through the years. "I want to forgive the slave traders for what they did to me, and Tarek, even Cyril, for the death of Hypatia and our beautiful library. I do not want to carry the weight of that hatred and that regret with me, with us, even one more hour." Then with the cry of a falcon on her lips, Hannah tipped the jar over the rail, letting a cloud of ashes pour out like snow. The dust of bones lifted into the sky and then settled in the white ruffles of the ship's wake, the sea folding its ancient song into the ashes, washing them away.

Alaya clapped and squealed, bouncing on her toes.

That gossamer cloud was followed by another, and still another, until the alabaster jar was empty as an eggshell, and the city of Alexandria and Alizar's ship were separated by a floating white veil that slowly settled on the sea.

"To the wind," said Hannah.

Gideon smiled and kissed her.

To the wind.

Epilogue

(Spoiler Alert)

Historically, it is still unknown how or when the Great Library of Alexandria burned. Credible sources diverge, creating a window of possibility that spans over seven hundred years during which the Great Library may have been destroyed, perhaps even more than once. Legends vary, probably because original sources are sparse due to the library having burned. Some sources argue that the main stacks were burned by Julius Caesar when he lit the harbor on fire as part of a military strategy, while others attest that the Arabs used all that was left in the library to fuel the city's bathhouses for six months after their conquest. I found it a worthy coincidence that the last known librarian of the Great Library is in many sources acknowledged to be Hypatia of Alexandria and that very few references to the Great Library can be found after her death. Thus, the account that I have offered here of the Great Library's demise is purely fictional, although plausible.

Though very little is known of Hypatia's actual life, it is evident from Synesius's letters that Hypatia was well known and adored throughout the Mediterranean. She is looked upon as one of the last Greek philosophers, holding significant sway among great leaders of her era who consulted her on matters of politics, science, mathematics, and astronomy. Her death has been cited by some bold scholars as the singular event that ended the Hellenistic era and invoked the Dark Ages that were to enshroud all of Europe until the Enlightenment many centuries later. Some sources even go so far as to suggest that Hypatia's murder set the stage for the persecution of women as witches and practitioners of black magic by the Christians in centuries to follow. We cannot know for certain. While much of Hypatia's life remains a mystery, her contributions to science and mathematics are still in use today, and she is currently recognized as the first female mathematician, philosopher, and astronomer in history.

What is referred to in this story as the Celestial Clock of Archimedes is known today as the "Antikythera Mechanism." It was found by Greek divers off the coast of Antikythera in 1901, and later reconstructed by scientists, some of whom suspect it to be an invention of Archimedes, though there is as of yet no conclusive evidence.

Hypatia, Bishop Cyril, Heirax, Ammonius, Peter the Reader, Orestes, Emperor Theodosius II, Pulcheria, Synesius, Alexander the Great, Ptolemy, and Hypatia's father, Theon of Alexandria, are all historical figures. I attempted to alter their lives as little as possible, though a few liberties have been exercised, as with Synesius, who did not expire in Alexandria but had already taken up residence in Cyrene as the bishop by the time of Hypatia's death. In fact, it is through his letters that we know most of what we do about Hypatia today. The legend of Alexander the Great and the Indian mystic Kalanos, as well as the origins of the Emerald Tablet, are ancient and varied, and I explored them in depth by inventing the Nuapar. Although the Temples of Isis and Poseidon did stand on the isle of Pharos, almost nothing is known about their rituals or lineages.

Cyril's exile of the Jews from Alexandria, the stoning of Orestes, and the burning of the daughter library at the Serapeum are well-documented historical incidents I have attempted to alter as little as possible. However, the specific details of Hypatia's death (such as where her body was disposed of) have been slightly altered to suit this narrative.

While Cyril's involvement in Hypatia's death was widely suspected over the centuries, it was never proven. Though Cyril was never brought to trial, in 416 C.E. an Imperial Edict was made to disband the Parabolani permanently.

More than one saint came out of the city of Alexandria from this era. For nearly a thousand years, Saint Catherine of Alexandria was one of the most venerated saints in all of Christendom. She was known as the patron saint of nurses, philosophers, spinners, teachers, jurists, and clergy. But there is a lack of evidence that Saint Catherine ever existed, eventually causing the Catholic church to discredit her. There are, however, certain indisputable similarities between her and our Hypatia. For one, she was tortured, dismembered, and murdered. She was also a virgin, like Hypatia, and held a standing among philosophers, claiming the title of martyr. Though the story bears a few dissimilarities as well, such as Hypatia remaining a Platonist to her death while Saint Catherine was a loyal Christian, the parallel between them is undeniable. Because Hypatia was adored by such a vast number of people, it is entirely possible that the myth of Saint Catherine was constructed so that the life and death of Hypatia could be remembered and honored without endangering the lives of her followers.

Many centuries after Hypatia's murder, Bishop Cyril was canonized St. Cyril of Alexandria in recognition of his contribution to Christianity, namely, that the Virgin Mary became recognized as the Mother of God at his behest. A great many of his writings have survived the centuries. He died in Alexandria in 444 C.E.

I must make a note to serious scholars and historians. While I utilized original source materials from university libraries wherever possible, it is clear that many of these sources and the commentaries about them, especially when having anything to do with Egypt, commonly disagree and more often than not, completely contradict one other. Inevitably, I would follow a promising thread to have it conclude by saying, "And whatever else might be known on this subject was probably lost in the burning of the Great Library." Thus, wherever sources diverged, I chose the text most complimentary to the structure of my work or simply imagined what may have occurred.

This novel in your hands is a synthesis of legend, history, and imagination. Had I opted purely for history, this would be a bland tale, indeed. Thusly, you will find a sprinkling of intentional anachronistic details. For instance, I opted for a more liberal expression of sexuality than the era was known for. Also, I made Hannah twenty years old at the beginning of the story, when, if I truly followed history, she would have been closer to thirteen—a choice I knew modern readers would shun for obvious reasons. The same was true but reversed for Alizar, as his seventy years of age would have exceeded the average life expectancy of the era for men by more than twenty years. To list other details here would be trite. It is my hope that a playful reader will enjoy searching them out with alacritous curiosity.

While the character of Alizar is not based on any living historical figure, I must say he prompted me to write this novel. When I learned of the discovery of the assorted Gnostic Gospels and texts of the Nag Hammadi library, I imagined some wise individual during the early centuries after Christ had the prescience to realize that certain texts were in danger and needed to be concealed for discovery in later centuries. I like to imagine we have not found them all, but will one day, and in so doing, discover more hidden truths of history. For history, dear reader (to paraphrase Napoleon), is incomplete, and merely a fiction that people agree upon.

Though Hannah was not a historical figure, she presents the very real story of human trafficking that I regret to tell you is still very much with us today. As of the writing of this novel, some sixty-million to one-hundred-million girls and women are missing—from countries all over the world, and for this very reason. Slavery is no archaic plight. If you felt moved by Hannah's story, I strongly encourage you to stay connected to me through my website and to get involved in the global efforts to help those affected. When entertainment gives rise to awareness, and awareness gives rise to action, there is enlightenment.

Image by K. Hollan Van Zandt.

Acknowledgements

Gratitude is too small a word to contain what I feel toward the supportive and understanding people in my life that helped bring this book to life.

Thank you to my mentor, novelist Tom Robbins, for spurring my inspiration and dedication to the daily art of crafting and refining language, and for insisting that the writing can always be improved.

My sincerest appreciation to Claudia Boutote at Harper One, who stood by this book and its publication with the kind of dedication authors dream of. Claudia, you are the reason. Warmest gratitude to my editor, Anna Paustenbach, and the rest of the brilliant staff at Harper Legend who contributed their geniuses to this book in many wonderful ways.

Deep thanks to my loving parents, my beautiful mother Shannon and bonus dad Scotty Peck, whose longstanding support for my work and faith in this book (and in its author) are the only reason you are able to read it. And to my father, who always knew I would be a writer, and believed in what he did not understand. Thank you also to my son Atticus, who is ever an inspiration, in birth as in life. And to Stu, for believing in me when I lost faith in myself, and for encouraging me to stay the course.

A heartfelt acknowledgment to my English teacher at Palisades High, Mary Redclay, who knew better than to give me an easy 'A'. Also thanks to my ninth grade school history teacher, Daryl Stolper, who shared obscure and fascinating stories from history instead of just making us memorize dates. Thank you to Jamba

Dunn, for opening the door to Egypt with our agonizing debates about ancient gods and light bulbs, and for providing photos, maps and a modern account of the Siwa Oasis.

Thank you to early readers Andrea Reitman, Toby Shaw, Kia Miller, Michelle "Fayde" Heit, Jacqui Lalita. My appreciation goes out to research assistance from David Michaels, the ancient coin director at Heritage Auction Galleries, and the firemen at the Los Gatos Fire Station. Thank you to beautiful Sofia, whose poetry crowns this novel. Also a big hug and a cold Guinness to Jack Lamb for introducing me to Cleopatra's Needle in Central Park, New York, one of two that once stood in the Caesarium gardens of the Great Library of Alexandria; the other is in London.

My gratitude goes out to the California university libraries and staff at Berkeley (UCB), Los Angeles (UCLA), and Santa Cruz (UCSC), Cabrillo College, and to professors Kathryn Pope at Antioch University and Professor Claudia Rapp Ph.D. If I had one wish it would be to possess a skeleton key to all the oldest libraries of the world, especially those that denied me access for my research (ahem, Oxford's Bodleian.)

Warm posthumous gratitude to Shannon Richardson, beloved friend and feminist—a daughter of Hypatia if ever there was, and also to Manolis, my tour guide to Delfi. Shannon, may you always have irises at your door, and Manolis, if there are warm seas in heaven, I pray you sail them in the arms of Eros.

Special thanks for early encouragement from Jacques de Spoelberch, Garry Shandling, Dan Fauci, Leigh McCloskey, Mark R. Harris, Robin Maxwell, and yogis Seane Corn and Rusty Wells. Also thanks to the kind baristas who served me bottomless cups of black tea in cafes around the world.

And last, but in no way least, a special thank you to two kitties who will never know what an impact their companionship had during the challenges of writing this story: Mooka and Zee Zee Bug. They both make cameo appearances in this book.

Characters are real people to their writer, and so I must convey to you, reader, the thanks of Hannah, Hypatia and Alizar for reading their story. Thank you. I pray you are always honored in return by having a wonderful story to read, to live and to tell.

Glossary

The following italicized words in the text are of Greek, Roman, Latin, Hebrew, Aramaic, Sanskrit, and Egyptian origins. Some are still in use today.

agora—A town square.

amenti—Egyptian heaven.

amphora/amphoriskos—A ceramic vase with two handles and a neck thinner than the body. The amphoriskos are smaller amphora. Both held liquids such as wine or olive oil.

armaria—A wooden or stone cupboard, usually labeled.

brucheon—The royal quarter where the noble and wealthy live.

challah—Holy bread baked on Shabbat by Jewish women.

corona—A wreath worn on the head by men for festivities.

dolmas—Spiced cooked grain wrapped in grape leaves.

fellah—Egyptian peasant.

fibula—A large pin fastened at the shoulder of a garment to hold it in place, originally Celtic and then borrowed and popularized by the Romans.

fuul—An Egyptian breakfast of bean stew.

gabbeh—A traditional variety of Persian carpet.

himation—A light or heavy woolen mantle worn by women when going out of the house.

hydria—A vase used for carrying water.

impluvium—The rectangular pool in an atrium designed to catch rainwater.

kairos—The eternal moment, the feeling of time standing still, often experienced in sacred ritual.

kalimera—Good morning.

kalispera—Good evening.

Kemet—The "black land," the term the ancient Egyptians used for the fertile land around the Nile River.

khamsin—Refers to the hot and fierce North African winds that blow for fifty days across the desert starting in March/April, from the Arabic word for "fifty."

khiton—The common clothing of the day. For men, a khiton (also *tunica*) was a garment of simple rectangular cloth belted at the waist, hanging to the knee. For women, the khiton was a longer flowing linen cloth that fell beneath the knee. It could be worn with or without sleeves and was often decorated with decorative strips along the bottom edge, or simple designs, and was occasionally pleated.

klamys—A woolen cloak with a decorative stripe along the bottom edge typically worn by Greek travelers and horsemen.

Kolossofia (author's creation)—The two reigning masters of the Nuapar and which is Greek for "Great Wisdom."

kronos—Linear time as it occurs in the passing of hours, days, nights, months, and years. Also the god known as Cronus, father of some Greek deities.

Kukla or kuklamu—A Greek term of endearment, like sweetheart or darling.

merles—Roman board game much like chess.

mudra—A hand gesture performed in religious Indian dance or meditation with specified meaning, often to indicate a deity.

neh—Yes.

Nuapar (author's creation)—The sect of yogic Egyptian monks, founded by the mystic Kalanos and Alexander the Great, who protect the ancient teachings of the Emerald Tablet.

palla—The Roman style of himation that was worn as an outer garment, simply a long length of cloth, often with a border, pinned at one or both shoulders with a fibula or penannular.

Parabolani or Parabolan—A sect of Christian priests in Alexandria created by bishop Cyril to help the poor, later used as a small militia.

penannular—A Celtic design of fibula the Romans were fond of using, shaped like an unfinished "O" with an adjustable pin down the center.

peripatos—A sheltered colonnade often used for walking in contemplation.

petasos—Greek hat with a wide brim often worn by travelers.

pinakes—Literally "lists," typically refers to the lists created by Callimachus who created the library classification system in 50 B.C.E.

pythos—A large pot used to store wine.

raks-sharqi—The tribal predecessor of modern belly dance.

rython—A drinking cup meant to be held and not set down, made of a broad range of materials from simple ceramic to decorous silver or gold, often in the shape of a horn.

shabbat—The Jewish Sabbath.

shema—The most sacred of the Jewish prayers, traditionally only recited by men.

taenia—Headband.

tholos—A circular outdoor platform for sacred ritual surrounded by columns, sometimes roofed, typically Greek.

tribon—The long grey or white robe commonly worn only by philosophers.

triclinium—A seated arrangement for guests and hosts of three couches popularized by the Romans.

tunica—In the Egyptian style of dress, usually a simple over-shirt belted at the waist, often pleated, that hung to the knee, or in some instances to the floor.

yaffe—Beautiful (Hebrew).

Money

nummus/nummi—Tiny bronze coin, the least valuable currency.

siliqua/siliquae—Silver coins sometimes referred to by citizens as *drachma*.

tremissis—A smaller gold coin worth about one third of a nomisma.

solidus/solidi—A solid gold Roman coin used all over the empire.

Translations

The Shema

(Hebrew prayer from the Torah)

> *Veahavta et Adonai eloheikha bekhollevavkha uvekholnaf-*
> *shekha uvekholmeodekha.*
>
> Hear, Israel, the Lord is our God, the Lord is One. (the
> Lord alone).
>
> Blessed be the Name of His glorious kingdom forever and
> ever.
>
> And you shall love the Lord your God with all your heart
> and with all your soul and with all your might.

The Emerald Tablet

Translation by Isaac Newton from the Latin

1. Tis true without lying, certain most true.
2. That which is below is like that which is above. That which
   is above is like that which is below to do the miracles of one
   only thing.
3. And as all things have been arose from one by the mediation
   of one: so all things have their birth from this one thing by
   adaptation.

4. The Sun is its father, the moon its mother,

5. The wind hath carried it in its belly, the earth its nurse.

6. The father of all perfection in the whole world is here.

7. Its force or power is entire if it be converted into earth.

8. Separate thou the earth from the fire, the subtle from the gross sweetly with great industry.

9. It ascends from the earth to the heaven again it descends to the earth and receives the force of things superior and inferior.

10. By this means ye shall have the glory of the whole world thereby all obscurity shall fly from you.

11. Its force is above all force. For it vanquishes every subtle thing and penetrates every solid thing.

12. So was the world created.

13. From this are and do come admirable adaptations whereof the means (Or process) is here in this.

14. Hence I am called Hermes Trismegist, having the three parts of the philosophy of the whole world.

15. That which I have said of the operation of the Sun is accomplished and ended.

Discussion Questions

1. How does Hannah change throughout the story? What wisdom does she acquire on her journey?
2. What central symbols does the author employ? What symbol do you relate to most? What meaning does it hold for you?
3. How do the characters of Gideon and Julian represent different aspects of love? Why do you think Hannah stays with Gideon? Do you agree with her choice?
4. Bishop Cyril was canonized by the Catholic Church—for his contribution of Mother Mary's role as Mother of God. How do you feel about how the author portrayed his journey of transformation that led to his eventual sainthood?
5. What kind of values does Hypatia stand for in the struggle between pagans and Christians? What does she represent in Hannah's life?
6. How do you interpret Hypatia's fate at the end of the book?
7. Do you see any commonalities between the problems faced in fifth century Alexandria, and today's world, and in your country? What has changed and what is the same?
8. Why do you suppose the author chose to make the hero of this story a woman instead of a man? Do you think a heroine's journey is different than a hero's? If so, how?
9. Which character did you most relate to? Why?
10. Why do you think the fate of the Emerald Tablet was left a mystery in the novel? What do you imagine may have happened if it had played a role in history?
11. How do you think the world might be different today if the

Great Library of Alexandria had been saved and maintained through the centuries?

12. Why do you think the author chose the title "Written in the Ashes" for her novel? (Discuss, and then reference the poem "The Journey" by Irish poet David Whyte.)

A Special Invitation from the Author

Dear Beloved Reader,

As an author, there is no one in the world more important to me than you! To honor your interest in my work I created a special club that is free to you called "Hannah's Friends."

You will receive insider access to several unpublished chapters from this book including Hannah's initiation as a priestess of Isis, rare video interviews of me talking about the behind-the-scenes of writing this novel, special bonus gifts, and stories about learning from my mentor, author Tom Robbins, as well as updates about my writing.

To become one of Hannah's Friends, please visit www. WrittenInTheAshes.com and enter your name and this book's ISBN (9780062570123).

I invite you to find me on Twitter and Instagram, as well as my blog and the K. Hollan Van Zandt page on Facebook. I'm always delighted to hear from you and answer your questions.

May the arms of the Goddess surround you, always.

In Truth and Beauty,
K. Hollan Van Zandt

About the Author

K. HOLLAN VAN ZANDT was born and raised in Pacific Palisades, California. She has performed in a touring magic show, led yoga retreats to swim with wild dolphins, and taught writing to students all over the world. She is a mother, a bird watcher, a pagan, and a graduate of Antioch University. This is her first novel. Find out more at www.kaiavanzandt.com.

Discover great authors, exclusive offers, and more at hc.com.